Keep Smiling Through

DAISY STYLES

PENGUIN BOOKS

PENGUIN BOOKS

UK | USA | Canada | Ireland | Australia
India | New Zealand | South Africa

Penguin Books is part of the Penguin Random House group of companies
whose addresses can be found at global.penguinrandomhouse.com

Penguin
Random House
UK

First published 2021
001

Set in 12.5/14.75pt Garamond MT Std
Typeset by Jouve (UK), Milton Keynes
Printed and bound in Great Britain by Clays Ltd, Elcograf S.p.A.

The authorized representative in the EEA is Penguin Random House Ireland,
Morrison Chambers, 32 Nassau Street, Dublin D02 YH68

A CIP catalogue record for this book is available from the British Library

ISBN: 978-1-405-94521-9

www.greenpenguin.co.uk

PENGUIN BOOKS

Keep Smiling Through

Daisy Styles grew up in Lancashire surrounded by a family and community of strong women. She loved to listen to their stories of life in the cotton mill, in the home, at the pub, on the dancefloor, in the local church, or just what happened to them on the bus going into town. It was from these women, particularly her vibrant mother and Irish grandmother, that Daisy learnt the art of storytelling.

For Jon Styles,
my guide to the Lake District, thanks for all
the wonderful memories

1. Mrs Jamie Reid

Walking through Mary Vale's post-natal ward, Ada stopped in her tracks as she felt her baby changing position inside her womb. Tenderly laying a hand over the swell of her belly, she smiled to herself as she murmured under her breath, 'You're lively this morning, little one.'

In just a few months' time, she herself would be on this very ward, hopefully holding her own baby in her arms. What would it be like? Ada wondered. In the years she had been Senior Staff Nurse at Mary Vale's Home for Mothers and Babies, she had delivered umpteen babies but never her own. One of the youngest patients, calling out from her bed, broke through Ada's line of thought.

'Sister Ada, I'm so sore from the baby feeding. Have you got anything I could use to ease the pain?'

Ada smiled warmly as she approached the girl, who had delivered a mewling little boy into the world in the middle of the night.

'I've got some marvellous cream,' she announced brightly. 'Made by a friend of mine who specializes in using only natural products; I always keep a good supply of it,' she added, as she unlocked the medicine cupboard and reached for a jar of the herbal cream that the chemist in Kendal kept a good stock of. 'Apply liberally three times a day – it will soon soften those cracked nipples of yours.'

The grateful girl took the cream eagerly. 'Thanks very

much. I think it's because my little boy fed so much during the night that I'm so sore.'

'He's fast asleep now,' Ada informed her. 'I left him in Nurse Dora's good care.'

The girl gave a smile of relief. 'Dora always knows what the babies want,' she replied. 'Whether it's changing, feeding, cuddling or playing, she senses their little needs right away.'

'She's a complete natural, with a heart of gold,' Ada agreed.

Thinking of what her dear friend and colleague had suffered, the deaths of her twin boys, both lost in active service – one at Dunkirk, the other on a minesweeper in the North Atlantic – brought tears to Ada's dark-blue eyes. After she suffered a nervous breakdown, it had looked like Nurse Dora Saddleworth would never return to work, but her love of new-born babies and her loyalty to Mary Vale had lured her back. Though now physically half the size of the woman she had been and with hair that had turned pure white almost overnight, Dora was back among them and the Home was a happier place for her presence.

As Ada assisted the young girl, her thoughts drifted to the many other girls she and her devoted colleagues, nuns and nurses alike, had assisted through hard times when nobody wanted to know them. Some poor wretches had just been dumped on the streets; others whisked off to the Home the moment their pregnancy began to show; some came alone and in secret. Rich and poor, educated professionals and ignorant girls who didn't even know where their babies had come from, they all went to Mary Vale in search of sanctuary. And the generous spirit of the place never failed them. The foundations of the building had been a tenth-century monastery, originally a refuge and stop-off point for pilgrims bound for Furness Abbey. For over nine centuries the ancient house which looked out over the ever-changing face of the vast Irish Sea and the majestic sweep of Morecambe Bay had never failed to provide sanctuary for travellers in need. Ada loved every aspect of it and was especially fond of the view of the valley from the back of the Home. Dotted with sheep farms, the rocky ground steadily rose higher and higher, until it merged into the lower fells of the Lake District, where Ada had spent her honeymoon and later conceived the child that she was carrying.

Buttoning up her nightie after applying the herbal cream, the young girl interrupted Ada's reverie. 'Thanks, Sister, that feels much better already.'

'Don't forget – three times a day,' Ada told her patient before she went on her way.

Though now Mrs Jamie Reid, Mary Vale's Senior Staff Nurse was always referred to as Sister Ada Dale. Thinking of her husband, Ada's eyes sparkled as she pictured Jamie's dear face: tawny golden hair that constantly flopped over his brow, bewitching hazel eyes with golden flecks, a firm full mouth, and a strong rangy body that she had grown to adore. How she missed him. The smell of his skin, the warmth of his smile, the pleasure of his soft lips. Married less than a year, they had seen each other only when Jamie was granted leave from the Front Line medical clearing station where he worked. On each visit Jamie had begged that they stay in the farmhouse where they had spent their honeymoon. '*Darling,*' he had written,

*Much as I love Mary Vale, I really don't want to spend all of my
precious leave in a single bed in your nurses' quarters. I want to be
in a room of our own, with a big double bed and a spectacular
view of the lakes out of the bedroom window.*

So Ada had each time booked them into the old-
fashioned farmhouse in the Borrowdale Valley, which she
knew for sure had a very big bed and a breath-taking view
from the window of Watendlath Tarn and the majestic
mountains surrounding it. It was there on his last leave
that Jamie had lovingly examined her rapidly changing
body. Wriggling in his strong arms, Ada had protested,
'I'm not one of your patients, Dr Reid.'

Holding her fast, Jamie had kissed her pouting lips.
'No, you're my darling wife,' he had insisted. 'And I am
examining you.'

Lifting Ada's nightdress over her head, Jamie gazed
adoringly at his wife's beautiful young body before running a cool hand over her growing belly.

'If you keep your hand there a bit longer, you might
feel Baby kick,' Ada had whispered excitedly.

Sure enough, after waiting patiently, which he was quite
happy to do, Jamie thought he felt the lightest flutter of
movement.

'How wonderful,' he sighed as he kissed her tummy.
'I'm not surprised you're pregnant,' he chuckled. 'We
hardly got out of bed the last time I was home on leave.'
Holding her tight, Jamie murmured, 'God, I hope I'm
here for the birth.'

Though Ada desperately wished for the same thing,
she was realistic enough to know that men called up to

4

fight for their country were rarely given leave to return home just for the birth of a child.

Suddenly anxious, Jamie gripped her hands. 'Darling, what if I don't get back in time?' he whispered.

Ada couldn't stop herself from bursting out laughing. 'Jamie!' she cried, as she stopped his questions with a kiss. 'I'll be in a maternity hospital, surrounded by trained staff – I'll be perfectly all right. All that matters,' she continued with determined optimism, 'is that you return home as soon as you can to hold your baby and kiss your wife. Now come on,' she laughed, dragging him from under the warm covers. 'Let's have breakfast, then climb Scafell Pike.'

'SCAFELL PIKE!' he exclaimed. 'In your state, young lady?'

'I'm as fit as a flea!' Ada giggled, dancing around the room stark naked. 'Beat you down to breakfast,' she teased, and she tossed his underpants and trousers into the air.

'Wild woman!' Jamie laughed too, as he struggled into his clothes, then crossed the room to open the curtains. 'Oh, my . . . what a morning.'

The morning mist had lifted, revealing the tarn like a vast mirror reflecting a stunning duck-egg-blue sky in its still waters. Around the edges of the tarn Muscovy ducks waddled or preened their feathers while Canada geese honked crossly as they chased each other in the shallows. In the tarn, wild trout rose and flipped before landing back in the clear water with a loud plop.

When Ada joined Jamie to share the view, he gently kissed the top of her head. 'I could stay here forever,' he murmured.

'Tell me the names of the mountains,' she asked as she cuddled closer into him.

With his eyes tracing the grey-green backbone of the hills that undulated away into the distance, Jamie dreamily replied, 'Grange Fell, High Seat and Ashness Fell.'

'I want to climb every fell in the Lake District with you,' Ada whispered.

Looking down at her tummy, Jamie asked, 'Are you sure about climbing Scafell Pike? It's difficult walking on the top, scree and ice.'

'Certain,' Ada answered with gusto. 'I want to stand on top of the highest mountain in England and admire the view with my husband.'

2. Interviews

It was obvious to Ada's friends how upset she was after Jamie's leave was up and he left to return to his medical team on the Front Line. Sister Theresa, a young postulant and a former patient who simply adored Ada, spoke of her concerns with Sister Mary Paul, the old nun who was both the Home's cook and housekeeper. Rolling out pastry for half a dozen cheese-and-onion pies in the Home's big kitchen, Sister Theresa blurted out, 'Ada looks like she's been crying all night.'

Sister Mary Paul straightened her stiff back and gave a heavy sigh. 'The child shouldn't be running around on the mountaintops in her condition.'

Stepping out of the pantry from where they had just picked up the daily supply of milk for the nursery, Sister Ann and Dora exchanged a smile: they knew how the young postulant and the old nun regularly got into a flat spin over Ada's health and well-being. Approaching the large kitchen table, Sister Ann, the Home's Matron, said soothingly, 'It's inevitable that Ada will be upset after parting from her husband.'

'It's hard to keep smiling and putting on a brave face after saying goodbye to somebody you love,' Dora added, with a catch in her voice. 'It might break your heart into a thousand pieces, but it's not you that's going off to fight the enemy. The least you can do is send your loved one away with a smile on his face.'

'Aye, you're probably right,' Sister Mary Paul sighed.

Knowing how the old nun liked to fuss, Sister Ann suggested that she might make Ada a hot cup of tea. 'She's busy doing some paperwork in her office.'

'Good idea,' Mary Paul immediately agreed. 'I'll pop along there right away.'

Ada was grateful for the cup of tea that Sister Mary Paul delivered to her, along with thin slices of warm home-made bread spread generously with butter from Mary Vale's own farm.

'Thank you, Sister.' Ada smiled, then sipped the strong hot tea and nibbled the bread. 'I need to build up my strength before Matron and I select the interviewees for my maternity-leave cover,' she joked.

'There'll be none as good as you,' Sister Mary Paul answered staunchly.

'You never know,' Ada teased. 'They might be even better.'

Matron, known as Sister Ann in the convent, had initially rejected Ada's offer of help.

'You've got more than enough to do; I can handle the shortlist myself,' she had insisted but Ada had remained firm.

'When I leave Mary Vale to have my baby, I want to go secure in the knowledge that I can trust the person who will replace me.'

Seeing the steely determination in Ada's steady gaze, Sister Ann conceded. 'If you put it like that, I have no choice,' Matron smiled. 'We've had quite a number of applicants,' she went on to explain. 'Mostly nurses with little obstetrics experience; I've whittled the list down to three candidates.' She laid three application forms on her desk. 'They're all skilled midwives with considerable experience but . . .'

'But what?' Ada enquired.

'One's nearing retirement age; another I really liked the sound of, but she has a history of back injuries.'

'An occupational hazard with midwives,' Ada pointed out. 'Who's the third applicant?'

'A Sister Edith Mann from Harrogate,' Matron replied. 'She has excellent references and is available to start work immediately.'

Early the following week, Matron, Ada and Father Ben, the convent priest who ran all the convent business including the adoption arrangements, interviewed the three candidates whom Matron had shortlisted.

Though Ada took an instant shine to the young midwife with the back problems, she agreed with Matron that they simply couldn't take the risk of employing her.

'The last thing we want to do is send the poor girl away with more injuries than she arrived with,' she remarked.

There was no doubt that Miss Mann was the best person for the job, but there was something about her that niggled. After she had accepted the position, Ada had taken her on a tour of the wards and the delivery room, where she certainly asked all the right questions. Stopping to chat to a few of the patients, Miss Mann seemed friendly enough, though Ada noticed she hurried through the noisy nursery seemingly uninterested in the tiny babies Dora and her team were feeding. After Miss Mann had taken the train back to Harrogate, Dora made exactly the same observation as Ada.

'Miss Mann is certainly qualified enough, but she's a bit of a cold fish,' she said, as she and Ada refilled the nappy buckets with fresh sanitizing liquid. 'Didn't talk much or ask many questions, and she showed not the slightest interest in our babies,' Dora added in a slightly offended voice. 'I don't know how anybody with a beating heart could resist those little ones lying there all innocent-like in their cribs.'

Ada nodded. 'She was a bit detached.'

Dora continued, 'I wonder how well she'll go down with the girls; a lot of our residents are the salt-of-the-earth type – Sister Mann was a lot more formal than that.'

Not wanting to stoke any fires, Ada answered diplomatically. 'She was probably on her best interview behaviour.'

'Mebbe,' Dora grunted, lugging the heavy galvanized bucket out of the big ceramic sink. 'It'll be hard for anybody to step into your shoes, lady, that's for sure.'

Ada gave her colleague a reassuring pat on the shoulder. 'It won't be forever, dear. Hopefully I'll quickly recover from the birth and be back with you all in no time.'

Dora, who had suffered too many of life's hard knocks, didn't look convinced. 'Who knows what the future will bring?'

Desperate that Dora shouldn't fall into the deep depression that she had only so recently beaten, Ada gave a bright smile. 'You never know,' she said cheerfully. 'Now that the Americans have joined forces with us, the war could be over with sooner than we all think.'

Dora threw her a dirty look. 'They took their time,' she

muttered. 'It was only the Japanese bombing Pearl Harbor that forced the Yanks to get their finger out.'

Seeing she was going to get nowhere with grumpy Dora, Ada decided positive action was the best way forward. 'Come on, dear,' she said, as she hauled her heavy bucket out of the sink too. 'We're needed in the nursery – the babies will be screaming the place down by now.'

Just a mention of her darling babies instantly brought a smile to Dora's face. 'Best not keep the little lovies waiting,' she said fondly and hurried to the door.

Walking behind her, Ada recalled how Mary Vale's babies had saved Dora's life after her beloved sons had died fighting the enemy; Dora's tiny, helpless charges in the nursery had given her a reason to go on living, something which Ada repeatedly thanked God for.

3. Sybil Harwood

Sybil Harwood was not in a good mood. Her lover, Brigadier Monty Baldwin, had not been able to get tickets for the cabaret show she had been longing to see, and for which she had bought the most gorgeous, full-length, sleek, Grecian-style dress in shimmering emerald satin that perfectly set off her striking witch-green eyes and long, dark, lustrous hair. Glaring crossly at her reflection in the bevelled dressing-table mirror that matched the other bedroom furniture in her elegant Mayfair flat (on loan from her father since she had been appointed to the War Office), Sybil sighed moodily. In normal circumstances beautiful and thoroughly spoilt Sybil wouldn't have given Monty Baldwin the time of day. In peacetime she had been a debutante who effortlessly worked all the young men in the room – handsome, titled, rich, witty and educated, Sybil had the pick of the crop. But now, two and a half years into the war, they were all gone, fighting on active service or killed. Though married to the beautiful and very wealthy Lady Veronica Baldwin, the Brigadier was a great one for the ladies. Overweight and full of himself, the Brigadier was a powerful figure both in and out of the War Office. In no time at all after Sybil's appointment, Monty had set his sights on her small curvy body and glamorous film-star looks. Clever Sybil with a gift for maths and languages had risen effortlessly through the ranks, until she was appointed Monty's own personal private secretary.

As a senior Army officer, Monty was renowned for his brutally quick decision-making; the same instinct applied when it came to women; Monty always got what he wanted, whatever the cost. It came as little surprise to the department that the philandering Brigadier had wasted no time in getting his pretty private secretary into bed. Sybil had undoubtedly enjoyed the perks that came with becoming Monty's mistress: the endless social whirl of dining out in the most fashionable restaurants in town (for the rich with connections in high places, rationing hardly impacted), cabaret shows, opening nights at the Drury Lane theatres and ballroom dancing in exclusive West End clubs. Her envious gaze would occasionally drift towards young men on leave, dashing in their smart military uniforms, but ever the realist Sybil knew that in a blink these same young men could be whisked away to the Front Line and never come back. She would stick it out with Monty, at least for the time being.

Everything had been perfectly satisfactory, until Sybil had stupidly fallen pregnant. At first, she had point-blank refused to accept the fact; she had always insisted Monty used condoms, though when drunk and over-needy he could be a fumbling fool and tear the wretched things. After she had missed her third period, Sybil could no longer allow herself to be in denial. Determined to take care of herself, she sought help from a professional with specific skills whom a friend had recommended. After making an appointment Sybil had endured the woman's ghastly poking down below before she had returned home, where she had been assured bleeding and back pains would soon commence. Unfortunately, neither of these things happened, so Sybil, furiously disappointed, had been forced to accept that she was still carrying a baby that she didn't want. If there had been any doubts in her mind about keeping the baby, they would have flown out of the window when she announced her predicament to her lover.

'Jesus Christ Almighty!' Baldwin had seethed. 'Do you know what you have done, woman?'

Giving him a cool haughty look, Sybil answered in a steely voice, 'I think it would be more appropriate to say, do you know what YOU have done?'

Knowing it was true, that he had indeed made a hash of things, caused Monty to bluster even more loudly: 'You'd bloody well better get rid of it.'

'I've tried that,' Sybil snapped. 'It didn't work.'

Lowering his voice, Monty attempted a more reasonable tone. 'Now listen here, Veronica puts up with many of my indiscretions, but she would throw everything at me if she thought I might introduce a bastard into the family.'

'Then you had better make arrangements for me to disappear until the baby is born,' Sybil retorted.

Turning his back on her, Monty growled as he reached for the whisky decanter.

'Leave it with me.'

'I most certainly will,' she assured him.

Though Sybil's family were comfortably wealthy she knew they were far more likely to disown her rather than assist her in such a sordid matter, which could bring disgrace to the family name.

'Anyway,' Sybil fumed. 'Why should they pay for Monty's catastrophic clumsiness? He's the idiot that messed up; it's his responsibility to at least pay for me to stay in a decent nursing home.'

When Sybil discovered that her lover had booked her into the Mary Vale Home for Mothers and Babies, she went through the roof.

'I thought I could trust you to book me into a discreet nursing establishment in the Home Counties,' she furiously declared. 'Instead you're planning on sending me off to bloody Grange-over-Sands!'

'I've heard it has a reputable name, run by nuns –'

Monty got no further as Sybil exploded, 'NUNS! Jesus, now I've heard it all. They'll have me scrubbing the floors and saying the Rosary from dawn till dusk.'

'Darling, don't be ridiculous,' Monty had soothed as he attempted to pull her struggling body close to his. 'I posted off a few discreet enquiries to regimental chums with operational centres up north, pals who know the way of the world, if you get my drift.'

Knowing full well what he was inferring, Sybil scowled. 'You mean chaps who have arranged terminations for their mistresses?' she asked.

'Sweetheart, please don't be cross – this is a fine way to keep in touch,' he coaxed. 'I'll be able to visit you when I'm up there checking on our Northern bases.'

Fumbling with her blouse, he grasped Sybil, who pulled away in order to dodge his odious wet kiss; as her pregnancy advanced and powerful hormones took hold of her body, she found Monty's amorous advances increasingly loathsome. She had imagined that one of the perks of her enforced absence would be not having to put up with Monty, but now he was suggesting that he would visit her on a regular basis, even when she had been exiled to the far North of England. The thought of seeing Monty when she had a swollen belly and sore breasts revolted Sybil, but she knew she had to keep him sweet; otherwise she would finish up paying the fees for her stay in a Mother and Baby Home – which, as far as she was concerned, was the least the Brigadier could do.

'Let's drive you up there together,' he volunteered, adding with a lascivious wink, 'Stay over in a fine hotel along the way, what do you say?'

Sybil took a deep breath before answering coldly, 'No, thanks. I'd prefer to make less of an occasion of it. I'll go alone, by train.'

Smarting at her rejection, Monty had said huffily, 'Then make it soon – you're beginning to show.'

And that's how Sybil found herself on a train bound for Lancaster, where she changed trains in order to connect with the local line that dropped her off at Kents Bank. It was twilight by the time she disembarked, and, as she walked along the short station platform built on marshland that edged the Irish Sea, Sybil heard the plaintive call of roosting curlews, who, along with sandpipers and oystercatchers, were settling down for the evening. Following the guard's instructions, spoken in a thick Lancashire accent that she could barely understand, Sybil crossed the narrow lane outside the station and entered a small ash wood, where she inhaled the pungent sweet smell of bluebells and narcissi. After rapping on Mary Vale's front door, Sybil was welcomed by a smiley-faced Sister Mary Paul.

'Good evening to you, please come on in, won't you?'

Sybil followed the nun into the sitting room, where, even though it was fast going dark, the windows were wide open to allow in the fresh evening air.

'Can I get you anything, dear?' Sister Mary Paul enquired. 'A cup of tea and some nice buttered toast perhaps?'

Suddenly starving, Sybil eagerly accepted the nun's kind offer, which was delivered to her not by Sister Mary Paul but by a strikingly good-looking nurse with dark-blue eyes.

'Welcome, we've been expecting you,' she beamed, and set a loaded tea tray on to a side table. 'I'm Sister Ada, and you must be Sybil. How was your journey?'

In between mouthfuls of hot strong tea and nibbles of hot toast, Sybil responded to the nurse, finding that she'd taken an immediate liking to her. 'Grim, but I'm here now, for which I am truly grateful. The journey out of London itself seemed to take hours, stopping and starting, shunting back and forth past cities and towns almost razed to the ground by bombing raids. If that wasn't bad enough, the carriages and corridors were full of weary troops, half of them sleeping on the carriage floors.'

Seeing Sybil's pale face and tired eyes, Ada suggested she showed her to her room.

'Thank you,' Sybil quickly agreed. 'I'm exhausted.'

Ada carried the newcomer's case and led her up the dark, winding, mahogany staircase to the first floor, where, Sybil was relieved to discover, she had her own single room equipped with a sink.

'You'll share a bathroom with the other girls on the first floor,' Ada explained.

Though dismayed at the prospect Sybil answered diplomatically, 'Well, at least I have my own room.'

After giving the new resident a brief introduction to the running of the Home, seeing her weary expression Ada suggested she continue the conversation the following day, when Sybil would be more refreshed. Completing her duties on both the ante- and post-natal wards, Ada then shared supper with the residents in the dining room before she busied herself helping Sister Mary Paul to clear away the dishes.

'Well, what do you think of the newcomer?' the old nun whispered the second she and Ada were alone together. Before Ada could open her mouth to reply, the old nun rushed on. 'From the look of her, with her fine clothes and posh voice, I'd say she's in for a bit of a shock.'

Arching her fine black eyebrows, Ada said, 'Now, now, Mary Paul, we've had rich girls here before and they've all survived.'

'That's as may be,' Sister Mary Paul answered lugubriously. 'But Miss Harwood looks like the sort that's used to getting her own way, and that attitude won't go down well at Mary Vale.'

'Everyone here is in the same boat,' Ada grinned as she patted her tummy. 'And that includes me too!'

Just a mention of Ada's pregnancy sent the nun off at a tangent. 'I'm worried to death about you leaving here,' she blurted out. 'You need taking care of,' she declared indignantly.

Seeing the nun agitated and upset stirred Ada's gentle heart, and, drawing Mary Paul into her arms, she hugged her tightly. 'Darling Sister, I'm no different from the thousands of other pregnant women all around the country who are on their own.'

'Why can't you stay here with us?' Sister Mary Paul implored with tears in her eyes.

'Because I can't live in the single room in the convent building, and I certainly don't want to join the residents in the Home,' Ada patiently explained for the umpteenth time. 'I'll go back home to Leeds when the time comes for my baby to be born – now *please* stop worrying.'

Sister Mary Paul gave a grudging smile; if she could have had her own way, she would have locked her beloved Ada in the pantry and kept her there until she went into labour.

Upstairs in the privacy of her single room, Sybil unpacked her clothes and hung them in the rickety old wardrobe: cashmere twinsets, pretty dresses, pleated skirts, brand-new black suede court shoes.

'Ridiculous!' she scolded herself out loud. 'Did you think you were going to the Ritz?' Running her hands along the line of clothes, she sighed miserably. 'This lot hardly fits me now – goodness only knows what size I'll be by the time I give birth.'

Mary Vale – a grand old house, albeit spotlessly clean with old-fashioned furniture and worn linoleum – wasn't what she had had in mind. Feeling utterly miserable, she walked over to the window, which she flung wide open so that she could inhale the first breath of fresh air she had breathed all day. She leant out and gazed at the marsh, silvery sage-green by the light of the almost full moon that was rising over the sea. From the rippling pools left by the tide came the sound of roosting birds and the echoing hoot of a hunting barn owl, sweeping on ghost-like wings over the ground.

'There's no turning back, Sybil,' she firmly told herself, as she closed the window and prepared for bed.

London was another country, far away; for now she was stuck in the North for the duration of her pregnancy.

4. First Impressions

The following morning dawned wet and windy. Feeling hungry after barely eating the day before, Sybil struggled into an expensive tweed skirt and a pretty pink cashmere twinset. She was grateful that she had her own sink – at least she could wash herself and clean her teeth in private. Examining her face in the mirror over the sink, she was tempted to apply a little make-up – she would certainly never have gone to work without applying foundation, mascara and luscious red lipstick – but this morning, with the rain lashing at the window and the smell of food drifting up the stairwell, Sybil simply couldn't be bothered.

When she arrived in the dining room, Sybil was taken aback by the number of women gathered around the large dining table, where places were laid and crockery set. As all eyes turned to the newcomer, Sister Mary Paul swooped in bearing a large teapot.

'Good-morning, Sybil,' she cried. 'Sit yourself down and I'll pour you some tea. The toast is still hot, and there's some butter there from our Mary Vale Farm and blackberry jam I made last autumn.'

Sister Mary Paul, still bustling around, placed Sybil between two women: one looked like she was going to give birth any minute; the other was probably about as far gone as Sybil.

'Irene and Mavis will show you the ropes, won't you, girls?' Sister Mary Paul commanded rather than requested.

Looking awkward, both girls did as instructed, passing butter, jam, toast and a jug of milk towards Sybil, who gave a polite but distinctly weak smile.

'How long have you got to go?' Irene, the larger of the women, with a broad Yorkshire accent, asked.

Rather put out by the intimacy of the question, Sybil prevaricated. 'Do you mean how many months pregnant am I?' she asked rather pedantically.

Looking annoyed, Irene snapped, 'Aye, in't that what I just said?'

By now everybody around the table was listening to their exchange, some trying to hide their smiles behind their hands as Sybil, put on the spot by Irene's bluntness, replied in a voice that could have shattered crystal, 'I'm not entirely sure.'

Bursting out laughing, Irene did a perfect imitation of Sybil. 'Oooh, you're not entirely sure!' she mocked.

Now annoyed by the girl's rudeness, Sybil concentrated on buttering her toast and drinking her tea, the uncomfortable silence broken by Mavis, the girl on Sybil's other side, quietly offering her some jam.

'Thank you,' Sybil smiled. 'That would be nice, thank you.'

Clearly trying to make conversation, poor Mavis struggled on. 'How was your journey here?' she politely asked.

Knowing that everybody in the room was listening to them, Sybil answered in a rather high voice. 'It took hours, and the train was full of soldiers.'

Again, Sybil was aware of hidden smiles and little nudges

as the residents reacted to her responses. Quickly finishing her tea, she reached down to pick up her rather expensive crocodile-skin handbag. 'Excuse me,' she said curtly, as she made to leave the room.

'Where might you be off to?' Irene called after Sybil. 'We've all got our morning jobs to do, no exceptions,' she added pointedly.

Not having a clue what the girl was talking about, Sybil exited the room and then, with a low groan, closed the door behind her.

'God . . .' she murmured. 'What have I let myself in for?'

Mary Vale's daily chores were essential to the working of the Home. Whether residents paid their way or not, they were expected to be on the cleaning rota, which was pinned up every week in the dining room. Because Sybil was so weary on her arrival, she hardly took in the information that Ada had passed on to her; as a consequence, she had no idea that the Home's rota system existed. When Sybil didn't turn up to commence her work, which was usually done by the residents in pairs, she received a gentle knock on her bedroom door.

Sybil, who was lying down and reading a magazine, was momentarily startled. 'Come in,' she called.

Smiling self-consciously, Mavis creaked open the door. 'You're on cleaning duty with me this week.'

'Cleaning?' Sybil spoke as if it were a dirty word.

'It don't take long, a couple of hours, then you're free for the afternoon, unless you fancy attending Sister Ada's relaxation classes,' Mavis explained.

Sounding like a parrot, Sybil couldn't stop herself from repeating Mavis's words. 'Classes?'

'Aye, Sister Ada says they're right good at relaxing you, especially when it comes to giving birth – she's a proper good teacher. Now that she's pregnant herself, she joins in and does all the exercises with us.'

'God spare me the detail,' Sybil thought to herself.

'We'd better get started,' Mavis urged. 'We're expected to mop and polish the entrance hall, dining room and sitting room.'

'Nobody told me about mopping and polishing hallways!' Sybil protested.

Mavis gave a nervous little sigh, as she struggled to find the right words – she needed to convince Sybil of the importance of her moral duties.

'Mebbe they forgot,' she muttered apologetically. 'I think it's o . . . o . . . obligatory, you know, we have no choice in't matter.'

Livid Sybil swung her slim legs over the edge of the bed. 'For heaven's sake!' she cried crossly.

'You'll have to change your clothes: them's too posh for cleaning,' Mavis said, pointing at Sybil's twinset and tweed skirt.

'Have you got now't else, like a pinnie or an overall?'

Appalled, Sybil gazed at her. 'I've never worn a pinnie or an overall in my entire life!' she cried.

'I think my old overall might fit you,' Mavis said, as she scrutinized Sybil's body. 'Better than getting your best stuff mucky.'

Five minutes later Mavis returned with a faded patched

overall, which (after removing her 'best' clothes) Sybil put on.

'And do up your hair,' Mavis added. 'You get right hot mopping yon surfaces.'

Hardly able to understand half of what Mavis was saying, Sybil angrily did as she was told, then followed Mavis downstairs, where she caught sight of herself in the hall mirror. Appalled at her reflection, a pale-faced woman in a threadbare overall with her long hair tied up in a tight knot on top of her head, Sybil literally stopped dead in her tracks.

'God Almighty!' she gasped. 'I look like a rag woman.'

Mavis was right: mopping and polishing three floors, then dusting down the stairs and banisters, brought them both out in a sweat. While breathless Sybil laboured, Mavis (who suffered no shortness of breath) cheerily chatted away.

'It's a regular turn-around on all the chores; next week it'll be fireplaces and coal buckets, then it's window cleaning and washing, and then there's the nursery rota.'

When Sybil paused in her mopping, she noticed she seemed to be creating pools of soapy water on the lino tiles, while Mavis swished quickly and efficiently without leaving a mess in her wake.

'Isn't the nursery the responsibility of the staff?' Sybil enquired.

'Aye, but there's not enough of them to feed the babbies – sometimes there's as many as ten little 'uns in there, and they all need feeding every four hours, night and day.'

Sybil's heart sank. 'Christ,' she thought.

Working as a char lady was bad enough, but feeding babies around the clock was simply too much. She would have to have a word with the staff, she thought haughtily; the situation was simply intolerable!

While Mavis staunchly defended Sybil (who in her simple generous way Mavis accepted for what she was), the rest of the residents hadn't much time for the newcomer.

'Bloody snob! Coming here with her fancy ways and posh voice,' Irene grumbled. 'Now, if you don't mind, ladies, I'd quite like to retire,' she said in perfect mockery of Sybil's haughty tones. 'We're all up the duff,' she added scathingly. 'So she needn't think she's any better than us.'

'Southerner,' another girl sneered. 'I bet she's never had to mop a floor in her life – not to mention fill up a bucket of coal or empty a piss pot!'

'Aye, well, she'll soon have her eyes opened,' Irene continued. 'You can't dodge jobs in this place, even if you do walk around swinging your handbag like the Queen of England.'

As both women laughed, Mavis intervened on Sybil's behalf. 'Give her a chance – she's only just arrived.'

'She should have stayed down South where she rightly belongs,' hard-hearted Irene insisted. 'I'm not going to be treated like dog muck just because Miss High and Mighty thinks she's above me.'

Mavis gave a resigned sigh. What was the point of trying to defend Sybil, who did have a cool haughtiness about her; maybe Irene was right – maybe she did look down on the other, poorer girls.

'If the new girl doesn't try harder,' Mavis thought grimly, 'she's going to have a hell of a long, lonely pregnancy.'

It was Nurse Dora who put Sybil in the picture when it came to the feeding rota, which was entirely Dora's domain. After explaining that without the residents' help the babies simply wouldn't be fed around the clock, Dora added, 'And of course there's the nappy changing too.'

Sybil's pretty elegant face paled. 'Nobody mentioned nappies,' she gasped.

'Yes, I'm afraid there's that too, but don't worry about it,' Dora added cheerfully. 'The feeding rota comes around only once about every five weeks, so it's not that bad.'

Sybil raised her perfectly manicured eyebrows. 'Not that bad?' she thought. 'Sounds like hell to me!'

5. Bombshell

Early one morning, when an easterly wind was whipping the waves of the outgoing tide into a foam and squawking seagulls straddled the air trying to keep their balance, Sister Ann, Matron of the maternity unit, arrived as white as a sheet. Leaving Dora in the nursery with the babies, Ada hurried after Matron, who, as soon as she had shut her office door, came straight to the point.

'Oh, Ada, I've had some rather alarming news.'

Seeing the stricken expression on Ann's gentle face led Ada to assume the worst. 'Is one of the sisters ill in the convent?' she quickly asked.

Matron shook her head. 'No, no, not that kind of news; everybody is fine, thank God.'

Now thoroughly agitated, Ada begged, 'Please, Ann, just tell me what's going on.'

Looking her friend square in the face Matron replied, 'The Reverend Mother has just heard that there's a rumour circulating.' She paused nervously before continuing. 'Apparently the Army has expressed an interest in requisitioning Mary Vale.'

Ada was so shocked she literally flopped into the nearest chair.

'They can't do that!' she exclaimed.

'Oh, they most certainly can, my dear,' Matron assured

her. 'You yourself know how many Army-training bases there are around here,' she pointed out. 'With the war raging, military authorities can snap their fingers and requisition property in a blink.'

Still in shock Ada murmured, 'But we have new-born babies here, and vulnerable pregnant women – they can't just up sticks and clear off just because the Army says so. Surely there's some protocol to the procedure?'

'I'd like to think so,' Matron agreed.

Flabbergasted Ada asked, 'But where would all the girls go if the Army went ahead, and the babies too?'

At this point Matron also sat down in the chair behind her desk. Stricken and on the verge of tears, she sighed. 'God only knows. The Reverend Mother believes that the convent would be seized along with the Home. We'd be thrown out too.'

Seeing her dearest friend and strongest ally seriously upset, Ada jumped up and hurried to her side.

'Our order was established here years ago,' Matron continued, as she fretfully stroked the large silver cross that she wore over her dark habit.

'I know there's a war on,' Ada soothed. 'But the Army can't just fling a whole community on to the streets!'

Completely distracted, Matron muttered miserably, 'I don't know what to say to the residents . . . it seems wrong not to notify them of what's going on.'

Holding up one hand, Ada said firmly, 'I'd hold fire, Matron,' she advised. 'Making an announcement at this particular time when, as you yourself just said, it might be nothing more than a rumour might alarm the residents unnecessarily. Give yourself a little time to find out more. Please don't go sounding alarm bells until you have more substantial information.'

'You're right, but I need to be very careful here. If requisition goes ahead, we're morally obliged to give our residents time to make their own plans, if it should come to that,' Matron fretted.

With a sinking heart Ada couldn't help but see her point.

'And what about the ones that can't go home, the girls that have been thrown out for bringing shame on their families?' Struggling to hold back tears, Matron blurted out, 'Oh, this is too awful for words.'

Even though Ada's heart sank too when she thought of all the vulnerable residents she had been nursing over the last few months, she nevertheless put on a brave face. Laying her arms around her friend's shoulders, she spoke firmly. 'One step at a time, eh?'

Matron gave a weak smile.

'And, if the worst comes to the worst,' Ada continued with a strong ring in her voice, 'we'll put up a fight and present a good argument before we allow our beloved Mary Vale's doors to be closed to our patients.'

Knowing how much Dora adored 'her babies' (as she always referred to them), Ada took her to one side and, treading carefully, she confided in her about the alarming rumour.

'The Army? Taking over Mary Vale!' Dora cried.

'I'm sure it's nothing more than idle gossip,' Ada quickly replied. 'I only mention it in case any of the residents get wind of it – it's important that we keep everybody calm.'

Being the compassionate professional that she was, Dora nodded as she bit her lip. 'God, I pray it doesn't happen,' she said with a catch in her throat. 'After losing my two sons, my life revolves around my sweet little Mary Vale babies.'

'For sure, we would all be devastated,' Ada agreed.

'And where would you go, lovie, in your condition, if the place does get closed down?' Dora asked.

'I could always go home, but my parents' house is a bit cramped for a new-born baby's paraphernalia . . .' Her eyes strayed to the window, from where she could see the storm was passing and a weak sun was making its way through the rain clouds, dappling the Home's spring garden where the birds were singing. 'I'd miss Mary Vale so much; it's become home to me, and all of you feel like a second family,' Ada confessed, now on the verge of tears herself.

'I just can't imagine the House without the girls bustling about here, their laughter and chatter everywhere, and the line of little cots in the nursery,' Dora said, as she searched for a handkerchief to wipe her eyes.

Ada took a deep breath before she continued, 'It's not come to that yet, and I only brought it up in case some of the residents start asking awkward questions.'

Dora gave a sharp nod. 'Forewarned is forearmed,' she agreed. 'And, as you say, it's not come to that – yet.'

Inevitably, as in all small communities, the rumour was leaked and in no time at all talk of a possible Army takeover was all over the Home. As panic replaced the initial shock, the outraged residents asked questions of Matron.

'But what about us?'

'Where will we go?'

'I'm due any time now, I can't go home in this state,' one girl sobbed.

'Given all the bloody big houses round here, you'd think the soddin' Army could pick somewhere else!' one bold girl protested.

'Yeah!' another cried as she supported her enormous tummy. 'Why pick on us pregnant women?'

Holding up her hand, Matron calmly tried her best to assuage her patients' fears.

'Please, you must understand, from what I can gather this is nothing but speculation, *nothing* is official. Mary Vale, along with several other establishments in the district, is under consideration by the Army.'

As cries of protest and dismay echoed around the sitting room, where staff and residents alike had gathered, Sybil appeared to be the only one who registered no emotion; in truth she found it hard not to stand up and start cheering. Could this apparent rumour be the answer to her prayers? Sybil's brain whirled with all the possibilities that the closure of the Home would bring about.

'I could relocate to the kind of expensive nursing home I envisaged in the first place,' Sybil thought feverishly. 'One with an en suite bathroom, carpeted floors, maids to serve me breakfast in bed, a private telephone line in my own room, no damned chores! And a sound-proofed nursery that I need never enter.'

In the days that followed, Sybil, almost delirious with joy, wasted no time in doing some research into select nursing homes at the very opposite end of the country. She had had more than enough of the North, with its smell of wet sheep, endless rain, gloomy mountain ranges and people talking in a grating Northern accent. This time, free of manipulative Monty, she would make her own personal arrangements, informing Monty only of her transfer when it came to the point of handing over money, which as far as she was concerned was his moral obligation and nobody else's.

'Paying for this unwanted confinement is the least the brute can do,' Sybil thought with great satisfaction. Determined, galvanized and happy for the first time in months, Sybil took the local train to Grange-over-Sands, where in the little town library she read every nursing magazine that she could get her hands on. With several addresses jotted down in her diary, Sybil returned to Mary Vale intent on immediately writing letters of application to the nursing homes she had singled out as exclusive enough for her purposes. So focused was Sybil on her plan that she failed to notice a car parked up by the front door, so it was an enormous shock when she walked slap-bang into Brigadier Baldwin in the Home's entrance hall.

'MONTY!' she gasped.

'Sybil, darling!' he cried, as he gathered her into his arms and squeezed her so hard it hurt.

Quickly disentangling herself from his arms and stepping away from him in order to avoid his dreadful bad breath, Sybil was flustered. 'What on earth are you doing here?'

Looking blasé he answered, 'I'm briefly in the area, visiting one of the bases, thought I'd pop in and see my best gel,' he added with a lascivious wink, as his hand slipped over her pert bottom.

Desperate to get him out of the building before he started pawing her again, Sybil babbled, 'I . . . I . . . er, maybe we should talk somewhere more private?'

She stopped short as Matron came hurrying into the hall. 'Hello,' she said, smiling politely. 'Sister Mary Paul told me we had a visitor.'

Grabbing Monty's arm, Sybil almost dragged him to the front door. 'Sorry, Matron, we were just heading out for a walk.'

Keen to introduce himself, self-important Monty, looking smart and impressive in his Army uniform, slipped from Sybil's grip and hurried to shake Matron's hand.

'Pleased to meet you – Brigadier Monty Baldwin at your service.' He clipped his heels and gave a smart salute before barking, 'Just heading over to Boswell Army base, doing a spot of training with the lads up there, thought I'd drop by and see Sybil, an old chum of mine from the War Office.'

Matron's jaw dropped. 'Boswell Army base?' she exclaimed.

Monty gave a curt nod. 'Know it?'

'As a matter of fact, I do,' Matron replied. 'We've had several Boswell representatives in the area recently. Rumour has it that they're keen to requisition property for the Army. Possibly even our Home.'

Monty's florid face was startled. 'I've not been notified of any such order.'

Sybil, who hadn't said a word throughout, quickly added, 'It's only recently come to light.'

Trying to control his temper, Monty snarled, 'I should have been bloody well told of this before I even left London.'

Seeing that Matron had heard more than enough from the uncouth Brigadier, Sybil ushered him to the door.

'Why don't we get some fresh air?'

'My car's outside,' Monty retorted as he followed her, grumbling and grunting under his breath.

Once outside, Sybil, keen to dispense with the requisitioning discussion, immediately hopped into Monty's car, while he breathlessly clambered into the driver's seat and started up the engine.

'Let's find a nice private spot and make up for a bit of lost time, shall we?' he suggested, as he steered the car down the drive and out of the front gate.

Groaning inwardly, Sybil guided him to a narrow sandy lane that flanked the empty marsh. In the short space of time it took him to drive there, Sybil frantically tried to work out a diplomatic plan of action. When he pulled up and drew her into his arms, she blurted out, 'Monty, please stop.'

'What kind of a welcome do you call that?' he complained, in a voice heavy with self-pity. 'When a fellow drives two hundred miles to see his gel, he expects more than a rebuff.'

Knowing she had to sweeten the old fool up, Sybil gave him the briefest of kisses on the mouth.

'Sorry, darling, but I need to tell you right away,' she said as she feigned tears. 'That I want to come back down South, I miss you so much, darling,' she fawned.

Looking rather pleased with himself, Monty answered

with a bit of a swagger. 'It's a bally awful situation,' he agreed. 'I can quite understand your feelings, sweetheart.'

Sybil took a deep breath before she moved on to the more delicate matter of the move.

'When I heard the staff talking about the Army's possible plans for Mary Vale, I decided to take the law into my own hands.'

With his little piggy eyes bulging indignantly, Monty blurted, 'Did you indeed?'

Before he started blustering all over again, Sybil pressed on. 'As you well know, I'm not the sort of girl that lies back and does as she's told.'

Eyeing her full voluptuous breasts, Monty leered as he fiddled with buttons on her blouse. 'Now you're talking.'

Regretting her choice of words, Sybil announced as she pushed his hands away from her breasts, 'So I've arranged to go into a rather lovely nursing home in Haywards Heath. Don't you think that's clever of me?'

Monty stopped mid-grope. 'You did what?' he demanded.

'I'm moving out of Mary Vale; I never liked the place to start with. Stuck in the middle of nowhere surrounded by poor ignorant girls and nuns,' she mocked. 'The Elms will suit me down to the ground.'

'What bloody "Elms" are you talking about?' he snapped.

'The nursing home near Haywards Heath, of course,' she explained quickly, adding, as his face yet again went puce, 'Don't worry, darling, I'll be discreet, I won't mention a word about our relationship, nobody will ever know that you're the father of the child – I promise.'

Not a fool, Monty snarled, 'I suppose you want me to cover the costs for this exclusive Elms place?'

'Well, of course, darling, I can't possibly pay for your little faux pas.'

Hoping to quickly conclude the conversation and send Monty on his way, leaving her free to write the letters she was desperate to post that evening, Sybil leant close to stroke his cheek. 'Aren't you pleased with little old me for sorting everything out?'

Instead of smiling, Monty gave a sharp grunt. 'I'm going to look into this Boswell business,' he announced. 'If I find some spotty little upstart has jumped the gun and thought to sideline me, he'll be in for a bally court martial.'

Desperately hoping that the requisition order would go through if only to facilitate her escape from Mary Vale, Sybil did her best to soothe. 'I can see why the Army might be interested in taking possession of the place. It's perfectly positioned for their transportational needs, so near to all the major train lines, and its proximity to local shipyards will be vital too.'

Annoyed that she was one step ahead of him, Monty bluffed, 'I don't need you to tell me what the Army needs.'

'Try not to get too cross, darling,' she gushed, as she offered up her pouting lips.

Suitably distracted, Monty's hands once again returned to caressing her breasts, which, because of her pregnancy, were fuller than they had previously been.

'Don't you go worrying that pretty little noddle of yours with men's talk,' he murmured throatily, as he reached under her skirt. 'Jesus, I've missed you so much, Sybil.'

Before he could suggest they had sex in his car, Sybil wriggled free and flung open the door. 'I must get back to the Home – we have chores to do,' she said, and, making a little moue of distaste with her mouth, she added, 'Such a ghastly, barbaric place.'

Looking distinctly put out, Monty snapped, 'For women up the duff it looked like a decent enough set-up to me.'

Suppressing the urge to hit him, Sybil feigned a cheery smile. 'Don't worry, I can easily walk back from here.'

Revving the engine, Monty called over his shoulder, 'I'll phone you after I've got to the bottom of this bally Boswell business.'

Standing on the edge of the marsh, where the wind snatched the words from her mouth, Sybil gave vent to her fury. 'PIG!' she exploded as he roared away. 'You never even asked how I am.'

6. Finsbury Park

Rosie Pickles would never know how she got herself and her two children, Ronnie, seven, and Sally, five years old, from Finsbury Park to Morecambe Bay. If her local doctor hadn't brutally informed her that her children would soon lose their mother as a result of Rosie's poor health, she wouldn't even have considered such a journey.

Finsbury Park was where Rosie had been born and where she planned to die. She had met her husband, Mick, at primary school; they had got married in the Catholic church attached to the school and lived in a run-down tenement block (crawling with cockroaches), where both their children had been born. Patriotic Mick had joined the Navy almost as soon as war broke out, and she had seen him once since and fallen pregnant as a consequence of his only home leave.

It had been a terrible pregnancy, nothing like the ones she had experienced with her other two kids. Rosie simply couldn't keep any food down her, and the doctor had given her condition a grand name, hyper-gravida something – she could never remember the long, foreign-sounding name. All it meant (as far as she was concerned) was she couldn't stop vomiting from dawn till dusk. As a consequence, as her pregnancy advanced, she became unbearably weak and useless. Mercifully, after a while the sickness gradually eased up a little, but, after barely eating for months,

Rosie hardly had the strength to get out of bed. Life descended into chaos. The children, without a father and in effect a mother too, ran wild around the council estate. Occasionally neighbours would bring in some soup or a pie, but if Rosie didn't drag herself to the local shop to pick up their meagre rations, the family subsisted on bread, marg and strong black tea.

The doctor had been adamant. 'You simply can't have your baby in these conditions – you need to get out of this slum; otherwise I might be forced to take the law into my own hands,' he had threatened.

Terrified that she might be taken into hospital and lose sight of her children, Rosie had begged him for help.

'There are Mother and Baby Homes all over England,' he had told her.

'Ain't them for unmarried mothers and their bastards?'

'That's one way of putting it,' the doctor had sniffed. 'Evacuees, pregnant evacuees like you, have access to these places too.'

Immediately on the defensive, Rosie had cried out, 'I ain't being parted from mi kids.'

The doctor eyed the dirty, scruffy, scrawny boy and girl standing by their mother's bedside; Ron was picking his nose, while Sally was scratching the nits in her hair. Who in God's name would want them under their roof?

'I wasn't suggesting parting you from your children, Mrs Pickles, merely that you should go to a place where you can be taken care of,' the doctor replied. 'I'm told these homes take in mothers and their children too.'

'Is there one here in Finsbury Park?' Rosie asked hopefully.

'I'm afraid not,' the doctor told her. 'They're in the countryside.'

'So we'd have to travel to get there?' Rosie asked weakly.

'Yes,' he told her bluntly.

'I can barely get out of bed, never mind board a train with two kids,' she wailed.

Bored with the circuitous conversation, the doctor rose to go. 'Then stay here and die and leave your children to go into an orphanage.'

Tears coursed down Rosie's ravaged face, which might once have been pretty, but now, with barely any teeth, sunken cheeks and hair that clung greasily to her scalp, looked cadaverous.

'Can you arrange it, please?' she asked limply.

'I'll try,' he told her curtly as he left.

When the letter came telling Rosie that Mary Vale House had a place for her and her children, she told Ronnie to pack a case, while with Sally's help she had unearthed a tin at the back of the kitchen cupboard in which she had squirrelled away her paltry savings. Leaving Ron to carry the cheap cardboard suitcase, Sally helped her mum on to the tram for Euston Station, where they took a steam train (packed with soldiers chain-smoking in the crowded corridors) north to Lancaster. Leaving their mum slumped in the corner of a carriage fast asleep, Ron and Sally ran up and down the train, cadging anything they could – a sandwich, a bit of cake, a boiled sweet, a drink of tea, before they too fell fast asleep beside their exhausted mother.

When the steam train clanked to a halt in Carnforth, Rosie, Ronnie and Sally caught the little local line that dropped them off at Kents Bank, from where, many, many hours after they had left Finsbury Park, they walked to Mary Vale House in the dark. Luckily the light from the half-moon guided their way through the wood and along the path to the front door of the Home, which was as usual opened by Sister Mary Paul. Even though she was expecting the new arrivals, the nun's jaw dropped at the sight of the rag-and-bone family standing on the doorstep. The mother looked like a corpse propped up between her two filthy children, who stared at her with wide open, frightened eyes.

'We've brought our mum here to 'ave a baby,' Ron announced. 'Can we have sumfink to eat, we're bloody starved!'

Sister Mary Paul didn't dare take Rosie and her family into the sitting room for fear of passing other residents who might be shocked at the sight of them. Instead she whooshed them upstairs to their large, airy, spotlessly clean bedroom laid out with three single beds, a wardrobe, a chest of drawers and a rickety table with three small spindle-backed chairs. When Rosie saw the clean sheets and cosy eiderdowns that covered the beds, she started to cry.

'Rest now, dear,' Sister Mary Paul urged, as she settled the weeping woman on to the most comfortable bed by the large bay window, which she quickly opened to let in some fresh air. Leaving Rosie and Ron bouncing on the beds like cheeky monkeys, Sister Mary Paul scooted downstairs as fast as her feet would carry her and all but ran in search of Ada.

When she found her checking her patients on the post-natal ward, she cried out, 'God Almighty, Ada, come upstairs right now!' Gasping for breath, Sister Mary Paul wheezed on. 'The family from London have just arrived, you should see the state of them – they look exhausted! I put them in Room 3 at the front of the House,' she babbled, as she hurried after Ada, who, even though pregnant, was far more fleet-footed than she was. 'The children need bathing before they get in between those clean sheets – they're nothing short of feral.'

'And the mother?'

'I'd say on the point of collapse,' cried Mary Paul. 'God alone knows how the three of 'em got up here unassisted.'

'Desperation, I imagine,' Ada said, and took the stairs two at a time, calling over her shoulder, 'Make a pot of strong tea and a plate of meat-paste sandwiches if you can spare it.'

The children stopped their wild bed-bouncing when Ada entered the room and took control.

'Hello, I'm Sister Ada, welcome to Mary Vale,' she said, as her eyes swept over the rags Ron and Sally were wearing. 'Now,' she said, as she hunkered down in order to talk directly to the children, 'how about having a nice hot bath after the long journey you've just had?'

Both Ron and Sally looked like they would rather face a firing squad than take a bath.

'NO!' they shrilled together.

Rosie rose from the bed she had been stretched out on, and, with her dark-brown eyes blazing in her haggard face, she summoned up all her strength to take control of her wayward children.

'Apologize to the lady right away, you two,' she commanded.

Shuffling their grubby, worn-out shoes, they muttered in unison, 'Sorree, miss.'

'Once you've had your bath I promise I'll fetch you something nice to eat,' Ada coaxed.

Aware that she needed to talk to the mother in private, Ada rang the emergency hospital bell that was in every resident's room, knowing Dora would come to help with the children while she checked on the mother's state of health.

Competent Dora was there in a jiffy. 'Leave the kiddies to me.'

Five minutes later Rosie, urged by Ada, was sipping a bowl of nourishing barley broth soup which Sister Mary Paul had quickly heated up for her, along with providing sand-wiches for the children.

'I don't know what you must think of us,' mortified Rosie murmured in between sips of soup.

'I think you're all exhausted,' Ada soothed.

'The kids are out of control,' Rosie admitted. 'I've not had the strength to even belt 'em for being naughty.'

Ada gave a sympathetic smile. 'Maybe that's not a bad thing.'

'I just hope they'll settle down now that they're here,' Rosie fretted, as she dipped a slice of home-made bread into the broth. 'Mmm,' she sighed gratefully. 'This is proper tasty.'

'I'm not going to trouble you with too many questions tonight,' Ada continued. 'We'll get to know each other more tomorrow, but just tell me how you managed to get up here in such a weak state, and with the children in tow?'

Rosie laid down her spoon and repeated what the doctor in London had told her.

'So, you see, after he told me I might well die, and mi kids would be sent to an orphanage, I had no choice, had I?'

Ada gave a solemn nod just as Ron and Sally burst into the room, both wearing the nursing-home nighties generally used for pregnant patients, which almost drowned them.

'The water was right hot, mother,' Ron said as he ravenously eyed the meat-paste sandwiches.

'Nurse Dora said we're crawling with nits,' Sally announced. 'She put some smelly stuff on our 'eads and she ses she'll chop our 'air off tomorrow morning.'

Completely unphased, Dora added firmly, 'The nits will come back if we don't get rid of the eggs – we need to de-louse you two before everybody in the Home catches them too. If you don't mind, Sister Ada, I'd better get back to my work on the ward.'

'Of course, Dora, I'll be down there soon,' Ada promised.

As soon as Dora had closed the door behind her, Ron said, 'She's a strict old cow.'

'Ron!' Rosie cried in shame. 'I'm sorry,' she said contritely to Ada, 'I don't know where they've picked up such bad language.'

Helping himself to a sandwich, which he crammed whole into his mouth, Ron mumbled, 'On the streets, when we go begging.'

Seeing Rosie blushing with embarrassment, Ada threw her a reassuring smile before she rose to leave.

'I'll let you all get some sleep now, but I'd like to see you first thing in the morning, Mrs Pickles, to do some more medical checks, if you don't mind?'

'Call me Rosie, lovie,' the patient replied. 'First thing is fine with me. Goodnight to you, and thanks for all your kindness to me and mi kids.'

Leaving the ravenous children, now with shiny clean faces, tucking into the pile of sandwiches left for them by Sister Mary Paul, Ada said a sweet 'Goodnight, God bless' as she left the room.

The following morning, when Rosie and her brood turned up in the dining room for breakfast, the usual clatter and chatter fell silent as the residents surveyed the scruffy newcomers. It was cocky Ronnie with his cheeky gap-toothed grin and high squeaky voice who broke the ice by pointing to the butter dish in the centre of the table.

'Blimey, Mother, look at all that bleedin' butter!'

'RONNIE!' Rosie's anguished cry was drowned out by a loud roar of laughter from the residents.

Trying to ignore Ronnie's swearing, Sister Mary Paul sat the family at the end of the table – unfortunately right next to Sybil, who looked like she had been introduced to a viper. Throwing down her napkin, she flung back her chair and glared at Sister Mary Paul.

'You seriously don't think that I am going to eat with filth like this?' she snapped and, grabbing her very expensive handbag, she stalked out of the room.

'Don't worry, little lad,' Irene indulged the naughty boy. 'She's just a snob, we'd much rather have your company than Mrs Hoi Poloi.'

Further encouraged by Irene's wink and a few indulgent

smiles from around the table, Ronnie got stuck into his breakfast, and his sister quickly followed suit. Spreading creamy butter, delivered daily from the nearby Mary Vale Farm, which supplied the Home with plenty of dairy, plus vegetables and fruit in season and sometimes meat, Ronnie sunk his teeth into the hunk of fresh warm bread. Little Sally did the same in between earnestly telling the girl next door to her that she had nits, which immediately made every resident in the room shuffle their chair further away from the infected children. Seeing how uncomfortable their presence was making the diners, Rosie urged her children to finish their breakfast, something she was, in fact, struggling to do herself.

'I could eat an 'orse, Mother!' Ronnie protested, as he lathered butter on to another slice of bread.

'Leave some for others,' his mother said sharply.

At which point Ada came breezing into the dining room. 'Morning,' she called in her happy uplifting voice. 'How are you all today?'

Before her mother could open her mouth to speak, Sally said, 'It's nice having an indoor privy.'

Which brought on another round of laughter from the entertained residents. Seeing Rosie squirming with embarrassment, Ada suggested that the children should play in the garden while she examined Rosie in private.

Up in her room, Sybil was seething. She simply could not have been more appalled or outraged. It was bad enough being at Mary Vale as it was; she didn't like the residents and they didn't like her. Fair enough, she could live with that, especially if her transferral plan came to fruition, but

47

in the meantime was she seriously expected to cohabit with a bunch of savages? It was a downright bloody insult to a woman of her standing – how dare the wretched Home even contemplate such a scenario!

'There's nothing for it, I'll have to leave sooner rather than later,' Sybil declared. 'In the meantime, I shall complain to Matron about this unacceptable lowering of standards.'

When Sybil swanned into Matron's office, Sister Ann – normally the kindest person on earth – felt her hackles rise. She resented Sybil's tone and was shocked by her outright snobbery.

'I'm quite sure you are aware, Miss Harwood, that Mary Vale, which is a charitable foundation, accepts unmarried mothers awaiting the birth of their babies, and since the outbreak of war we are obliged by the government to accept evacuees too,' Matron patiently explained. 'We have welcomed family units of evacuees in the past when they have turned to us for help, just as we welcome the Pickles family now.'

'But the children are running wild, and the mother appears to be completely ineffectual,' Sybil pointed out.

Matron actually agreed that Ronnie and Sally were indeed running wild, but there was no way she was going to allow high and mighty Miss Harwood to crack the whip over her authority. Without doubt they would settle down once they got used to the House and the countryside; after all, they had been cooped up in a bombed-out city for some time now. Matron didn't want to think about the fact that if Mary Vale were to be requisitioned by the Army, they would all be out on their ear very soon, the Pickles family included.

'Mrs Pickles suffers from a rather grave condition of continuous morning sickness, which has left her weak and anaemic; we're hoping that a better diet and good care will ease her situation and she will improve as her pregnancy progresses,' Matron informed Sybil, who, looking sulky, continued with her list of grievances.

'It's thoughtless and irresponsible to allow people like *them* to live under the same roof as decent, upright, law-abiding citizens.'

'We were instructed to accept them,' Sister Ann retorted sharply. 'Are you suggesting that we go against government instructions?'

'I'm told the brats have lice too!' Sybil added grumpily.

'That's being dealt with,' Sister replied.

'Who is actually responsible for them while they're charging around the place unsupervised?' Sybil icily enquired.

'Sister Mary Paul and Sister Theresa keep an eye on the children, and some of the residents,' Matron added pointedly. 'They have kindly offered to help while the mother is incapacitated.'

Thinking she would rather take a gun to herself than babysit the uncouth brats she was presently cohabiting with, Sybil raised a cynical arched eyebrow. Thinking that now might be the time to inform Matron of her new plans, she continued in a casual manner. 'By the way, I should inform you that, because Mary Vale is soon to be requisitioned by the Army, I'm making plans to move back South, to another nursing home closer to my family. As a consequence of the arrival of the Pickles family,' she virtually spat the word out, 'I now plan to go sooner rather than later.'

Matron looked genuinely surprised. 'As far as I know at

this point in time Mary Vale is just one of several large estates under consideration.'

Sybil waved a dismissive hand in the air. 'It's perfect for the Army's purposes.'

Annoyed by Sybil's arrogance, Matron snipped back at her, 'Your kind friend, the Brigadier, mentioned he would look into the matter last time he was here.'

Completely sure that Monty for all his bluster would do no such thing, Sybil gave a careless shrug. 'I think you might have the wrong end of the stick, Sister.'

'On the contrary, Miss Harwood. The Brigadier recently wrote to me saying that he thought Mary Vale served the community well and was vital to the stability of the Home Front.'

Sybil gaped at her in disbelief: why on earth would stupid Monty say that a run-down dump of a home for unmarried mothers and their babies was vital to anyone or anything? Convinced that Matron had got carried away by Monty's ridiculous blagging Sybil gave a tight smile before she continued, 'As I said, I'm making arrangements to leave. I'll let you have the details of my departure soon.'

Once Sybil was out of the office, she slumped against the corridor wall. What the hell was bloody interfering Monty up to? The Army's issuing a requisition order to close down Mary Vale was her exit strategy. If the place were to be kept open, she might be well and truly stuck at Mary Vale for the length of her pregnancy; and, if that were the case, there was a very good chance that she would strangle the evacuee brats with her own bare hands before she or their miserable mother gave birth.

7. Running Wild

Poor Sister Mary Paul was run ragged by Ronnie and Sally. Though her gentle heart ached for their mother, whom she nurtured with wholesome soups and broths, her patience was frayed by the children. Their common swearing and blaspheming offended her; their bad habits, like refusing to wash their dirty hands before meals, literally meant forcing them into the bathroom three times a day, which was exhausting. And when they did arrive in the dining room, they ate like savages, pushing and shoving each other to get the last fish-paste sandwich or slice of pie. As time passed and the novelty of having children around the place passed, Sybil wasn't the only resident who got fed up with Ronnie and Sally. She was without question the most opinionated on the matter, but a few of the other residents, especially the ones nearing their delivery dates, found Ronnie and Sally loud and tedious. There was no question that their arrival plus their constant bad behaviour had upset the Home's peaceful equilibrium.

To add to Sister Mary Paul's woes, old Alf Arkwright, who took care of Mary Vale's farm and livestock, had complained that the children had chased his sheep and stolen eggs from the hen coop. Though a kind man, Alf had threatened to bang Ronnie and Sally's heads together if he found them on his land again. The only person that seemed to have any patience with the children was Sister

Theresa, the convent's youngest nun, who had a heart of gold. A former resident named Shirley before she took Holy Orders, she had arrived at Mary Vale some years ago, pregnant as a consequence of her father's repeated abuse. Mary Paul gave a tender smile as she recalled the nervous young girl, barely more than a child herself, who had fled the horrors of her home life to seek sanctuary with the nuns at Mary Vale. Nowadays it was difficult to connect that helpless, damaged waif with the radiant, caring young nun that Shirley had become. She had found joy and peace in her vocation, and her love of God simply glowed out of her. Maybe it was because her former life had been so hideously cruel that Sister Theresa was instinctively compassionate to anybody in trouble.

'Or maybe she's just a much better nun than me,' Mary Paul reasoned to herself.

As if reading her thoughts, Sister Theresa asked, 'Can you spare me for ten minutes while the bread dough's rising? I'd like to check on the kiddies in the garden.'

'Certainly, please do,' Mary Paul smiled. 'You never know what they'll be up to next!'

Sister Theresa eventually found the children running wild on the marsh on the other side of the railway track. Waving frantically, she caught up with the pair of them – they were chasing wild birds.

'Don't do that,' she said mildly. 'Some of them will be sitting on their eggs – it's not a good idea to chase them away.'

'Why are they sitting on eggs – won't they flatten them?' Sally asked.

'No,' laughed Sister Theresa. Hunkering down so she was on the same level as the children, she explained, 'Mummy birds lay eggs, which they sit on to keep warm; when the baby birds inside the eggs hatch out, they stay with their mummies until they're strong enough to fly away and build their own homes on the marsh.'

'I'd like to fly away,' said Ronnie with a wistful smile. 'I'd like to fight the Germans with mi dad. Boom! Bang!' Ronnie made loud repeated noises like a cannon or a rifle going off.

'You're too young to fight, thank God,' Theresa said firmly.

'But I don't want to be here with all these bloody women with their big bellies – I'm a man!' Ronnie swaggered.

'You're a little boy,' Theresa reminded him. 'And you really have to stop swearing so much, Ronnie. It upsets the ladies and the nuns, and your mother too.'

'Mum's too weak to care,' Ronnie said angrily. 'The doctor in London told us she might die, and we might get put in an orphanage.'

Little Sally's dark eyes filled with tears.

'I don't want our mother to die!' she wailed. 'I don't want to be a horphan,' she sobbed pitiably.

Theresa gathered the frightened little girl into her arms. 'Sweetheart,' she soothed, 'your mother brought you here so that we could look after all of you. Sister Mary Paul's good food will make Mummy better, and when the war is over she'll take you home.'

'R . . . r . . . r . . . really?' hiccupped Sally.

'*Really*,' Theresa assured the child. Turning to Ronnie,

she added, 'Now promise me you'll stop your horrible swearing?'

'S'pose so,' Ronnie said reluctantly.

Then to Sally. 'And you'll do your best not to worry your mother.'

Sally bit her lip as she earnestly nodded.

'If you keep your promise, I'll take you into Grange on the train tomorrow and I'll buy you a treat for being good.'

Sally's dark eyes sparkled. 'I'll be good, Sister Trees,' she solemnly said. 'I want a lollipop.'

When Sister Theresa returned to the kitchen, she found Sister Mary Paul having a cup of tea with Ada.

'Ada's just told me that Miss Harwood is planning on leaving the Home,' the old nun said in a low voice.

'Not surprising really,' Ada commented. 'She's never been happy here.'

'She's a woman who's used to getting her own way,' Mary Paul said knowingly.

Sister Theresa smiled to herself as she popped the risen dough into the big old Aga oven.

'Nobody gets preferential treatment here,' she said. 'Everyone is in the same boat.'

'Including me,' giggled Ada, as she pointed to her own growing tummy.

'Glory be to God, you grow bigger by the day,' exclaimed Mary Paul.

'That's the general idea, Sister,' Ada smiled.

'You certainly look well,' Theresa commented.

'I'm fine,' Ada agreed. 'I think when the time comes for me to leave, I'll be ready for it,' she admitted.

'I'm worried sick about you living on your own,' Sister Mary Paul fussed. 'No woman should be on her own when she's expecting.'

'Dear Sister,' she soothed. 'I'm no different from all the other thousands of pregnant women who are on their own these days.'

Tears welled up in the old nun's eyes. 'I shall miss you,' she confessed.

'And I'll miss you,' Ada assured her. 'But hopefully I'll come back as soon as I'm fit for work, and in the meantime,' she said with a mischievous wink, 'you'll probably get to like the new staff nurse more than me.'

'Never!' Mary Paul exclaimed. 'Nobody could replace you, dearest Ada.'

Though Sally tried her best to be good, she was always led astray by her fearless, wilful brother, who one day went way too far in his dangerous antics. He was spotted by the station master at Kents Bank walking along the railway track that led to Grange-over-Sands. Outraged, the indignant man penned a letter of complaint to Mary Vale's Reverend Mother, who immediately took matters into her own hands. Summoning Matron into her office, the Reverend Mother came straight to the point.

'Sister Ann,' she declared. 'The evacuee children simply cannot go on like this. They need firm handling and a regular routine.'

'Reverend Mother, with all due respect, Ronnie and Sally are extremely hard to control.'

'We can't just let them run wild,' the Reverend Mother

reminded her. 'They're a danger to themselves and the community.'

Sister Ann vehemently nodded her head. 'They definitely need strong discipline.'

'Exactly,' the Reverend Mother responded. 'So I had a talk with the primary school headmaster in Grange this morning and he's kindly agreed to take the children immediately.'

'That's excellent news,' Sister Ann replied, though a frown soon appeared on her smooth pale brow. 'But how do you plan to get them there?'

'By train, of course,' the Reverend Mother answered.

'They can't be trusted to travel alone on a train,' Sister Ann cried. 'They would cause chaos left to their own devices. Probably pull the alarm cord and bring the train grinding to a halt.'

'I hear Sister Theresa has established a bond with the children,' the Reverend Mother said thoughtfully. 'Perhaps she would agree to escort them to Grange every day?'

Sister Theresa was given the task not only of escorting Ronnie and Sally to school but also of breaking the news to them. Mutinous Ronnie, immediately on the defensive, announced he wasn't 'going to no bleedin' school'.

Sister Theresa took a firm line with him. 'We've been as considerate as we can, giving you enough time to settle into your new home, but really now you are required by law to attend school, or else we'll get into trouble,' she told him.

'I never bothered with school in London – why should I bother with it 'ere?'

Praying for strength, Sister Theresa patiently pointed out, 'Because, as I just said, Ronnie, it is *the law*. If you refuse to attend school, the local bobby will come knocking on our door and he will frogmarch you to school, whether you like it or not.'

Frightened of being man-handled by a policeman, Sally instantly complied. 'I'll go to school, Sister Trees.'

The nun smiled at the earnest little girl. 'Good, and so will your brother if he knows what's good for him.'

Getting the Pickles children washed and dressed for school was quite an undertaking, but, once they were scrubbed cleaner than they had ever been in their lives, and after they had polished off a huge breakfast, the children were accompanied by their mother, holding Ronnie by one hand and Sally by the other, as well as Sister Theresa to Kents Bank Station.

Standing on the platform, Rosie waved cheerily as the train pulled away. 'Be good, I'm proud of you.'

Sitting in between the children and watching pale-faced Rosie, Sister Theresa realized what an effort the short walk from the Home to the station had been for her.

'At least she's doing her bit to support them,' Theresa thought to herself. 'Let's hope Ronnie does his bit to support his poor mother.'

As soon as they disembarked from the carriage, Sister Theresa led the wildly overexcited pair through the narrow, grey-stone streets to the primary school, where Ronnie's expression immediately darkened. Determined to ignore his scowling face, Theresa chatted cheerfully to Sally, who, unlike her rebellious brother, seemed curious as to what might happen once they reached the little Church of England school.

'You'll do some writing and some sums, and you'll be able to play with your new friends after you've had your dinner. At the end of the day I'll pick you up and take you home to Mum,' Theresa explained.

When it came to the handover, Theresa was relieved to find the children's class teacher was a lively young woman with a warm, welcoming smile. After showing Ronnie and Sally to the cloakroom, where they hung up their coats, she gave a discreet nod in the direction of the door, which was Theresa's cue to leave.

Back at Mary Vale the residents were grateful for the peace and quiet that descended on the place without Ronnie and Sally charging around.

'Thank God,' Sybil said when she heard they had gone to school. 'If only they had been packed off to boarding school like I was.' She gave a wistful sigh. 'We wouldn't see them again for months.'

'Yeah,' one of the girls muttered under her breath to her friend, 'then they'd turn out as weird and snobbish as you are, dearie!'

Sister Theresa assured the children's mother that everything had gone better than she had expected.

'I hope Ronnie didn't start swearing,' Rosie asked anxiously.

'Well, he did start, but I told him it would get him into trouble,' Theresa answered truthfully. 'I'll collect them later, then you'll be able to hear all their news yourself.'

'Oh, dear,' Rosie fretted guiltily. 'It's a lot of work for you, Sister, going back and forth like this every day.'

'Hopefully, once they're confident about getting the train, I'll be able to leave them to it,' Theresa replied.

'But, in the meantime, what about your work, and your duties?' Rosie continued to fret. 'I mean, shouldn't you be in the chapel, doing good works, praying the Rosary and the like?'

The young nun smiled. 'I'm doing good works looking after your children,' she pointed out. 'Anyway,' she added realistically, 'the school board would soon be knocking on our door if we didn't pack them off to school.'

Rosie looked defeated. 'I feel like I've failed them both; Sally's never even been to school, and Ronnie spent half his time there running away from the place. He was always in trouble and getting the cane.'

Trying her best to stay sunny and positive, Theresa grinned. 'This is a new start, Rosie – let's look on the bright side and hope for the best.'

8. A Little Bird . . .

Shortly before the new sister was due to arrive, two women in Mary Vale House were pre-occupied in very different ways with getting a new roof over their heads. Ada, still unclear about which way the requisition order might go, was now seriously considering returning home to Leeds sooner rather than later to have her baby.

'We want to look after you, love,' Ada's mother repeatedly insisted when she wrote to her daughter, which Ada never doubted. However, she also knew that a crying baby waking everybody up in the middle of the night would put a lot of pressure on her dad, a foreman who worked shifts at the local coal mine.

Sybil meanwhile was busily planning what she hoped would be her imminent move to the South and a luxury nursing home of her choice. Loaded with coins, she made regular trips to the local telephone box, from where she regularly tried to persuade Monty that Mary Vale was the perfect site for an Army training centre.

'Like I've said before, sweetie, it's perfectly situated for the Army's transport purposes, bang on the main train line north and south.'

Livid at again being bossed about by a woman who should have known her place, Monty exploded, 'Dammit, stop pestering me, woman!'

'Darling, I was only trying to help,' Sybil coaxed to no effect.

Now thoroughly riled, Monty turned to another source of irritation. 'And, while we're at it – don't run away with the idea that I'm going to pay for you to move to the South.'

Sybil caught her breath; perhaps she had overplayed the requisition card? No matter how humiliating it was, she had to backpedal fast if she stood any chance of keeping the old goat sweet.

'Don't say nasty things like that, Monty baby,' she purred. 'I'm sure once I'm back to normal I can cover the cost of The Elms in ways that only I know.'

Smirking Monty humphed loudly on the other end of the phone. 'That's my girl – always did know how to please a chap.'

'So no more horrid naughty threats, eh?' Sybil said through gritted teeth. 'Mustn't scare your little lady, that's not nice.'

Feeling rather disgusted by her act, Sybil put down the phone and returned to Mary Vale deep in thought. From now on she had to prioritize her move South, rather than getting Monty's back up with requisition talk.

Back in London, Monty was thoughtful too. He actively liked the fact that his pregnant mistress was isolated in the far North-Western corner of England; he'd chosen Mary Vale for that specific reason alone. As far as he was concerned, the further away from society that Sybil was, the better. He was damned if he were going to change his mind and let her travel to an extortionately expensive nursing home in the South, which would be too close to London for his comfort.

Knowing ambitious Sybil as he did, the Brigadier suspected that once among her own kind she would inevitably gossip. No, he determined, the spirited little filly was damn well staying in the back of beyond until all this messy business was over with, and when she did return to work it wouldn't be in his office. There were plenty of lively young gels who could keep him entertained, hopefully ones that didn't go and get themselves pregnant like Sybil had.

Monty's thoughts moved on to Mary Vale.

'The longer the place stays exactly as it is the better,' he'd already decided.

He would do everything in his power to ward off any potential requisition interest; it suited him to keep the Home open. He actively wanted Sybil exiled up there until her bastard baby was born and well out of sight; then for all he cared wretched Mary Vale and its snivelling unmarried mothers and their brats could go to hell.

If he could save it from requisition, albeit short term, he most definitely would. The only fly in the ointment was if he saved Mary Vale then he would have to find a viable alternative, and dammit, Sybil was right: Mary Vale was perfectly placed, with its proximity to main train lines and the Barrow shipyard, but he certainly wasn't going to admit that to Sybil.

Ada was taken aback one bright morning when Sister Mary Paul came bustling up.

'The Reverend Mother wants a word with you, dear.'

A shiver went down Ada's spine; was this something to do with the Army's looming requisition order, she wondered. Hurrying along the corridor that connected the Home to the convent, Ada wondered why she might want to see her. Though not a Catholic, Ada automatically crossed herself as she passed the life-sized, carved wooden statue of Our Lady of the Sea, which marked the dividing line between the convent and the Home. Little votive candles flickered around the feet of the statue alongside vases of fresh flowers that were always placed there no matter what time of the year it was.

Ada found the Reverend Mother in her book-lined study and sat across the desk from the rather imposing senior nun.

'Good-morning, Reverend Mother, you asked to see me,' Ada said nervously.

Clearly amused, the Reverend Mother gave an indulgent smile. 'It would appear that Matron and all of your loyal friends don't want to lose sight of you, Ada. They have expressed a sincere interest in your staying local when you start your maternity leave.'

Confused Ada blushed. 'I'm not quite sure how I would do that, Reverend Mother – much as I love this area, and my friends too, I can't possibly afford to live here without a job.'

'Nevertheless,' the Reverend Mother's smile widened, 'I thought I'd just mention, on the off-chance, that our convent has a small cottage on our farm estate that is due to be vacated by the tenant very soon.'

Ada's dark-blue eyes sparkled with excitement; she

knew exactly which cottage the Reverend Mother was talking about.

'Is it the pretty stone cottage at the end of the lane, just past Mary Vale Farm?'

The Reverend Mother nodded. 'Yes, Mary Vale Cottage. The tenancy is in the gift of the convent, which means we could offer it to you for a peppercorn rent as soon as your maternity leave starts, if that would suit you and your family,' she finished diplomatically.

'Mary Vale Cottage!' Ada's eyes brimmed with tears of joy. 'That would be wonderful!' she exclaimed, then her face dropped. 'But what about the requisition threat? If the Army were to take over the Home, surely they would take over the entire estate too. I'd be homeless, just like you.'

The Reverend Mother shook her head. 'We've been in discussion with our friend Brigadier Baldwin, who is doing all he can to point the Army elsewhere,' she replied. 'But, God forbid, if we have to give up the Home, the farm and its adjacent land wouldn't be needed by the Army, so you would still be safe.'

'It would be wonderful to stay here in this place that I have grown to love so much, and hopefully still be close to my friends and colleagues,' Ada exclaimed.

The Reverend Mother offered a word of advice. 'Be careful that everybody doesn't come knocking on your door, Ada. You know better than most how important it is to rest in the last few months of pregnancy.'

Ada gave a quick nod of agreement. 'I also know how comforting company can be too.'

Pushing back her chair, the Reverend Mother rose to

her feet. 'Well, the offer is there: take your time, perhaps discuss it with your husband,' she suggested.

Ada sprang to her feet too. 'I don't need to take my time and there is no chance of discussing anything with my husband, who is on the Front Line,' she blurted out. 'The answer is yes, *yes, please*!' Her eyes went dreamy as she breathlessly concluded the conversation. 'Jamie and I have never shared anywhere together – Mary Vale Cottage will be our first home.'

With wings on her feet, Ada sped back to the ward, where she told her friends what had transpired in the Reverend Mother's office.

'She's offered me Mary Vale Cottage!' she rapturously declared.

Standing between Matron and Sister Theresa, naughty Dora raised her eyebrows in an expression of complicity.

'Well, you don't say!' she cried.

Seeing Sister Theresa blushing to the edges of her white wimple, Ada stopped gabbling.

'The Reverend Mother told me you'd all been involved.'

Dora gave a throaty giggle. 'Believe you me, hardly a person in Mary Vale wasn't involved.'

Ada's eyes filled with grateful tears, and turning to Sister Ann who, she was sure, would have led the delegation, she said, 'Thank you, all of you, I'm so happy!' Unable to control her emotions and regardless of her big tummy, Ada spun round in a circle and cried, 'I'm soooooo happy!'

Giddy with excitement, Ada immediately wrote a letter telling Jamie the good news; then, in the few quiet minutes that she had to herself during her break, she sat at her desk dreamily doodling.

Mary Vale Cottage:
TO DO LIST
Clean, Paint, Decorate
Furniture – cot/bed, linen
Kitchen – utensils

'Our own home,' she sighed. 'It's like a dream come true.'

When Ada went to inspect the cottage a few days later, the old lady who was leaving kindly showed her around the place, which was spotlessly clean and smelt of lavender soap and wax candles.

'My daughter in Lancaster has built a modern annexe for me and furnished it too,' she proudly explained. 'So you're welcome to all the furniture, if you like it, that is.'

Ada's big eyes widened in delight.

'Take another look round on your own,' the old lady urged. 'I'll make us a nice pot of tea.'

The two-up, two-down cottage had a large double room with a window in the gable end that gave on to beautiful views of Cartmel Forest, while the second smaller room, next to a tiny but serviceable bathroom, looked out over the farm fields, where a herd of sheep and their young were grazing on the rich grass. The larger room had an old-fashioned wooden bed, with a matching wardrobe and set of drawers, while the smaller room had a small wardrobe and not much else. At the bottom of the steep flight of stairs was a sweet parlour with an open fire and a small cottage three-piece suite. Last of all was the kitchen, which was a delight. There was a rocking chair beside an old-fashioned black range that kept the room snug and cosy, a large wooden table scrubbed spotlessly clean and an ancient slop sink with a pump handle to provide running water for washing and cooking. Pretty pottery hung from a neat little dresser, and cooking utensils dangled from hooks over the range.

'It's just lovely,' Ada sighed as she sank into the rocking chair and gratefully accepted a cup of scalding hot tea.

'It's that all right,' the old lady agreed. 'If you're as happy here as me and my husband were, you won't go far wrong,' she said, with an emotional catch in her voice. 'For sure it will be a good place to start a family,' she added as her eyes lingered on Ada's swollen tummy. 'I wish you all the luck in the world.'

9. One Last Ditch

After her last emotional conversation with the Brigadier, Sybil resorted to desperate measures. There was only one thing that ever worked with Monty and that was sex. She could have kicked herself for being so cold with him on his last visit to the Home; he had certainly lusted after her then, but she had in no uncertain terms rejected his advances. Not a good move, she crossly told herself. Though she hadn't seen Monty since, she instinctively sensed that he was cooling, which inevitably meant she was losing control of him. At her wits' end, Sybil reasoned that if she could entice Monty back to Mary Vale she might make up for her foolhardy rejection of him and bring him round (one way or another) to her way of thinking.

Even with the vagabond evacuee kids out of the way, Sybil was finding the atmosphere in the Home stifling, and the sight of the ill-bred, ill-educated, dreary residents dragging themselves around was starting to make her feel hysterical.

'I *have* to get out of this hole before I die of bloody boredom,' Sybil muttered through gritted teeth. 'I have to get away.'

Back in London the Brigadier smiled to himself when he received Sybil's fawning letter; knowing what a wilful young filly she was, he rather flattered himself on the success of his *Treat 'em rough, treat 'em tough* policy, which had certainly brought hot-headed Sybil to heel. Here she was abjectly apologizing for her behaviour on his last visit North, her excuse being she felt unattractive due to her condition.

'She certainly looked damned unattractive,' Monty grunted. 'Red-eyed and drab as a fish wife . . . mind you,' he mused, 'she still had a good figure.'

In fact, Monty was due to visit a base close to Barrow-in-Furness soon, and now that he had brought his headstrong mistress into line he might just drop in on sassy little Sybil.

'If she plays her cards right, I'll book us into a discreet country hotel, where we can pick up where we left off,' he chuckled to himself.

Sybil was thrilled to receive his letter in which he agreed to meet her at Mary Vale. In an uncharacteristic fluster she fretted, 'This could be my last chance – I have GOT to make it work.'

Going through her wardrobe she painstakingly chose clothes that enhanced her appearance. Obviously, she couldn't hide her big tummy, but she could draw the eye away from it, directing attention to her full, voluptuous breasts. Accordingly, she went shopping in Grange, where she bought a soft, silky, Empire-line, midnight-blue crêpe dress with little gathers under the bust, which emphasized her shape but gracefully draped over her tummy. Before Monty arrived, she took great care with her lustrous long hair, which she had washed and rolled into a slick shiny victory roll. After carefully applying foundation and mascara, she dabbed her checks with a warm-coloured rouge, then painted her lips with the glossy Victory Red lipstick she had bought in Mayfair a lifetime ago, or so it seemed now. Before she left her room, she liberally dabbed Chanel No. 5 (a gift from Monty's amorous courting days) on to her neck and behind her ears as she stood before an inadequate cracked mirror examining her reflection.

'Good job,' she said in a satisfied voice. 'Now keep calm and seduce the bastard!'

When Sybil went downstairs, she found Monty and Matron in deep discussion, with Sister Mary Paul hovering close by in order to overhear what passed between them – which wasn't difficult, given the Brigadier's booming voice. As Sybil approached, she heard Monty saying, 'My dear lady, I'm doing everything I possibly can on your behalf, but if it's decided by those senior to me to take over the Home, then I would be powerless to stop the order going through. However' – puffing out his chest self-importantly – 'the British Army has a heart when it comes to women and children, hey what?'

'I'm sure of it, Brigadier,' Sister Ann replied gratefully. 'Your efforts to help us keep the Home open are never forgotten – you are always in our prayers.'

Seeing Sybil's furious expression, the Brigadier beamed as he held his arms out wide to greet her. 'How lovely to see you, dear,' he said, as he gave Sybil an avuncular kiss on both cheeks. 'My, you've grown,' he added with a cheeky wink.

Ignoring his sarcasm, Sybil smiled.

'Lovely to see you too, Monty,' she gushed. 'Shall we?'

Knowing that at least half the residents would be watching her leaving on the arm of a loud, overweight Army officer made Sybil cringe with embarrassment. Guiding him out of the front door, she couldn't fail to hear some of the comments that followed her.

'Must be her fancy man.'

'Wouldn't fancy him!' somebody giggled.

'He's old enough to be her father,' another sniggered.

With all the hustle and bustle of the visit, no one had noticed how quiet the newest resident was at the sight of the Brigadier swaggering into Mary Vale. Without any question of doubt, Rosie immediately recognized Brigadier Monty Baldwin – how could she ever forget the man? Florid with thick, wet lips, bald, overweight and overbearing, he had only to open his mouth and his barking voice could be heard half a mile away. Terrified that the Brigadier might see her, Rosie pressed herself against the thick, full-length sitting-room curtains; though realistically, she thought to herself, how on earth would he associate the woman she was now with the pretty lady's maid she had been, another world away before she had married Mick and become financially destitute? Not that Mick wasn't a hard grafter and a good husband: he had worked all the hours that God sent on building sites all over London.

The outbreak of war and Mick's tragic disappearance during armed combat had sent the family he left behind spiralling into poverty. An official letter from his regiment stated that Mick was 'Missing in Action', which had left poor Rosie in an agony of uncertainty. She had written back asking for more details, but the Army was unable to supply them. The constant gnawing worry of never knowing whether her husband was dead or alive didn't help Rosie's health, either physically or mentally, something that without a doubt had a negative effect on the children she was left alone to bring up.

In those days, when she had worked at Dowry House, one of London's most fashionable Knightsbridge establishments owned by Earl Stow of Stowupland, she had cut quite a dash in her maid's black uniform with a pretty white-lace trim that set off her raven-black hair and big dark eyes. She'd had good skin before the babies were born, and good teeth too.

Rosie had adored her mistress, Lady Veronica Baldwin, who was kind, patient and thoughtful with her staff; they in return worshipped the ground she walked on. A gentle smile lit up Rosie's face as she recalled her mistress's beautiful thick golden-blonde hair, which Rosie had brushed a hundred times every night before her ladyship settled into bed and Rosie switched off the gilded bedside lamps.

Rosie had loved preparing her ladyship for those special grand occasions – society balls, opening nights at the theatre or a splendid dinner in Dowry House. Rosie closed her eyes as she recalled Lady Veronica's fabulous wardrobe: dozens of ballgowns, cocktail and little silk tea dresses, stylish tweed suits, and breathtaking tiaras that were kept locked in a safe in his lordship's private study.

'Be a sweetie, Rose,' her ladyship would call out as she bathed in her private bathroom. 'Fetch the pink taffeta and the white mink' or 'Bring the black sequin with the Dowry tiara.'

Excited, Rosie would scurry into the wardrobe, where

she would run her small hands over the different luxurious fabrics, all the time inhaling the perfume of Dior or Givenchy that lingered in the air like a fading dream. Even the invitations her ladyship received, arranged on the white marble mantlepiece in her en suite bedroom facing the park, fascinated Rose, as she was called in those glamorous days. Though a poor reader, she managed to make out the wording on the thick white embossed paper.

'An Invitation to the Palace . . .'

'Drinks at the Savoy . . .'

'A day out at the races . . .'

'Lunch in the Lords . . .'

Oh, what a world of luxury, beauty, opulence and extravagance – and how she had loved every minute of it. Rosie never minded if she had to stay over for the night, even though it meant sleeping in a chair in the hallway waiting for her ladyship to return in the small hours around dawn. Those were the very best and the most personal moments, when Rosie would help to disrobe her slender mistress. Freeing her of her lacy undergarments and fine stockings, she would slip her mistress's manicured feet into soft slippers, before easing a long silk nightgown over her head; then, after seating Lady Veronica in front of her wide antique walnut dressing table with bevelled mirrors, she would brush her hair and remove her make-up before settling her between silk sheets. As she closed the windows on her mistress, Rosie always felt she was locking up a rare treasure for the night.

'Goodnight, ma'am,' she would whisper softly.

'Goodnight, Rose,' a gentle voice would whisper back.

Below stairs, the staff often gossiped as to why their

gracious, charming mistress had married an oaf like the Brigadier.

'When she's got the pick of London, why *him*?'

'She could have anybody – the handsomest, richest and most brilliant men – why settle for dreadful, lecherous Monty Baldwin.'

Hiding in the shadows of the curtains, Rosie's skin crept as she listened to the Brigadier assuring Matron that he was on her side.

'Fighting the good cause,' he boomed.

Her eyes widened in surprise when she saw the Brigadier extend an arm to Sybil. My God, she had seen that look of lascivious lust on the man's face many times before – the look he kept for his special ladies, of which unfortunately she had met many at Dowry House.

'She was definitely scraping the barrel if she had any dealings with him,' Rosie thought. 'Randy old bugger – he'd chase anything in a skirt.'

Peeping through a crack in the curtains, Rosie waited until the Brigadier and Sybil had exited the building, then, sighing with relief, she slipped out of her hiding place, stepping right in front of Ada on her way to the kitchen.

'Heavens, Rosie,' Ada cried. 'You gave me a fright.'

Looking awkward, Rosie gave an embarrassed shrug. 'I was avoiding Miss Harwood's gentleman visitor,' she mumbled.

'Would that be Brigadier Baldwin?' Ada enquired. 'Somebody mentioned they had seen him arrive.'

Rosie gave another embarrassed shrug.

'Do you know him?' Ada enquired.

'Knew him,' Rosie stressed. 'I worked for his wife, Lady Veronica Baldwin.'

Surprised by this very unexpected information, Ada smiled. 'Lady Veronica – sounds very glamorous.'

'You wouldn't believe it to look at me now, but I was once a lady's maid in Knightsbridge,' Rosie said with an unexpected ring in her voice. 'It was the best time of my life; Lady Veronica was a lovely woman, way too good for *him – the Brigadier*,' she finished with a sneer. Then, suddenly nervous, suspecting that she had said too much to a member of staff, who, for all she knew, might approve of the Brigadier, Rosie dashed towards the open front door.

'I'd better see what the children are up to,' she cried over her shoulder.

Standing watching her go, Ada frowned – why was Rosie hiding from the Brigadier, and what on earth could he have done that made her clearly dislike him so much?

10. The Smugglers' Inn

Monty swaggered into the Smugglers' Inn, Grange's smartest hotel, which overlooked the esplanade, in high spirits. Good food, good beer and a pretty woman were the ticket tonight, but when he looked at his ex-lover her former seductive witch-green eyes looked edgy and her skin, which used to be so luscious and creamy, was pale and spotty. Disappointed, Monty's beady little eyes wandered around the bar admiring one buxom waitress after another, until he finally locked eyes with the blowsiest, who approached their table for their order. As Monty ordered a pint for himself and a glass of lemonade for Sybil, she warily watched him flirting with the fulsome waitress, trying to keep her emotions under control. The minute they were left alone, she snuggled up to Monty, purring, 'Darling, it's been ages.'

'Better make the most of it, old girl,' he replied.

Snuggling even closer, Sybil murmured, 'We've so much catching up to do.'

She sighed irritably as the waitress returned with their drinks. Before he could flirt all over again, Sybil said sharply, 'Just leave them on the table.'

Giving her a filthy look, the waitress laid down their full glasses, purposely slopping the contents on the table as she did so. Knocking back a good half of his pint of bitter, the Brigadier muttered through the froth on his lips, 'Got plenty of business to attend to up here, ya know.'

Sybil gave a teasing smile. 'Not that silly old requisition business?'

In reply Monty gave a curt nod. 'Needs to be settled.'

'Then I do hope you've decided to take over Mary Vale? It would so suit the Army's needs,' Sybil enthused.

Though he knew she spoke the truth, the Brigadier continued to rudely fob her off. 'And what would you know about the Army's needs?' he scoffed.

'I did used to work for you,' she gently reminded him. 'Remember, when I was your right-hand girl?'

'Until you got knocked up,' he crudely remarked.

Swallowing her pride, Sybil continued, 'Matron, and everybody in the Home, is saying that we have a lot to thank you for.'

Gulping back what was left of his pint, the Brigadier guffawed. 'Bloody Matron doesn't know her arse from her elbow!' he sneered. 'Though the old girl did say that most of the residents, unlike *you*,' he added witheringly, 'consider themselves lucky to be there in the first place.'

Resisting the urge to shake Monty, Sybil counted to ten; she simply had to make this meeting work for her, and from the confrontational mood Monty was already in she would get nowhere fast if she challenged him. The arrival of the tiresome waitress with their food brought a smile to Monty's face.

'Now here's a sight for sore eyes,' he smarmed, as she set down their order in such a manner that Monty had a fine view of her full breasts, sensuously outlined by the sweetheart neckline of her clinging sweater.

'There you are, sir, can I get you anything else?' the waitress saucily enquired.

Seeing Monty's wide eager smile, Sybil snapped, 'That will be all, thank you.'

When she turned her attention to the fish pie steaming on the plate in front of her, Sybil's stomach churned; not so with Monty, who eagerly tucked into his meat and potato pie. As the smell of fish overwhelmed her, Sybil struggled unsteadily to her feet.

'If you'll excuse me,' she murmured as she hurried off to the ladies' toilets, where she was violently sick.

'Damn! Damn! Damn!' she seethed as she slumped against the wall and wiped herself down. Though faint and dizzy, Sybil focused hard as she tried to reapply her scarlet lipstick, which contrasted harshly with her ashen grey face. 'This really isn't going according to plan,' she thought anxiously.

Taking deep breaths to steady her nerves, Sybil walked back into the restaurant, where the sight of the wanton waitress virtually perched on leering Monty's knee didn't improve her flagging spirits. Dismissing the silly girl with a haughty glare, Sybil sat down again and realized she simply hadn't the strength or even the ability to play silly games any more; all she wanted were the facts, and if they weren't to her liking then for all she cared bloody Monty could go to hell.

'Please, Monty, just tell me the truth about the requisitioning situation at Mary Vale House?'

Monty feigned a guileless expression. 'How many times do I have to tell you? The decision is not solely mine to make.'

Weary of his lies, Sybil's temper began to fray. 'Then please explain why Sister Ann fawns all over you whenever you visit Mary Vale.'

Going bright red with indignation, Monty muttered through a mouthful of pie, 'Dammit, woman, I'm getting sick of your bally questions.' Seeing Sybil looking mutinous, he added, 'Look at it this way: you're up the duff and not fit for society – isn't Mary Vale your best option, for the time being at least?'

Sybil had to bite her lip to stop herself from screaming every known word of abuse at him. She had always known that it suited him to isolate his pregnant mistress in the middle of nowhere, two hundred miles away from any gossip and sideswipe jokes that might reflect on his own misconduct or offend his precious wife. Knowing she was beaten and that he was running rings around her completely defeated Sybil, who once more got to her feet.

'Take me home immediately,' she demanded in an imperious voice that everybody in the bar could hear.

Looking both embarrassed and furious, Monty quickly rose to his feet too, wiped his greasy chin on his perfectly laundered napkin and spoke in an overloud, solicitous voice. 'Not feeling well, are we, dear? Come along, let me help you.'

'I can manage,' Sybil muttered as she barged past him.

'Sorry to cause a fuss – it's her delicate condition,' the Brigadier murmured, as he passed the goggle-eyed waitresses and the drinkers at the bar.

Once outside, his tone changed immediately. Livid at her behaviour he demanded, 'What the hell do you think you're playing at?'

Ready for clawing Monty's eyes out, Sybil vented all the bitterness and anger she had bottled up during her exile at Mary Vale. 'How dare you treat me like a bitch that's about to whelp?' she snarled in his face. 'It's because of you and your stupid bloody fumbling that I'm dumped up here where you have guaranteed by your devious manipulations that I will stay, whether I like it or not.'

Monty threw her a look of withering contempt. 'You should be bally grateful I've forked out the money to support you.'

'You talk as if you have nothing to do with my being pregnant – it takes two to tango, you know,' she cried.

Giving her a dangerously cold look, Monty sneered, 'You really make me laugh,' he mocked. 'You and your family have plenty of money; there's nothing to stop you leaving the Home if you're that dissatisfied.'

Ready to throttle the man with her bare hands, Sybil snapped back, 'Wouldn't that suit you perfectly? Getting somebody else to foot the bill, while taking absolutely no responsibility for anything that has happened.'

'Don't play the innocent with me, lady,' Monty snarled. 'You knew exactly what you were taking on when you didn't reject my approaches,' he reminded her.

Knowing she couldn't argue with that, Sybil turned on her heel and set off walking home alone.

'You're despicable, loathsome,' she called furiously over her shoulder, 'and one day, when all this bloody awful business is over, I vow I will have my revenge on you.'

'What revenge?' he mocked. 'How can you ever get close to me? I'm married to one of the most highly ranked women in the realm. Do you think her family will ever listen to a little tart like you, snivelling on about how badly you've been treated? You made your bed, now lie in it.'

As Sybil set off walking through the wet windy night, he yelled after her departing back, 'To hell with you!'

Then, without a backward glance, Monty re-entered the Smugglers' Inn, where several eager waitresses welcomed him back.

11. Plans

Normally immensely energetic, Ada was daily more aware of how she was starting to flag at certain times of the day; sometimes she even felt like she could fall asleep standing up. Seeing her smothering yawns behind her hand while they were doing their morning round caused Sister Ann to speak up.

'The sooner you start your maternity leave, dear, the better.'

Smiling apologetically, Ada assured her that she was fine. Smiling back, the nun said, 'I can see you're fine, Ada, in fact, I've never seen you look better – pregnancy suits you – but that doesn't mean to say you have to keep pushing yourself.'

Ada nodded. 'You're quite right, sister, it's just that I'm a bit –' Catching sight of Ann's knowing expression, Ada gave a resigned shrug. 'You know me.'

'Putting everybody before yourself,' Matron finished.

'There's always somebody here with a need bigger than mine,' Ada explained.

'Of course – it's a Mother and Baby Home, what would you expect?' Matron answered realistically. 'There's always some cause of concern.'

'We're not doing too badly at the moment,' Ada added.

'Apart from Rosie, who's a huge cause of concern,' Matron pointed out. 'We can feed her up and make sure she gets all the rest she needs but hers is a very delicate pregnancy.'

'I know – her anaemia's not improving fast,' Ada agreed. 'I'm amazed she's got this far, to be honest.'

'The baby's heart-beat remains weak,' Matron sighed. 'She might not make it until the end, you know.'

'Really, the things women go through,' Ada remarked. 'At least Rosie's married, so she's not got that unmarried mother stigma to bear. But she does have the terrible fear of not knowing where her husband is,' Ada added. 'Imagine not knowing if your husband is alive or dead, captured, imprisoned, wounded.' Thinking of her own beloved Jamie, Ada shivered as a chill of fear shot down her spine. 'Apparently he doesn't even know his wife is pregnant.'

Matron sighed. 'So many issues are stacked against her.'

'On the positive side she seems a lot better since Ronnie and Sally started school,' Ada said, smiling. 'At least she gets a bit of a break during the day when the kiddies aren't roaring around.'

'Poor Rosie – she tries her best to take care of them until bedtime, but you can see it's a strain,' Matron said sympathetically. 'Nevertheless, she still makes the effort, which is to be admired.'

'I'm increasingly worried about Sybil at the moment too – she's not been right since Brigadier Baldwin's last visit,' Ada noted.

Sister Ann raised her eyebrows in a quizzical look.

'I know, I know how difficult she is,' Ada quickly responded before Matron could say the obvious. 'She's a downright snob and she invites trouble.'

'She's never once attempted to integrate with the other

residents,' Matron reminded Ada. 'Moving to another nursing home is the best thing she can do – she will never be happy here unless she changes her habits.'

'I agree that she would be much happier in a place with women of her own kind – she's certainly a fish out of water in Mary Vale – but these days she seems depressed; she barely eats and stays in her room as much as she can. I'm convinced that brigadier chap did something to upset her.'

Sister Ann frowned. 'I admit he is a pompous man, but he is working hard on Mary Vale's behalf,' she pointed out.

A flush spread across Ada's pretty face and her big blue eyes looked troubled. 'Is he *really*?' she questioned. 'I'm seriously beginning to wonder if it isn't all talk and no action. I mean, why hasn't he involved us in his discussions with the local Army officers, some of whom we already know and are on good terms with? Have you ever thought that he could be stringing us along?'

Matron's brow furrowed in concern. 'Why would he waste his time doing that?' she enquired. 'And why would he draw attention to the matter if he didn't think he had some chance of succeeding?'

'To be honest, I just don't trust him – and I stick to my point, Sybil's not been the same since his last visit to the Home.'

'Mmm,' Matron murmured thoughtfully, then, reminding herself of what they had originally been discussing, she added, 'We've somehow managed to move away from the subject of your departure date, Ada.'

'I don't want to be here for too long after Miss Mann

has joined us,' Ada said. 'It wouldn't be fair on her, apart from anything else.'

Matron nodded. 'Perhaps you could work in tandem with Miss Mann for a week?'

'I think I can manage a week,' Ada smiled.

When Ada took Dora and Sister Theresa to see Mary Vale Cottage, Dora, worried about the requisitioning rumour which was always at the forefront of her mind, came straight to the point. 'If the Home gets closed down and we're all sent elsewhere, you might well find yourself on your own in the middle of nowhere – and with a new-born baby too.'

'You know what, Dora, I'm prepared to take that risk,' Ada answered frankly. 'I've got to know a lot of good people in this beautiful valley, where I think I would be happy to live forever.'

Theresa gave a cheerful smile. 'Anyway, the Home might not be requisitioned,' she said optimistically. 'All this nasty scaremongering could just be a silly storm in a teacup.'

After a tour of Mary Vale Cottage, dewy-eyed Dora said, 'It reminds me of when me and mi husband set up home. We started out renting a little place just like this on't other side of Kendal, eeh, they were happy days.' Ada couldn't help but notice the catch in her friend's voice.

'It's like a doll's house,' Theresa exclaimed in delight. 'So neat and trim and tidy.'

Ada slipped an arm around her friend's slender waist. 'You're welcome any time, darling,' she said sincerely. 'Both of you,' she added as she teased, 'You never know, I might get lonely.'

Dora gave a loud hoot of disbelief. 'YOU, lonely? Pull the other one!' she mocked. 'Anyway, you won't have time for socializing, you'll have your hands full with a newborn baby.'

Ada gazed around the little kitchen the former tenant had left meticulously clean. 'I'm longing for Jamie to see it,' she sighed.

'Are you planning on any changes?' Dora asked, as she walked into the pretty little parlour.

'I was thinking of giving the kitchen another coat of paint,' Ada told her. 'I rather like the pretty old-fashioned floral wallpaper in here, so I thought I'd leave it as it is.'

'You could smarten it up with a lick of gloss paint on the door frames and skirting boards,' Dora suggested. 'I'll see if I've got some spare pots of paint in the shed when I get home later.'

'I'd love to make some curtains for the baby's room,' Theresa said shyly.

Moved by her generous offer, Ada called the young postulant by the name that was hers before she entered the convent.

'That would be lovely, Shirley, of course I don't know the sex of the baby, so I leave the colour for you to decide.'

'I could paint the baby's room too?' Theresa eagerly asked.

'That would be so lovely.' Ada smiled. 'I'm not sure how nimble I am up a ladder these days,' she said as she stroked a hand over her tummy.

Busy with all sorts of arrangements both in the Home and at the cottage, Ada nonetheless decided she would try to have one more talk in private with Sybil. Spotting her sitting on a bench one warm afternoon, Ada crossed the lawn to sit beside her. At the sight of her Sybil edged away, which didn't bode well.

'Hope you don't mind,' Ada said brightly. 'It's such a lovely day, I just thought I'd get a bit of fresh air before I return to the ward.'

Sybil shrugged and didn't respond. Determined not to take offence, Ada cheerfully continued. 'This is the best time of the year here,' she declared, throwing out a hand to take in the spectacular views of Morecambe Bay and the lower foothills of the Lake District. 'The sea, the bay, the mountains.'

Looking completely unimpressed, Sybil gave a rude grunt.

'Have you thought about attending my ante-natal classes?' Ada enquired. 'They're every afternoon, after dinner, just for an hour.'

Sybil gave her a long, level look. 'I find the company of most of the women here odious,' she said coldly. 'Why would I want to spend even more time with them than is absolutely necessary?'

'The classes are about helping mothers prepare for their delivery,' Ada told her.

'Look, can I be crystal clear?' Sybil asked. 'I don't want your help, or anybody else's for that matter. I just want to get this wretched business over with, then I'll be on the train back home before you even know it.'

Ada was shocked by the vitriol in Sybil's voice, but she answered steadily. 'I'm sorry to hear that.' Their conversation got no further, as Ronnie and Sally, fresh back from school, came tearing into sight, yelling. Waving an imaginary rifle in the air, Ronnie was hollering, 'BANG! BANG! You're dead.'

'ARGHHH!' shrieked Sally at the top of her voice, as she fell in a fake slump at Sybil's feet.

Outraged, Sybil leapt up. 'This place is second only to a lunatic asylum,' she cried.

Storming away, she almost bumped into Rosie, who was struggling to catch up with her children.

'Have you no control over your brats?' Sybil demanded.

Huffing and puffing for breath, Rosie spluttered, 'I'm so sorry . . . I couldn't keep up with 'em.'

'Oh, really?' Sybil retorted as her eyes raked up and down Rosie's skinny frame and threadbare clothes. 'You do surprise me.'

Ronnie made a rude sign after Sybil's upright departing figure. 'Bloody snooty cow!'

Concerned about Rosie's physical frailty, Ada sprang indignantly from the bench and addressed the wayward boy. 'That's enough, Ronnie!' she cried. 'We don't behave like that at Mary Vale – I suggest you stick to our rules as long as you are here.'

Seeing that Rosie was about to start making apologies on her son's behalf, Ada intervened. 'I'm sorry, but I'm talking to Ronnie, Rosie. If he continues in this rude way, I will have no option but to take him to see the Reverend Mother, who won't tolerate his bad behaviour.'

Ronnie visibly paled under the sheen of dirt that always seemed to be smeared across his scrawny face; it seemed like the only person he was afraid of was the senior nun at the convent.

'Now run off and play while I have a word with your mum,' Ada told the naughty Ronnie and his embarrassed little sister. 'And make sure you wash your hands before tea-time,' she called after them.

Clearly weary, Rosie slumped on to the bench that Ada had just vacated. 'We always seem to be in trouble,' she said, with tears in her eyes.

Ada quickly sat down again. 'It's much better than when you first arrived here,' she pointed out.

'It's forever two steps forwards and one back,' Rosie sighed. 'I don't know why any of the residents put up with us.'

'They're kind women,' Ada started.

'Apart from one,' Rosie interrupted. 'That woman, Sybil Harwood, has got it in for me and my kids – you can see it every time she lays eyes on them.' She shrugged. 'If looks could kill.'

'The rest of the residents are fairly understanding,' Ada continued diplomatically. 'And things are much better since the children started attending school.'

'Yes, until they get back here again and start playing their noisy games,' Rosie answered realistically. 'We should never have come in the first place.'

'I don't think you had much choice, did you?' Ada enquired.

'S'pose not,' Rosie answered with a resigned shrug. 'One thing's for sure, we're not popular, wherever we go.'

12. Feeling Broody

Ada thoughtfully suggested to Sister Ann that her replacement should have one of the guest rooms in Mary Vale House.

'I have never minded being in the convent,' she told Sister Ann as they walked upstairs to the Home's guest rooms. 'In fact, I loved the cool quietness of my little cell room there, but it might not be to everybody's taste.'

'A private room might suit Miss Mann more,' Sister Ann agreed. 'But,' she added as her eyes swept around the room, 'they are a bit on the shabby side.'

'Shabby, but clean and with good views down the valley,' Ada pointed out.

Sister Ann gave a heavy sigh. 'If I'm honest, I must confess to feeling a bit nervous; I'm so used to working alongside you, dearest Ada – we will all miss you so much.'

Though edgy too, Ada nevertheless stayed calm. 'We're a tight little team,' she agreed. 'Look how devastated we all were when Dora lost her sons and left Mary Vale for a while. But my going isn't permanent, Ann, I'll be back before you know it.'

Feeling slightly ashamed of her outburst, Sister Ann moved on to less emotional territory. Glancing around the rather stark guest room, she murmured, 'I'll make sure there are plenty of fresh flowers in here to welcome Miss Mann.'

Ada answered brightly, 'Good idea – that should cheer the place up.'

Overjoyed at the thought of taking possession of Mary Vale Cottage, Ada couldn't wait until the official handover date to move in. At the earliest opportunity, when she had a break in her shifts, with a briefcase in one hand and a suitcase in the other, she made her way down the farm track to the cottage. Hurrying up the stairs to the baby's room, Ada smiled to herself as she stood in the doorway, inhaling the combined smell of fresh paint and lavender furniture polish. Darling Sister Theresa had kept her promise: the room, now painted a soft, pale, primrose colour, glowed warmly and the pretty lined patchwork curtains Theresa and Sister Mary Paul had made added a childish gaiety to the place. Dora's gift stood in the corner – an old cot she had bought at a local jumble sale for two shillings and sixpence. Washed and sanitized in readiness for the new arrival, Dora had also left on the little chest of drawers, also painted a soft primrose colour, a supply of baby linen and winceyette blankets that she had borrowed from the hospital storage cupboard.

Seeing the room bathed in the luminous golden light of the now setting sun, Ada's heart contracted with a mixture of love and excitement.

Only weeks now and she would be holding her son or daughter in her arms, Jamie's child. The thought brought tears rushing to her eyes; when would she see her darling again? Love letters regularly passed between them, outpourings of their passion and longing which kept the pair of them going during long periods of absence.

Oh, my dearest love,

Even though life at the clearing station is round the clock, I see your beautiful smiling face before me so much. Your lovely eyes, so blue and gentle, and your red lips, pouting and kissable. The line of your neck and the sweep of your full breasts, silky smooth and soft to the touch . . . my love, you have no idea how much I dream of your gorgeous body and the wonderful love-making we share so joyfully when we are alone together.

At first Ada had blushed at the intimate detailed descriptions in her husband's passionate missives, but, as she read them over and over again, she rejoiced in Jamie's wild freedom of expression. What harm or embarrassment was there in a husband telling his wife how much he desired and admired her?

Perched on the side of the old-fashioned double bed with noisy rusty springs that she and Jamie would share, Ada patted the slippery silk purple eiderdown (a gift from the old lady before she left for her new home in Lancaster) and gazed dreamily out of her bedroom window. The valley before her was steeped in a crimson sunset light that flared deep indigo as the sun dropped over the skyline, casting a dark shadow over Cartmel Forest, where the tallest conifers spiked a filigree pattern against the glowing orb of the sinking sun.

Feeling suddenly tired, Ada made up the bed with clean linen and cosy blankets that she had borrowed from the convent stores, then she went downstairs to build up a fire in the old black kitchen range. After putting the kettle on to make a pot of tea, Ada sat in the creaky wooden rocking chair, where her eyelids slowly started to droop.

'If I don't move soon, I'll sleep here all night,' she firmly told herself, as she staggered to her feet to brew a pot of tea.

Later, after washing her face, cleaning her teeth and brushing her long, thick brunette hair, Ada slipped between the cool bed sheets and, as the moon rose over the mountains, she fell into a deep peaceful sleep in her new home.

Waking up bright and early the next morning, Ada closed the door of her sweet little cottage, then smiling at the novelty of walking to work, set off along the narrow country lane that passed Mary Vale Farm. Seeing Farmer Arkwright inspecting his sheep bleating plaintively in their pen, she waved happily.

'Morning,' she called. 'Gorgeous day.'

Farmer Arkwright gazed up at the azure-blue sky, where swallows and house martins zipped and dived in their search for small insects to feed to their young.

'It's that all right,' he beamed. 'Settled in all right?' he queried.

'Oh, yes,' Ada enthused. 'It's thrilling to have a home of our own – I still can't believe it.'

'Let me know if you need any help shifting furniture and the like,' he added kindly. 'Don't want you lugging stuff about in your delicate condition.'

'That's very kind of you,' Ada answered gratefully. 'And thank you for the milk and butter you left on the doorstep for me.'

'There'll be a bit of Lancashire cheese later,' he promised with a grin. 'You can't beat fresh, strong, crumbly Lancashire cheese.'

'Thanks again,' Ada cried as she almost skipped up the lane.

When Ada walked into the hospital, she spotted Sister Ann giving Miss Mann a tour of the hospital. It was actually a relief to see her replacement doing the morning rounds with Matron; even though they had only just met, Ada thought (as she watched them through the window) that they seemed fairly relaxed in each other's company. Dora grinned at Ada when she joined her in the delivery room, where she was sterilizing the surgical equipment.

'The new staff nurse made a good impression on the patients in the post- and ante-natal wards,' Dora told Ada. 'Stopped at every bed to enquire after the health of each of them.'

'That's nice,' Ada replied.

'No interest in the nursery, though, hardly a second glance,' Dora continued. 'Just like last time: she peered into the occasional little white cot, but there was no cooing or clucking noises, the likes you or me would make.'

Ada threw her a teasing smile. 'And I bet she didn't pick the babies up and kiss them on both cheeks before giving them a cuddle like you always do?'

Offended Dora shook her head. 'Sister Mann was clearly not carried away at the sight of the little darlings.'

'Don't worry, dear, not everybody is like us,' Ada smiled. 'Miss Mann probably doesn't express her emotions in the same way we do.'

'Obviously not,' Dora replied.

'Has she met all the residents?' Ada asked.

'Only the girls on the wards.' Dora dropped her voice to a conspiratorial whisper. 'Everybody's talking about her, though, comparing her to you – you'll be a hard act to follow, for sure.'

Ada shook her head. 'Don't be silly – they'll soon forget about me! Out of sight, out of mind.'

Dora didn't think that in the present circumstances the old cliché rang true: there were some residents, like Rosie, who were needier than others. The staff, from the top to the bottom, did their best, but Ada was especially compassionate with the young mothers, an invaluable quality in a nurse which no amount of money could buy.

'Staff Nurse Mann is supposed to be shadowing me,' Ada said, as she busily laid the metal instruments in the sterilizing machine. 'But I'll leave her and Matron alone to finish the ward rounds before I catch up with them.'

Dora grinned as she nodded towards the instruments Ada was loading up. 'Make sure they're spotless,' she joked. 'You never know, you might be needing them yourself soon.'

13. The New Staff Sister

After her late arrival at Mary Vale the previous night, Edith Mann had walked into her room, where her heart sank. Even though it had been polished until it positively shone and the garden flowers in vases on the windowsills filled the air with a fresh perfume, there was no getting away from the worn carpets, faded rugs and rickety furniture. Nevertheless, Edith threw back her rather stiff shoulders; she had made her decision and now she must live with it. Working at Mary Vale was a necessary move – a sacrifice she had made for the greater cause. Admittedly it wasn't as smart or as comfortable as her previous place of employment, a rather select nursing home in Harrogate full of snobby young mothers whose every whim was indulged virtually around the clock.

'Compared to this place it was like Buckingham Palace,' Edith thought.

Taking a deep, determined breath, Edith critically checked her reflection in the small mirror hanging on the wall. At thirty-nine she was still strong and fit, her long rather horsey face offset by an abundance of thick, dark, wiry hair, now flecked with streaks of silver; her grey eyes were assertive; and her chin firm. She was a woman who had worked hard all her life in order to support her tyrant of a mother, who had never allowed her only daughter so much as a look at any young men. Mrs Mann controlled

Edith with violence and threats, and Edith, terrified of her mother's volatile temper, had towed the line until she fell for the married consultant gynaecologist at her former place of work. That her beloved was a married man with an invalid wife hadn't dissipated Edith's passion; if anything, it had enhanced her determination to comfort and support him. Over the past five years they had enjoyed a clandestine relationship which perfectly suited them both and would have gone on for years had it not been for one of the night nurses spotting him sneaking out of the dormitory in the early dawn light. Terrified that their affair would damage Charles's career and enrage her deranged mother, Edith had immediately resigned her post and looked for work elsewhere. Mary Vale was the first place to offer her a job, and she had snatched at it like a rope thrown to a drowning woman.

'Charles is my first priority,' grim-faced Edith told her reflection. 'And anywhere on earth is better than living at home.'

After completing the ward rounds, Sister Mann met up with Ada in Matron's office, where they swapped notes on the hospital's filing and record system, after which they were joined by Father Ben, who explained his role to the new staff nurse.

'I'm the convent's resident priest,' he started. 'I officiate at all the Masses and services, plus I'm in charge of the Home's adoption procedures.'

Ada beamed. 'Father Ben always manages to find the best matches for all our babies,' she said, as she threw the priest a loyal smile. 'We always encourage our residents to discuss their arrangements with Father Ben.'

Edith expressed her surprise. 'In my former place of work adoptions were always arranged by a representative from the board of governors.'

Loyal Ada said, 'We trust Father Ben's guidance and expertise; he has more insight than anyone on Mary Vale's governing body.'

The priest responded with a modest smile. 'Over the years I've learnt how important it is to get to know the residents and when possible their backgrounds too; it helps me enormously when it comes to choosing the appropriate adoptive parents.'

Edith gave a polite smile. 'Heavens!' she thought. 'Priests and nuns in preference to official governing bodies – Mary Vale is like some archaic institution out of the Middle Ages!'

Edith was in for another surprise when Ada briefed her before they went to meet the residents at tea-time.

'Most of our girls are from poor backgrounds and depend heavily on the charitable trust fund the convent extends to the destitute; you'll find some of the younger girls are frightened and nervous,' Ada explained.

Within minutes of entering the dining room, it became clear to Edith that Ada was immensely popular among the young women sitting around the table.

'How are you feeling this afternoon, Sister?' a cheery girl asked.

'Marvellous,' Ada beamed. 'You're looking better, Irene – have you been taking one of your long walks across the marsh again?' Turning to a small quiet girl across the table, Ada brightly enquired, 'Have you heard more news from your little sister, Josephine?'

When all the diners were assembled, a polite silence fell after Ada tapped her teacup.

'I'd like you all to welcome Staff Sister Mann, who is replacing me.'

Though the residents smiled or nodded politely, it was impossible for Edith not to miss the flickers of sadness and disappointment that flashed across almost all of their faces; clearly none of them wanted to say goodbye to Sister Ada. Edith couldn't avoid seeing their curious eyes straying from herself to the vibrant young woman beside her; she knew they would inevitably be comparing Ada's stunning looks and sparkling eyes with her own plainer, more middle-aged appearance. Steeling herself Edith thought, 'Hopefully sometime soon they'll learn to appreciate my professional skills. I'm quite sure in that department I will not be a poor comparison.'

The familiar sense of inferiority that Edith had carried all her life, the enormous weight of being unloved and feeling inadequate, reared its ugly head. Fortunately, since meeting Charles and finding love, Edith had become more aware of her own self-worth. Theirs might have been an illicit affair, but the effect it had had on Edith had been to turn her world completely upside down. Throughout their time together Edith had always been realistic enough to know that Charles's feelings for her amounted to nothing more than affection, and she was happy to take without complaint any crumbs that fell from his table. Her feelings for him amounted to adoration, and being wanted, touched and kissed had turned her former bleak emotional landscape into a paradise of joyful fulfilment. Life was indeed grim again without Charles, but at least she had had passion in her otherwise empty life, and for that she would always be grateful.

During the wholesome meal Edith chatted to her neighbours, but her

attention was constantly drawn to Sybil, who remained aloof from the residents gathered around the dining table; the woman wore good shoes, expensive clothes and seemed to ignore everybody in the room. Once she had finished the tasty shepherd's pie made mostly of suedes, onions, a little well-cooked mince subtly flavoured with fresh herbs and heaped with creamy potatoes, Sybil departed the room without a backward glance.

'Thank God, her ladyship's gone,' a girl said over-loudly.

'I don't think the food was up to scratch,' another tittered. 'Bloody Southern snob.'

Ada gently rebuked them. 'Ladies, let's not be unkind.'

Under her breath Edith tactfully enquired, 'Who is that proud young woman?'

'Miss Harwood,' Ada answered in a whisper. 'She rather keeps herself to herself.'

'Mmm, I can see that,' Edith murmured.

Their exchange was interrupted by the noisy arrival of Rosie with her brood, which caused a stir around the room. The residents shuffled to make way for the restless children, who were kept under reasonable control by their mother and Sister Mary Paul, but, as far as Edith (who had no idea how much the school in Grange had reined in some of the children's wildness) was concerned, their behaviour was appalling. Little did she know that at least they now washed their hands before meal-times (or they wouldn't get a crumb, Sister Mary Paul threatened them daily), and they sat down to eat instead of racing around the table throwing crusts of bread at each other.

Edith stole a secret peep at pale, tired Rosie, sitting across the table from her. Again, in a quiet voice, Ada explained, 'That's the Pickles family, Rosie, Ronnie and Sally, our only evacuees, who recently arrived from London. The mother has been suffering from anaemia and hyperemesis gravidarum, from which she is slowly recovering.'

'She looks very poorly indeed,' Edith quietly commented. 'Has she shown any improvement since she arrived at the Home?'

'A little,' Ada answered cautiously. 'Her appetite is poor, but she's getting more rest throughout the day now that her children are at school.'

Edith glanced again at the noisy children. 'Mmm,' she murmured disapprovingly. 'They do appear to be quite a handful.'

After tea, just as Edith and Ada were about to leave the room and return to work, one of the girls asked, 'Will you be taking over Ada's breathing and relaxation classes, Sister Mann?'

Taken aback, Edith shook her head. 'I don't think I'll have time,' she prevaricated. Seeing a look of disappointment on the girls' faces, she quickly added, 'I will of course discuss it with Sister Ada and find out more.'

Edith conducted the evening ward rounds with Matron and Ada, the latter, unless called upon, staying as much in the background as possible. As they were crossing from the post- to the ante-natal ward, Edith surprised Ada with a sudden question. 'I was never briefed about taking over your exercise and breathing classes?'

Knowing just how much the patients enjoyed the classes and the camaraderie that existed within the group, plus the undoubted benefits to be had from the exercises themselves, Ada answered eagerly. 'It would be marvellous if you could?'

'Well, I'm not trained,' Edith quickly explained, looking far from enthusiastic.

Anxious about the girls she had been teaching and whose babies were due about the same time as her own, Ada persisted. 'I could continue for a while and train you in the process if you like? It would benefit me as well as the other ladies.'

Edith gave a slow nod. 'We could see how I get on,' she answered cautiously.

'They're daily, every afternoon,' Ada continued. 'Indoors if it's wet or windy, outside if the weather's fine – they usually last for about an hour.'

Edith gave a bleak smile; it really was the very last thing she wanted.

'I'm sure they do the girls a world of good,' she said limply.

14. Tension

Though Sybil didn't seek out friendship in the Home, she nevertheless had a grudging respect for Staff Sister Ada Reid, who would soon be replaced by Staff Sister Mann. Sybil had taken an instant dislike to her. After observing the new nurse on the job, Sybil's instincts calcified; she didn't like Edith's false smile or the way the woman smothered her Yorkshire accent with a feigned posh one. Though Sybil was by no means a fan of the Northern drawl, she much preferred it to Miss Mann's tortured pronunciation, which grated on her nerves. She wondered if the new Ward Sister had Ada's sensitive birthing knowledge and skill, which Sybil had heard a great deal about.

'She definitely needs something to make up for her haughty manner,' Sybil thought harshly.

In truth nothing agreed with Sybil. Neither the Home nor the inmates nor pregnancy itself. The nauseous months were well past, giving way to enlarged, painful breasts, indigestion, backache, sleepless nights, and rushing to the lavatory almost every hour. All pretence of being a glamour girl fell away as Sybil's depressing life engulfed her. She had stopped caring about what she looked like: her long, dark, lustrous hair was becoming thin and straggly, and her previously fine-spirited green eyes showed more defeat than pride these days. She had run out of foundation, rouge and mascara, and had not the slightest interest in replacing any make-up; really, what was the point? For now, life was on hold until she returned to London, where she would grasp life again with a passion – though NOT with Monty by her side, Sybil vowed.

To her everlasting shame, Sybil had overheard some of the residents gossiping about a local girl who worked in the Smugglers' Inn, where Sybil and Monty had argued when he had last visited.

'She said he paid her ten bob to spend the night with him, gave her a packet of fags too,' one of the residents said loudly as Sybil passed by. 'The fella said he were visiting his girlfriend' – she winked cheekily in Sybil's direction – 'but she was sick – up the duff, so not in't mood for any slap and tickle.'

Sybil's pale cheeks flared crimson. 'God! How utterly humiliating,' she seethed as she stalked past the gossips with her head held high.

As if her public shaming weren't enough, loud praise for the Brigadier regularly grated on Sybil's frayed nerves.

'Thanks to the Brigadier's kind intervention,' she overheard Matron telling an anxious resident, 'there's less fear of the Home's closure, though I must stress,' she added cautiously, 'we're nowhere near out of the woods.'

'So, are we staying put, then?' the nervous girl enquired.

'As I just said,' Matron answered patiently. 'We're still holding our breath and hoping for the best. If the Brigadier succeeds in persuading the powers that be to look elsewhere, hopefully the sword of Damocles hanging over our heads will pass us by, and we shall be saved.'

The questioner gave an irritated shrug – she hadn't a clue who the hell Damocles was or why he was waving his sword over Mary Vale; all she wanted was a straight yes or no. While Matron was speaking, Ada caught sight of Sybil's bitter expression. Feeling sorry for her patient, Ada shot her a smile that was not reciprocated.

'Poor woman,' Ada thought compassionately. 'She must be the loneliest woman in Mary Vale.'

Like a caged animal, Sybil had grudgingly resigned herself to her fate, but even as she accepted the changes she was undergoing physically, her mind grew sharper and more vindictive. Like a spider in its web, Sybil had plenty of time to think of how she would wreak her revenge on Monty for what he had done to her. She had no choice but to endure what lay ahead, but, exiled as she was, she at least had time to concoct malevolent schemes to bring Monty to his knees; wicked pleasures in the long drab days of her pregnancy.

With her head buzzing, Sybil was hardly aware that the residents in collusion with the nuns were planning a surprise farewell tea-party for Sister Ada. Sister Mary Paul had baked scones, which she planned to serve with damson jam made from last year's fruit crop, along with a scraping of Farmer Arkwright's creamy best butter. While Ada was busy on the wards, the giggling residents decorated the dining room with bowls of fresh garden flowers and colourful bunting. Delighted with their efforts, the residents waited excitedly for their guest of honour to arrive. There was just one fly in the ointment, in that Ronnie and Sally arrived home from school before Ada had finished her shift. Having spent all afternoon on the shameful dunce's chair in the schoolroom, Ronnie barged into the dining room like a bear with a sore head. Seeing him crashing around, Sybil raised her eyes to heaven: why in God's name did nobody land him a hefty whack and send him off to bed for the entire evening? Much to everybody's relief, Rosie managed to coax her bad-tempered son and whimpering daughter into the garden, but Ronnie, furious that yet again he was being excluded from events, tore back into the dining room and wilfully ripped down all the bunting and hurled half of the flowers (arranged in vases on the sills) out of the window – and just at the very point at which Ada, with a happy expectant smile on her face, came sailing into the room. Seeing the entire Pickles family screaming and swearing at each other, Ada typically put their needs first.

'Let's have tea,' she said, taking charge of the scones and jam, which immediately assuaged Ronnie's fury, but the boy's outrageous behaviour still left most of the residents feeling resentful and angry.

'Brat!' Sybil seethed loudly.

At the first available moment Rosie herded her bothersome children out of the room, but the happy, anticipatory mood had been spoilt by Ronnie's acts of wanton destruction. Sister Theresa busily set the vases that weren't smashed to rights, while a couple of the girls tried to rehang the bunting, which dangled rather forlornly from the cornices of the room.

Once fresh tea had been made by Sister Mary Paul, Ada received a gift from the residents, a tiny creamy-white wool layette, which one of the girls had knitted herself.

'Thank you,' she said with genuine pleasure. 'It's perfect,

just what I need, seeing as I'm such a poor knitter myself,' she joked.

'We'll miss you, Sister,' a young girl chirped up.

'As I keep saying, you'll see me around,' Ada assured her patients. 'I'll continue with my breathing and relaxation classes as long as possible, so no excuses for giving up, ladies,' she teased. 'And I might well meet a few of you on the ante- and post-natal wards,' she added with a warm smile. 'Look after Matron and Dora for me and of course Nurse Mann.'

After Ada's rather anti-climactic farewell tea, Sybil slipped out of the room, but, as she headed upstairs, she caught sight of cheeky Ronnie imitating her proud walk, while swinging an imaginary handbag. Livid at the child's relentless rudeness and his sister's sniggering laughter, Sybil gritted her teeth; what they were both short of was a firm hand, which the Grange school certainly administered, but once back at Mary Vale the pair of them returned to their wild feral ways.

'Life here is no picnic,' Sybil thought as she entered the privacy of her bedroom. 'But those wretched little hooligans don't make it any easier.' With a malicious glint in her eye she had a sudden thought. 'There must be a way to get rid of them? God!' she exclaimed. 'How much better this place would be without them.'

15. Ada's Nest

Once she had handed over her job to Staff Nurse Mann, Ada was astonished at how quickly she took to not working at all. Waking up and lying in bed was sheer bliss; not having to rush around washing and starching her uniform was an unexpected relief; going for long peaceful morning walks on the lower fells or in the lovely woods close by was a strangely new and relaxing experience. Ada realized that without even knowing it she had been pushing herself hard during her last few weeks at work, worrying about leaving her patients and handing over to her replacement, and now it was all over she acknowledged that it had been quite stressful. Free to do whatever she chose, Ada slept a lot or sat in the garden on warm days with her hands over her growing tummy. It was a real luxury to have the time to feel her baby grow, and when a little foot or fist kicked her, Ada laughed out loud in delight. She was so excited about having her first child; she dreamily wondered if it would have Jamie's beautiful gold-flecked hazel eyes or his full, smiling mouth, or her rich brunette hair and big blue eyes. The biggest question of all was what sex would their baby be? Jamie had written saying he really didn't care, just so long as it was healthy, and Ada didn't care either, except that she knew she ultimately really wanted both a girl and a boy, but she didn't mind which came first.

Ada enjoyed cooking for herself too, good nourishing

food like broths and soup that didn't bloat her or cause indigestion. Sister Mary Paul regularly dropped by with a warm crusty loaf of bread and a bit of tangy Lancashire cheese. Though she always commenced her visits by breathlessly declaring that she couldn't stop, she could always be persuaded to sit and have a cup of tea in front of the old cooking range, where (after settling herself in the rocking chair) she brought Ada up to date on all the latest news in the Home.

'The little lass, Maureen, she gave birth last night, and the girl whose little boy you delivered last week, she's raring at the bit to go home.'

'It's a bit early,' Ada murmured.

'Matron said the same thing,' Sister Mary Paul told her. 'Way too early, but Sister Mann seemed to think otherwise. She told the lass she could leave when she felt up to it, which I don't think best pleased Matron.'

Ada's brow creased. 'I'd never go against Matron's opinion,' she responded. 'She's an expert on post-natal complications, plus we have no idea what living conditions our patients are returning home to. We need to be sure that they're fit and strong when they leave Mary Vale, ready to face whatever's around the corner.'

'Aye, the last thing we want is them picking up an infection just after giving birth,' Sister Mary Paul agreed, as she drained her cup and, groaning with effort, rose to her feet. 'My back gets no better,' she muttered.

'You overdo it, dear,' Ada fretted.

'I wouldn't miss popping in to see my favourite lass,' Sister Mary Paul smiled. 'Now I must get back: I've a ton of springs greens waiting to be chopped and boiled.'

Ada gave a knowing smile. 'Sister Theresa will have done the job by the time you get back.'

Standing by the door, the old nun's eyes swept around the immaculately clean kitchen.

'Looks like you've settled in nicely,' she remarked.

'Oh, yes,' Ada exclaimed. 'I'm so very happy here in my sweet little cottage.'

Sister Mary Paul looked at her friend's glowing face and sparkling eyes. 'I've never seen you looking better,' she said fondly.

'If I could just see Jamie, I would be the happiest person in the world,' Ada sighed.

Sister Mary Paul gave her a quick hug. 'Try not to fret too much about Dr Jamie – he wouldn't want you worrying yourself. Anyway, I'm sure he'll be home just as soon as he can,' she assured Ada before she went on her way.

When her visitor had left, Ada strolled around her cottage garden, pretty with bobbing hazy blue delphiniums and foxgloves. As the peace of the quiet garden filled her senses, Ada inhaled the sweet mountain air that drifted down the valley, but, instead of smiling with pleasure, she was suddenly filled with guilt. Here she was, happy and safe in a beautiful part of England, while Jamie and millions of other men and women were out there in Europe, North Africa and the Far East fighting for the freedom she was enjoying. The ability to walk in peace and enjoy the natural beauty of the world seemed indulgent when she thought of others, some even younger than she was, fighting or dying for the privileges she took for granted. Almost three years into the war with the death toll inevitably rising and rationing getting harder by the week, the nation wearily wondered when it would ever end. Admittedly now that America had joined forces with the Brits there was a lot more military activity and national morale was certainly higher, but for how many years could this go on and at what expense to the nation?

'No matter what we throw at the enemy, they manage to throw even more back at us,' Ada thought gloomily, as she deadheaded her flowers. 'When will we ever be strong enough to break the Nazis?'

Ada had noticed that, as the months passed by, Jamie's love letters touched more on his emotions than on the actual events he was living through. Was he omitting to tell her things because he thought they might worry her or more realistically because the censors would delete any sensitive information? It was so frustrating and annoying, Ada thought crossly; she didn't even know where her beloved was. He had been in France, then there was talk of his team being transferred. She prayed he wouldn't be moved to a medical clearing station in the scorching deserts of North Africa. Suddenly deflated, Ada sat down on the garden bench and brushed tears from her eyes.

'Stop it!' she said out loud.

She knew that if she had been at work, busy on the wards, she wouldn't have had a minute to dwell on such sad, defeatist thoughts; when she was working, she was always steadfastly cheerful and optimistic, especially when her patients' morale was low. She couldn't afford to be so pathetic now, she impatiently told herself; but when she allowed the dreaded thought to cross her mind that she might lose the man she adored, that her unborn child might never know his or her father, she was filled with a blind panic. Springing to her feet, she hurried into the cottage, where she took a writing pad and pen from the bureau in the parlour and returned to the little garden bench to write.

My dearest, darling Jamie,

I'm finally settled into our cottage, our first home and it's wonderful!

Jamie might not be with her, but the least she could do was to brighten his world and hopefully bring a smile to his weary face at the end of a long shift with buoyant news from home.

The garden is drenched in perfume of rambler roses and is presently a sea of colour, and right now the blazing delphiniums nodding in the breeze are my favourite. There are wonderful views of Cartmel Forest just down the winding cart track, and when the cloud lifts there are tantalizing glimpses of the fells, which I know, if you were here, you'd be itching to climb. Maybe one day soon we can walk over to the Langdales with our new son or daughter and introduce them to all our special mountains. When the wind drops, I can hear the sound of the tide going out over the marsh and sea-birds calling to each other as they soar high over the Irish Sea. It is a perfect place to live, Jamie, I just can't wait to share all of this beauty with you.

Though I was sad to leave Mary Vale and my patients, I have to admit it was a big relief to stop running around, and now, rather heavy on my feet as I try to manoeuvre my way around the cottage with my ever burgeoning tummy, I can relax and enjoy this time waiting for our baby to be born. Of course, I miss my friends in the Home and the residents too, but I have regular visitors, Sister Mary Paul, Sister Theresa, Dora and sometimes Alf Arkwright, the farmer who pops by with eggs and milk. So, I'm not short of company, or food! I think of you so much, my love, and worry if you're getting enough food and sleep. I know your work never stops and that you will always put your patients' needs before your own, but please, my dearest love, remember how precious you are to me and take the greatest care of your sweet self. Write when you have a moment, I long to hear your news.

At the very moment Ada sat writing in her cottage garden, where newly arrived swifts, busy nest-building, swooped and dived in the eaves, Jamie was also sitting writing his own missive on a stone-cold cellar floor, dog-tired and starving hungry. Back on the Front Line in northern France, he had once again to deal with the bombing of his casualty clearing station. With shells exploding all around them, the medical crew had lifted the survivors on to stretchers, then staggered with them along the edges of the battlefield, until they found shelter in the cellar of an evacuated bomb-blasted chateau. Unfortunately, the pump there was dry because the water supply had been cut off.

'Bastard Germans!' a fellow officer raged as dying thirsty patients cried out for water.

Luckily Jamie found another well at the back of the chateau where the water hadn't been cut off, so at least he could appease some of the wounded's needs if not their hunger. Even though many of the survivors were in urgent need of surgery, it was impossible to perform any theatre work amid the filthy dust and rubble. All Jamie and his colleagues could do was to carry patients to places of comparative safety and tend to their needs as much as they possibly could. As one group worked with the living, another had the gruesome task of burying the dead. Exhausted by a gruelling day but too tired and wound up to sleep, Jamie had snatched a few minutes to write to Ada, something he tried to do every day no matter what had befallen him. Sitting or standing, sometimes even crouching in dugouts, he felt there was something about writing a letter to his wife that centred his thoughts and made his chaotic, blood-soaked, mad world just about bearable.

Summoning up Ada's image, he could almost smell the perfume of her long, lustrous hair, he imagined the sparkle in her big blue eyes and the seductive smile on her lips. He could never quite believe that he had been lucky enough to marry such a beautiful, talented, wonderful woman, or that she returned his love with passion and fervour and seemed to be as proud of him as he was of her.

'When this bloody war ends,' he thought to himself as he lit a cigarette and stared out at the night sky, 'I pray to God that I will enjoy a long and happy life in the Lake District with my wife and family, who I will fight with my life to protect from the horrors of Hitler's Nazi empire.'

16. Spider's Web

Back at Mary Vale, Staff Sister Mann was settling into her new role. With Ada gone, she felt confident and more in control, though, when it came to her first birthing experience, she had not been impressed by the behaviour of the young girl on the delivery table. Screaming and writhing, the silly girl became hysterical, losing all self-control, begging in turn either to die or to be with 'her mam' throughout the entire labour. Eventually she gave birth to a mewling daughter, whom Dora whisked off to the nursery after throwing what Edith was convinced was a dirty look in her direction. She had delivered the child efficiently enough; and, though she lacked Dora's ability to gush over every baby that drew breath, there was no doubt about Edith's ability to do her job.

Seeing Dora in the nursery bathing the sleepy newborn, before dressing her in one of the Home's sweet little white nighties hand-stitched by the nuns in the convent, Edith watched her tenderly rocking the baby to sleep in a manner she knew she could never do. She knew she was a competent midwife, but mothering and cuddling were not within her remit. Having been raised by a woman with a heart of stone, Edith was simply not empathetic.

Venting her disapproval, Dora, now in the sluice room with Sister Theresa, grumbled on about Sister Mann's lack of emotion.

'Ada helped her patients breathe through their pain but

this new one' – Dora rolled her eyes as she nodded over her shoulder in the direction of the delivery room – 'doesn't seem to have an instinctive bone in her body. Once she'd checked the baby was breathing and cut the cord, she didn't give the poor little mite a second glance.'

'You mustn't judge too harshly, Dora,' Theresa earnestly whispered. 'It's really not fair.'

Stubborn Dora set her jaw at a firm angle. 'I can only judge on what I saw,' she insisted.

'Give Sister Mann a bit longer before you jump to conclusions,' gentle Theresa pleaded. 'And please don't go mentioning this to Matron,' she anxiously added.

Dora gave a dismissive shrug. 'Don't you worry, I won't need to mention it. Matron's bound to see Nurse Mann's bedside manner for herself before long, and, believe me, Sister, she's in for a bit of a shock.'

Sybil's opinion of Ada's replacement had worsened too if anything; with Ada gone, it was impossible not to notice that the new staff sister quickly assumed superiority in a way that irked Sybil and other residents too. Unlike Ada, Sister Mann took to eating her meals in her office, saying she was far too busy to have extended meal-times in the communal dining room, which the residents took as a rebuff. If Sister Ada could pass the time of the day with them, why not Sister Mann – weren't they good enough for her? Sybil was one of the few who didn't actually articulate her disapproval – how could she when she herself spent as little time as possible with the residents? Anyway, she was far too busy with her own plans, which had unrolled far more quickly than she had initially imagined.

Unable to get at Monty (at least for the time being), Sybil's vindictive thoughts turned to Ronnie and Sally, who remained a thorn in tetchy Sybil's side. As far as she was concerned, their continued presence here was the straw that broke the camel's back. The Home had never been acceptable, far from it, but, loud with the clamour of two intolerable kids (Sally was marginally more acceptable than her odious brother), Sybil's frazzled nerves were constantly on edge.

'If I could only get rid of them,' she wished every time she laid eyes on the children.

Then one afternoon fate unexpectedly provided Sybil with the means to do so. Walking into the dining room in search of her magazine, she found Ronnie and Sally peering hungrily at the sandwiches and scones on the serving table.

'What are you two doing in here?' she snapped.

'What's it to you?' cheeky Ronnie snapped back.

'Tea's not served till five o'clock,' Sybil pointed out.

'So we can admire it, can't we?' he replied.

Resisting the urge to hit the lippy child, Sybil turned to Sally, who cringed beneath her steely glare.

'We're just hungry,' the little girl muttered nervously.

It was at that precise moment that Sybil had a wicked thought; why not encourage them to eat before the other residents turned up for their meals; it certainly wouldn't go down very well with the holier than thou nuns, and it wouldn't impress the residents either.

Mustering up a smile, Sybil turned to Sally. 'What does it matter if you pop in a few minutes before the others? Don't worry about it – take a few sandwiches and a scone too – nobody will notice,' she urged as she piled up two plates. 'Now run upstairs and enjoy your tea before anybody sees you.'

Wide-eyed Sally gratefully snatched the plate and ran out of the door, while Ronnie shoved more sandwiches in each of his trouser pockets before bolting after his sister.

Sybil smiled to herself. 'That should put the cat among the pigeons,' she smirked.

Though hardly anybody noticed the disappearance of a few sandwiches and scones at tea-time, the following morning found Sister Mary Paul baffled, not to mention irritated, when she noticed that food she had laid out for breakfast had mysteriously disappeared.

'I swear I put four fresh loaves out this morning,' she told Sister Theresa, who was helping her to lay the table.

'There are only three now,' Sister Theresa pointed out.

When the same thing happened the very next day, both nuns were dumbfounded. This time it was Theresa who expressed her dismay. 'I know for certain, I put four loaves out just now,' she insisted.

Mary Paul nodded in agreement. 'I saw you walk out of the kitchen with them on a tray.'

Both nuns stared at each other.

'Who on earth is taking the food?' Sister Theresa asked.

'Somebody who thinks they're not getting enough in the first place,' Mary Paul answered crossly.

But, as the days progressed, steadily more and more food began to disappear: coconut biscuits, cheese pasties, potato cakes, corned-beef fritters, and every morning bread from the breakfast table.

'This is just ridiculous!' cried Mary Paul in sheer frustration. 'There's not enough food to go round as it is. We simply can't allow stealing under our roof!'

'There's no choice but to keep a lookout,' Sister Theresa said grimly. 'And catch whoever it is red-handed.'

Within a few days both Theresa and Sister Mary Paul knew exactly who the culprits were. Taking it in turns, they had monitored movements in the dining room before every meal-time. Separately they both spotted Ronnie and Sally entering the dining room alone, and, after checking that nobody was watching them, sneaking up to the serving table to grab food – bread, butter, cheese, a cake, sandwiches, whatever was available – stuffing it into their school-bags before slipping out of the room.

'We should have guessed,' Sister Mary Paul sighed, after they had shared their evidence.

'We had to give them the benefit of the doubt,' Theresa replied.

Frustrated at how the situation had escalated, Sister Mary Paul cried, 'Why didn't they just ask rather than steal the stuff?'

Theresa shrugged. 'They probably thought we would refuse them – after all, we have other mouths to feed three times a day at Mary Vale,' she pointed out.

'So they just took it instead,' Sister Mary Paul said. 'You know we'll have to report them to Matron.' Wearily shaking her head, she continued. 'A verbal warning from me or you isn't going to have much of an impact on those two wilful kiddies.'

'If only Ada were still working here,' Sister Theresa said wistfully. 'She could handle Ronnie and Sally better than anybody.'

'Sadly, she isn't,' Sister Mary Paul said. 'Now don't go

telling Nurse Mann,' she quickly added. 'She'll come down on them like a ton of bricks.'

When Matron called the children and their mother into her office with Sister Mary Paul and Theresa, Ronnie went ballistic when the thefts were brought up.

'I didn't take nuffink!' he exploded.

Matron gave the mutinous little boy a long cold look. 'Then please explain how Sister Mary Paul and Sister Theresa saw you both on separate occasions stealing food out of the dining room.'

'There's no point in lying, Ronnie,' Sister Theresa started gently. 'I saw you several times.'

Shocked rigid, Rosie turned on her children. 'Is this true?' she cried.

At which point Sally burst into tears. 'Ronnie made me do it,' she bawled. 'He's been selling stuff at school during play-time.'

Rosie slumped into the nearest chair. 'Ronnie, how could you? And Sally, you too? Stealing from the Home, it's a disgrace,' she cried.

'I needed money for marbles,' Ronnie blurted out. 'You never give us anything,' he grumbled.

'What money have I got?' his mother protested.

'That's what you always bloody say, *I haven't got any money*,' he cruelly mocked her. 'Well, I'm sick of being broke and I'm sick of being the poor kid who's always in trouble.'

Seeing that tempers were about to fly, Matron firmly took the situation in hand. 'You'll be in a lot more trouble if you don't stop stealing, Ronnie,' she told the scowling child. 'This must not happen again, do you understand?'

Shuffling his dirty, worn-out shoes, Ronnie made an angry grunting noise. 'Do you understand?' The senior nun repeated her question even more firmly. 'You too, Sally?' she added, turning to the little girl, who was clutched weeping in her mother's arms.

'Yesss . . .' Sally sobbed.

Rising with her daughter clasped to her chest, Rosie spoke with as much dignity as she could summon up. 'It won't happen again – I'll see to it.'

With the family gone, the three nuns stared anxiously at one another.

'I'll have to report this to the Reverend Mother,' Ann told her sisters.

'Of course,' Sister Theresa nodded.

'Do you *really* think Rosie can control Ronnie?' Sister Mary Paul asked.

Sister Theresa, who had escorted the children to Grange when they first started school and knew them better than most, answered cautiously. 'She's just about got Sally under control but as far as Ronnie goes?' She shook her head in despair. 'He runs rings around his poor mother.'

Matron stared thoughtfully out of the window. 'The Reverend Mother will not countenance theft,' she said quietly. 'I've given them a second chance, but, if this happens again, I'm in no doubt that the Reverend Mother will remove them from the Home.'

Inevitably news of the dining-room thefts spread around Mary Vale, and people held varying views on the children's behaviour.

'Greedy little sods, stealing our food,' some grumbled.

'They don't know any better,' others said in the children's defence.

'Dragged up, that's their problem.'

'It's the mother I feel sorry for.'

'She's about as effective as a condom in a brothel,' somebody sniggered.

'Better lock up your riches!' a resident joked. 'Those kiddies could be nicking from us next.'

This remark was followed by a loud hoot of laughter.

'What riches?' someone chuckled.

Sybil's witch-green eyes swept over the women assembled around the table. 'Now there's a thought,' she mused.

Her fellow residents, poor as they might be, surely had a few precious trinkets that they would seriously resent anyone meddling with.

In the midst of all the mounting gossip, Sybil smirked like a cat that had got the cream. It hadn't taken long for the children and their ineffectual mother to fast lose whatever popularity or pity the residents had originally had for them. Now on a warning from Matron, Ronnie and Sally had to be on their best behaviour, the mother too for that matter, or face the dire consequences. Sybil decided to give it a week to let things settle down before she activated the next stage of her plan. If her ambitious complicated plot were to succeed, it required clear advanced planning and would have to be precisely executed to create maximum impact. Like a malevolent spider in its web, Sybil had time to plot, plan, and weave a drama that would successfully remove the Pickles children from Mary Vale.

17. On a Knife-edge

A week later Sybil specifically chose her day to take action. After careful observation she established Ronnie and Sally's daily schedule; accompanied by Sister Theresa, and sometimes their mother on the occasional day that she was strong enough to make the journey, they were taken to the little Kents Bank Station, where they boarded the steam train into Grange. They weren't seen again until their return from school around four thirty in the afternoon. Though why the nun bothered was beyond her, as she watched Theresa trail after Ronnie and Sally, who went roaring up the garden path yelling (as ever) at the top of their voices.

'Hooligans,' muttered Sybil, as she slammed down her bedroom window to drown out their racket.

Rosie Pickles proved to be the biggest stumbling block, because her poor health dictated that she spent most of her time resting in the family bedroom.

'Surely the woman must go out sometimes?' Sybil fumed, as she stalked Rosie's movements.

As luck would have it, she overheard Rosie one lunchtime talking to Sister Theresa, who was as usual lending a hand in the busy dining room.

'Did the children get off all right this morning?' she asked.

Smiling, Theresa replied, 'Good as gold.'

'Don't you think the guard might chuck the pair of them off the train?' Rosie joked.

'We might have to glue their bottoms to the seats,' Theresa joked back. After wiping down a table with a damp cloth she remarked, 'Dora tells me you've got a hospital appointment in Lancaster on Thursday. Is it a regular check-up?'

Looking anxious, Rosie shook her head. 'No, Matron and Ada are concerned that the baby's not as big as they'd like it to be, so they're sending me off to Lancaster for some tests.'

Seeing Rosie looking nervous, Theresa gave a bright cheery smile. 'Good idea – always best to get a second opinion, don't you think?'

Rosie nodded miserably. 'Of course, but it seems to be one problem after another with this pregnancy.'

After hearing the conversation, Sybil quickly picked up her expensive leather handbag, which she always held in the crook of her arm, and left the room.

'Thursday it is, then,' she thought with a satisfied smile.

On Thursday morning Sybil watched Ronnie and Sally leave for Grange, and a short time later she observed Rosie heading off to the station to catch the train to Lancaster. Once Sybil heard Rosie's train pulling away and saw a plume of black smoke cloud the sky, she grabbed her shopping bag and the piece of paper on which she had scribbled down the names of the residents and their room numbers.

After making sure the coast was clear, Sybil slipped upstairs to one of the resident's rooms, which she rummaged through. After going through a set of drawers, she removed a rusty tin containing some coins from a battered old handbag. On a lower floor, she took some cheap earrings from a little glass dish on the dressing table, and from another room she filched a gilt powder-compact case and lipstick. Hurrying back to her own room, Sybil hid the stolen goods in her suitcase, which she kept locked inside the wardrobe. With her heart beating as loud as a drum, Sybil checked her watch: nearly eleven. She would have to complete her tasks by four o'clock, when Ronnie and Sally got home, and for that matter Rosie too; for now, she could take a breather.

While the residents were at lunch, Sybil faked tummy ache and took to her room. In the short space of time available to her, Sybil sneaked into several empty bedrooms, removing a few more trinkets that she added to her stash. Her final bit of filching centred around the kitchen, which meant she had to hide in the corridor until she saw Sister Mary Paul bustle out and she could slip into the store cupboard. Squinting as her eyes grew accustomed to the gloom, Sybil froze as she suddenly heard footsteps in the corridor that stopped right outside the store cupboard. When she saw the door handle turning, sweat broke out on Sybil's brow – what would she say when the door swung open? Mercifully she heard Dora calling from the other end of the corridor. 'Sister Theresa, have you a minute to lend me a hand?'

The door handle was released as the young nun called back: 'Yes, of course, Dora.'

Sybil slumped with relief as she heard the voices of the two women recede; then, quickly recovering, she reached up to a shelf and removed several silver teaspoons and a small silver cream-and-sugar set. Slipping the spoons into her pockets and the rest into her handbag, Sybil sneaked out of the store cupboard and fled to her room.

To the growing pile of stolen goods Sybil added her own leather wallet, containing bank notes. Then, just after three in the afternoon (later than she had originally planned), she made her way to the room that Ronnie and Sally shared with their mother. Precious time was wasted as Sybil hid in the shadows under the stairs waiting for two residents to dawdle by – then she shot into the family's bedroom, where, with her heart pounding, she had to take several deep breaths.

'Keep cool, take it easy,' she told herself.

Removing the stolen goods from her shopping bag, Sybil went around the room secreting them in Ronnie and Sally's higgledy-piggledy chest of drawers, under the bed, at the back of the wardrobe, even behind the little sink unit in the corner of the room. Her wallet she slipped into a cardboard box containing some old rusty cars; then, when everything had been deposited, Sybil fled the room with barely ten minutes to spare before Ronnie and Sally returned home from school.

Lying exhausted on her narrow bed, Sybil wondered how long it would be before someone noticed something missing and raised the alarm. All she had to do now was wait for her plan to unfold.

As it turned out, she didn't have long to wait, as during the course of that first evening and the following day various residents discovered that articles that belonged to them had disappeared.

As questions were raised, Sybil added hers to the list. 'My wallet's disappeared too.'

'So's my powder compact and lipstick,' a girl chimed up. 'I left them in my room, but they're not there now.'

When Sister Mary Paul breathlessly reported that some silver cutlery had gone missing from the store cupboard, Matron looked at the mounting list of missing articles that had been reported throughout the day.

'This is ridiculous!' she exclaimed in sheer frustration. 'I have no choice but to report this to the Reverend Mother immediately.'

After each resident with a claim to being robbed had been thoroughly questioned about their missing goods and their value, the Reverend Mother turned to Sister Mary Paul, who mournfully said, 'The teaspoons were all silver-plated, but the little cream-and-sugar set was solid silver and worth quite a lot of money. We used them only on special occasions.'

Bridling with indignation, the Reverend Mother announced to a very flushed Sister Mary Paul, 'We cannot allow a thief to live under our roof. I have absolutely no choice but to call in the police.'

Sometime later a young, rather self-conscious police constable, holding a notepad and the stub of a chewed pencil, questioned the residents who had had articles stolen. When it came to Sybil's turn, sitting primly in an armchair with her ankles neatly crossed, she, like several others, mentioned that Ronnie and Sally had recently been discovered stealing food from the kitchen.

'I'd make sure I thoroughly questioned those two,' she

said in all innocence. 'They can't seem to stop themselves. It must be in their blood.'

The Reverend Mother, Matron, Sister Theresa and Rosie were in attendance when the policeman finally got around to questioning Ronnie and Sally. After he had patiently outlined the gravity of the situation, Ronnie typically went on the defensive.

'I don't know a bleedin' thing about nicked stuff!'

Visibly shocked by the boy's pent-up fury, the Reverend Mother spoke sharply. 'I will have no swearing, young man!'

Ronnie scowled but wisely kept his mouth shut.

'If you cannot behave decently when questioned I shall ask the policeman to remove you to the police station – now answer his questions civilly.'

'Did you have anything to do with these thefts, young man?' the policeman formally asked.

'Nuffink,' Ronnie growled.

'And you, young lady . . .' the policeman continued, turning to Sally, who was wrapped around her mother's skirt. 'Do you have anything to tell us?'

Utterly terrified, Sally mutely shook her head.

The policeman addressed Rosie. 'I will be inspecting all of the residents' rooms, Mrs Pickles – have I your permission to search your room?' Rosie, knowing her children had only recently been caught stealing food from the dining room, could barely speak. Could they really have robbed again and so soon after their first offence? As the blood drained from her face, she nodded in mute agreement.

*

The conscientious policeman set about systematically searching the residents' rooms, Sybil's included, but it was of course only when he came to the Pickles' family room that he found what he was looking for: irrefutable evidence that firmly sealed the children's fate. Breathless with shock, Rosie slumped on her bed and watched the policeman gather up the goods squirrelled away under the bed, at the back of the wardrobe and behind the sink.

'They weren't here yesterday,' she protested. 'I'm sure I would have seen them.'

'Well, I'm afraid they're here now, ma'am,' the policeman said politely. 'And I'm afraid your youngsters have some explaining to do.'

Ronnie, Sally and poor trembling Rosie were this time brought before the Reverend Mother, along with the policeman, in the dining room.

'If you did *not* steal any of the articles, why were they all found hidden in your bedroom?'

'I dunno!' Ronnie cried. 'I never put 'em there.'

The policeman cleared his throat. 'I'm told you two were caught stealing food not that long ago,' he started.

Poor Rosie flared crimson with shame. 'They were,' she declared. 'For which they have been reprimanded.' Clutching her children close as if to protect them from what might follow, Rosie's voice wobbled as she continued. 'For God's sake, they've had an 'ard time since we moved here, and it was only because of my health that we came here in the first place.'

'I wanna go home, go back to London,' Ronnie said, as his resolve crumpled and he started to cry.

'I want my dad!' little Sally bawled.

The policeman turned to the Reverend Mother, who rose from the ornately carved chair behind her vast desk.

'Thank you for all that you've done, young man,' she replied with dignity. 'We'll take charge from here, if you don't mind?'

'I should advise you –' he muttered.

The Reverend Mother gave a tight little smile as she shook her head.

'A formal charge would be all over the papers,' she rightly pointed out. 'It would do them no good,' she added, nodding in the direction of the weeping children. 'And it would certainly smirch the reputation of our Home. No,' she said on a heavy sigh. 'We'll settle this matter internally, if you don't mind?'

18. Hope Farm

Ada was appalled when Sister Mary Paul told her the next day of the recent goings-on at Mary Vale.

'I don't believe it!' she gasped, as she supported her heavy tummy in one hand and a mug of hot tea in the other.

Nodding glumly, the old nun (who even in her haste to get to Ada's had not forgotten to bring as much as she could spare of a loaf of freshly baked bread) filled in her friend further.

'The evidence was stacked against those kiddies, but I have to say they did look pole-axed with shock. I don't know how they ever thought they could get away with it.'

Ada didn't look totally convinced. 'It seems like a heck of a lot of stuff to steal,' she said.

'Mebbe it was stolen over a period of time,' Sister Mary Paul suggested, as she topped up her tea from the pot on the table.

Ada still didn't look convinced. 'If things had gone missing, wouldn't residents have raised the alarm earlier, one by one as they noticed? What you're talking about seems to have happened suddenly, almost overnight,' she said thoughtfully. 'I know Ronnie's sharp, but that kind of systematic thieving would take a lot of planning.'

'I agree, it was complicated, but the young policeman had no doubts about it. He definitely thought the kiddies were guilty; how could he think otherwise with all the stolen stuff hidden away in corners all over their family room? If that young bobby had his way, I believe he would have charged them,' Mary Paul declared. 'Imagine what the press would have made of that.'

Ada nodded. 'It would have been terrible for Ronnie and Rosie.'

'And it would have reflected badly on the convent too,' Mary Paul added.

Ada looked thoughtful. 'You know, it might have actually swayed the requisition decision. So far the Army have been sympathetic to Mary Vale's cause on the grounds that we're good for the Home Front, but if they had read in the papers that we were harbouring thieves they might not look upon us quite so generously any more.'

'The Reverend Mother took control, thank God,' Sister Mary Paul said gratefully.

Moving on, Ada asked, 'How's Rosie? She's in no state to withstand a shock like this.'

'She all but fainted away once it was all over with – Dora rushed her on to the ward and into a bed.' Sister Mary Paul rolled her eyes. 'Dora said Staff Sister Mann didn't look best pleased.'

Ada looked surprised. 'Was she annoyed that Rosie had been brought on to the ward?'

'Well, I wasn't there myself, but Dora said she looked at Rosie like something the cat had dragged in.'

Knowing that Dora regularly swopped stories with Sister Mary Paul on her many visits back and forth to the kitchen for nursery milk, Ada, now in full professional mode, pressed on. 'Try to remember, dear, what exactly did Dora say about Rosie?'

Mary Paul crinkled her brow as she tried her best to recall Dora's exact words. 'She said Rosie's blood pressure was sky high, and the baby's heart-beat was weak.'

'Oh, dear,' Ada murmured under her breath. 'Is she still on the ward?'

Mary Paul nodded. 'Dora thinks that if there's any chance of the baby surviving, Rosie will probably need permanent bed-rest from now on.'

'Gosh!' Ada cried. 'Who is going to look after those poor children? First, they're dragged up here where they're clearly not wanted, then sent to a new school which they hate, and their mother is still in no state to care for them despite all our best care.' Ada gave a sad sigh. 'I feel so sorry for them both.'

'The Reverend Mother is looking to have the kiddies fostered out. Just until their mother's back on her feet,' Mary Paul informed Ada.

'Heavens above, their situation just gets worse,' Ada cried.

'What else can we do with Rosie ordered to her bed?' Mary Paul asked. 'Though God knows how Ronnie and Sally will take to leaving their mother.'

The Reverend Mother talked to saintly Sister Theresa about preparing the children for a possible move.

'Prepare the way, just in case we have to foster them out,' the Reverend Mother requested.

'They're pretty subdued at the moment,' Theresa told her. 'What with their mother sick on the ward and them only allowed one visit a day after they get home from school, they're both a bit tearful.'

'Hardly surprising,' the Reverend Mother responded. 'Are they still adamant about not stealing from the residents?'

'Completely – they never stop insisting on their innocence,' Theresa replied. 'So much so that I'm beginning to wonder if we're doing them an injustice by sending them away.'

'Come, come, child,' the Reverend Mother answered firmly. 'If they do have to leave us, they might well benefit from joining the family I have in mind. The Larkins are a no-nonsense, salt-of-the-earth couple with four children of their own. They run a sheep farm in the next valley and have been fostering for years.'

'How can we be sure that Ronnie and Sally will behave themselves once they leave here?' Sister Theresa fretted.

'There's no guaranteeing it, Sister, all we can do is pray,' the Reverend Mother answered fervently.

Feeling guilty that she doubted the power of her Lord, Sister Theresa wondered if prayer could undo the colossal damage done to Ronnie and Sally, who seemed to ricochet from one tragedy to another.

After a great deal of heart-searching and several discussions with the Larkins, the Reverend Mother decided that it was in Rosie's best interest to briefly foster the children out. Though Rosie was heartbroken, and the children were mutinous, their departure was softened by the fact that Farmer Arkwright had to deliver some fluffy bleating lambs to the Larkins' farm. Ronnie and Sally, accompanied by Sister Theresa, were so excited by the bouncy drive in the farm pick-up truck they hardly gave Mary

Vale a backward glance as they drove away down the winding lane.

The previous night had been altogether another story. Dora had closed the curtains around the bed when Ronnie and Sally had visited their mother on the ward, thereby affording the family a little privacy. Sister Mann raised her eyebrows when she heard the sobbing and weeping coming from behind the curtain.

'Really, it isn't the end of the world,' she muttered to Dora. 'Leaving Mary Vale and their mother in peace is the best outcome all round.'

Dora, who had suffered the loss of both of her beloved sons to the war effort, looked mutinous. 'It's not easy breaking up a family.'

Unaware of Dora's tragic past, Sister Mann rambled on. 'Ronnie and Sally will be able to visit their mother regularly, and Mrs Pickles – once her children are out of the way – will most likely thrive.'

Dora gave her a hard look. 'Well, let's hope it works out that way,' she said, and she stubbornly remained in front of the drawn curtains, determined that nobody would interfere with the children and their mother as they said their farewells.

Marge Larkin was feeding her hens when Sally and Ronnie arrived. Standing in the doorway of the coop with hen poo blobbed on her cardigan, she watched the children scamper after Farmer Arkwright as he approached her burly husband, Tom, who was smiling a welcome with a lamb tucked under each arm. The newcomers were about the same age as her youngest two but thinner and scruffier.

Her experience at fostering gave her the confidence to believe that as much good healthy grub as they could manage during rationing combined with firm handling, lots of fresh air and regular prayers usually worked wonders. Obviously, she had read the children's report and gathered that they were a handful, but Mrs Larkin had fostered many a 'handful' before. The first thing she did in every case was to wipe the slate clean and start afresh. If she started off prejudiced and judgemental, she'd get nowhere. The Pickles kids had had a hard time; they hadn't seen or heard from their dad for months through no fault of their own and now their mother was sick and ailing. She would do her best; the rest she left to Nature and God.

Sister Theresa took her charges to their room, which they seemed to like; she for one was charmed by the old-fashioned oak-beamed room with a creaky, uneven, polished wooden floor. Sally and Ronnie seemed more interested in a box of toys and some comics they found on their bedside tables, little gifts of welcome that instantly helped them to relax. After Sister Theresa had helped the children unpack their sparse belongings, they all clattered downstairs to the big, untidy but homely kitchen that smelt of sheep and dogs. Mrs Larkin laid a whopping big teapot on the table and some hot toast with the thinnest scraping of their precious butter, which was shared out among six children in a flash. Seeing the newcomers looking awkward, Mrs Larkin turned to May, her eldest and only daughter. 'Why don't you take little Sally into the garden to feed the rabbits?'

Sally's eyes grew round as saucers. 'Real hoppy rabbits?' she squeaked.

'Aye,' May laughed as she extended her hand to Sally. 'Come on, we'll change their bedding too.'

Enthralled, Sally followed the older girl, while the three boisterous boys roared out on to the fell, dragging Ronnie in their wake.

'Do you think they'll be all right?' Theresa finally asked the question that had haunted her all morning.

Marge Larkin gave a confident nod.

'They might be a challenge, and I do believe they'll be all right, but if they're not I'll be the first to let you know.'

'It's Ronnie I'm most bothered about,' Theresa blurted out. 'He's wild, to put it mildly.'

'Let's see how he gets on with us,' Mrs Larkin chuckled softly. 'If anybody can handle an unruly little boy, it's three other unruly little boys.'

'Thank you for your kindness,' Theresa said, as she rose and straightened her habit. 'I'd better be heading back to Mary Vale. Their mother will want to know how they settled in.'

After Farmer Arkwright had dropped her back at the convent, Sister Theresa reported immediately to the Reverend Mother, then hurried over to visit Rosie, who was sitting upright in bed drinking a cup of tea.

'How were they?' she cried, setting her cup and saucer down on the bedside table.

'Surprisingly well, given the circumstances,' the young nun assured the anxious mother.

Rosie's tired eyes flew wide open. 'You wouldn't lie to me, would you, Sister Theresa?'

'Never,' Theresa replied. 'I left Sally feeding dock leaves

to some sweet pet rabbits and Ronnie chasing after the Larkin boys, who were heading for the beck. I don't think I've ever seen him quite so excited before.'

Rosie slumped back against her pillows. 'Thank God,' she sighed. 'Thank God,' she repeated earnestly.

Theresa patted the sick woman's hot trembling hand. 'Now all you've got to do is get your strength back, Rosie. God will take care of the rest.'

19. Edith

Though Sister Mann had little interest in Rosie, the relief of not having to suffer the presence of her wretched children made her considerably kinder to the expectant mother, who was responding well to bed-rest, though her baby, according to the Home's visiting doctor, still remained small and underweight, which was a cause of constant concern. Now that Rosie was restricted to bed, Edith hoped her sickly condition would improve, and she did all she could as a professional nurse to improve her situation, but really life at Mary Vale was turning out to be one big disappointment after another.

The residents weren't her kind of people: the nuns were simply alien to her and Dora seemed to actively disapprove of her. In the Harrogate nursing home where she had previously worked, the babies were the responsibility of the nursery nurses, leaving Edith and her team of nurses free to concentrate on their patients, who had expressed their gratitude with very often illegal war-time luxuries such as chocolates, cigarettes, nylons, a bottle of sherry, even an occasional silk scarf. At Mary Vale, Edith was more likely to get a tin of baked beans or a bag of split peas as a thank-you gift. She had hoped that she might pal up with well-spoken, smartly dressed Sybil Harwood, but her attempts at friendship had been sharply rebuffed by haughty Sybil, who kept herself strictly to herself.

Edith's Harrogate ladies had been altogether a better class of people, wives of bankers, tradesmen, engineers, mill owners and teachers. Edith had once personally nursed the wife of a distinguished local Member of Parliament. The Mary Vale residents were younger, poorer and had no finesse. Not that Edith didn't know about poverty; she had dragged herself single-handedly out of that hole. Affecting a posh voice and saving whatever money her mother hadn't snatched from her wages, Edith had reinvented herself from back-street kid to genteel professional lady. Unfortunately, Edith had not initially had the resources to leave her miserable home, and the end of every day saw her back in the poky two-up, two-down terraced house with her gin-soaked abusive mother, whom Edith yearned to break free of.

It had been a battle for Edith to train as a nurse. Her widowed mother had whined constantly that her only daughter should join her brothers in the local mill, in the weaving shed, which paid good money, but Edith's eyes were set on higher things. Nursing was her ambition, a possible way out of the life she detested, but it had been a fight right from the start.

'You're too stupid to be anything other than a mill girl,' her mother had cried. 'You should be bringing money home, putting your wage packet on the table every Friday night.'

'Right,' Edith bitterly thought. 'So, you can spend all of it at the out-door licence.'

By studying every hour that God sent, Edith had achieved the grades required to commence her training and, after promising to give her penny-pinching mother all her wages (which she never entirely did, always squirreling away something even if it was only sixpence a week), a deal was finally struck between mother and daughter. Slowly and patiently adding to the tiny amount of money she had saved and hidden in the coal shed next door to the outdoor privy, Edith began the process of transforming herself into a 'lady'. She had worked with enough posh patients to know what 'ladies' looked like, and many of her colleagues were from good middle-class backgrounds, so it was easy to copy their style.

Edith deduced that the essential elements to the perfect female image were a good haircut and make-up, smart clothes, decent shoes and handbag, a trim figure, and a posh voice with no hint of a Morley accent. Though the women she emulated took for granted their stylish haircuts and expensive clothes, undoubtedly paid for by their well-heeled husbands, Edith had acquired her luxuries the hard way. Over the years, scrimping, saving and buying wisely, always with a good eye for detail, Edith's wardrobe grew. Now consisting of one smart pair of heeled brogues, one crêpe summer frock, a well-cut coat, a sage-green twinset, a tweed skirt, and her pride and joy, a leather handbag. Knowing that if she left her precious clothes at home, her mother would pawn them for drink or, worse, burn them in a fit of rage, cautious Edith hid her precious wardrobe in her work locker, in fact, her two work lockers, one of which she had slyly claimed when a fellow nurse left.

To complete the transformation, it was essential that Edith changed her voice, affecting posher tones and dropping her Northern accent; she worked hard to sound like the women she nursed and worked alongside. Knowing she would be mocked if she ever spoke anything other than rough Northern in front of her family, Edith became adept at switching between the two. Confident that she was no longer the poor gauche outsider, Edith was able to mix more easily with her colleagues, and, as time went by and she became more established, she was regularly invited to the staff drinks events and retirement parties.

When these precious invitations arrived, the first thing that Edith did was to organize an overnight stay at the nurses' dorm, where she would have loved to have lived permanently but simply couldn't afford to. On these special occasions she revelled in the luxury of solitude, without her mother breathing down her neck about wasting hot water or occupying the outdoor privy for too long. Of course, Edith had to pay for the accommodation, but, oh, it was worth every penny. The thrill of taking a bath in private instead of in front of the fire, of taking her time applying her make-up, then slipping into a new dress that she might have saved a whole year to buy, was worth any amount of money as far as Edith was concerned.

It had been at Matron's retirement drinks some years ago that she had first *really* talked to her colleague, Mr Charles Lamberty, a consultant high up in the nursing home. Of course, they had exchanged a few words in the delivery suite when he was performing a caesarean or had been in charge of a complicated delivery, but it had never been intimate talk. Suddenly and alarmingly she found Mr Lamberty gazing into her dark eyes enquiring about where she had trained, information she was happy to share with him, and where she had been educated, information she was less happy to share. Some weeks after the retirement party another social event followed, and this time there was no doubting that their relationship had suddenly slipped from professional to personal. When Charles had suggested driving her home, Edith had demurred, saying she was sleeping on site, and it was in the nurses' dorm in a very narrow bed, aged well over thirty, that Edith had lost her virginity.

It was a perfect secretive arrangement; Edith simply couldn't have asked for more. She was happy with her wealthy, good-looking older consultant who treated his mistress to luxuries she could never have afforded: a gold watch, a string of pearls, the occasional silk underwear and nylons when he could get them, all of which Edith sneaked into her locker to be worn on the rapturous occasions she spent with Charles.

When the news got out and gossip spread, Edith immediately handed in her notice. She didn't want to be in the nursing home or the area itself when the scandal broke; her primary concern was to avoid at all costs bringing shame upon her beloved, for whom she was prepared to sacrifice her life. Her mother, ever a loose cannon, had to be played carefully; if she heard about Edith's affair with a married man (fortunately in Harrogate, which Mrs Mann barely frequented), she would without question use it as another means to threaten or blackmail Edith whenever she wanted money from her. If Edith acted swiftly, she could get away from her mother, whom she would continue to pay weekly if only to keep her drink-sodden and quiet.

Recalling having to leave Charles brought tears to Edith's eyes; he had been simply wonderful. Grateful for the sacrifices she had made in order to protect his reputation, he had arranged a weekend away in a discreet hotel in Whitby. There he had showered her with gifts and promises of working together and continuing their relationship in the dim and distant future. Edith had been touched by his promises, but, ever the realist, she held out no long-term romantic hopes. Charles was a married man and showed not the slightest inclination to leave his wife, and neither would she want him to. She wasn't cut out to be a consultant's partner: she had enjoyed being his devoted mistress, but beyond that she had no further hope or expectations.

Keeping her emotions firmly under control, Edith hadn't begged Charles to keep in touch; she hadn't even left him her forwarding address. If he ever needed to communicate with her, Edith reasoned that Charles could always locate her current address through the nursing-home records. Though sad and disappointed that she hadn't heard from him, Edith was hard-headed enough to accept the truth of her situation and live with it.

Her time with Charles had undoubtedly been too short-lived, but Edith never regretted a single moment; it had been the most perfect time of her life, and nobody could ever take that away from her. Giving a long, resigned sigh, Edith straightened her stiffly starched, white lace-edged cap. Would there ever be another Charles? She couldn't imagine it, but, if there were, she hoped that he wouldn't be stupid enough to be spotted sneaking away from the nurses' dorm in the dead of night carrying his shoes in his hands.

20. Sybil and Rosie

Sister Mann reluctantly and very occasionally attended the breathing and exercise classes, where Ada was by far the most pregnant woman of all the women there. It was a time of cheerful camaraderie, when the women could bond as they lay on their backs (usually in the sunny garden) with their legs up in the air. Much to Ada's surprise Sybil had recently started attending her classes, speaking little but concentrating hard on her breathing. When the class was over, Ada made a point of chatting to Sybil, who was hunkering down putting on her shoes.

'Are you finding the sessions helpful?' Ada enquired.

Sybil cocked her head to one side. 'Now, Sister, I can't give you a true answer to that question until after I've given birth.'

'You know what I mean,' Ada said, smiling.

Sybil gave a slow nod. 'It's nice that we can exercise outside in the fresh air,' she conceded.

Ada agreed whole-heartedly. 'It's lovely to lie back with the sun on your face and feel your baby kicking.'

'Well, I'm not sure I'd go that far,' Sybil grimaced. 'The sooner this baby is outside of me rather than inside, the happier I will be.'

'It's a pity you don't relate much to the other girls,' Ada said tentatively. 'After all, we're all in the same boat.'

Sybil shrugged, and avoided eye contact as she busied herself with tying her shoes laces.

'You know that I have little in common with my fellow residents,' she reminded Ada, who couldn't stop herself from bursting out laughing.

'You have a huge thing in common with us,' she cried. 'We're *all* pregnant!'

'That doesn't mean to say I have to spend every blessed moment talking about the state of my uterus and my bowel movements,' Sybil declared.

Knowing she was treading on thin ice, Ada continued cautiously. 'I understand that you're not happy here – is it because you miss your former life?'

For the first time ever, Ada saw a fleeting sign of vulnerability in Sybil's witch-green eyes.

'I desperately miss London and my war work,' Sybil admitted. 'You met the Brigadier when he visited the Home; he was my boss.'

Ada nodded. 'Matron speaks very highly of him.'

Sybil could have kicked herself; why had she gone and mentioned Monty's blasted name and the fact that she had worked for him? The last thing she wanted was another conversation about the blessed Brigadier and his so-called good works on their behalf. Little did the foolish nuns know that all the bastard really wanted was to entomb his mistress in Mary Vale for the duration of her pregnancy, after which Sybil knew, without a shadow of a doubt, he would turn his back on the place forever. Seeing Sybil's face visibly harden, Ada suddenly remembered the surprising conversation she had recently had with Rosie.

'By the way, did you know that Rosie Pickles used to work for the Brigadier's family?'

Sybil looked thunderstruck. The two people in the world she would never have put together actually knew each other.

'Rosie Pickles worked for Monty?' she spluttered.

'Actually, I think it was his wife,' Ada corrected herself.

'Are you sure?' flabbergasted Sybil enquired.

'Yes, as I recall she was a lady's maid.'

Instantly recalling Monty's wife's name, incredulous Sybil spluttered on, 'Rosie worked for Lady Veronica Baldwin?'

Ada nodded. 'Bit of a coincidence, isn't it?'

With a frown on her face, Sybil watched Ada walk away. Could it really be possible that the poorest, dowdiest, most pathetic woman she had ever met had been glamorous Lady Veronica Baldwin's maid? Ada must have got her facts muddled, Sybil decided; there was simply no way that Rosie's path could ever have crossed with Monty's beautiful, wealthy, socialite wife.

Though Sybil had dismissed Ada's news as preposterous, she nevertheless couldn't get it out of her head. The conversation had brought back happy memories of the time she had mixed with the cream of London society, so much so that on the spur of the moment Sybil caught the bus into Kendal in order to buy some fashion magazines. Irritated that there was little more than farming weeklies and knitting magazines in the newsagent's, Sybil eventually came across a couple of old back copies of *Vogue*. Flicking through them, she found an article, 'This Season's Top War Hostesses', and promptly bought both issues.

On the smoky bus back to Grange, Sybil flicked to an article which caught her eye. 'There's More than One Way to Beat Gerry!'

Underneath were photographs of glamorous women in glittering sequinned ballgowns serving champagne and canapés to handsome, war-decorated heroes. It was no surprise to find Lady Veronica, by far the most stunning and best dressed of them all, smiling alongside her husband, who looked ridiculous as he beamed for the camera with a Pekinese dog tucked under each arm.

War hero Brigadier Montague Baldwin now works from behind a desk in Whitehall. A sad loss to the troops in the field but a bonus for the War Office responsible for the movement of tanks across Europe. One of our bravest and most honoured men, he still manages to spend time with his charming wife, Lady Veronica, their young daughter, Marigold, and their two Pekinese dogs, a gift from doting Monty to his wife on their tenth wedding anniversary.

The jerky movements of the stuffy bus winding its way along the narrow country lanes and breaking at every junction started to make Sybil feel nauseous; the article she'd just read didn't help either. Feeling the bile rise in her throat, Sybil's hatred of the man returned with venom.

'The bastard,' she seethed under her breath.

He had done *nothing* to ease her burden, quite the opposite in fact: when she could have flown the coop, he had slammed her cage door shut. She would have vengeance on Monty for treating her like dirt; somehow, she would drag him down from his privileged society perch.

'If only people knew what he was *really* like,' Sybil thought bitterly.

At which point her thoughts drifted to Rosie Pickles. Though she had scoffed at the idea of Rosie once being Lady Veronica's lady's maid, she nevertheless couldn't stop herself from wondering if it were actually true. Given the circumstances, it would be useful to get to know somebody (even a servant) who had known Monty in the past. Previously, she wouldn't have given the time of day to Rosie, but now, Sybil calculated, Mrs Pickles might be able to recall some juicy, useful gossip about Monty. The question was how on earth could she approach a woman whom she had been consistently rude to and whose children she had effectively (by her lies and plotting) exiled from Mary Vale?

21. Happy Days

Lying on her hospital bed and fretting about her children, Rosie inevitably started to think about her husband. Life hadn't been bad when Mick had been around; he had religiously brought home his pay packet (from the various building sites he worked on) every Friday tea-time, when they had always had fish and chips from the corner chippy for supper. In those days little Ronnie had been biddable while Sally had only been a baby. For the umpteenth time Rosie wondered what had happened to her husband. She had seen him some months ago – the baby in her womb proved that – but, apart from a brief letter telling her that he had arrived safely back at the barracks after his home leave, she had heard nothing until the letter came from the Army reporting Mick 'Missing in Action'. But what did that *really* mean? Had Mick been shot during a charge and fallen down dead into a ditch, never to be seen again? She had read of men being captured by the enemy and thrown into prisoner-of-war camps, where they lived in appalling conditions, eating rats and starving to death. The very thought made her blood run cold and sent her troubled mind spiralling into further fear and confusion. Lost in dark thoughts, she jumped when Dora came bustling into the room.

'How are we?' the kindly nurse asked cheerfully.

'Worried sick about my children,' Rosie confessed.

'You should be thinking about your own health, lovie,'

Dora urged. 'You're not stuck in that bed for the fun of it; we're trying to sort out that anaemia of yours and build up your strength with good wholesome grub.'

Sticking to what was troubling her, Rosie persisted, 'The Reverend Mother was kind enough to show me the letter that Mrs Larkin had written telling her that Ronnie and Sally have settled in well,' she told Dora. 'But I need to know how they *really* are.' Her big eyes filled up with tears as she gazed beseechingly at Dora. 'Do you think you might have time to pop by and see them for yourself?'

Knowing that Rosie would only continue worrying if she didn't hear more news, smiling Dora agreed readily – she couldn't possibly say no.

'I could swing past Hope Farm on my way to work in the morning,' she promised.

A happy smile briefly illuminated Rosie's sunken eyes. 'Oh, thank you, Dora, I'd really appreciate it.'

Dora didn't thank Rosie when the next morning she had to get up an hour earlier than usual in order to keep her promise. But, once she was outdoors, skimming along on her sturdy old bike, she actually didn't mind at all. It was a glorious morning, with the sun rising high, shedding golden light into dips and hollows where heather and bracken grew on craggy slopes. Sheep and their lambs ambled around the side of the mountains, bleating and baaing as they took it in turns to catch up with one another. Swallows dipped and swooped overhead, and Dora was sure she heard the sound of a cuckoo calling for a mate in the nearby woods.

Being outdoors brought a flood of memories of her twin boys, who had grown up and thrived in this wonderful landscape. Dora sighed from the depth of her soul – God, how she had worshipped her boys. Beautiful, strong, sturdy lads who raced each other up the fells and down again. Tears flooded her eyes and spilled on to her cheeks as she remembered their sweet grinning faces when they arrived home late for their tea after a day out exploring the becks and tarns.

'We got lost, Mam,' they used to say in unison.

Dora had always found it hard to be cross with them, the two like peas in a pod, covered in mud and ruddy with health. Her smile melted any anger she might have felt about their tea going cold.

'Wash your hands before you sit down,' she would say in a pretend firm voice as she produced their tea from the oven.

'Thanks, Mam,' they'd cry as they rushed to hug her on their way to washing their grimy hands in the sink.

Now they were both dead; her pride, her joy, her hope for the future; Percy at Dunkirk and Jack in a minesweeper in the North Atlantic. She had gone out of her mind when they had died; all she had wanted was to die herself and join them in eternity. Without her husband and the constant support of her devoted Mary Vale friends, Dora would have gone under; there was no doubt that death had seemed a sweeter alternative to living. It wasn't that she had 'pulled through', an expression the papers regularly trumpeted; she had merely survived and limped back to a life that was poorer and harsher without her boys. If it hadn't been for Ada urging her to return to Mary Vale, she might well have been institutionalized in the lunatic asylum in Lancaster. As it was, Ada had gently and repeatedly begged Dora to return to the nursery, where she was so desperately missed.

Without a doubt it was the babies who had saved Dora. Lined up in neat rows in their pristine white canvas cots, the Mary Vale babies were in need of love and care. Dora had poured all her emotions into the infants, who of course regularly came and went throughout Mary Vale's year. They could never be her babies, nor did she want them to be, but she could set them on the road to life, cuddled and loved. This was now her life's work, her mission, to be the interim mother before the real one took over.

When Dora arrived at Hope Farm, it was breakfast-time. Mrs Larkin invited Dora indoors with a welcoming wave of the hand.

'Sit yourself down and I'll get you some tea. Tom's out with the cows,' she added, as she pulled out a chair at the top of a long, scrubbed kitchen table around which six noisy children were assembled. 'You lot,' she called over the chatter, 'have some manners and say good-morning to Nurse Dora.'

Dora was astonished at the visible change in Ronnie and Sally in such a short time. It had been only a couple of weeks since they had left Mary Vale, but they both looked taller and stronger.

'Marge's good farmhouse grub,' Dora thought, as her generous host set a soft-boiled egg and toast in front of her, along with a mug of hot strong tea.

'I bet you a shilling you've had no breakfast,' Mrs Larkin said knowingly.

'You're right there,' Dora beamed. 'Thanks very much.'

When they had finished their breakfast, Sally and Ronnie hurried eagerly to her side.

'How's Mother?' the little girl asked.

'Is she getting better?' Ronnie added.

'She's much better,' Dora assured the anxious pair.

'Is she still in bed?' Sally enquired.

Dora nodded. 'She won't be getting up very soon,' she gently explained. 'Though she is a bit stronger than she was.'

'I hate that kid she's having,' Ronnie growled. 'It's nothing but trouble.'

Marge Larkin was on Ronnie like a shot. 'Enough of that talk, lad,' she said firmly. 'You'll mind your tongue, or you'll have me to answer to.'

The eldest boy winked at Ronnie. 'Watch it! Mam will have no bad talk in the house,' he said knowingly.

Expecting Ronnie to explode, which had usually been his response when checked, Dora was surprised when he apologized. 'Sorry, Marge,' he said, grinning sheepishly; then, turning to Dora, he added politely, 'I'm glad mother's improving.'

Ten minutes later the children were on their way to the local village school, all six of them racing each other down the lane, their laughter floating out behind them. Dora shook her head as she lit up a Woodbine.

'Well, Marge,' she said and exhaled a ring of smoke. 'You've worked wonders with the Pickles kids.'

'I won't deny Ronnie was a handful to start with,' Marge admitted, as she too lit up a cigarette. 'It was my three lads that knocked him into shape – they know the rules in this house, and they soon put Ronnie in his place.'

'Your lads certainly did a lot better than we did at Mary

Vale,' Dora admitted. 'They ran rings round us – Ronnie was like a caged animal half the time.'

'Well, he's the youngest lad here, so last in the pecking order, plus being in the same class as my youngest has helped, well, at least I hope so.' She smiled as she poured them both another cuppa from the big brown pot on the table. 'Sally's a lovie – she idolizes May, who's a regular little mother to the child. They feed the hens together, help milk the cows and she's fallen in love with the kittens the farm cat's just produced.' Marge gave a warm smile as she recounted Sally's achievements. 'She's settled into school too; our May's been teaching her to read and write, and she's made really good progress, even got a star for her work t'other day. All in all, they've both settled down nicely.'

When Dora reported the good news back to Rosie, she burst into tears of relief. 'Thank God!' she cried. 'I thought our Ronnie would upset the apple cart in no time, and they'd kick him out,' she admitted.

'Well, he's not, believe me,' Dora laughingly reassured her. 'You wouldn't recognize the pair of them, they've grown so much, and they love their new school, Marge says.'

Rosie shook her head incredulously. 'Mebbe it's all worked out for the best,' she sighed. 'It couldn't have gone on the way it was when they were here, shouting and swearing, upsetting the residents and the nuns too,' she said with a shame-faced blush. 'Though till the day I die I'll never believe they did that thieving. I don't know who did, but I just know in my bones it wasn't my kids,' she added staunchly.

22. Ward Rounds

As Sybil thrashed her brains trying to think how she could approach Rosie, who was still in bed, out of the blue Dora came up with the solution. When it was Sybil's turn to do the hospital ward chores, Dora allocated her to meal-time duty.

'Could you do the teas and lunches, lovie?'

Sybil, who had never been called 'lovie' in her entire life, gave a curt nod.

'Oh, and please encourage Rosie to eat as much as you can get down her,' Dora urged.

Sybil's ears pricked up. 'Rosie Pickles?' she asked.

'Aye, we've got to build up her strength somehow.'

'What bed is she in?' Sybil asked.

'No. 8.' Dora nodded in the direction of the bed. 'Sister Mann's with her at the moment.'

Sister Mann in her usual fussy way was not impressed by Rosie's nightdress.

'It's rather grubby,' she complained, as she removed it in order to give Rosie a bed-wash.

'It's actually clean,' Rosie protested, while Edith scrubbed her back a little too vigorously. 'Just well worn.'

Seeing her patient's skinny body swollen only in the pelvic area, where her feeble baby grew, Edith felt a stab of pity for Rosie, who, given the unrelenting harshness of her life, hardly ever complained.

'I'll get you a nice fresh nightie from the laundry store once I've finished washing you,' she promised.

Walking to the store, Edith let out an involuntary sigh; Mary Vale's functional linen nightshifts (made by the nuns with no embellishment) were a far cry from the silk pyjamas and lace nighties she had handled in her former nursing home. Charles had, in fact, bought her a ravishing cream lace negligee which was locked away with all her other treasures in the suitcase on top of her wardrobe. Sometimes at the end of a long and weary day Edith would unlock the suitcase and run her hands over the treasures of the past that Charles had lavished on her: pearls and silk she had worn on heavenly nights with him.

As Edith searched for the right-sized gown for Rosie, she thought with regret of the irksome links she still had with her mother. Ideally, she would have liked nothing more than to never communicate with Mrs Mann again, but Edith knew that in order to keep her happy (in other words, drunk) she had to regularly supply her mother with money. Without it, Mrs Mann would unquestionably kick up a stink, start asking questions, possibly even drag herself to Harrogate and make mortifying enquiries at Edith's genteel former place of work. The thought of her mother bumping into Charles or any of her posh colleagues, reeling drunk and slurring her speech, brought Edith out in a hot sweat. Cunningly she made sure that she never sent any correspondence bearing her Mary Vale address – that would be asking for trouble. The appeasement money she allocated to her mother was in the form of a postal order sent from the post office in Kendal; though Edith was uncomfortable with the fact that the postmark would appear on the envelope, she comforted herself in the knowledge that her mother wouldn't know where Kendal was, and would probably be too drunk to catch a train or a bus these days even if she did. No, Edith couldn't risk upsetting her mother while she was working at Mary Vale; she would bide her time and wait until she was absolutely sure that any gossip surrounding her scandalous affair had run its course; then she would look for work elsewhere and start to withdraw from her family altogether.

After Sister Mann's thorough bed-wash and change of clothes, exhausted Rosie lay back against her bank of pillows.

'Dinner's on the way,' Edith announced.

With no appetite at all, Rosie smothered a groan; she wasn't looking forward to her dinner at all, and she certainly didn't want it delivered by Sybil Harwood. Forcing a cheery smile, Sybil laid the tray down on Rosie's bedside. 'Here we are, tasty liver and onions, make sure you eat up – it'll do you the world of good.'

As soon as Sybil was out of sight, Rosie grimaced as she pushed the tray aside. She wouldn't trust that young madam as far as she could throw her, and for all her hearty words there was a wary look in Sybil's eyes that suggested the feeling was mutual. Little did Rosie know that the snooty young woman wheeling the loaded dinner trolley up and down the ward was desperate to make friends with her for reasons she could never have imagined.

23. Sweet-talking Rosie

Every morning, while she was on ward duty, Sybil tried her hardest to smile as she wheeled the tea-trolley, but it was still only seven o'clock and she had had a hell of a night, with back pains and dashing to the lavatory almost every hour. The loaded trolley she was pushing weighed a ton and rattled loudly on its creaky wheels, warning all the slumbering patients that early-morning tea was on its way.

Though she tried her best to encourage Rosie to eat, as instructed by Sister Mann, who was on a mission to build Rosie up, Sybil simply hadn't the right bedside manner. She hadn't a clue how to coax Rosie to eat the mashed potatoes and swede that she herself gagged at, but a day didn't pass without Sister Mann urging her to try harder.

'It's imperative we build up Rosie's strength.'

'We can't force her to eat,' Sybil remonstrated.

Edith gave her a hard look. 'Have you heard of the word "persuasion"?' she asked sarcastically.

'I'm trying my best,' Sybil answered irritably. 'But she shows no interest at all in food.'

Giving up on Sybil, Sister Mann took on the challenge of monitoring Rosie's daily intake, sitting by her patient's bedside and gently urging her to take just another spoonful of semolina or tapioca pudding – which showed an admirable, caring side of Edith's character – but sadly even that was wasted on Rosie, who regularly brought back up the meal she had tried so hard to swallow.

An hour later Sybil was on another tour of the wards, yet again with the noisy trolley, this time loaded up with yet more tea plus toast, a scraping of Mary Vale butter and Sister Mary Paul's rhubarb jam bulked out with turnips. By the time she had completed the breakfast round, Sybil really needed a cup of tea herself, but, seeing Rosie sitting up in her bed, she seized the opportunity and quickly approached. Just as she was about to offer Rosie a second cup of tea, Sybil's baby gave her a hefty kick in the ribs.

'Ouch!' she exclaimed.

'Oh, dear, are you all right?' Rosie asked nervously.

'Active baby,' Sybil explained.

Rosie pulled down the corners of her mouth. 'Unfortunately, mine's not active – occasionally it moves a bit, but compared to the other two it's a weak, little scrap of a thing.'

Turning towards the open window through which the morning sun streamed, Rosie caught the fragrance of early roses combined with lily of the valley.

'It's beautiful out there,' Rosie sighed wistfully. 'Pity I can't enjoy it.'

Sybil gave an inward sigh; never having been a chatterbox, she struggled with small talk about gardens and babies, but she had to stick with the banal if she were going to make any progress with Rosie.

'I'm sure your children will be enjoying the warm weather?' she said feebly.

Rosie's face lit up like a sunbeam that had just popped out from behind a dark brooding cloud.

'Oh, yes,' she enthused. 'They'll be loving this weather, running up and down the fells, chasing each other around the school playground. Dora says they're loving Hope Farm,' she added happily.

A pang of guilt shot through Sybil; here she was chatting about Rosie's children, who had literally been evicted from Mary Vale because of her devious scheming.

Mercifully Rosie started another thread of conversation. 'The new sister seems to be settling in,' she remarked. 'Though she doesn't hold a candle to Sister Ada.'

Seeing this as a possible segue, Sybil said as casually as she could, 'Talking of Sister Ada, I saw her at her exercises classes the other day.'

'Good God!' Rosie yelped. 'Is she still doing them classes?'

'She says she really benefits from them, now that she's so close to her due date.'

'She's a lovely woman – I miss seeing her bright smiling face around the place,' Rosie enthused.

Determined not to be side-tracked, Sybil ploughed on. 'She mentioned after the class had finished that you and I have somebody in common.'

Looking suspicious, Rosie asked, 'And who would that be?'

'Apparently you used to work for my boss's wife.'

Wondering if Rosie would rise to the bait, Sybil held her breath.

'Lady Veronica Baldwin?' Rosie asked.

Sybil nodded. 'I never met her,' she continued. 'I just worked for Brigadier Baldwin. I was his secretary at the War Office.'

'And a bit more than that, from what I've seen,' Rosie thought as she fiddled nervously with her bedspread.

She knew all the gossip in the dining room about Sybil and the Brigadier; as one of the saucy residents crudely put it, 'Her Majesty was his bit on the side.'

Looking even more wary, Rosie's response was non-committal. 'I did work for Lady Veronica.'

'I've heard she's a lovely woman,' Sybil gushed. 'Though God knows how she puts up with that wretched husband of hers,' she added and artfully rolled her eyes. 'I know he's perceived as a war hero and a perfect gent, but, after working closely with him for nearly a year, I'd say he was quite the opposite.'

Rosie's dark eyes flew wide open. 'Would you now?'

Wondering again if Rosie would take the bait, Sybil eagerly continued. 'He was a monster to work for – hands everywhere. We ladies avoided him like the plague,' she lied through her teeth.

A look of real contempt flashed across Rosie's pale face. 'I know all about him,' she said in a voice thick with loathing. 'The man's lucky to have a saint for a wife.'

A patient calling out for another cup of tea dragged Sybil reluctantly away from Rosie's bedside.

'I'd better get a move on. Let's have another chinwag about the wicked Brigadier soon, eh?' she said with a cheeky wink.

Moving off with her trolley, Sybil smiled to herself. 'Rome wasn't built in a day,' she thought. 'Now I've started I can always go back for more.'

*

Once they had established a tacit understanding that neither of them could stand the Brigadier, it became easier to stop by and chat to Rosie.

'I worked my way up from housemaid,' she told Sybil with an uncharacteristic ring of pride in her voice. 'Course it didn't just happen overnight – I had to be trained proper for the role. I thought when I applied for the more senior post Lady Veronica would turn me down, me being common and that, but she took me on and trained me up herself.'

Sybil checked her wristwatch – she would have to bring the conversation to a stop very soon or get a ticking-off for delivering cold food to the entire ward. Seemingly oblivious of Sybil's body language, Rosie rambled on.

'Dowry House belongs to Lady Veronica's father, the Earl Stow, though watching the Brigadier striding around the place like lord of the manor you'd wouldn't have guessed it.'

'He certainly thinks he rules the universe,' Sybil said encouragingly, but was immediately disappointed by Rosie's reaction. Instead of rubbishing the Brigadier, Rosie returned to eulogizing her former place of work. Sighing, Sybil smothered a yawn.

'Dowry House was a big beautiful place, hundreds of windows to clean, balconies back and front overlooking the wide streets and the grand white stucco houses. Massive marble-floored entrance hall with stairs running off either side, and chandeliers everywhere,' Rosie burbled on. 'Summer was wonderful, with the rose garden in full bloom and . . .'

Interrupting Rosie mid-flow, Sybil lumbered heavily to

her feet. 'I really mustn't let the food go cold,' she said, as she playfully wagged a finger. 'Now eat all your dinner, Mrs Pickles, or you'll get me into a lot of trouble with Sister Mann!'

'Then do me a favour,' Rosie joked. 'Bin that blasted plate of liver and onions that you keep shoving at me!'

By the end of the week Sybil knew the colour of just about every set of curtains that hung in Dowry House, the brand of Lady Veronica's expensive perfume (Givenchy), where the family tiara was kept (in a vault in the library), what her ladyship preferred for breakfast (salmon and scrambled eggs) and what her favourite cocktails were (Dry Martini and Pink Lady). She also knew everything there was to know about her only child, Marigold, whom the Brigadier had barely mentioned in all the time Sybil was having an affair with him. Sentimental Rosie could barely stop talking about her.

'Such a lovely little girl,' she sighed. 'And her clothes! The most gorgeous party frocks that you've ever seen. I wish my Sally could have seen her expensive clothes; she would have just loved them.'

By Friday, when Sybil was coming to the end of her week working on the wards, she had little to show for all the long-winded conversations she had had with Rosie. Conversations had ranged from Marigold's toys to the weekly butcher's bill, the wine list, the gardener's dismissal for stealing brandy, Lady Veronica's extensive wardrobe and how often Rosie starched her maid's uniform. How on earth was she going to get anywhere when she wasn't daily in Rosie's company? Sybil realized that if she were to proceed – and she wasn't giving up now that she had started – she would have to invent reasons to visit Rosie, whom she almost *quite* liked now that she was removed from her wretched children.

'I'll have to engineer excuses to visit her,' Sybil decided. 'Drop by with a slice of cake, or a bit of gossip, anything that justifies my turning up at her bedside asking questions.' Her eyes strayed to the garden. 'I could pick her a little posy – that would be a nice alibi for popping in for a visit.'

Recalling the wary look of distrust that had flashed across Rosie's face right at the beginning of their exchange about the Brigadier, Sybil knew she was on to something; there had to be a good reason why downtrodden Rosie had reacted so visibly when Sybil had mentioned his relationship with Lady Veronica. It was perfectly clear that Rosie couldn't stand the man, but Sybil was hoping for more than that: some dirt, some secret that Rosie might be holding back.

'It's just a question of sweet-talking her until I entice the truth out of her,' Sybil thought hopefully. 'If Rosie eventually reveals some dark scandalous secret about Monty, it will be well worth the wait.'

24. Confidences

The following week Sybil was on her least favourite chore, laundry duty; working in the laundry was steamy hot and the carbolic soap cracked the skin on her small, delicate hands. Groaning as she hauled big heavy wet sheets out of the boiler, Sybil comforted herself that she would not be doing this kind of grim work for much longer. By the end of the summer she would be long gone from Mary Vale and everybody in it, but hopefully (if Rosie obliged) she might leave the place with some interesting juicy gossip on the Brigadier.

The previous afternoon Sybil had popped on to the ante-ward with a small slice of cake for Rosie, but, as she entered, she spotted Sally and Ronnie by the side of their mother's bed. Sybil immediately scurried away before any of the family spotted her. She would try again later today, after Sister Ada's exercise class.

In the few weeks that Ada had been away from Mary Vale she had bloomed into a radiant mother-to-be; her rich, thick brunette hair was long and lustrous, and her tanned skin glowed with good health. It was clear from the shape of her that Ada's baby was also blooming, growing so big and round that the girls attending the class insisted it was a boy.

'You're carrying it all high up front,' one insisted. 'Nice and neat, a sure sign that it's a boy. Girls sit lower, more spread out, making your bum look enormous!'

'Baby or not I've always had a big bum,' one girl giggled.

Ada burst out laughing. 'Stuff and nonsense!' she declared.

At the end of the class Ada approached Sybil. 'A little bird tells me that you've finally found a friend,' she smiled.

Sybil's witch-green eyes widened. 'I wouldn't go that far,' she demurred.

'From what I've heard you and Rosie have palled up,' Ada continued.

'We just chatted a bit when I was on ward duty,' Sybil answered with a dismissive shrug.

'Well, I'm delighted to hear it,' Ada beamed. 'Bed-bound as she is these days, Rosie needs all the friends she can get.'

Anxious that her behaviour shouldn't arouse suspicion – after all she had previously been the most anti-social resident in Mary Vale – Sybil insisted, 'I wouldn't say we were friends. I just delivered her meals three times a day and sometimes stopped for a chat.'

'I think it's very thoughtful of you,' Ada added. 'With her children gone, Rosie must be awfully lonely.'

Feeling uneasy, Sybil recalled Rosie's happy smiling face as she had gazed at her children on the ward. Washed and scrubbed up, wearing clean clothes, possibly hand-me-downs from the older children at Hope Farm, Sally and Ronnie looked almost unrecognizable. Sally's former straggly hair had been cut into a neat bob which empha-sized her sweet little heart-shaped face, and Ronnie had lost his two front teeth, which made him look uncharac-teristically cute.

'It's because of me that they're no longer at Mary Vale

with their mother,' Sybil reminded herself, but, before guilt got the better of her, she also reminded herself that she had never seen the Pickles kids looking better. 'Maybe I've done them a favour after all?'

Just before tea-time, which, from the smell issuing from the kitchen, was cheese-and-onion pie, Sybil, bearing a pretty posy of flowers which she had popped into a little vase of water, appeared at Rosie's bedside with a rather sheepish smile on her face.

'Thought these might cheer you up,' she said, as she plonked the vase on the bedside table.

'Oh, they're lovely, Sybil,' delighted Rosie exclaimed and leant over to inhale the delicate smell of sweet peas. 'They smell lovely too, thank you so much,' she said with genuine gratitude.

'Can I fetch you anything?' Sybil enquired, even though she actually wasn't officially on ward duties.

'No, I'm fine, sit down,' Rosie urged. 'You look like you need a bit of looking after yourself, love.'

Unexpectedly touched by the warmth of her kind words, Sybil did indeed sit down.

'It's been a long day, starting with damn laundry duty.' She pulled down the corners of her pink pouty mouth to form a grimace.

Rosie leant across to squeeze Sybil's chapped hand. 'Never mind, you'll soon be out of here,' she said softly.

As tears pricked the back of Sybil's eyes, she wondered if her brain was going soft; she was on a ruthless mission to coax information out of Rosie, yet here she was going all soppy because Rosie was being kind to her.

'I've missed our little chats,' Rosie continued cheerfully. 'The time just flew when I was talking to you about Lady Veronica. I hope I didn't bore you to death,' she added with a self-conscious blush.

'Not at all: it made a nice change from the usual run-of-the-mill conversations here at Mary Vale,' Sybil said, grinning. 'If I have to sit through another meal listening to pregnant women talking about their toilet habits, I swear I'll scream!'

'The way you talk reminds me so much of Lady Veronica,' Rosie laughed. 'Maybe it's your posh accent or just the outrageous things you say.'

'We probably moved in similar circles too,' Sybil said as casually as she could.

'Maybe,' Rosie agreed. 'The Brigadier often invited members of his staff to Dowry House.'

Sybil averted her gaze to the floor, trying not to look too obviously interested.

'Maybe not the ones he was knocking off,' she thought bitterly, before she said, 'He was such a big head, I bet he was an awful show-off.'

'Oh, yes, he loved being the centre of attention,' Rosie replied. 'Especially when it came to the women.'

'Don't overstep the mark,' Sybil quickly warned herself. 'Let Rosie unravel the tale in her own time.'

'Sometimes it was embarrassing for us staff,' Rosie confessed. 'Especially when, you know – we caught him at it.'

Feigning innocence, Sybil asked, 'Kissing and cuddling?'

'No!' Rosie exclaimed, then lowering her voice to a whisper she hissed, 'More than that; you know, at it, with other women.'

Sybil gave a theatrical gasp. 'He betrayed the lovely Lady Veronica in his own home?'

Rosie gave an indignant snort. 'More than once too.' Having gone this far, Rosie suddenly didn't seem in the mood for stopping. 'He couldn't keep his hands off any new young woman.'

Sybil well remembered being a new woman herself. Smart, well educated, with a plummy, alluring voice, an hour-glass figure and neat ankles. Knowing Monty as she did now, she knew she must have been like a flame to a moth.

'He'd be all over them,' Rosie continued. 'Removing their coats, which was *our* job to do as servants,' she added indignantly. 'Serving them one too many drinks, leading them into dinner, all in front of Lady Veronica, who just rose above it all, like the lady of quality that she is.'

'Maybe that was the only way the poor woman could survive,' Sybil mused. 'Rather than arguing in public, she turned a blind eye to her husband's sordid excesses and got on with raising her young daughter and looking after the country estate – that's enough to keep anyone busy.'

'Indeed, her ladyship spent a lot of time at Stowupland, especially during Marigold's holidays. She always took me with her – I loved it.' Rosie positively glowed at the happy memory. 'I would pack up the car, then we'd set off for their country seat, where the staff would be awaiting our arrival. Oh, the food they prepared for us, all fresh from the estate, fish, meat, cheese, fruit.' Rosie licked her lips as if she were tasting the food afresh.

Hoping Rosie wouldn't dwell too long on food, Sybil

quickly asked, 'Did you always attend Lady Veronica on her trips?'

'I did when I became her lady's maid, but before that I used to stay in the London house along with the rest of the staff.'

'You must have missed your mistress when she was absent?'

'We all did, for sure, especially because that's when the Brigadier came into his own,' Rosie replied darkly. 'Him and his cronies, eating and drinking till late into the night, playing cards and billiards till dawn.' Rosie gave a contemptuous sniff. 'There were always ladies present too, not all of them the respectable type, I can tell you,' she ended contemptuously.

'While the cat's away the mice will play,' Sybil joked, but Rosie didn't laugh.

'It was a humiliating spectacle,' she grumbled. 'The things the Brigadier's valet told us after serving the master breakfast in bed.' She quickly looked around to check that nobody was listening. 'Some of the servants thought it amusing, hearing about tripping over knickers and suspender belts, but us maids were embarrassed. I had no time for the Brigadier's debauchery – it was always a marvel to me that her ladyship didn't walk out on the brute,' Rosie said crossly.

'It's a wonder she married him in the first place!' Sybil exclaimed. 'A beautiful young woman like her must have been overrun with proposals of marriage when she came out into society.'

'I wasn't working for her at the time, but I know she was Deb of the Year. I saw some smashing photos of her ladyship in a photo album one of the little kitchen maids kept.' Rosie gave a proud sigh. 'She looked like proper royalty. She was better looking and better dressed than the royal princesses, and that's saying something.'

Sybil sat back in the hospital chair she had been tensely perched on. 'All I can say is the Brigadier is a very lucky man,' she declared.

Rosie wriggled her thin body to the side of the bed so that she could be nearer to Sybil.

'There was a bit more to it than luck on his side,' she whispered. 'My friend Daisy, the little kitchen maid with the photo album I just mentioned, she *worshipped* her lady-ship. Well, she heard it from the Stowupland chauffeur who she was engaged to that –'

And at that precise moment Sister Mann appeared at Rosie's bedside.

'The doctor's due to see you in fifteen minutes, Mrs Pickles,' she said briskly. 'I need to take your temperature and check your blood pressure before he arrives.' Turning to the visitor, she added, 'If you'll excuse us, please.'

Feeling like she might scream in sheer frustration, Sybil rose to her feet.

'Nice talking to you,' she said lamely as she left Rosie.

Walking down the hospital corridor, irritated Sybil seethed under her breath. 'Damn, blast and buggeration! *Why* did we have to get interrupted?'

Too restless to stay indoors, Sybil stomped along the garden path that led down to the marsh, where the tide was out, and sea-birds pecked and dibbled in the silvery sage-green grass that grew on the sandbanks. Cooled by the salty sea-breeze, Sybil followed a track that skirted the edges of the bay. Standing staring out across a sea that was so blue it merged with the blue of the sky dotted with seagulls soaring and dipping on the warm air currents, Sybil gave herself a good talking to.

'Be patient for a bit longer – at least you know that you're on the right track.'

25. Home Sweet Home

At the same time that Sybil was staring out across the Irish Sea, Ada was busy in her cottage garden digging in the tomato and strawberry plants that Farmer Arkwright had recently given her.

'Plant 'em south facing and water 'em well,' he had advised. 'You should get a fine crop afore long.'

Though it hurt her tight tummy to bend over too far, Ada was enjoying being outdoors in the fresh air. A cheeky little robin followed her every move before popping down from the hawthorn bush and perching to peck at a fat earthworm Ada had just uncovered. With the sun shining on her tanned face and her hair caught loosely in a blue ribbon, Ada gave a little smile as her baby changed position.

'Sorry, darling,' she murmured, as she briefly stopped digging in order to let her baby settle back down again.

Turning her gaze to the fruit trees that edged the garden – apple, plum and pear, all of which showed signs of bearing fruit – a sudden thought brought an excited smile to Ada's face.

'I'll ask Sister Mary Paul for her jam recipes and make pots of my own jam for Jamie. He'll love that,' she thought happily.

The unexpected arrival of Sister Ann tearing down the farm track on a rickety old bicycle that was always kept in the garage in the convent yard widened Ada's smile.

'Hello,' she cried, as she waved a welcome.

The look of concentration on her friend's face made Ada's heart skip a beat; was she here on a social visit or the bearer of bad tidings?

Seeing Ada's anxious response, Sister Ann immediately guessed what might be running through her mind.

'Nothing to worry about,' she called out, as she parked her bike up against the garden wall.

Visibly relieved, Ada hurried over to her friend, whom she kissed on the cheek.

'How lovely to see you,' she enthused. 'Shall I put the kettle on?'

'Yes, please,' Sister Ann said breathlessly. 'But first I must tell you that Jamie's just got through on the ward phone – he's coming home!'

Flabbergasted, Ada slumped weakly on to the garden bench, where she murmured incredulously, 'Jamie's coming home?'

Ann nodded. 'He said he's got some leave due and he's hoping to be home by Thursday afternoon.'

'So soon!' Ada gasped in delight.

Seeing her friend in a daze, Ann quickly said, 'Stay right where you are, dear, *I'll* put the kettle on.'

Left alone, Ada could only smile in delight, while the little robin who had become her gardening companion trilled from the holly bush.

'Did you hear that?' Ada called out to the bird. 'My darling's coming home on Thursday.'

Sister Ann reappeared with a tray set with a pot of tea and cups and saucers.

'Here, drink this while it's hot and strong,' she said and

handed Ada a cup of tea. 'I must have given you a bit of a shock.'

'The best shock possible.' Ada smiled. 'Completely out of the blue too.'

'Jamie also said,' Ann recalled, 'that you are by no means to try to meet him at Preston or Lancaster Station – he said he would make his own way here.'

'But he doesn't even know where I live!' Ada exclaimed.

Matron burst out laughing. 'He knows where Mary Vale Farm is – the cottage is just down the road from there.'

'I suppose so. I'm not thinking straight,' Ada confessed, as she thoughtfully sipped her tea. 'Isn't it awful how war has affected us all in so many ways? When I saw you cycling towards the cottage, I instantly thought the very worst.'

'I could see that from the way your face dropped,' Ann replied.

'I can't be the only young wife who thinks the worst when she sees a car pulling up, or a cyclist approach. You hear so many heartbreaking stories about telegraph boys arriving with terrible news, shattering families and all their hopes of future happiness.' As tears filled Ada's big blue eyes, she added with an emotional catch in her throat, 'You've got to grasp life by the throat and squeeze every bit of joy out of it while you can.'

'Life's very precious,' Sister Ann agreed. Laying aside her teacup, she rose to her feet. 'I left the end of a fresh loaf of Sister Mary Paul's bread on your kitchen table; she handed it to me as I was leaving.'

'Sweet Mary Paul,' Ada murmured. 'How lucky I am to have you all.'

After Sister Ann had cycled off, Ada went into a flat spin, washing the kitchen curtains, sweeping the garden path, ironing sheets and ploughing through recipe books intent on finding a dish she could make out of her meagre rations for her beloved. In the end she decided on corned-beef fritters and dark, sticky gingerbread for pudding.

'That's if I can borrow some spices and black treacle from Sister Mary Paul's larder,' she said out loud.

By the end of the day, Ada, worn out with sheer over-excitement, went to bed early, but, as she lay back against her pillows listening to owls calling in the nearby forest, her thoughts flew to her husband. Where was he? On a troop ship crossing the Channel, sleeping on a bench at a draughty railway station waiting for a train to pull in?

'Stay safe, my darling, we're waiting for you,' she murmured, and she stroked her tummy, where her baby lay peacefully sleeping.

The following morning, nice and early before the day warmed up, Ada set off for Mary Vale, where she was welcomed by Sisters Theresa and Mary Paul.

'Look at the size of you,' the older nun lovingly fretted. 'You shouldn't be out walking in this heat.'

'I picked the coolest time of the day,' Ada protested, as she willingly accepted a glass of water from Theresa.

'You look marvellous,' the younger nun smiled. 'Bonnier than ever. And we know why you've got such a happy smile on your face,' she said with a conspiratorial wink. 'You must be so excited?'

'Oh, I am,' Ada earnestly replied. 'I'm sick with longing, it's been months since we met.'

'Don't go overdoing it,' Mary Paul urged.

'I did way too much yesterday,' Ada admitted. 'I want Jamie to love the cottage as much as I do, so I spring-cleaned it yet again.'

'He's bound to love it,' Theresa exclaimed. 'Though to be honest I think he'll only have eyes for you,' she giggled.

Thinking of being in her husband's arms and kissing him made Ada blush; what a thought to have in front of two consecrated nuns!

'Well, today is all about cooking,' she announced briskly. 'I want to feed my husband well, so I thought I'd get some dishes ready in advance. I don't want to spend every precious minute while Jamie's home sweating over a stove.'

'I can give you a meat-and-onion pie to take back; it'll be all right for a day or two in that nice cool larder of yours, and I could drop off an egg custard and jelly tomorrow if you like?'

'That would be marvellous,' Ada smiled. 'I always said you were an angel,' she added and planted a kiss on her favourite nun's wrinkled old cheek. 'Could I cadge some ground ginger and black treacle to make sticky ginger-bread slices, please?' Ada begged.

Sister Mary Paul nodded, then trotted off to the pantry to find the precious cake ingredients, leaving Ada chatting with Sister Theresa.

'I'm sure that once he's home Jamie will want to do some fell-walking,' Ada said.

Gaping at her friend in disbelief, Theresa cried out incredulously, 'You can't possibly be thinking of joining him?'

'The fresh air will do me good,' Ada assured her. 'And I'll only do what I can.'

Rolling her eyes, Sister Theresa declared, 'I'd let Dr Jamie be the best judge of that.'

A few days later, as Jamie's train made its way across Morecambe Bay, chugging slowly over metal tracks built on stout wooden plinths drilled deep into the seabed, his thoughts were only for his wife. Darling, sweetest Ada. How he admired her strength and determination, and how she always faced the future with a brave smile on her beautiful face. As ever, he thought how lucky he was to have her as his wife. Her image was a constant in his mind, as he carried out grim amputations and tended the dying in the Front Line clearing station where conditions had been growing grimmer and grimmer as the Germans made their relentless advances.

Determined to think of only the positives in his life, at least for the time being, Jamie wondered what it would be like to finally share a home with Ada. No more slipping away to the Watendlath farmhouse where they had spent their honeymoon and other subsequent holidays. Now he and Ada could lie in bed late and make breakfast at leisure – in their underwear if they chose, he thought with a broad grin. Gazing out across the wide sweep of the bay with its vast stretch of sparkling golden sand, Jamie willed the train to pick up speed. His heart pounded with excitement as it rattled along the margins of the marsh, filling up fast as the incoming tide swilled into rock pools dumping shrimps, cockles, mussels and aquatic insects for the oystercatchers and avocets to gorge on.

Leaping out at Kents Bank (barely before the train had stopped), Jamie slung his duffle bag over his shoulder, then sprinted through the small wood that skirted the grounds of Mary Vale House. Following the track that led to Mary Vale Farm, Jamie spotted a little plume of smoke rising from the cottage just beyond the farm gate. Jumping over the drystone wall, he rushed to the front door that was standing wide open.

'ADA!'

'Jamie, Jamie!' she answered and flew into his open arms. 'Darling,' she sobbed, as her tears mingled with his kisses.

'Oh, my love,' he murmured into her glorious hair, which had grown even thicker and longer in his absence. Holding her close to his heart, Jamie could have willingly stayed right there for a very long time, but their baby, complaining at being squeezed too hard, gave Ada a protesting kick in the ribs, causing her to laughingly pull away.

'Gosh!' Jamie exclaimed, as his eyes swept over Ada's vast burgeoning tummy. 'You've grown.'

'I should jolly well hope so,' Ada grinned.

Tenderly feeling the shape of her tummy, Jamie enquired, 'Aren't you uncomfortable?'

'I was when I was working full time,' Ada admitted. 'Less so now – at least I get to lie down and rest when I need to.'

Jamie pulled her close again but this time less forcefully. 'I have been worrying myself sick about you,' he confessed.

Seeing the tears in his hazel eyes, Ada gently stroked his thick, tawny-brown hair.

'I've been very well,' she soothed. 'My only complaint is your child has very strong legs and powerful little fists.'

'Then I'll have to have a word with him or her,' he answered in a mock stern voice. 'No more kicking Mummy!'

'Come on,' Ada urged and drew away. 'My mission is to feed you up while you're home, so sit down while I make you some tea and you can sample my first-ever gingerbread.'

'Not until I've had a tour of our cottage,' Jamie insisted.

After inspecting the cosy little sitting room, the baby's room and finally their large airy bedroom with breathtaking views of Cartmel Forest, loud with the call of songbirds and cackling pheasants, Jamie returned to the kitchen, where, while eulogizing about Farm Cottage, he polished off most of the gingerbread and a whole pot of tea. Finally, his long journey, excitement and non-stop talking got the better of Jamie, who, as his energy levels dropped, visibly slumped before Ada's eyes.

'Come on, my darling,' she said tenderly, as she took him by the hand. 'You need to catch up on your sleep.'

Obediently following his wife upstairs, Jamie grumbled, 'I don't want to waste our precious time together sleeping.'

'If you don't get some rest, you'll nod off with your head on the kitchen table,' she teased.

Once upstairs in their bedroom, bleary-eyed Jamie struggled to get his clothes off.

'Here, let me help you,' Ada said, and she helped him undress, then settled him on the bed; once his head touched the pillow, Jamie fell into the deepest sleep.

Seeing his body naked apart from his underclothes,

Ada was visibly shocked to see how thin Jamie had become since his last visit home: his ribs poked out of his ribcage, and his arms and legs were thinner too.

Filled with love for her sweet husband, Ada lay down in the curve of his arm and, with her head pressed against his chest, listened to the regular beat of his heart. All she wanted to do was to fold him into her arms and keep him there, loved and safe, never to leave her. Feeling her baby gently changing position, Ada held her husband's hand in one hand while with the other she held her tummy. For a few minutes she felt a feeling of complete and utter joy; all that she had ever wanted was right here with her now.

26. Jamie

Jamie slept solidly for almost five hours, and when he did next appear in the kitchen he was smiling, refreshed – and starving hungry.

'Mmm, what's that delicious smell?' he asked, as he sniffed the air appreciatively.

'Corned-beef fritters, baked potatoes and fresh peas and green beans from Farmer Arkwright's vegetable garden.'

'The man's a miracle worker,' Jamie joked and circled his arms around Ada's thick waist.

'And,' she added, as she nodded towards two bottles of beer on the kitchen table, 'he thought you might appreciate a drink.'

Opening a bottle, Jamie downed half the beer in one thirsty gulp. 'Just what the doctor ordered.'

After Ada's hearty supper, which Jamie demolished with great appreciation, Ada suggested they went for a stroll before it went dark. Hand in hand, they walked down the lane that ran alongside a gurgling beck, chattering happily to each other about anything but the war. Occasionally they stopped to gaze at the distant northern mountains of the Lake District towering in a twilit sky. They watched in awe as the sun burnished their summits in a blaze of gold and crimson before it sank, and the mountains were engulfed in darkness.

Throwing up his arms, Jamie gave a joyful cry. 'God! This place is heaven on earth. What a piece of luck you were offered Farm Cottage,' he said gratefully.

'Luck and a lot of friendly intervention,' Ada chuckled. 'As I said in my letter to you, Sister Mary Paul, Sister Theresa and Sister Ann put the idea into the Reverend Mother's head; secretly I think they never stopped nagging her, and she was probably worn down by their insistence, and so eventually offered the place to me.'

'And you're not too lonely, all on your own?' he earnestly enquired.

Ada burst out laughing. 'Lonely!' she exclaimed. 'I have numerous visitors, all bearing gifts, from rhubarb jam, to a sliver of Lancashire cheese, to baby's bootees, and when I'm really lucky freshly baked bread. I've got Farmer Arkwright next door with his herd of cows and sheep, not to mention his ducks and chickens, and little one here.' She smiled as she rolled her hand over her tummy. 'Believe me, sweetheart, I have no time to be lonely.'

'It's such a relief to know that I can leave you in safe hands, darling,' Jamie said sincerely. 'Now that I've been granted this present leave, there's no chance of any more in the near future,' he said, as he anxiously watched her face for a reaction.

Brave Ada stuck out her determined chin, which had a little dimple in its centre.

'You're here with me tonight, that's all that matters,' she whispered as she leant against his warm shoulder. 'We have each other for a few days,' she continued as she swallowed back her tears. 'Why ask for the moon when we have the stars?'

'My sweetest girl, I love you more than life itself,' Jamie whispered into her hair.

Standing on the edge of Cartmel Forest, they clung tightly to each other, while in the forest the roosting song-birds serenaded each other to sleep and an adult barn owl, white as snow, glided out of the dark woods, swooping past them on strong, silent wings.

Having arranged to borrow Farmer Arkwright's old Bedford van that smelt of sheep, collie dogs and the vegetables that he regularly transported to sell at Kendal market, Jamie and Ada set off for Keswick the next day. After dropping a picnic basket into the back of the van, Ada settled herself in the passenger seat beside Jamie and asked excitedly, 'Where are we going?'

Jamie answered cautiously. 'Seeing as you're fell-walking for two, we need to be careful. I don't want you getting overtired.'

'I will be careful,' Ada promised. 'Now, please, will you tell me where we are going.'

'You'll know when we get there,' he teased.

And she did. The moment Jamie pulled up by the side of Derwentwater, Ada exclaimed, 'Catbells, Mrs Tiggy-Winkle's mountain.'

'One of the best,' Jamie sighed, as he stepped out of the van in order to admire the mountain that soared high over twinkling blue Lake Derwentwater, cupped in the folds of the surrounding mountains.

Grabbing the picnic basket, Ada clambered out of the car. 'Come on, let's get started,' she said eagerly.

'I mean it, darling,' Jamie cautioned. 'You *must* take care.'

'Stop fretting, love,' Ada answered. 'I'll go as far as I'm comfortable and then I'll stop and have a cup of tea.'

Holding the picnic basket, Jamie led the way up the steep, narrow, winding track that quickly gave them height; in no time at all they could see the sweep of the Borrowdale Road, which wound its way circuitously through rocky crags and belts of woodland, until it came to the village of Grange, where the road ran parallel with the clear bubbling river all the way into the village of Rosthwaite. As the morning sun rose higher in the sky, Ada began to flag. Finding a cool grassy spot on a rocky outcrop with stunning views both ways, Jamie settled a blanket on the ground and Ada gratefully sank down on to it.

'Off you go, have fun,' she urged. 'I promise I won't eat all the sandwiches.'

Once her husband had gone leaping and bounding up the mountainside, Ada drank a mug of tea from the Thermos they had brought along with them, then settled back on the blanket, where, shading her eyes against the blinding bright sun, she watched swallows swooping and diving high up in the vaulted blue sky. Suddenly overcome with fatigue, she closed her eyes and in no time at all was fast asleep. When she awoke, it was to find Jamie grinning down at her.

'The hunter warrior returns,' he joked, as he slumped beside her. 'Mmm, these sandwiches are delicious,' he said, as he took a bite from one of the egg-and-cress sandwiches Ada had prepared for their picnic.

'There's cheese and pickle too,' she said as she poured out more tea. 'And a bit of the gingerbread cake and apples, another gift from Farmer Arkwright, from his apple cellar.'

'Here's to Farmer Arkwright,' Jamie cried, raising his mug of hot tea. 'The man's better than Father Christmas!'

Once they had demolished their picnic, Ada sighed with contentment as she leant against Jamie.

'These are days that memories are made of,' she said dreamily.

Jamie stiffened as if he were suddenly uncomfortable. 'Darling,' he said, 'there's something I have to tell you.'

Suddenly alert, Ada sat bolt upright. 'What is it? What's wrong?'

Drawing her back towards the warmth of his body, Jamie finally told Ada what he had been dreading telling her since he arrived home. Now that he had made his opening gambit, he came straight to the point.

'My team are being posted to North Africa.'

Rigid in his arms, Ada found herself unable to speak. 'The Eighth Army are out there,' he started.

Ada gave an impatient nod. 'Yes, I know,' she said shortly.

She had read all about the North African campaign, which was being fought in the Libyan and Egyptian deserts; she just never imagined, goodness only knows why, that Jamie would ever be caught up in that campaign.

'They're desperately in need of medical clearing stations,' Jamie explained.

Ada's thoughts were all over the place. Jamie was being moved from Europe to Africa. The thought of his being on another continent – even further away from her – gripped Ada with fear. Feeling her tremble, Jamie quickly added, 'Ada, dearest, I'll be doing the same job that I do now, attending the wounded; it's no different nor is it any more dangerous.'

Unable to stop herself from reacting like a frightened child, Ada burst into tears.

'Darling, please don't cry,' he begged. 'Please don't upset yourself.'

But Ada just couldn't stop crying. She had been strong and positive for so long, but this sudden news of Jamie's new posting tipped her right over the edge. She didn't want him to go anywhere, she thought wildly – she didn't want him to leave her at all. As her tears subsided and her reasoning returned, Ada let Jamie rock her in his arms.

'When?' she finally asked.

'No date yet,' he replied.

Ada sighed. Of course not, she thought bitterly. The Army drops a bombshell then keeps you waiting, dangling, holding your breath, until the order gets the official stamp and men are on the move, travelling on trains and ships to new battlefields. Smiling tenderly, Jamie rose to his feet and held out his hands to her.

'Come on, love,' he urged. 'Let's not sit here moping; there won't be many more days like this before I have to go back.'

Seeing the sad pleading in his lovely golden-hazel eyes, Ada struggled to her feet.

'Yes, let's walk,' she said, then thought to herself, 'Let's make the most of our time together and be happy while we can.'

*

Eager as she was, Ada didn't get very far. Seeing the highest peaks of Catbells looming overhead, she soon groaned and flopped down into a bed of heather, where she was quickly joined by Jamie. Lying on their backs until they had caught their breath, they rolled towards each other. As they lay facing each other, Jamie recalled a line from one of their favourite Vera Lynn songs: 'Keep smiling through, sweetheart,' he whispered, before kissing her softly on the lips.

After responding passionately to his kisses, Ada whispered back, 'I never stop smiling when I'm with you, my love.'

'It's only when you're gone that smiles fade and tears come,' she thought, 'but that's for me to bear and not another burden for you to carry.'

27. A Shock

Sybil got the shock of her life when she turned up on the ward to visit Rosie, only to find the bed stripped and all the usual clutter littering the bedside table removed.

'Where's Mrs Pickles?' she asked Sister Mann, who bustled busily by with a bedpan.

'She's been taken to the hospital in Lancaster,' the nurse informed her. 'I'm afraid to say she's not at all well.'

Anxious Sybil asked, 'What's the matter with her?'

'Like I said, she's not well,' Sister Mann replied in professional mode. 'She's having tests, that's all I can say.'

As she went on her way, Sybil gazed thoughtfully at the empty bed, which without Rosie looked sad and forlorn.

'This damned place has turned me soft in the head,' Sybil muttered under her breath. 'I used to hate Rosie and now I'm missing her – ridiculous!'

It's true, though, Sybil thought; she had grown fond of the only friend she had made in Mary Vale. Admittedly the relationship had started with Sybil determined to milk everything she could out of Rosie about her time at Dowry House, but the daily visits and the laughs at Monty's expense had become something Sybil actively looked forward to. The camaraderie that had developed between them; two women both miserably pregnant for very different reasons, had been something neither of them could ever have imagined. At opposite ends of the social spectrum, they had one vital link: Monty Baldwin. Feeling yet again so near and yet so far away, Sybil made her way back into the Home, wondering when she would see Rosie Pickles again.

At Hope Farm, Ronnie and Sally, having been told of their mother's removal to another hospital, were both very upset.

'When can we see her?' little Sally asked tearfully.

'When she comes back to Mary Vale,' Mrs Larkin assured her.

Ever the pessimist, Ronnie demanded, 'Is she going to die?'

'Of course not!' Mrs Larkin explained. 'The doctors in the Lancaster hospital are going to make your mother stronger, then send her back home.'

'Home?' Ronnie cried. 'Send her back to London?'

'No, the Home where she lives with the other ladies.'

Ronnie's pinched face fell; that wasn't home, he thought bitterly. Though he worried about his mother, Ronnie couldn't deny he was happier now that he wasn't living at Mary Vale; he preferred living on the farm and playing on the fells; the village school was much nicer than the one in Grange too. In fact, Ronnie was settling in nicely, until he overheard the big boys talking in the playground.

'Some of our lads are coming back,' he heard the gang leader say.

'How can they leave the Army without permission?' a knowing lad asked.

Another one answered, 'They might be injured or home on leave.'

The gang leader gave him a shove. 'Are you listening, cloth ears?' he scoffed. 'They sneak back here into the country, then sneak back out again,' he explained in a melo-dramatic whisper.

'Why would they do that? They could get shot?' a wiser boy queried.

'To check their families are okay, make sure that their missis ain't knocking off other fellas,' the gang leader sniggered.

Shocked momentarily speechless by this remark, the other boys fell silent, until one shocked kid scoffed, 'That can't be true.'

'I'm only telling you what I heard in't pub t'other day,' the leader told his captivated audience.

'What were *you* doin' in't pub anyway?' his friend demanded.

'Buying fags for mi mother,' the gang leader snapped. 'Any more bleedin' questions?'

Wide-eyed Ronnie, years younger than the boys he had been eavesdropping on, became haunted by this piece of completely fictitious information. Obsessed, he began to wonder if his dad might have sneaked into the country like the ringleader had said. What if he had come back to their Finsbury Park block of flats where they had lived as a family? A recurring thought went around and around Ronnie's confused little head: what if his dad had risked his life to visit his family and found them all gone? How would he have felt? The very thought reduced Ronnie to tears and nightmares. Had his mother left a forwarding address? Remembering how ill she had been when they left London, Ronnie couldn't imagine she would have had her wits about her and done just that; and, even if she had, there was a good chance that whoever she had left it with had been bombed out or had left London too.

Frantic with fear, Ronnie worried that his dad, like the boys at school had whispered, might have been shot for deserting his post if he'd tried to get home to see them. Wild speculation blurred with an overactive imagination led poor bewildered Ronnie to devise a crazy plan which involved him running away, back to London to search for his dad, or at least returning to what had been his home and leaving his Mary Vale address with any neighbours that he spotted. Ronnie reasoned that if his dad could risk being shot just to check up on his family's safety, he could at least risk something in return.

Ronnie's sketchy run-away plan did not involve Sally; it was a dangerous journey which he planned to do solo. Though Ronnie worried about leaving his little sister behind, the very last thing he wanted was Sally trailing along with him. He could travel more quickly without her, and anyway (Ronnie convinced himself) Sally would be far better off and safer with Mrs Larkin.

Several days later Sybil was delighted to hear that Rosie was back on the ward. Knowing she would get little information from Sister Mann, she approached Dora, who told Sybil that Rosie was still to be bed-bound.

'The sooner her pregnancy is over the better,' Dora confided in Sybil. 'It's taking all the strength out of the poor woman.'

Sybil did a quick calculation. 'It can't be long now – we're due about the same time.'

Dora cast an appraising glance at Sybil's tummy. 'Yes, but you're strong and healthy; I only wish I could say the same for Rosie. Hopefully she'll perk up a bit when she sees her children this afternoon.'

*

Rosie's thin, drawn face did indeed light up when she saw Ronnie and Sally hurrying up the ward towards her bed.

'Kiddies!' she exclaimed as she cuddled each in turn. 'How lovely to see you.'

'Look, Mother, pretty flowers,' Sally cried, as she thrust a bunch of wilting white roses into her mother's hand. 'The thorns pricked my fingers and made them bleed, so Mrs Larkin gave me a bandage – she said I was a brave soldier.'

'How kind of her,' Rosie said, inhaling the roses' delicate perfume. Seeing her anxious son hanging back, she smiled. 'How are you, sweetheart?'

'Are you better now?' Ronnie mumbled, as he shuffled awkwardly.

'I'm better for seeing you, lovie,' Rosie said and planted a kiss on Ronnie's cheek. 'I always feel much better after seeing the two people I love most in the world,' she added with a catch in her voice. 'Now come on,' she urged. 'Tell me all your news.'

As Sally chattered on about her favourite kitten at Hope Farm and explained to her mum how she helped Mrs Larkin milk the cows and stir the cheese in the dairy, Ronnie kept quiet. His mother's loving words had moved him – he knew how much she needed both her children – but he was not going to change his plans.

'You never know,' Ronnie thought to himself. 'If I do manage to track Dad down, I could reunite our family and we could all be happy again.'

He blinked tears from his eyes as he imagined such a scenario; it was really all the little boy had ever wanted.

28. The Secret

The next day Sybil appeared by Rosie's bedside with a box of chocolates.

'For me?' Rosie squeaked in complete delight. 'How on earth did you lay your hands on them?'

Sybil gave a teasing wink. 'If I told you I could go to prison.'

'Oh, thank you, thank you,' Rosie gabbled, as she tore open the box and gobbled a chocolate. 'Mmm,' she sighed. 'I've not had a chocolate in years.'

Sybil smiled to herself. The chocolates were, in fact, Monty's last gift to her on his final visit North. She had never once been tempted to open the box, always associating it with how much she loathed him. She had shoved it in the back of her wardrobe and forgotten all about it, until she was searching around for a gift for Rosie.

'Lovely,' Rosie murmured, as she reached for another chocolate.

'How are you feeling?' Sybil enquired, pulling her chair closer to the bed.

'Not much different,' Rosie mumbled with her mouth full. 'Here,' she said and thrust the box into Sybil's hands. 'Put them in the cupboard before I eat the lot and make myself sick.'

After the chocolates had been stashed away, Rosie continued. 'The doctors at the Lancaster hospital did some tests, more on the baby than on me – like I've said all along, it's a weak little thing,' she said sadly. 'No wonder, it's never really had a chance. I fell pregnant during Mick's leave when we had hardly any food in the house, then I came up here with barely the energy to even walk, then mi kids were taken away. The shock of that all but killed me – what kind of effect must it have had on a poor little baby? Still, I suppose life goes on.'

Gripped with acute guilt, words simply failed Sybil, but Rosie, after requesting another chocolate, to 'cheer her up', surprised Sybil by remembering their last conversation, about Monty, and picking up almost exactly where she had left off.

'So I never did finish telling you about my little friend, Daisy the kitchen maid, the one who got engaged to the Stowupland chauffeur,' Rosie said, pulling herself up in bed.

Sybil nodded; how could she ever have forgotten?

'You certainly left me on a cliff-hanger.'

Settling back on the pillows again, Rosie continued her story. 'She was a sweet little kid, only eighteen years old, then out of nowhere the poor kid got consumption. It was terrible to see her go down so quickly, coughing up blood, short of breath, thin as a rake. Course she had to leave her post right away for fear of spreading the disease.'

Sybil's shoulders sagged in disappointment. 'Please don't let the little maid's departure be the end of the story,' she prayed.

Looking pensive as she recalled the incident, Rosie added, 'But something really strange happened just before Daisy left . . .'

Sybil's green eyes brightened. 'Thank God, there's more to the story.'

'She called me out into the kitchen garden, where she handed over all the precious photo albums she had put together while she was working for her ladyship,' Rosie gulped, as she tried to control her emotions. 'Then, though the poor soul could barely catch her breath, she told me a secret that her fiancé had passed on to her.'

Trying to fit the pieces together, Sybil asked, 'The Stowupland chauffeur?'

Rosie gave a quick nod. 'Her young man told Daisy about a love affair Lady Veronica had before her marriage, with the game-keeper's son. It was all supposed to be hush hush, but them below stairs knew that they were walking out together, and that it was a relationship Lord Stow would strongly disapprove of – apparently his lordship always had high ambitions for his precious only child. Anyway, Daisy told me the poor young man died in a shooting accident on the estate, died never even knowing that he had left his girl in the family way.'

'That's tragic,' Sybil murmured.

'Yes, and when his lordship found out he was adamant that the child should be adopted.'

'Not such an unusual outcome,' Sybil murmured.

'But Lady Veronica was having none of it,' Rosie added. 'Daisy's fiancé heard them arguing in the back of the car when they were out on a drive: she was as adamant about keeping it as he was about adoption.'

Genuinely riveted and beginning to piece it all together, Sybil asked breathlessly, 'So that's where Monty came in?'

Rosie gave her a long provocative look. 'Indeed. The

valiant Brigadier stepped in and saved her ladyship's good name – why else would Lady Veronica ever settle for the likes of him?'

Speaking out loud, Sybil tried to work out the possible sequence of events. 'He must have proposed and promised to rear Marigold as his own, then come to some sort of agreement with Lord Stow.'

'A FINANCIAL agreement,' Rosie stressed. 'Using family funds, I bet.'

'How sad – a lovely young woman like her, with the world at her feet, wasted on Monty,' Sybil cried. 'What rotten luck.'

'She must have accepted him rather than lose Marigold,' Rosie concluded. 'It has to be said she worships her daughter.'

'So Monty's privileged lifestyle is all down to the arrangement he made when Lady Veronica was pregnant with another man's child?'

Rosie nodded grimly. 'Like I say, this is all second hand to me: I didn't witness any of it myself,' she admitted. 'Though I've never doubted it,' she insisted. 'I mean, why would Daisy make up a story like that when she was at death's door? She could have taken her secret to the grave, but instead she told me just before she left Dowry House.'

'I agree,' Sybil said. 'There must have been a good reason why she would bare her soul like that.'

'I've thought about it a lot,' Rosie confessed. 'Did Daisy think that sometime in the future I could use the information to protect her ladyship if the Brigadier really did try to reveal the truth about Marigold's father.'

'Did *you* ever hear him threaten Lady Veronica?' Sybil asked.

Rosie shook her head. 'No, but I've heard them many a time arguing behind closed doors about him sleeping with other women. Like I said, none of us could understood why her ladyship put up with the Brigadier. It was only after Daisy had revealed her secret that it all made sense, to me at least.'

Sybil shivered in disgust. 'So, while Monty was banking Lord Stow's family funds, he was simultaneously blackmailing his wife. God, really, the man's capable of anything.'

Swiping away a tear, Rosie said, 'If the truth be told, I've fretted that I could have done more, said more. But who would listen to me, a poor servant girl?'

'If you had told Lord Stow the truth about Monty, Marigold's name would have been dragged into the mud along with her mother's,' Sybil reasoned.

Rosie sadly shook her head. 'I couldn't have done that; I love them both far too much.'

Later, back in the privacy of her room, Sybil reran Rosie's story over and over in her head. Not for a single minute did she doubt that it was the truth. Though Lady Veronica's story was far more tragic than her own, it nevertheless had Monty's trademark all over it: bullying, threatening, manipulating – she recognized them all. She, like Lady Veronica, had been forced to accept what he had thrust upon her; she had, in fact, got off lightly compared with his poor wife. Though Sybil hugged the long-awaited knowledge to herself, there was little gratification in knowing of somebody else's misery.

'Now that I've finally got something on Monty, what am I actually going to do with it?' she asked herself.

Like Rosie, she didn't want anything to do with information that was detrimental to Lady Veronica and her little girl. Sybil's vendetta was with the Brigadier; he was the one she wanted to turn the tables on, not his wife and child. But, as long as Monty had Lady Veronica's daughter's illegitimacy as his ace card, the poor woman was a prisoner within her own marriage. It would take some time to work out a strategy, but there had to be one, Sybil determined.

'If there's any justice in this world,' she said through gritted teeth, 'Monty must pay for what he thinks he's got away with.'

29. Ronnie

Ronnie's plan to run away was almost foiled by his little sister. Usually the Larkin children, plus Ronnie and Sally, got the bus home from school, Sally sitting alongside May at the front of the bus, while Ronnie sat with the Larkin lads at the back. On this particular occasion, just as the bus was about to pull away from the bus stop, one of the boys yelled out, 'Oi, Sal! Where's your Ronnie?'

Sally, who hadn't even registered her brother's absence, stood up to take a look around. Baffled, she replied that she had no idea. 'Don't worry, lovie, he's probably playing marbles,' May said comfortingly.

Knowing how unsociable Ronnie was, Sally was quite sure that he would never stay behind after school to play marbles when he could be running up the fells with the Larkin boys. Immediately sensing something wasn't quite right, she jumped up before the bus pulled away.

'I'll go and look for him,' she called over her shoulder, as she hopped off the bus.

Seeing May's concerned face through the bus window, Sally gave a cheery wave, then ran back into the school playground to search for her brother, who was nowhere in sight. When she saw the caretaker sweeping the long corridor that connected the girls' part of the school to the boys', Sally asked him if he had seen her brother.

'Aye, he went down t'road into Grange,' the caretaker

informed an astonished Sally. 'Towards t'railway station from t'looks of it.'

Thinking Ronnie might have gone to visit their mother at Mary Vale, Sally ran as fast as she could to Grange's pretty red-brick station, where she dashed on to the platform just in time to see the Kents Bank train noisily chugging away. Out of breath and worried, Sally slumped on to a nearby bench and, as the noise of the departing train subsided and the plume of inky-black smoke blew away, Sally saw to her complete astonishment Ronnie standing on the platform straight opposite her.

'RONNIE!' she yelled.

Springing to her feet, Sally hurried down the dark subway to join her brother on the other side of the station.

'What the 'ell are you doing here?' he barked.

'Looking for you!' she snapped back, offended.

'You should mind your own bloody business, Sal,' he scowled.

'I was worried when you weren't on the bus.' Shaking him by the arm, she demanded, 'Where are you going?'

Ronnie sighed; he knew how irritatingly tenacious his little sister was. 'Can you keep a secret?'

Sally nodded. 'Cross my heart and hope to die.'

Pulling her close, Ronnie whispered, 'I'm running away – I'm going to find Dad.'

Bewildered Sally gasped. 'Dad? But he's fighting the Germans.'

Ron's voice dropped to a low growl. 'He might've come home. I've heard talk,' Ronnie told her.

'Does Mother know?' she asked.

'No, and she ain't gonna know either,' Ronnie told her sharply. 'I'm gonna go and find Dad myself.'

Sally gave a little sob. 'No, Ron, it's too dangerous – anyway,' she added as an afterthought, 'you ain't got no money.'

Ronnie winked as he clinked the coins in his trouser pocket. 'I got plenty,' he assured her.

Looking down, Sally saw a little packed rucksack at her brother's feet, and started to cry. 'You can't go on your own, please let me come with you.'

Ronnie glared at her as if she had lost her mind. 'I ain't dragging my kid sister around London.'

The distant rumble of an approaching train caused Sally to panic and, grabbing hold of Ronnie, she cried, 'Take me with you, Ron, *pleeeease, pleeeease*,' she implored.

Shaking her off, Ronnie hissed, 'Stop drawing attention, Sal. Go away – get lost!'

Pushing her to one side, Ronnie scoured the carriages of the approaching train, which blasted smoke as it clanked to a halt. Waiting until the guard and the station master were busy clipping tickets at the end of the platform, Ronnie bolted almost the whole length of the train, until he came to the luggage compartment piled high with leather-bound trunks, large suitcases and a crate of clucking chickens. In a blink he had opened the door and was inside the compartment, where he quickly burrowed under a pile of empty mail bags. Hardly daring to breathe, Ronnie waited tensely for the train to pull away from the platform; when it did, he let out a long sigh of relief, at which point he heard his little sister's whimpering close by. 'Ronnie, Ronnie, where are you?'

*

Back at Hope Farm, Mrs Larkin was sufficiently alarmed to phone Mary Vale when neither Sally nor Ronnie returned home with the rest of her brood. Thinking they might have taken it into their heads to pay a visit to their mother, Mrs Larkin picked up the big old-fashioned phone which stood on a marble-topped table in the hallway of the farmhouse. Speaking into the mouthpiece, she asked Sister Mary Paul if Ronnie and Sally had dropped by.

'I'll go and check if they are with their mother,' the kindly nun replied. 'Hang on a tick.'

It certainly took longer than a few ticks for the arthritic old nun to walk down the length of the ante-natal ward to make enquiries of Dora, who assured Mary Paul that she had seen no sign of the Pickles kiddies. Passing on the message, she said, 'They're not here, Mrs Larkin – nobody's seen them.'

Not wanting to cause panic, Mrs Larkin replied, 'Not to worry – maybe they decided to walk home. I'll let you know when they turn up. By the way, don't mention anything of this to their mum. I wouldn't want to worry her when it's all probably a storm in a teacup.'

'Of course not,' Mary Paul assured her.

Calling her children together, Mrs Larkin announced, 'Everybody in the farm truck – we're going to look for Ronnie and Sally.'

After they had driven into Grange, Mrs Larkin and her children split up into separate search parties. Two of the boys she sent to the park and the town centre; the other two hurried off to search the Esplanade; while she and May went to the railway station.

'Meet back here in half an hour,' she instructed.

*

Thirty minutes later, when the train Ronnie and Sally were on was pulling into Carnforth Station, the Larkins regrouped, none of them with good news.

'Not a sign of them anywhere,' they all concluded.

The eldest lad, who was starving hungry, suggested the missing pair might by now have returned on foot to Hope Farm.

'Pray to God they are there,' Mrs Larkin mumbled, as they all clambered back into the truck.

At Carnforth the train shunted slowly into the station and the guard called out, 'Everybody off, everybody off.'

The wide-eyed children looked at each other from behind the huge trunks they were pressed against. They both jumped in fear when the door of the luggage van was flung wide open and a deep gruff voice barked, 'Give us a hand here.'

Staying perfectly still, they saw through the gaps in the piles of teetering luggage an older porter and his young assistant walk in.

'You take that lot,' the older man instructed, as he nodded towards the heavy trunks. 'I'll get them noisy bloody hens!'

Seeing the interior door to the next carriage hanging wide open, Ronnie gave his sister a sharp dig in the ribs, after which he slipped silently from his hiding place. Crawling along the floor, he waited until both the porter and his assistant had their backs to him, then he bolted through the open door, from where he frantically beckoned to his trembling sister who was too scared to move.

'Come on!' Ronnie mouthed.

Checking that both men were still occupied shifting luggage, Sally scampered on all fours to join her brother, who, after yanking her to her feet, grabbed her hand in his and jumped out of the nearest door.

30. Runaways

Though the local constabulary in Grange assured Mrs Larkin that they would alert the bobbies on the beat to the disappearance of the children, they didn't seem unduly worried. They explained to her that children often went missing, particularly when they lost track of time, but they usually turned up sooner or later, tired out and starving hungry after their adventure. Though this information was meant to reassure Mrs Larkin, it had the opposite effect: she didn't voice her fears, but she knew in the short time that she had known the Pickles kiddies that they would NEVER miss a meal. Food was their god. As a gnawing anxiety gripped her stomach, Mrs Larkin simply didn't know what to do for the best. Should she notify the Home of the children's disappearance? If, like the avuncular policeman said, they turned up later cold and hungry, she would have worried a lot of people unnecessarily, but if they didn't show up those same people in the Home would be within their rights to question her judgement. In the end she took advice from Mr Larkin, who characteristically didn't beat about the bush.

'You don't need to sound the alarm bell to everybody in the building, but you should have a word with somebody in charge,' he wisely suggested.

Holding her breath Mrs Larkin again dialled Mary

Vale's number on the old phone in the hallway; as it shrilled out she wondered who would pick up and gasped in relief when she heard Dora's warm familiar voice on the other end.

'Oh, thank God it's you,' she cried.

After blurting out the whole story, Mrs Larkin asked, 'What's the best thing to do, Dora? Should we tell Rosie? It seems wrong not to.'

Having just taken Rosie a simple supper of tea, bread and butter, Dora said, 'I'll notify Matron and let her decide that.' Then she quickly added, 'Please let us know if they do turn up, Mrs Larkin, whatever the time of day or night.'

After Mrs Larkin had promised to keep her in the picture, Dora laid down the phone and sighed heavily. With Rosie being so ill, was it wise to worry her unduly? Yet again she wished Ada were around to support Rosie and advise the staff.

'At least we've got Sister Ann,' Dora thought to herself, as she hurried down the corridor to Matron's office. 'I certainly wouldn't want Sister Mann to be handling this.'

Matron was indeed concerned both for the missing children and for their very delicate mother, who despite eating as much iron-rich liver as they could muster in wartime, still remained weak and anaemic.

'This is terrible news,' she murmured. 'If we tell Rosie, she'll be awake all night and get no rest at all.'

'And that naughty pair might well turn up first thing in the morning, so all the fretting and worrying will have been for nothing,' Dora pointed out.

Matron sat back in her chair. 'I think we must wait and

pray that Ronnie and Sally are both found safe and sound by morning.'

As Dora was helping one of the residents on ward duty serve early-morning tea to patients, she heard the ward phone ring out and hurried to fetch Matron, who answered the call.

'Mrs Larkin,' Matron said breathlessly 'Any news?'

'Nothing, nothing at all,' Mrs Larkin answered on a long sigh. 'I've just phoned the police, who just said they'd look into the matter.'

Sister Ann's heart-beat quickened; there was no choice now: she would have to inform her patient, because deceiving Rosie any further was totally unacceptable.

'I'll let you know if they turn up,' Mrs Larkin said with real yearning in her voice. 'Oh, God, if only they would.'

With Dora by her side, Sister Ann drew the curtains around Rosie's bed. 'We've got some rather bad news, dear,' she started gently.

Dora, perched on the bedside chair, placed a supportive arm around Rosie's skinny shoulders.

'The children!' she gasped. 'What've they got up to now?'

Momentarily lost for words, Matron gazed appealingly at Dora, who continued. 'It's like this, sweetheart. I'm sure they will turn up very soon, but the truth is they didn't go home last night.'

'Didn't go home?' Rosie cried, as she struggled to get out of bed. 'Where have they gone? Who's taken them?'

Holding her firmly while trying her best to keep her

calm, Dora tried to explain. 'The police think they've gone on a little adventure, they think –'

But she got no further. Throwing Dora's arm from her shoulder, Rosie struggled to stand upright. 'I'm going to find them!' she cried.

Matron hurried forward to prevent Rosie from getting out of bed. 'No, dear, you're in no state – please stay calm and think of the baby.'

With both nurses on either side of her, Rosie started to scream hysterically. 'I've got to find them! *I've got to find my children!*'

Before Rosie fell to the ground in a dead swoon, Matron and Dora caught her and, between them, they got her back in bed. Stroking the lank hair that fell over Rosie's damp brow, Dora prayed with all her heart: 'God help this poor woman, God help her.'

Completely unaware of the drama that was unfolding on the ante-natal ward, Sybil was picking some sweet peas in the garden to make a little posy for Rosie, whom she planned to visit after her exercise class.

'Odd.' Sybil smiled as she stood on her tiptoes to pluck the blooms that were fragrantly flowering against the old red-brick garden wall. 'Instead of picking Rosie's brains, I'm picking flowers for her. It's just nice to see her and keep her company.' Then she thought ruefully, 'Or maybe it's Rosie who's keeping *ME* company.' She gave a heavy sigh. 'If she were ever to find out it was me who got rid of her kids, Rosie would never speak to me again.'

After eating her lunch, Sybil left the dining room as usual, swinging her handbag, barely giving her fellow residents a backward glance. Picking up the fragrant little posy from her room, Sybil made her way to the ante-natal ward, where she was stopped in her tracks by a stony-faced Sister Mann.

'Where are you going?' she demanded.

Annoyed by her haughty manner, Sybil bridled. 'To see Rosie,' she snapped, as she all but thrust the posy in Sister Mann's moody face.

'I'm sorry, but Mrs Pickles is in no condition to receive visitors,' Sister Mann barked, and she stood in front of Sybil, blocking the entrance to the ward.

Seeing she was going to get nowhere, Sybil turned on her heel and retraced her steps. Worried sick, she thought to herself, 'Heavens! What's happened to Rosie now?'

Though Ada was now bigger than most of the residents in the exercise class, she still enjoyed the weekly afternoon relaxation classes, lying on the lawn with the sun on her upturned face. Her soft voice with a hint of a warm Northern accent was both soothing and reassuring to her pupils as she repeated the familiar set of instructions.

'Legs up, nice and slowly, breathing deeply . . . hold the position as long as you're comfortable with it.' She stopped speaking as she too tried to control her breathing, before releasing her body from the pose and lowering her legs to the ground.

'Phew,' Ada gasped.

'You've grown even bigger since last week,' one of the girls teased.

Ada patted her huge tummy. 'If this little one had his

way, he would be out of there right now,' she joked. 'Right, shall we give it another go before we all fall asleep in the sunshine?'

In the company of wheeling swallows circling overhead and the occasional gull drifting upwind on a warm air current, the class recommenced, only to be interrupted by Sister Mann, who had absented herself yet again from attending the class.

'Sister,' she called urgently as she almost ran across the lawn. 'May I have a word, please?'

Struggling to her feet, Ada followed her colleague till they were a discreet distance from the class, at which point the two women conversed in low voices. Visibly shocked, Ada turned back to the group. 'I'm so sorry, ladies, something urgent has come up – I'm going to have to abandon you.'

Leaving the class goggle-eyed with curiosity, Ada hurried after Sister Mann.

'What's going on?' the women whispered among themselves.

'Summat must be wrong,' a girl remarked ominously. 'Dragging Ada off like that.'

'Aye,' another gloomily responded. 'Somebody's in trouble.'

'I wonder who?' another mused.

Sybil instinctively knew exactly who was in trouble.

'Oh, God! Rosie!' she thought.

31. Reparation

Hurrying after Sister Mann, Ada was trying her best to steady her breathing.

'Are you sure it's a good idea involving me?' she asked.

Sister Mann answered brusquely, 'We've no choice: as soon as she went into labour, Rosie started calling out for you. We're all more than capable,' she added huffily, 'but clearly that's not enough for Rosie.'

Not wanting to get on the wrong side of Edith, especially if they were going to be in the delivery suite together, Ada answered self-deprecatingly, 'I'm sure it's nothing other than familiarity. Rosie and I have known each other since she arrived from London.' Moving quickly on, she added, 'What happened?'

'It was the shock that brought it on.'

Mystified, Ada asked another question. 'What shock?'

'Haven't you heard?' Edith enquired. 'Rosie's children have run away. Rosie collapsed and went into premature labour after Matron broke the news to her this morning.'

Ada reeled and had to stop to catch her breath. 'This is terrible news,' she declared, utterly shocked.

Sister Mann nodded. 'The police are searching for them, but it's still very worrying.'

Horrified that two little children could be wandering lost and alone in a strange dangerous world, Ada shivered in fear, before forcing her thoughts back to Rosie, who was the one she was in a position to help right now. She quickly focused on the practical.

'How is Rosie now?'

'The prognosis for a healthy birth was never good; a combination of malnutrition at the beginning of her pregnancy plus ongoing anaemia.' Sister Mann gloomily shook her head. 'And now this, early onset of labour brought on by shock.'

Ada didn't need any more information; she was an experienced midwife and she knew the combination of Rosie's problems was unlikely to add up to a happy outcome.

Worried sick about Rosie too, Sybil (like Ada) abandoned the relaxation class. Heading into the hospital, where she knew she would get nothing out of Sister Mann, she searched out Dora, who in the past had always been more helpful. Finding her in the nursery, sterilizing the bottles in readiness for the next scheduled feed, Sybil cautiously approached.

'I'm sorry to trouble you, Dora, but I've heard Rosie's poorly and, well, I'm worried,' she said with obviously genuine concern. 'She's the only friend I have here in the Home, and I'd like to help her, if I can.'

Dora had been surprised when she'd noticed that the two vastly different women had become friends. It seemed genuine enough, though; from the laughter and chatter that passed between them, they obviously enjoyed each other's company, and Sybil's friendship had certainly improved Rosie's spirits.

'If you could just tell me what's going on,' Sybil begged, 'I really would be grateful.'

Dora nodded in the direction of the nurses' station. 'Over there – I don't want us to be overheard.'

Once they had reached the big desk, Dora lowered her voice to a whisper. 'I shouldn't be telling you this, Sybil, but, seeing as you are the best of friends these days, well . . . Rosie's gone into labour. She collapsed after she heard that her children had run away.'

Thinking that she too might collapse with shock, Sybil gripped the side of the desk so hard her knuckles went white.

'Ronnie and Sally!' she gasped.

'Disappeared yesterday, nobody knows where,' Dora added.

'Oh, my God!' Sybil wailed as she slumped into the nearest chair. Covering her face so that Dora couldn't see the fear there, her thoughts became frantic. 'Jesus Christ! This is all *MY FAULT*. They would never have run away if they had been here safe with their mother.'

Dora's next words brought tears to Sybil's green eyes. 'It'll be the death of Rosie if those kiddies aren't found soon.'

Pulling herself up from the chair, Sybil tried to compose herself. 'Thank you, Dora, I'm grateful you shared that information with me, truly I am. Now I won't take up any more of your valuable time.'

Dora watched Sybil as she walked away: as usual her back was arrow straight and her head was held high, but Dora had seen real grief in her eyes.

'Who would have thought in the world of God that those two women would have a single thing in common?' she mused.

*

Desperate to get information that might give Rosie hope and a reason to live, Sybil paid a visit to Mrs Larkin at nearby Hope Farm.

'I hope you don't mind my turning up like this, unannounced,' Sybil started, as she was ushered into the big, untidy farm kitchen. 'I'm a friend of Rosie Pickles and I want to do everything in my power to help her. If there's anything, anything at all I can do to help in the search, or if there is any news at all that might reassure her, please let me know.'

'Poor woman, she must be going through hell,' Mrs Larkin said, as she lit up a Woodbine. 'Please sit down,' she urged and poured strong black tea into two mugs and added milk. 'I can't help but blame myself,' she murmured guiltily. 'I was responsible for them and they ran off on my watch.'

'Have you any idea where they might have gone?' Sybil enquired.

'I've gone over it a hundred times, in my head and with the police,' Mrs Larkin responded. 'One thing I do know, though,' she added. 'Ronnie planned it.'

Sybil raised her eyebrows. 'How do you know that?'

'His little rucksack has gone missing, and a few clothes, not that he had many, and the little bit of pocket money that he had – and two tins of baked beans. Sally seems to have taken nothing, though; my eldest said the little girl just jumped off the school bus and ran off down the road to find her brother.' Marge Larkin concluded, 'Like I said to the police, I think Sally had no idea of Ronnie's plans – for her it was more of a last-minute decision.'

Sybil visibly paled. 'God!' she exclaimed. 'I hope she

caught up with him, as I can't bear to think of them separated and lost.'

'The police told me that both of them were spotted by members of the public at Grange Station, so we hope they are still together.'

'Well, that's something, I suppose,' Sybil said. 'If that's where they were last seen, maybe I can take the train to Carnforth or Lancaster, to see if I can find out anything more there.'

Mrs Larkin shook her head. 'The police have already done that – anyway, shouldn't you be thinking of resting rather than running around the countryside in your condition?' she added and nodded at Sybil's big tummy.

'I suppose so – I just want to help Rosie,' desperate Sybil said, as she rose to go.

What she didn't say was the last thing on her mind was resting. With Rosie's two children lost and at risk, Sybil wouldn't get any peace at all until they were both found.

Instead of going back to Mary Vale, Sybil took the bus into Grange and, ignoring Mrs Larkin's wise advice, caught the first train to Carnforth. After a short journey across the bay, Sybil stepped on to the long platform, where she curiously looked around. If the kiddies had ended up here, where might they have headed?

'Could they be hiding in the lavatory?' Sybil thought to herself.

Entering the ladies' toilets, Sybil first used the facilities herself – she seemed to need to go on the hour these days – then cast her eyes around the ladies' waiting room, which was completely empty. Just as she was about to close the door behind her, it jarred against something lying on the tiled floor. Reaching down, Sybil removed a grubby, pink hair ribbon which she stared at thoughtfully. It was way too small for an adult to wear, so it must belong to a child, a little girl. Gripping the ribbon in the palm of her hand, she dashed out of the ladies' and went in search of the porter, whom she found sweeping the platform with a broom.

'Excuse me, I'm making enquiries about two little children,' she started.

'Oh, aye, them two what went missing t'other day,' he answered lugubriously. 'Police have been back and forth here asking questions of us all. Before you ask, I never clapped eyes on 'em myself. Other folks did, said they saw 'em sneaking on to another train on t'other side yonder.'

'And where could that train have been heading?' she asked urgently.

'Well, going by the time they were seen, it could be either the Leeds or the London via Manchester train,' he answered knowingly. 'That's what I told t'police when they asked the same question.'

Thinking there was no obvious reason why Ronnie and Sally would be making their way to Leeds, Sybil assumed they would have been aiming for London, since it was their home.

'Thank you,' she said politely. 'That's most informative.'

Seeing her tired expression, the guard kindly remarked, 'I wouldn't fret yourself, miss, the police have got it all in hand.'

As Sybil miserably retraced her steps, taking the next train back to Grange, she considered the guard's words, which she certainly didn't agree with. He might think that the police were on the case, but none of them knew wily little Ronnie, who could outwit a bag of monkeys. In the privacy of the empty compartment she had entered, Sybil sighed; she was quite sure Ronnie and his sister would be as difficult to find as a needle in a haystack.

32. Which Train?

In their dangerous, reckless journey, desperate not to be spotted by the ticket collector, Ronnie and Sally had foolishly darted on to the first train that left Carnforth Station shortly after they'd arrived.

'How do we know we're on the right train?' Sally whispered, as they hid once again in a baggage compartment that contained a crate of irate quacking ducks as well as luggage.

Ronnie, whose geography left a lot to be desired, shrugged. 'Stop naggin' – they all go to London.'

But when the train eventually pulled into its destination, it was 'LEEDS, LEEDS. All change here' that the guard called out.

Sally's eyes filled with tears. 'We're not in London,' she said on a smothered sob.

Starving hungry, dog-tired and constantly snapped at by her older brother, Sally wished she hadn't chased after Ronnie in the first place. She could be safe at Hope Farm right now, playing with the kittens, making bread in Mrs Larkin's warm kitchen or helping the farmer milk the cows. Instead she was on the run with her brother, who didn't seem to have much of a clue as to where he was going. It was cold, and it would soon be dark – then what would they do? Heavy footsteps approaching the luggage compartment made both children cower behind a pile of suitcases. As the guard struggled with the crate of squawking ducks, the children manoeuvred a path behind his broad back and bolted off the train.

Sitting in the refreshment room on the draughty platform, they tried to get warm in between begging for food or, in Ronnie's case, eating customers' stale leftovers. With his mouth full of dry bread, Ronnie went in search of information, leaving his sister shivering by a spurting gas fire. When a woman spoke to her, Sally all but jumped out of her worn-out T-bar shoes.

'Would you like a hot drink?' the kind-looking lady asked her.

'Yes, please, miss,' grateful Sally nodded. 'And a bun too, please, miss.'

The woman returned to the fireside table with two cups of tea and a spam sandwich.

'No buns,' she said cheerfully as she set the tray down.

After wolfing back the sandwich and gulping the hot strong tea, Sally felt fortified.

'Thank you, miss.'

'You're a bit young to be all on your own here,' the lady commented.

'I'm with mi brother, Ronnie. We're going to London . . . if we can find a train to take us there.'

Sally's weary voice trailed away as Ronnie returned with a scowl on his face, and, looking hungrily at his sister's empty plate, he demanded, 'What've you just had to eat?'

'A sandwich,' said the lady. 'Would you like one too?'

'Yes, please, two, if you don't mind,' Ronnie asked without reserve.

Like Sally, Ronnie talked more easily after he had eaten.

'We're going to see our dad in London, but we got on the wrong train and lost our bloody tickets.'

Sally glared at her brother for swearing in front of a genteel lady.

'And where's your mother?' the lady asked.

Scared that her big-mouthed brother would swear again, Sally quickly answered, 'She's in the hospital having a baby – we're on our own.'

Seeing the tears in Sally's eyes and the misery in Ronnie's grubby face, the woman's heart melted.

'I'm travelling as far as Peterborough,' she told the children. 'We could travel together, if you like?'

'Not without tickets we can't – we'll get arrested,' Ronnie mumbled.

The woman smiled. 'We don't want that, do we?' Rising, she added, 'I shall buy you both tickets and I'll also arrange with the guard at Peterborough to see you both safely off the train when it arrives at Euston Station.'

Overwhelmed with gratitude, Sally wrapped herself around the woman. 'Thank you, thank you,' she gabbled.

Much to Sally's astonishment, Ronnie held out his hand in a polite gesture. 'Thank you, missis, we're grateful to you.'

'I'm a bit concerned about how you're going to track your father down once you're in London,' the kind lady added anxiously.

'We'll go to our old address and search him out there to start with,' Ronnie said with a confidence that Sally certainly didn't share.

Relieved to be in a warm compartment and soothed by the steady rhythm of the thundering steam train, Sally laid her head against their benefactor's shoulder and fell fast asleep. With his nose pressed to the window, Ronnie watched the landscape mist over as the sun began to set over the rugged Pennine range that flattened out as they travelled further east and the vast sweep of fertile fenland began.

'I hope your mother isn't missing you too much,' the kind lady enquired of Ronnie.

'We promised her we'd go to our dad in London,' he muttered. 'She's not fit to travel, you see.'

The woman smiled sympathetically, but, as Ronnie didn't pursue the conversation, she too dozed off, leaving Ronnie sighing with relief. It could get awkward if she started cross-examining him and asking questions. Now that they were really on their way, Ronnie was racking his brains trying hard to recall where exactly in Finsbury Park their home Gladstone Gardens actually was; he could just about remember the name of the tenement block, that is of course if it were still standing. Confident that he would find their old home once he was back on familiar territory, Ronnie next worried if he would, in fact, find his dad.

Ronnie vividly remembered leaving Finsbury Park, half dragging Rosie to Euston Station. There was smoke and rubble dust everywhere, from bombed-out houses and tenement blocks, to stinking roads swimming with sewage leaked from smashed drains. What would he and Sally do if his mission to be reunited with his dad failed? Go back to Hope Farm and the happy Larkin family? Get into more trouble with the police for running away and endangering his little sister in the process? Ronnie felt a stab of guilt as he thought of his poor mum lying in bed worrying herself sick about her children. He was startled from his reverie by a gentle touch on his shoulder.

'My stop's coming up,' the lady they had befriended said softly. 'I hope you don't get held up too much on the way – trains are awful these days,' she fretted. 'Anyway, I've had a word with the guard, and he's promised me that once you get to London, he'll see you safely off the train.'

'Thanks again, missis,' Ronnie mumbled.

Nodding towards little Sally still curled up and fast asleep on the carriage seat, she added, 'Say goodbye to Sally for me, and good luck with finding your dad.'

Ronnie felt cold and quite alone when the lady disembarked, and, yawning widely, he snuggled up on the seat next to his sister, where he too fell into a deep sleep as the train thundered on through the long, dark night.

The sleeping children were rudely awakened when the train shunted into a siding and stood there for hours for no obvious reason. When it did move on, it stopped at every station along the way, picking up troops who wearily crowded into the corridors and compartments, some falling asleep where they stood, others smoking and singing. They finally reached their destination just as a misty cold dawn was breaking over Euston Station. Almost too exhausted to stand, Sally leant against her brother as the guard ferried them on to the heaving platform, where he waved them goodbye.

'Now what?' yawned Sally.

'Get the bus home,' Ronnie told her.

Staring at all the red buses chugging slowly into the crowded station, Sally tried to recall where the bus stop was, but when Ronnie asked a man which bus would take them to Finsbury Park, he was told to catch a trolleybus.

'Take the 653,' he advised. 'That should do you.'

In their ignorance the children hopped on to a trolley-bus going the wrong way, so they hopped off and waited for one that was going the right way. When they finally disembarked from the bus at Finsbury Park, it was gone eight and they were both now starving hungry. Almost in tears, weary Sally wailed, 'How far now?'

'Shut your moaning!' Ronnie barked.

Snivelling quietly, Sally asked, 'Do you know where we are?'

'Yeah,' he answered and pointed to a ruined pile of rubble from which dangled a shattered street sign: GLAD-STONE GARDENS. Ronnie laboriously spelt out the letters. 'This was where we lived.'

Cautiously making their way around tumbled metal arches and gaping huge holes from which filthy water gushed, they came across a gang of kids about their own age who, even in the early-morning light, were playing among the filth and dirt, yelling and screaming at each other as they foraged like feral animals for anything they could recoup from the ruin.

'We lived *here*?' Sally gulped. 'This was home?'

Close to tears, Ronnie swiped tears from his grubby cheeks before he mumbled, 'Not any more, it ain't.'

33. Shock Waves

Rosie's labour was gruelling for all concerned but especially so for the poor mother, who thrashed about on the bed in the delivery suite calling out her children's names in between crying out in pain as she tried to deliver her baby. With Ada by her side, Rosie felt a little easier, gripping Ada's hand and barely letting go of it through the long hours of her labour.

'Don't leave me,' she begged.

'Don't worry, I'm here, dear,' Ada soothed. 'You're doing well,' she lied – what else could she say? We're worried sick about you and the health of your baby? The most important thing was to reassure Rosie now that she was in labour and to hope that, against the odds, she would deliver a healthy child. 'Remember what we did in the exercise classes, dear? Nice deep breaths and slowly exhaling.'

In between contractions Rosie wildly asked about Ronnie and Sally. 'Any news? Are they safe? Have you called the police?'

Matron, who was monitoring the patient's progress at the end of the bed, shook her head. 'The police are out looking for them,' she assured Rosie. 'Remember, they were spotted at Grange Station?' she added for what must have been the fifteenth time. 'They won't have got far.'

'But they're so little,' Rosie gasped as another contraction started. 'Oh, God, what if something happens to my children?'

'Shhh, shhh,' Ada soothed; but, for all her attempts to keep Rosie calm and in control, her patient ranted, raved, and used up all of her precious energy until she lay on the bed limp, dripping with sweat and feverishly exhausted. Worried and needing to speak in private, Ada and Matron slipped briefly out of the room, and in the corridor they consulted in tense whispers.

'I think the baby's breech,' Ada whispered.

Matron nodded. 'One of them might not make it.'

Knowing how hard a breech birth would be, Ada said urgently, 'I must get back to her.'

Matron stopped her. 'Ada, Dora can replace you,' she said. 'It's important you don't take unnecessary risks at this stage in your pregnancy.'

'I'll stay with Rosie,' Ada answered firmly. 'It's the right thing to do, and after all I promised I would.'

After Matron had administered a sedative to ease Rosie's pain, Ada stayed by her side, wiping her brow, speaking softly and calmly, never letting go of her hand, while Sister Ann eventually eased Rosie's baby into the world. When it was finally over, there was no sound from either mother or child. Ada looked down at Rosie, who looked more dead than alive; she gasped in relief when she saw her eyelids flutter.

'Stay with her,' Matron instructed. 'I'll see to the baby.'

Ada stayed with Rosie until she mercifully dropped off to sleep, then she started the process of washing and tidying up before Rosie was removed to the post-natal ward.

Now completely exhausted and working automatically, Ada was grateful when Dora walked in.

'I'll take over now, lovie,' she said. 'Matron says you've got to go home and get some rest before you collapse.'

In no mood for arguing, Ada nodded. 'Thanks, Dora. How's the baby?'

Dora shook her head. Ada's heart sank.

Ada was inconsolable by the time she caught up with Sister Ann, who could do no more than give her a comforting hug.

'We did everything we could, dear. The rest is in God's good hands.'

'Poor Rosie,' Ada gulped. 'It's so heartbreakingly unfair that everything has gone wrong for her. The worry over her missing children was just the final straw. I'm amazed she survived her labour, to be honest. There were times during it when I was sure she would just give up and die.'

Matron agreed, almost as concerned for her dear colleague as she was for her patient.

'I'll take over now, dear. Promise me you'll go home now and go straight to bed.'

Weary Ada nodded as she sighed. 'I don't need to promise, Ann, I'm exhausted – all I want to do is lie down and sleep.'

Though bone weary, Ada slightly revived after deeply inhaling the soft, warm, evening air. Walking home down the farm track, she revelled in the intense perfume of wild honeysuckle brimming over the farm wall, and the screech of swallows enjoying their last flight before velvet darkness fell. Thinking of poor Rosie and her loss, Ada asked herself yet again if it were wrong to feel comforted by life and the beauty of the world when others were going through such terrible times?

Childbirth was her job, her profession; it had never ceased to amaze her how the female body could grow and change so radically, then produce another human being through the final, unquestionably difficult and painful part of the process. It was an everyday miracle which people took completely for granted. Most of Ada's experience of birthing had been with women who would be giving away the child they had just delivered; within weeks the baby would be adopted, and the mother would re-enter the world she had fled in order to hide away her shameful secret. Nevertheless, Ada had seen, albeit briefly, the joy and love on young mothers' faces as they beheld their baby for the very first time. It was absolutely heartbreaking that this could not be what Rosie experienced.

Glad to be home, Ada was drawn to the letter she had received earlier that day from Jamie. Reading it again would give her the only comfort she might find just now. Taking a cup of tea and the letter, she sat in the fading light on the garden bench with the pert little robin for company and eagerly opened the letter.

My dearest darling love,

How are you?

Ada instinctively pressed the letter to her face; was there the faintest hint of the tobacco Jamie smoked, or the soap he used, even the sterilized hospital scrubs he wore? Quickly continuing, she read on.

I think of you constantly, Ada, and our baby, though to be honest I barely have a moment to myself these days, as we're in the throes of preparing for our move to North Africa. I know how upset you were about this imminent move, my darling, and what a shock it was to you, but I want to reassure you that it won't be so very different to the usual routine here. The big difference will be the uniform, desert kit, and of course we'll be sailing to our destination rather than marching or driving medical trucks. I just pray that we'll land with enough equipment, as you know from what I've told you previously the worst thing is dealing with dreadfully wounded men with nothing to offer them but water – if they're lucky.

The team I work with, men and women (don't worry I have eyes only for you, my beautiful wife!) are a good lot, always helping each other out and easing the long hours, so that between us we do get some shut eye. We share our food rations too, especially when parcels arrive from home. Sister Mary Paul's coconut buns were a real treat – I'm sure she must have used half of Mary Vale's rationing coupons to provide enough for my gang!

Ada burst out laughing; she knew just how many buns Sister Mary Paul had made and where she had scrounged, borrowed and all but stolen the ingredients to make a big enough batch to feed Jamie's team.

The woman is a saint, without a doubt. Give her a big kiss from me, if that isn't too saucy a thing to do to a holy nun!

Oh, my sweet, I think of you in our cottage, or out in the

*garden waiting for the arrival of our son or daughter. I count
down the days to when I can hold both of you in my arms, when
we can be a little family, at peace with the world. If I don't get
time to write between now and our departure, please don't think I
have forgotten about you – you are always in my mind and my
prayers.*

*Your devoted, loving, home-sick husband,
Jamie xxx*

Ada carefully folded the letter and replaced it in its
envelope, and, after sipping her now cool tea, she leant
her head against the red-brick wall of the cottage, which
was still warm from the slow-setting sun, its rays spilling
over on to the flowerbeds heavy with the perfume of
phlox, sweet peas and rambling roses. Thinking of poor
Rosie lying bereft and lonely in her narrow hospital bed,
Ada felt a rush of gratitude. She had a wonderful husband, a strong, healthy baby presently kicking its little feet
against her ribs, and the sweetest home in the most beautiful valley; she was blessed, utterly blessed, and she thanked
God for it.

34. Gladstone Gardens

It wasn't long before the terrible news spread around the Home. As they went about their daily chores, in the kitchen, on the wards and in the laundry, the girls whispered among themselves.

'Poor Rosie – it's too much for any one person to bear.'

'I feel so sorry for her, lying there in that hospital bed all alone.'

'If only Ronnie and Sally were here, at least she would have something to hold on to.'

'Where on earth can those two kiddies have got to?'

After her fruitless trip to Carnforth, tired Sybil was busy on yet another hateful house chore, cleaning out the fires and laying new ones in the numerous grates all over the Home. Sybil was racked with misery. She was all too aware that she was totally responsible for the removal of Rosie's children from Mary Vale, and now her burden of guilt had doubled. If Ronnie and Sally hadn't run away, Rosie would never have gone into premature labour and lost her baby. It was as simple and as brutal as that and, as far as Sybil was concerned, it was she who had created this nightmare scenario and it was down to her to make reparation.

Having lain awake most of the night, Sybil woke up convinced, yet again, that Ronnie and Sally were now in London.

'After all, it's the only place they know apart from Grange,' she reasoned.

Resolved not to waste another minute, she sprang out of bed determined to find out where they had lived before they came to Mary Vale.

'I've got to at least try to find them and bring them safely home before they get into even bigger trouble,' she said out loud as she quickly dressed.

Unfortunately, in all her many conversations with Rosie about her family and home life, Sybil had never once heard her mention the address of her former home. All she knew was it was in the Finsbury Park area.

Judging from past experience, Sybil knew for sure that she would not be allowed to visit her friend on the ward, and, even if she were allowed entry by Sister Mann, Sybil would never dream of asking Rosie troubling questions. How could she get the information she required without arousing suspicion? Again, it was Dora she turned to for the information she needed.

After hearing Sybil's request, Dora cocked her head. 'I'll check her file,' Dora said, and slipped into the office. 'Wait there.' A few minutes later she reappeared holding a slip of notepaper that she handed to Sybil. 'No. 21 Gladstone Gardens, Finsbury Park, London. Let's hope the place is still standing.'

Sybil would have loved to have told Dora the honest truth – that she was bent on travelling to London to find the missing kiddies. She knew without a doubt that Dora in her professional capacity would block her undertaking, saying it was too dangerous for a woman in her condition to travel. A statement that Sybil would be unable to argue with – it was dangerous for her to set off on such a journey in her condition, but, really, what choice did she have? So instead of being honest Sybil took the easy route and lied through her teeth.

'You never know,' she told Dora. 'It's worth sending off a couple of letters to neighbours who may have spotted the kiddies.'

In actual fact the very last thing Sybil had in mind was messing about with time-wasting letters. If her hunch was right – and please God, she prayed, let it not be a wild-goose chase – immediate action was required. Hurrying to her room, Sybil attempted to cover her tracks by writing a letter to Matron explaining that she would be away for a few days.

An elderly aunt of mine who lives in Penrith, she lied, *has had a fall and is presently being nursed in a convalescent home, where I intend to visit her.*

After sealing the letter, Sybil dropped her wallet, identity card and ration book into her handbag, and found her gas mask. Then, after packing some underwear, a nightie and some toiletries into a small shopping bag (a suitcase would immediately arouse suspicion), she left the letter addressed to Matron on the hall table before setting off for Kents Bank Station.

Given Sybil's urgent desire for speed, the journey down to London could not have felt longer or more complicated; the government's ruling that goods trains and special troop trains were to have priority meant that innumerable passenger trains were held up at junctions and outside mainline stations, full of servicemen and women, itching to get home for a weekend pass or a spell of leave. Fretting at the long waits, some up to forty-five minutes, the endless delays inevitably resulted in passengers missing vital connections. Getting off one train and on to another was nothing short of a nightmare, with passengers, most in uniform, hurling themselves off trains as they slowed down, then racing down the platform or across connecting bridges to jump on another one. Inevitably in all of the confusion the trains were full to the gunnels, with desperate servicemen climbing on to the luggage rack if there were no seats. Sybil was in no condition to race or rush; instead she had to waddle from one platform to another with a hand laid protectively over her tummy in case some burly soldier bowled into her. Sweating and gasping for breath, she made her way along the corridors, peeping into compartments; mercifully, kind fellow passengers gave up their places for her.

Utterly exhausted, Sybil fell asleep against a sailor, who in turn was half leaning on her. The pair dozed throughout the last leg of the journey, only to be woken by the heavy clanking of the steam train as it rumbled and hooted its way into Euston Station.

'Sorry, miss,' said the sailor when he awoke. Shuffling with embarrassment, he stood up to retrieve his duffle bag from the luggage rack above his head, where his mate lay stretched out full length in a deep sleep. 'Oi, we're in London!' he said to his pal, as he rudely shook him awake and the train rumbled to its final stop.

Sybil waited for the worst of the crush to pass before disembarking and making her way out of the station, just as Ronnie and Sally had done only days earlier. Hailing a taxi, Sybil gratefully settled in the back seat, where she was regaled by the taxi driver with gory details of Hitler's bombing sprees. When he stopped at the destination Sybil had given him, she looked around the vast bomb-site littered as far as the eye could see with mountains of rubble, brick, twisted metal and broken pipes.

'Is this Gladstone Gardens?' she cried in despair.

'It is, or rather was,' the driver answered. 'Hitler had a fair bash at this too,' he added bitterly.

'But, b . . . I was hoping to meet somebody here,' she stammered in confusion.

'Well, you can see there ain't nobody here to meet, sweetheart, unless you have an appointment with a rat,' he said, as he nodded towards a skinny rat slinking its way through the debris.

'Where has everybody gone?' she asked. 'The residents who lived here?'

The driver shrugged. 'Who knows? They could be anywhere.' Aware of her condition and her pale, strained face, he added sympathetically, 'Shall I drop you off at Finsbury Park, love? There's a few pubs down that way and a couple of cafs,' he suggested.

Feeling utterly deflated, Sybil gave a feeble nod. 'Yes – yes, please.'

Sitting at a Lyons' Corner House, drinking strong tea and eating toast and margarine, Sybil considered her next move. She had come this far – she had to see it through and at least keep looking for the missing children. Right now, with her aching back, sore feet and throbbing headache, she could have cheerfully shaken the pair of them.

'What on earth possessed them to run away in the first place?' she thought for the umpteenth time. 'What hare-brained idea got into their silly little heads?'

After finishing her tea, Sybil hauled herself up from the table, then made her way warily along the main road in the sweltering heat of the summer morning. On all sides craters and crushed, misshapen girders lurched precariously from former apartment blocks. Sagging gable ends revealed bedrooms where shreds of filthy curtains flapped in the dusty air. Sybil stepped over stinking leaking pipes, jagged concrete slabs and coils of sharp barbed wire that were supposed to fence off the destruction but, in fact, was a menace to pedestrians, hanging loose as it did, gashing the legs of those struggling to pass by. Sybil shuddered; this was not the London she had worked in. Bombs had hailed around Whitehall, but this carnage was a brutal systematic ravaging of homes, families and communities. It was no wonder the Pickles had fled the scene.

Dodging the debris, Sybil continued deep in thought, until she was brought to an abrupt halt by a long queue snaking its way around a department store. Curious, she enquired of a passer-by, 'What's going on here?'

'It's the WVS,' a woman explained. 'They run a kitchen in the air-raid shelter in the basement, free tea and buns, fruit if you're lucky.'

Just as Sybil was about to sidestep the crowd, she heard a voice that she would have recognized anywhere.

'Oi, mate! You bleedin' well just pushed in.'

'Piss off, you snot-nosed brat!' an angry male voice responded.

As a skirmish broke out, the crowd stood to one side in

order to avoid the flying fists and kicking feet. As the two fighters were revealed, Sybil spotted Ronnie, eyes blazing, punching and hitting out as he was trying to dodge the blows the man was raining down on him.

'Bastard!' he cried, reeling from a hard slap around the head.

Incensed beyond words, Sybil boldly stepped forward and cried out in her poshest and most imperious voice, 'STOP! Stop that immediately!'

As her command rang through the air, the two came to a stumbling halt. Rounding on the man who was easily twice the size of Ronnie, Sybil raged, 'You should be ashamed of yourself.'

But before she even reached the end of her sentence, Ronnie had started to take flight.

'Sal!' he bellowed. 'Get away from her.'

Sybil did a double-take when she saw little Sally hesitating on the edge of the crowd, who were all goggle-eyed with amazement at the dramatic events unfolding before them. Running as if the devil himself were on his heels, Ronnie bellowed over his shoulder, 'RUN, SAL!'

With her eyes wide with fear, Sally didn't move as Sybil slowly approached her.

'Where's my mum?' the child whimpered.

'She sent me to fetch you,' Sybil told her softly. 'She needs you to come home.'

35. Jump for Joy

There was a discernible skip in Sister Mann's step as she went about her ward duties, and a small smile played constantly around the corners of her mouth, despite the tragic events that had taken place. Sybil's sudden disappearance didn't seem to trouble her much either; she had accepted her patient's absence due to family illness without any protest.

'Just so long as Sybil's back in time for the birth of her baby,' she cheerfully said to Dora after she had been told of Sybil's sudden departure. 'We wouldn't want her giving birth in Penrith, would we?'

Familiar with Sister Mann's moody manner and grudging smile, Dora was taken aback by her sudden lightheartedness.

'What's got into her all of a sudden?' Dora wondered.

Even she, a woman of the world and an expert on human character, could never have guessed what an unbelievably miraculous turn of events had recently taken place in Edith's otherwise drab life. The earth-shattering event manifested itself in the form of a letter that had appeared completely out of the blue. When Edith saw the embossed cream envelope sitting in her staff pigeon-hole, her heart almost stopped beating. Trembling, she had taken hold of it and read her name and address that were written in elegant copperplate, a style of writing that was imprinted in her brain.

Charles! *Her* Mr Charles Lamberty. Clutching the envelope like a precious jewel that might be snatched away from her, Edith had all but run into her office, where she locked the door and leant against it to get her breath back. As she lifted the envelope flap, her mind raced. Was Charles in trouble? Had the scandal she had sacrificed so much to avoid caught up with him? Reeling with nervous excitement, she read:

Mr Charles Lamberty
The Laurels Nursing Home
Granhams Road,
Altrincham
Cheshire.

My dearest Edith,

You may be surprised to note my new address. You see, you weren't the only one to leave Leeds. Maybe it was your rather abrupt departure, dear Edith, that triggered my transfer too. Be assured that I had no intention of losing sight of you, dearest. Before I left Harrogate, I made quite sure that I had secured your present address from Personnel, who had furnished your new employee with a reference.

I am presently employed as Senior Surgeon in a delightful nursing home just outside Altrincham, very close to the rolling green Cheshire countryside. I am of course with my wife, Beryl, who has taken to her bed with nerves since the move, which affected her very badly. Though domestic life is bleak, my professional life is deeply satisfying, the work is challenging and interesting; it is (to be blunt) my private life which suffers. To come to the point, Edith, I miss you and the occasions we spent together.

Feeling positively faint, Edith clutched the letter in her trembling hands, tense and barely able to breathe. 'He misses me, he actually misses *me*!'

I am amply paid and have a set of fine rooms in the nursing home. I think you would be impressed by the modern operating theatre where I perform my surgery. What I don't have is you, Edith. You are unquestionably the best and most competent theatre sister I have ever worked alongside – calm, controlled and thoroughly professional.

Edith's pulse raced as she reread the sentence out loud. '*Calm, controlled and always professional.* Oh, Charles . . .' she almost swooned.

I am looking to appoint an experienced theatre sister and I wondered if you might consider the position?

Shocked rigid, Edith smothered a loud cry. 'Oh, my God!'

There is an added perk to the post. The position comes along with its own private accommodation in the lovely hospital grounds. A small bungalow within easy walking distance of the nursing home. I'm sure you can understand how keen I am to see you installed in a place convenient to us both, where we can pick up where we left off. Please, Edith, do not presume that I expect you to fall in with my plans, though it would make me a very happy man if you were to do so. Quite simply, I would never forgive myself if I did not at least try to reinstate our tender relationship, as I have missed you enormously these last months. If you agree to my proposal, I shall discreetly take over the lease on the bungalow, which I am certain we shall both derive great pleasure from.

At this point Edith began to shake all over – his offer was all her dreams come true. To be close to Charles once more was more than she could ever have asked for, and to have her own home, shared by him on occasions (Beryl allowing, of course), was beyond all her wildest hopes.

I shall close now but hope sincerely that you will accept my offer. I impatiently await your answer, dearest Edith.

Yours ever,
Charles

Pacing her small office, Edith had gone around and around in ever decreasing circles, too restless and over-whelmed to sit down.

'Finally,' she thought. 'This is my chance to be free.'

With Charles forging a new life for her, Edith could throw off the shackles of the past, abandon the mother she hated and walk away from her family forever. Just thinking of her loathsome mother brought Edith out in a hot sweat of anger. The woman had bullied and beaten her since she was a child. If she did as Charles suggested this time, she would make absolutely sure that she disappeared altogether. She would take on a new name, a new identity, get rid of her car – do anything that allowed her to disappear into the blue, expunging her past like a bad dream.

'I must write back to Charles immediately,' Edith had thought wildly. 'I must let him know my feelings, *yes, yes, yes*!'

My dear Charles,

Your letter came as a most welcome surprise. I cautiously did not freely distribute my present address for reasons of privacy.

I am truly delighted at the news of your new appointment in Altrincham. As you will have most likely noted, I now work in a Mother and Baby Home near Grange-over-Sands. Compared to the working conditions I am familiar with, the Home is a somewhat grim and drab establishment, which I am keen to leave as soon as possible; plus, like you, I miss our former relationship. Therefore, my reply to your generous offer is an unconditional yes. I would love to join you in Altrincham at the earliest convenience. However, I must be blunt with you, dearest, I no longer want to be encumbered with my present name (particularly as it links me to you in the past), so I will be applying for the post under a new name, Emily Edgecombe. There are other details which I will need time to consider and plan for, and when I'm clearer (and calmer) I shall certainly inform you.

I simply cannot wait to see the bungalow you have so kindly secured for me. More importantly, I cannot wait to see you, dearest heart.

With affection,
Edith

P.S. I hope Beryl's health improves.

Sealing the envelope, Edith had run to the post-box outside the railway station, and, taking a little time after dropping her letter into the box before starting her shift, she crossed the railway line and, still wearing her starched nurse's uniform, wandered along the edge of the marsh, where the tide was slowly licking its way in. Hugging her secret to herself, Edith was oblivious to the call of the oystercatchers and sandpipers pecking at the edges of the shore; even the rushing swell of the Irish Sea over which squawking herring gulls drifted failed to catch Edith's attention. Her thoughts were focused entirely on the glittering blue horizon, on a new life with Charles, a bright and wonderful future that didn't include her mother.

Meanwhile, Edith told herself, she had work to do; it would do her no good if she appeared to be slacking. It was imperative that she kept to some semblance of normality, even if all she wanted to do was jump for joy. The secret she carried, the happiness that awaited her, made her glow, it was hard to keep a smile off her face or extinguish the excited twinkle in her eye.

'I must not arouse suspicion,' she firmly told herself. 'If I behave in any way that is uncharacteristic, people are bound to ask questions, which could be awkward. I need time to think and plan my departure carefully. This isn't just about accepting a new job and living a new life with Charles; it is about disappearing completely. Edith Mann must die in order for another woman to live. If I'm to take on a new identity, not a single thing must be left to chance.'

36. Return Journey

After tracking down Ronnie, who had run away and was found hiding behind a bus stop, Sybil spent a considerable amount of time persuading the two nervous children that she only meant well. Coaxing them into the Lyons' Corner House that she had only just left, Sybil gave a cheery smile in an attempt to break the frosty atmosphere.

'Now, then, what would you like to eat?'

Ronnie, sitting on the edge of his chair looking like he would run a mile at the slightest provocation, muttered, 'Spam fritters, mash potatoes, bread and butter – and gravy.'

Sally gazed longingly at the large sticky buns a waitress was serving to customers at an adjacent table.

'One of them, please, and some cocoa,' she replied with more manners than her brother.

After ordering the food and tea for herself, Sybil carefully chose her words. 'I know we got off to a bad start at Mary Vale,' she admitted.

'You can say that again,' Ronnie grunted.

Ignoring his rudeness, which in the circumstances was perfectly justified, Sybil continued. 'I came to find you because we've all been so worried about you. And your mother needs you – she's ill.'

Both children looked alarmed. 'Sicker than she was before?' Sally asked nervously.

'She's very poorly indeed,' Sybil explained.

'Why? What's happened?' Ronnie demanded.

Sybil trod carefully. 'The baby has made her very sick – the only thing that will really cheer her up and make her better is seeing you two.'

Sally asked with an incredulous smile, 'Can we really make her better?'

'For certain,' Sybil assured the little girl. 'But it means you have to come back to Mary Vale with me as soon as you have had something to eat.'

Suspicious Ronnie glared at Sybil. 'How do we know you're telling the truth?'

'The truth is I *really* want to help your mother, whom I am extremely fond of,' Sybil answered with all sincerity.

'You were never nice to us all the time we were in the Home with Mum – why are you being nice to us now?' Ronnie snarled viciously; then, turning to his sister, he grabbed her arm. 'Don't listen to her, Sal, you can't trust this lying bitch as far as you can throw her.'

Not convinced, Sally resisted. 'I want to go back to the Home and make Mum better, Ronnie,' she pleaded.

Terrified that she was going to lose them as soon as she had found them, Sybil quickly added, 'I swear I am not lying this time. I did before,' she readily admitted, 'but this time I am telling God's honest truth. Your mother has become my friend, which is why I want to help her. She's too poorly to come all this way to fetch you, so I'm doing it instead.'

Staring into their little faces, Sally's frightened, Ronnie's wary, Sybil felt thoroughly ashamed of herself. 'I behaved badly, for which I apologize,' she confessed. 'I just want to make things right now.'

The arrival of the welcome food stopped any further grumblings and accusations. Ronnie wolfed back everything on his plate, then asked for suet pudding and custard, after which he enquired, 'How do we get back to Mary Vale? We've no money.'

'I've got some money – I can pay for your fares,' Sybil told him.

'Do we not have to hide in the luggage van any more?' innocent Sally asked.

Sybil hid a smile. 'No, we'll travel in style,' she promised. 'If you can find it in yourselves to come with me, I can get you back to Mary Vale.'

After the children had eaten their fill and Sybil had paid the bill, she suggested they got a taxi to the station, but, standing on the kerbside outside the café, Sybil anxiously wondered if any cab would, in fact, stop for a heavily pregnant woman accompanied by two children who looked like vagabonds. Luckily a cab eventually pulled up and, after being dropped off at Euston, the three of them made their way through the teeming station, which was by now stifling hot. In all the clamorous commotion Sybil stopped for a second, aware of a sharp stabbing pain at the base of her spine, strong enough to make her gasp.

Steadying herself against a grubby brick wall, Sybil studied the platform notices.

'Over there,' she pointed. 'Up the stairs and over the bridge.'

Leading the children up and down two steep flights of stairs left Sybil feeling faint and weak. The heaving sea of servicemen with large duffel bags thrown over their shoulders seemed impenetrable, but, seeing her condition and the two kiddies at her side, the crowd parted just enough to allow them to board the train. After finding seats in a packed, smoky compartment, Sybil was grateful to be finally sitting down and groaned as Sally, shy of all the strange men, squashed in beside her, squeezing her distended tummy in the process.

It seemed to take hours for the train to fill up with passengers, then even more hours as it shunted painfully slowly out of the capital; then it picked up speed, stopping at the occasional station, until they eventually arrived on the outskirts of Crewe. It was here that the back-pain Sybil had hoped was a one-off started to resume. Asking Sally to get off her knee, Sybil tried to take deep breaths to counteract the pain but with little effect. Lack of space and dense cigarette smoke made her feel nauseous and claustrophobic all at the same time. Alarmed, she thought, 'Dear God, please don't let me give birth on a train!'

Struggling to her feet, she made her way out of the compartment and into the corridor, where weary servicemen were propped against the windows or lay sleeping on the floor. Struggling across prone bodies, Sybil finally made it to the lavatory, where she found three soldiers smoking with the door hanging open.

'Sorry, missis,' they muttered as they slunk away.

After closing the door, Sybil supported her enormous tummy in one hand, while with the other she tried to ease the increasing throbbing pain in her back. Trying to remember Ada's instruction about the length of the onset of labour, Sybil could only hope she would make it back to Mary Vale in time to give birth.

'That's if this damn train ever gets moving again,' she thought impatiently.

But what if she didn't make it back to the Home? She needed help, someone who could help her if the worst came to the worst. Sally, almost a babe herself, was out of the question but worldly-wise Ronnie might be useful.

Returning to the compartment, Sybil signalled to Ronnie to join her in the corridor, where in a relatively quiet corner she explained her predicament. It was embarrassingly essential that she asked him first off if he knew about the facts of life; if he thought that storks delivered babies overnight in a basket, then she was really in trouble.

Ronnie blushed and mumbled, 'They come out the same way they got in.'

Sybil gave a sigh of relief. 'You see, the thing is, I think I might be starting with my baby.'

Ronnie's horrified eyes locked on to her vast tummy. 'Now?' he panicked.

'It might not be for a while, but if it does happen I'll need you to empty the compartment and you might have to get Sally out of the way too, find a lady who can help me or call the guard,' she told him in as calm a voice as she could summon up. 'Can you do that?'

Looking tense, Ronnie just nodded.

'It might not come to that,' she added hastily. 'I just needed to put you in the picture in case it does happen. Will you help me?' she asked with a wobbly catch in her voice.

'Yeah, s'pose so,' he answered casually, but the look in his eye showed concern, which was as much reassurance as Sybil was going to get right now.

*

It was a huge relief when the train shunted out of the siding and went on its way fairly speedily to Manchester, where yet again they had to change trains and platforms. After hurrying along the length of the platform to catch the connecting train, Sybil gasped as the previous pains gave way to a dull thudding throb in her lumber region. Hearing her cry, then stumble, Ronnie used his small skinny body as a prop.

'Lean on me,' he told her, as he half dragged Sybil on to the train, which, compared to the one they had just vacated, was virtually empty. Laying Sybil along the length of the seat while keeping an eye out for Sally too, Ronnie removed her jacket and laid it under her head.

'I don't know what to do,' he blurted out.

'Remember what I told you earlier,' she reminded him. 'See if you can find the guard, or a lady who might help me.'

'What will I do with Sally?' he cried. 'She's scared and she keeps crying.'

'Leave her with me for the moment.'

Grasping the edge of the carriage seat, Sybil was overwhelmed at the speed of her next contraction, which gripped her body like a band of iron.

'Arghhh!' she groaned through gritted teeth.

Doing what she had always done to her mum when she was in pain, Sally stroked the hair back off Sybil's clammy forehead.

'Shhh,' she whispered. 'You'll get better.'

Sybil's body rose as the contraction peaked, then fell as it subsided. Weak and already exhausted, she slumped back on to the prickly plush pile of the seat, which is where the guard found her. Taking one quick look in Sybil's direction, he visibly paled.

'Bloody 'ell fire!' he muttered.

'How long to Kents Bank?' Sybil asked him.

'If we don't get shoved into a siding near Carnforth, then not so long at all.'

Struggling to sit up, Sybil said, 'Please could you get me some water?'

The guard gave a curt nod.

'Aye, I'll get yon lad here to fetch it.'

Clearly desperate to get away, he shot off with Ronnie trailing after him. Sybil closed her eyes as she listened to the steady rhythmic rocking of the train on the tracks.

'Please God,' she prayed. '*Please, please*, don't let the train get held up.'

God didn't quite answer her prayers; they were held up in Preston, where Sybil's waters broke all over the carriage floor. Wet through from the waist down, Sybil wondered if she would survive this ordeal. Alone in the carriage but for the children, she was in no position to time her contractions, but she knew for sure they were coming more quickly and lasting longer. Suddenly, when she was at her lowest ebb, Ronnie was at her side, having briefly taken off to remove his sister to another carriage, where a lady with her family said she would look after poor bewildered Sally.

'Thank God you came back,' she whimpered.

'You look properly poorly,' he murmured.

'Listen, I need you to do something very important,' she started. 'When I give you the signal, can you slowly count to sixty, then count another sixty and another until I give you the signal to stop?'

'Yeah, why?' he asked.

'Just do it, Ronnie,' she begged.

As the muscles around her uterus tightened, Sybil held up her hand, waiting for it to ease.

'Now!'

'1, 2, 3, 4, 5, 6, 7, 8, 9 . . .' Ronnie obediently started.

When the next contraction started up, Sybil turned to Ronnie, struggling to speak through the pain. 'How many sixties did you count?'

'Five,' he replied.

'Jesus, they're coming every five minutes,' she gasped.

'Shall I get you some more water,' he enquired.

Gripping his small trembling hand, Sybil cried out, 'No, Ronnie, please don't leave me, please stay with me.'

His tough little face contorted with emotion. 'I'll stay, don't worry, I won't leave you, promise.'

Tears streamed down Sybil's pale, tense face. 'I don't deserve your kindness,' she blurted out. 'I was an utter bitch to you and your sister, I completely set you up with the robbery at Mary Vale and had you kicked out of the Home because I wanted to hurt a man who had hurt me. But instead of punishing him, I took it out on two innocent children. I know it was a wicked thing to do. Can you ever forgive me?' she cried.

'Shhh, don't get so worked up,' the little boy soothed. Seeing the sweat breaking out on her brow, he handed her the water he had fetched. 'Drink,' he urged. 'Try to relax.'

Sybil had no choice but to stop talking – in the grip of yet another contraction, she was way beyond words.

'Start counting, Ronnie,' she told the anxious lad, as it came to a welcome stop.

'How many this time?' she asked when the next one started.

'That was three sixties,' Ronnie informed her, as she lay back weak and sweating, then added, as if she didn't already know, 'It looks like the pains are coming faster now.'

By the time they arrived at Kents Bank, Sybil was oblivious to her whereabouts, concentrating only on breathing through the contractions as Ada had taught her. Brave Ronnie had kept his word, staying with the patient and counting to sixty every time she told him to. When they were coming into the platform, Ronnie leapt off it before it had even stopped; running hell for leather out of the station, he called over his shoulder to the guard, 'I'm going for help – don't let the train go until I come back.'

When curious passengers poked their heads out of the open windows, Sally grandly announced, 'My auntie Sybil's on the train – she's having a baby!'

Just ten minutes later the extraordinary sight of two nuns bearing a stretcher running on to the platform with their wimples flying in the breeze came as a surprise to everybody.

'Where is she?' Matron cried to Sally, who was standing sentry by the compartment in which Sybil lay.

'In there!' Sally pointed to the door.

'Step aside, sweetheart,' Sister Mary Paul gently told Sally, who made way for the nuns.

Along with the goggle-eyed passengers, and the pole-axed guard, Sally and Ronnie watched Matron and Sister Mary Paul descend from the train with Sybil on the stretcher.

'Is she all right, will she die?' Ronnie asked.

Matron smiled. 'She'll be fine,' she assured the breathless boy. 'You've been very brave, Ronnie.'

Sybil momentarily gripped Ronnie's hand. 'Thank you for helping me, dear Ronnie,' she murmured feebly.

'Follow us back to the Home, children,' Matron said kindly. 'I know your mother is longing to see you.'

37. Action Stations

In the competent hands of Matron and Dora, Sybil's delivery was fast and furious. Pretty well dilated after her long arduous train journey, Sybil concentrated hard on her breathing throughout the swift bearing-down period, before eventually delivering a bumping baby boy into the world.

'Say hello to your son,' Dora said, as she presented the new-born to Sybil, whose first thought was, 'Oh, my God, he's the living image of Monty!'

The baby had his father's lungs and booming voice too; as Dora wiped him clean, Sybil thought her ears would pop if he screamed any longer. It was a huge relief when Dora swept the baby off to the nursery, leaving Matron to tidy up Sybil, who lay utterly wasted on the hospital bed. Grateful for the tea and bread and butter the nun brought for her, Sybil let out a long sigh of relief.

'I seriously thought at one stage in that nightmare journey that I was going to give birth in front of a trainful of servicemen.'

Matron shook her head as she stared earnestly at Sybil. 'I'm astonished you undertook such a journey – and on one of the hottest days of the year too.'

'I didn't have much choice at the time,' Sybil pointed out.

'We all believed your letter about going to Penrith to see your aged aunt.'

'You must have guessed by now that I'm rather good at telling lies,' Sybil said, blushing.

'Why did you set off like that in the first place?' Matron asked. 'Why didn't you leave the detective work to the police rather than go haring off in your condition?' She shook her head in despair. 'When I think of what could have happened to you,' she declared.

Too weak to go into detail, Sybil just raised her eyebrows. 'It was something I just had to do, a debt I needed to repay.'

Rearranging the pillows behind her patient's head, Matron smiled. 'Whatever your motives might have been, you paid a high price. Nevertheless, you have certainly made one mother very, very happy.'

'Rosie,' Sybil murmured. 'How is she?'

'If you could have seen her face when those children ran on to the ward,' Matron recalled. 'The relief and love, it took so much of her pain and suffering away.'

Tears welled up in Sybil's green eyes. 'That's all I wanted; I couldn't bear the idea of her suffering any more. She's been put through the mill and back again.'

'I have to tell you they arrived here filthy dirty,' Matron chuckled.

'They've been living on the streets,' Sybil informed the nun. 'You should have seen the place where I found them: bombed-out ruins everywhere, open sewers, shattered apartment blocks – they were even begging for food. God knows where they slept.'

'Or how they even got to London in the first place; they certainly didn't have the train fare,' Matron pointed out. 'They're really keen to see you, but I told them you must get some rest before you have any visitors.'

Grateful for her care, Sybil settled back on her pillows and closed her eyes. Five minutes later with the curtains drawn, Sybil was in a dead sleep while her new son, Monty's lookalike, kept the entire Mary Vale nursery awake for most of the night.

Ada, who had popped over to the Home to get an update on the runaway children, was thrilled to hear from Mary Paul that they were safely back with their mother.

'The police have been notified, along with poor Mrs Larkin,' the old nun informed Ada. 'The search is off.'

Sitting at the large, scrubbed wooden kitchen table, Ada gave a big sigh of relief. 'Thank God.'

Ada's big blue eyes flew open in surprise when she heard of Sybil's role in it all.

'Extraordinary.' Ada paused and cocked her head. 'How did Sybil manage to achieve what the police couldn't?'

Sister Mary Paul chuckled. 'Maybe they were looking in all the wrong places, while Sybil just followed her instincts. Believe me, much as I would have liked some answers, there wasn't much time for asking questions when we picked the poor girl up from Kents Bank Station.'

'Taking off alone like that,' Ada marvelled. 'There's no denying Sybil's got some guts.'

Lowering her voice to a dramatic whisper, Mary Paul added, 'And for sure it's cost Sybil, going into labour on the London train, surrounded by men in uniform.' The nun shuddered. 'Matron and I found her lying flat on her back, panting in pain. God Almighty, you should have seen the passengers hanging out of the windows watching us, two nuns struggling along the platform carrying between them a pregnant woman on a stretcher!' Mortified, she covered her flushed face with her wrinkled hands. 'And Ronnie and Sally telling anybody and everybody their auntie was having a baby on the train! I didn't know what to do with myself,' the old nun wheezed.

'Heavens, Sister! I'm surprised you had the strength at your age,' cried Ada.

'Glory be to God, as if there were any choice!' Mary Paul gasped. 'Dora took over once we got back here, while I took the children to see their mummy.' Dabbing her eyes with a handkerchief, Mary Paul wept. 'What a beautiful reunion that was. Those little kiddies snuggling up to their mummy, stroking her hair, kissing her hands, and she, poor woman, sobbing her heart out.'

Ada struggled to stand up in order to hug her favourite nun. 'Don't go upsetting yourself, dear,' she said softly. 'It's been very stressful for you, physically and emotionally.'

Leaning briefly on Ada's warm shoulder, Mary Paul let out a long sob. 'I'm just happy for Rosie, and for her little family too; imagine the alternative, if they weren't reunited. As far as I can see, Sybil, who in truth has not made herself popular here, is nothing short of a saint.'

'It is an amazing transformation,' Ada agreed. 'When I was working here, Sybil couldn't even be in the same room as the Pickles family; she was forever moaning and complaining about them.'

'Thank God something changed her mind,' Sister Mary Paul said fervently. 'Though,' she added in a low voice, 'the kiddies were sad to hear Rosie's news, especially Sally. Ronnie of course tried not to show his emotions, but you could see he was upset.'

'Hardly surprising,' Ada commented. 'It's hard to come to terms with a loss like that.' Sipping the cup of tea that the nun had thoughtfully set on the table for her, she asked, 'How are Sybil and her baby now?'

'She's still in the post-natal ward with Matron, but I'm told she's doing fine,' Mary Paul informed her.

Much as Ada wanted to see Sybil, she thought that it was best to stay out of the way.

'There's quite enough going on at the moment without my sticking my nose in,' she joked. 'But I might pop by later for a brief visit.'

Before she left, Sister Mary Paul gave Ada a little apple turnover she had made especially for her and the end of a loaf of freshly baked bread.

'To keep your strength up,' she said tenderly, as she bid her favourite girl goodbye.

After their emotional family reunion, the mood in the Pickles family settled down a bit, and Rosie was able to cradle her two children in her arms.

'What possessed you to run away?' she finally asked.

Sally by her side wriggled uncomfortably. 'I ran after Ronnie when he ran away without me,' she tried to explain.

Turning to her skinny son, who was lying stiffly at her side, Rosie said softly, 'So it was your idea, Ronnie?'

Guilty Ronnie averted his eyes. 'I wanted to find our dad.'

'Your dad's fighting for his country!' Rosie cried. 'What made you think he would be in London?'

With his cheeks burning bright red, Ronnie blurted out the truth. 'The big lads in the school playground said that soldiers were coming home to check out how their families were coping.'

'That's just wishful thinking, lovie,' Rosie said, as she stroked his untidy hair. 'Men get shot for desertion of their posts. How on earth did you think that your dad, fighting behind enemy lines, could sneak off and pay us a visit?'

Looking mortified, poor confused Ronnie started to cry. 'Because I wanted it – I *believed* in it because I miss my dad!'

'Sweetheart, we all miss Dad,' Rosie confessed.

'Why doesn't he write to tell us where he is?' Ronnie wailed. 'It's been so long since he left, how do we know he's not dead already?'

Though her son was, in fact, voicing her own worst fears, Rosie answered firmly. 'I won't lie and tell you that I'm not worried too, but there's a war on: there are thousands of people in the same boat. We have to do our bit, son; we can fight Hitler in other ways. We can stay strong and brave and pray for peace and that Dad will come home to us safe and sound one day soon.'

The grief and terror he had been bottling up inside for months on end spilt its banks, and Ronnie, really just a frightened little boy, poured out all his worries. Knowing he needed to get an enormous load off his chest, Rosie just held him until his sobs subsided.

'Please don't ever leave me again, son,' she implored. 'We must stay together as a family; you and Sal are all I've got now.'

Burying himself against his mother's scrawny breast, Ronnie hugged her tightly. 'I won't do it again, Mum,' he promised.

Sally, who was getting tired, whispered, 'Can we sleep in the hospital with you tonight, Mother?'

Rosie smiled. 'I think we'd all roll out of this narrow bed,' she joked. 'I'm sure Matron won't mind if you stay a little longer, but later on you must go back to Hope Farm.'

Sally suddenly brightened up at the prospect of returning to the farm. 'I like it there,' she volunteered; yawning, she added, 'I love the kittens and the cows.'

'I know you do – Mrs Larkin's a very kind lady,' Rosie said gratefully.

'How about you, son?' she asked, as she turned to Ronnie, who was staring at the ceiling. 'Do you mind going back to Hope Farm?'

'It's okay, but I hope that you won't have to be here too much longer, now that you've had the baby,' Ronnie said with a wobble in his voice. 'When can we all be together, like you just said, a family again?'

Desperately trying not to think of the baby she had lost, and what her children had put themselves through on behalf of their broken family, Rosie swallowed hard. She would grieve for the baby she had loved later when Ronnie and Sally were gone; right now she had to hold the situation together if only for their sakes.

'I've been thinking of just that myself,' Rosie admitted.

'We haven't got a house in Finsbury Park any more,' Sally chipped in. 'The Germans blew it up.'

'I know they did, lovie,' Rosie agreed. 'We can't go back to London until Hitler stops dropping bombs on the city.'

'So how will our dad ever find us if he does come looking for us?' Sally asked nervously.

'The people who look after evacuees know where we

are; they'll make contact with us when Dad comes home.' Feeling exhausted by all the questioning combined with the overwhelming relief of having her children close, Rosie slumped against her pillows. 'Let's cross that bridge when we come to it, shall we?' she murmured. 'For the moment let's just thank God we're all here, safe and sound.'

Wrapped around each other on the hospital bed, the three of them drifted off to sleep, a little family reunited once more.

38. The Truth Hurts

When Sybil woke up from her deep sleep, she couldn't at first ascertain where she was; her first thought was, 'Oh, God, am I on a train?'

Realizing with immense relief that she was, in fact, in a warm clean bed in Mary Vale's post-natal ward, Sybil tenderly felt her tummy. Though it was loose and flabby, she smiled: the baby she had been carrying for nine long months had been born. Monty's son was outside of her rather than inside, and from now on she was going to be fine. She could take up the reins of normality again and set about the business of returning to London and finding war work. As her mind wandered, Sybil heard a nervous giggle and saw the curtains surrounding her bed twitch.

'Hello,' she called, as she struggled to sit up straight.

The curtains parted to reveal Rosie, leaning feebly on a walking stick, with Ronnie and Sally by her side.

'Hello!' Sybil said again, but this time with real enthusiasm. 'Rosie! How are you?' she asked with genuine affection.

Rosie hurried to Sybil's side, followed by her children, both now smiling self-consciously.

'Dearest Sybil,' Rosie exclaimed as she laced her arms around Sybil's neck. 'I thought I'd lost everything, but you found my children and brought them home safe and sound. Of course,' she said as she nervously eyed Ronnie and Sally, 'there is so much sadness after what we've all been through, but we have each other and life goes on.' Fighting back tears, determined to stay strong if only for the children's sake, Rosie gulped. 'Keep smiling through, eh? It's the best we can do.'

Impressed by Rosie's stoicism, Sybil felt tears prick her eyes too.

'You're right, Rosie,' she agreed. 'Never give up and never give in.'

Suddenly aware of the pressure she might be putting on Sybil, Rosie said, 'We mustn't tire you out – just tell us how you're feeling, lovie.'

'Exhausted but *so* glad it's all over,' Sybil confessed. 'Ronnie and Sally were fantastic nurses when I needed help on the train. Ronnie especially,' she said, as she gave him a knowing smile. 'I couldn't have got through the ordeal without him.'

Ronnie gave a manly swagger.

'She told me if she started with the baby, I had to clear the compartment and keep Sally calm, then find a guard,' he said self-importantly. 'She told me to count to sixty over and over again. Dunno why.'

'You were so brave, and calm and kind,' Sybil assured the little boy. 'And Sally too, stroking my hair; then, when we finally got to Kents Bank, they even managed to hold up the train while Ronnie ran for help.'

Now it was Sally's turn to feel self-important. 'We brought Matron and a stretcher,' she announced.

Rosie gave a proud smile; then, catching sight of Sybil's tired expression, she said briskly, 'Come on now, I've got to get you two back to Mrs Larkin, so say goodbye to Auntie Sybil.' Seeing her friend's curious raised eyebrow, she added with a grin, 'That's what these two have started calling you.'

'Auntie Sybil – I like it.' Sybil smiled at the children. 'It makes me feel special.'

'You are special now that you don't frighten us any more,' Ronnie assured her with his funny gap-toothed smile.

'Good,' Sybil beamed. 'Let's keep it that way, shall we, Ronnie?'

After the children had bidden Sybil an affectionate if not a little bit of a shy goodbye, she waved cheerily as Rosie tried to usher them both away.

'Can we come back and see how you are tomorrow?' Rosie asked before she departed.

'Why not?' Sybil grinned. 'After all, we're both on the same ward, so not far to waddle, in my case.'

'I hope Mrs Larkin has a nice supper waiting for you,' Sybil called after the departing children.

'She makes us puddings,' Sally said. 'Jam roly-poly is my favourite.'

'Dead man's leg,' Ronnie joked. 'That's what the Larkin lads call it.'

After her own supper was delivered by Nurse Mann, who, for reasons nobody could quite understand, was less grim these days, Sybil tracked down Dora.

'How is the baby?' she asked.

'He's got the lungs of a lion and the appetite of a horse,' Dora laughed.

Sybil gave an inward sigh. 'So like Monty.'

'Would you like to see him?' Dora enquired.

Knowing she did not want to bond with her son, who hopefully would very soon be adopted, Sybil replied carefully. 'I'd like to see him tomorrow, if you don't mind, Dora.'

Early the following morning, as soon as the ward was stirring, Sybil felt strong enough to get out of bed and pay a call on nearby Rosie.

'Are you awake?' she whispered.

'Wide awake,' Rosie answered with a rueful smile. 'Have you forgotten they serve tea at six in this place and after that the place is jumping? I think I'll probably get more rest once I'm back in the Home.'

Sybil smiled as she sat on the edge of the bed. 'Really, are you okay?' she asked earnestly.

'Fine, promise,' Rosie responded.

Wriggling up the bed so she was nearer to her friend, Rosie dropped her voice to a whisper. 'Sybil, you took such a risk going in search of my children.' She shook her head in disbelief. 'You could have lost your baby in the process.'

'But I didn't,' Sybil declared pluckily, 'and luckily I found two of yours.' She held her breath in an attempt to steady her voice. 'I'm sorry for your loss, sweetheart, you must have suffered so much.'

Rosie didn't even attempt to hold back the tears she had managed to keep under control in the presence of the children.

'It was so, so sad,' she wailed. 'I knew in my heart it was

never a good pregnancy – like I've said before, everything that could have gone wrong went wrong – but I always prayed the little mite would survive. But for all Sister Ada's efforts and care it just slipped away . . .'

By this time Sybil was weeping too. 'I wish it could have been otherwise,' she sobbed.

Still overwhelmed by Sybil's heroism and feeling bad that she had upset her too, Rosie squeezed Sybil's hand hard. 'I'll be forever indebted to you, my friend; at least my two other children are safe, thanks to you.'

Sybil wriggled uncomfortably; this simply couldn't go on, she told herself; it was shameful to lie basking in Rosie's praise, all the time knowing what damage she had done to this poor woman in the first place. The time had come to unburden her terrible secret and tell the truth, even if it meant losing the only friend she had in Mary Vale. Gulping nervously, Sybil cautiously started the conversation she had been dreading for weeks.

'Rosie, my actions are not quite as selfless as they would appear,' she blurted out. 'You see, it was because of me and the lies I told the police that your children were forced to leave Mary Vale.'

Looking thunderstruck, Rosie gazed at Sybil uncomprehendingly. 'What do you mean?' she spluttered.

Having got this far, Sybil had no choice now but to keep on going. 'I was the one who stole from the residents, I was the one who left the stuff in your family room, *I* was the one who set your children up to look like thieves,' she explained.

Gasping as if she had been grievously wounded, Rosie looked at Sybil in total disbelief. '*YOU?*

Flame-faced with shame, Sybil nodded.

'Why?' Rosie gasped. 'Why would you do an evil, wicked thing like that?'

Sybil's answer was brutally honest. 'Sheer vindictiveness. I thought they were badly behaved and decided, quite arrogantly, that I'd get rid of them.'

'I knew you couldn't stand the sight of us,' Rosie blurted out. 'If looks could have killed, we would have been dead when we first set foot in the Home. I knew we were too poor for your liking, too common.'

With the knowledge of hindsight, Sybil murmured, 'More fool me – I know better now.'

'Bit late for that,' Rosie exclaimed.

Wanting to get the entire story off her chest, Sybil pushed on. 'On the train when I was in labour, I told Ronnie what I'd done to him and his sister.' Tears welled up in her eyes. 'Even though I had treated him so badly and caused him such pain and unhappiness, Ronnie stayed with me till the end.' She took a deep shuddering breath. 'His act of pure kindness shamed me to my soul.'

'I've always said he's a good lad deep down, my Ronnie,' Rosie said defiantly.

'I did a wicked, wicked thing,' Sybil admitted. 'Lying to the police and all the residents. Not to mention the effect it had on *you* and your innocent children.'

'Lucky Sally and Ronnie landed up in a good place with the Larkins,' Rosie answered carefully. 'Losing them was bad enough, but if they had finished up in an orphanage, I think I would have lost my mind.'

The two of them fell silent for a while, before Rosie persisted with her questioning.

'So what changed your mind about us?' she asked in bewilderment.

'You, Rosie,' Sybil said in all honesty. Having started down this road, she knew that she couldn't live with herself unless she revealed her other motive. 'It was when I got to know you better, when I was working on the wards. I knew you didn't like me, that you were quite rightly suspicious of me, but once we got chatting about Dowry House and the Brigadier's antics, we seemed to get on like a house on fire.'

'That's right – you were always asking me questions about Lady Veronica,' Rosie remembered.

'Oh, God!' Sybil thought. 'Now I'm going to have to tell her how I exploited her on those occasions too.'

Holding up her hand, Sybil stopped Rosie in her tracks. 'I've not finished,' she announced. 'There's something else.'

Shocked Rosie gasped incredulously, 'More wickedness?'

Sybil wriggled uncomfortably. 'Not necessarily wicked – more exploitative.'

Rosie's brow crinkled in confusion. 'What's that?'

'Using people for your own means,' Sybil muttered. 'You see, I started questioning you about Lady Veronica because I wanted to find a way to disgrace Brigadier Baldwin.' She let out a long sigh. 'Now you know everything, all my dirty secrets. Call me a bitch if you like, you'd be quite within your rights.'

'You're a bitch all right,' Rosie said without a moment's hesitation. 'You break up my family, then squeeze me dry for information. None of that is impressive behaviour.'

'I'm certainly not arguing with you,' Sybil readily agreed. 'But I can give you an explanation.'

'The truth would be a nice change,' Rosie said cynically.

'You must have guessed by now that Monty is the father of my baby.'

Rosie shrugged. 'Most people have.'

'When I informed Monty that I was pregnant with his child, he couldn't get me out of the War Office fast enough. Instead of setting me up in a nursing home of my choice, in a familiar environment, he sent me as far away from London as he could.'

Rosie gave a grim smile. 'The bastard got rid of you before he could be disgraced?'

'Exactly, packed me off up North,' Sybil agreed. 'I begged him to take me away, but the more I begged, the more determined he was to keep me here.'

'I nearly died of fright the first time I saw him strolling into the Home,' Rosie confessed. 'I thought after all those years I'd never see him again, but there he was as large as life, bragging about saving Mary Vale from being requisitioned. He had the nuns running after him like a clutch of frantic hens. They still think the sun shines out of his backside.'

'Monty may have saved Mary Vale for the time being, but, believe me, he only stopped the threat temporarily, until it suits him otherwise. Once I've left and the baby is adopted, he won't give a damn if the place goes up in flames.'

'Oh, my God!' Rosie cried. 'The requisitioning business could start all over again once Mary Vale has served the Brigadier's purposes?'

'I don't doubt it for a second,' Sybil answered bitterly. 'The good news, Rosie, is that all the information you have on Monty has helped me – enabled me to bring the bastard down.'

Rosie gave her a sly wink. 'If you play your cards right, you might be able to "persuade",' she said, grinning as she emphasized the word, 'the Brigadier into keeping Mary Vale open. I'm sure the Brigadier's superiors would be embarrassed to discover that one of their senior officers was using a Mother and Baby Home for his own private purposes.'

Sybil's witch-green eyes widened in surprise; clapping her hands in delight, she laughed gleefully. 'The final cherry on the cake! I'll have to work on that.'

After their joint laughter had subsided, Rosie gave Sybil a long level look. 'So all those chocolates and chats, and the posies too, were they just a way of milking me for useful information?'

Wriggling uncomfortably on the bedside chair, Sybil cleared her throat. 'Yes, to start with, but, to be honest, Rosie, it was during those hospital visits when you were stuck in bed, when we laughed and shared secrets, that I really began to like you – as a friend,' Sybil said shyly.

'We did have some nice times, given the circumstances,' Rosie reluctantly agreed.

Thoroughly ashamed of herself, Sybil murmured, 'As time went by and we got closer, I wanted to cheer you up, especially when you got upset about the children, who I, in effect, had banished from your side.'

Rosie shook her head as she tried to take the facts in. 'Yet, after doing all them wicked things, you went and risked your own health to put things right?'

'That was the very least I could do.' Sybil slumped

miserably back against Rosie's pillow. 'Can you ever forgive me for everything that I have done to you and your family?'

Unsmiling, Rosie stood up before she coldly replied, 'We'll have to see about that, won't we?'

39. Another Life

Throughout all the high dramas taking place at Mary Vale, Edith Mann's mind remained firm and focused on organizing her escape plan like a military strategy. She was sorry for Rosie's loss and the fact that her children had gone missing; in turn, she was impressed by Sybil Harwood's heroic rescue mission and the reuniting of Ronnie and Sally with their poor mum. But, if the truth were told, her only real thoughts were for her darling Charles. Now that the emotional floodgates were open, the passion she felt for her lover knew no bounds. The brutal upbringing she had endured at her mother's hands had hardened her heart previously to any kind of physical relationship. Men of her own age held no attraction for Edith; she considered them silly, young and foolish, and she, a plain-faced woman, certainly held no attraction for them. That was until she met her Mr Lamberty; sophisticated, mature, rich and accomplished, married he might be but that barely troubled Edith. That Charles's wife was a feeble invalid aroused a protective love in Edith; Charles needed her to look after him in ways that his wife couldn't. Edith was more than happy to step into that role; she would quite literally do *anything* for her beloved.

As more letters were exchanged between Edith and Charles, a clear plan emerged in Edith's head. As far as she was concerned, it was imperative that she slipped away from Mary Vale without leaving a forwarding address or any hint of where she might be going or what she might be doing. She acknowledged to herself that the Home deserved better treatment than her sloping off like a thief in the night, but there was no room for sentimentality in the execution of her plan. Though the residents weren't up to scratch, the staff and nuns had behaved more than decently to her. But, if she did the right thing by her employers – hand in her resignation, serve her notice and leave on an agreed date with her replacement already installed – she would leave a paper trail of where she might be going next and could therefore be traced. No, though her behaviour would be seen as sly and under-hand, and it would certainly leave the Home understaffed, Edith had no choice. Knowing that her Rottweiler-like mother would be on her tail, desperate to get hold of her money to feed her addiction, Edith delighted in the knowledge that this time, if all went to plan, the old witch would get nothing.

By changing her name, Edith would slip through the net and disappear into rural Cheshire, where she would shake off the bonds of a family and a life she had loathed. When Edith had informed Charles that she intended to change her name, explaining that she didn't want to be associated with the Harrogate nursing home where the scandal concerning their relationship had broken out, he appeared quite pleased. That was as much as she intended to reveal to her lover who had ingeniously tracked down 'a man who knew a man', someone whom, if paid enough, was prepared to forge new official papers for Edith.

Though they hadn't settled on an exact date, Edith had agreed with Charles that she would go to him as soon as her new position was approved.

'I'm sure it won't be long, dearest Edith,' he had written, adding that he had already prepared the bungalow for her arrival. 'Everything is in readiness, my dear,' he had promised.

'Our love nest,' happy Edith thought romantically.

Thinking it would be unwise and way too obvious to start packing a suitcase, Edith gradually squirrelled away most of her belongings in the little car that Charles had helped her buy when they were working together. Her mother didn't even know she owned a car; if she had known, she would have forced Edith to sell it, so Edith had kept it permanently at the hospital. Charles had taught her to drive in the grounds of the nursing home. She remembered how thrilling it had been sitting so close to him that their thighs rubbed together, his hand over hers, calmly guiding as she changed gears. As part of her plan to forge a new identity, that little car which she had become fond of would have to go too, something she had explained to Charles and he had agreed to, reassuring Edith that once she was firmly established in Altrincham he would buy her a smarter model that better suited a woman in her new position.

With the boot of her car full of her possessions, Edith was poised for flight at any time. Fortunately, since her arrival at the Home, she had hardly used her car at all, so there was still petrol in the tank; plus ever-practical Edith had carefully studied the route to Cheshire on a map she had bought in Kendal, along with another map showing the footpaths along the Manchester Ship Canal. The Home would have to report her sudden disappearance to the local constabulary, who just might trace her and then (God forbid) she would be hauled back into a life she detested. No. If she were to become Emily Edgecombe, Edith Mann would have to die. Of course, in order to pull off her plan she had been obliged to speak to Charles of her 'suicide plan', which he, clever chap that he was, had helped her to contrive. Ironically, Edith thought with some satisfaction, they would very soon both be living double lives, he behind his invalid wife's back, she behind a new identity.

The plan was that in some secluded spot close to the ship canal, with no nosy parkers watching, Edith would unload the contents of her car into Charles's Daimler and, sometime after he had driven away, she would abandon her car along with some identity papers, her ration book and a suicide note. After sloping away from the scene on foot, Edith would take a bus to join Charles in their love nest. For sure nobody would weep a tear for the loss of Edith Mann; her mother might snivel into the dregs of her last gin bottle; but apart from that who would even notice or care about her passing? Which suited Edith down to the ground. Like an actor in the wings, she held her breath, awaiting her cue from Charles and the paradise that would follow.

Meanwhile, Edith had plenty of work to do and a busy morning lay ahead. After helping several patients to freshen up with a bed-bath, Edith changed a number of dressings before she boiled all the recently used syringes and medical instruments in the sterilizer in the sluice room. After which the mid-day meal was served, Sister

Mary Paul's flaky cheese-and-onion pie followed by spotted dick and custard. As she served lunch, Edith couldn't help but notice that a certain coolness had developed between Rosie and Sybil, which surprised her, as before the children's disappearance they had been the best of friends. Sybil, suddenly keen to leave the post-natal ward, asked when she might be able to return to the Home.

'When the doctor gives his permission,' Edith replied, as she tidied Sybil's bed. 'What are your plans for the future?' she continued. 'Are you returning to your previous occupation?'

Sybil shook her head. 'I want to continue with my war work but not in the War Office. I've been thinking of going into radar signalling. It's vital work, intercepting the location of enemy bomber planes. Most of the radar stations are on the coast, though their exact location is top secret for security reasons. If I did follow that line of work, I wouldn't be going back to London.'

'Sounds thrilling,' Edith said, before probing a bit. 'Do you know of Rosie's plans for the future?'

'She certainly can't go back to Finsbury Park,' Sybil replied. 'You should have seen the state of the place, just a blasted, filthy bomb-site.'

'Ronnie and Sally are much better off up here,' Edith remarked.

'I saw them yesterday chattering away, nineteen to the dozen with Mrs Larkin when she came to pick them up. Now that Rosie's ordeal is over, she will no doubt want to be reunited with her children.'

'Yes,' Edith agreed. 'I wonder what they will do now?'

*

At visiting time Edith was surprised to see Mrs Larkin with Rosie's children.

'I hope you don't mind, Sister, but the kiddies were keen to see their mum,' the kind foster mother explained, knowing the Ward Sister had every right to turn the youngsters off the ward. But, given their exceptional circumstances, even strict Edith hadn't the heart to turn them away.

'Only an hour,' she warned.

'Thanks,' Mrs Larkin said gratefully. 'They've never stopped talking about their train journey back here with "Auntie Sybil". Different from what Ronnie used to call her – an old witch, and a lot worse too,' she chuckled. 'Their time in London with Sybil seems to have changed everything.'

Edith raised her eyebrows in surprise. 'Auntie Sybil, indeed,' she thought. 'My word, how things have changed.'

When Edith delivered the children to their mother's bedside, she smiled as Ronnie and Sally hugged and kissed Rosie, who flushed with pleasure at the sight of them.

'Back again,' she exclaimed.

'We missed you, Mummy,' Sally whispered.

'And I missed you too,' Rosie said, as she pulled her daughter close and kissed the top of her head.

While Edith was checking Rosie's medical chart, which hung on the end of the bed, Ronnie disentangled himself from his mother's arms to ask a question. 'Can we go and say hello to Auntie Sybil?'

Edith was taken aback when she heard Rosie's sharp reply.

'No, not now, son.'

'Why?' the boy persisted.

Hauling Edith into the conversation, she was clearly clutching at straws. 'Sybil's asleep, isn't she, Sister?'

Knowing full well that Sybil was, in fact, wide awake and reading a magazine in bed, awkward Edith mumbled, 'Er, I'm not quite sure.'

Seizing the moment, Ronnie cried out, 'I'll go and check.'

'No, Ronnie!' his mother called after the departing boy.

Seeing Rosie's tense face, Edith followed the boy down the ward, where she found him greeting Sybil. When Edith appeared, Ronnie announced triumphantly, 'See, she's not asleep.'

Feeling even more awkward, Edith said sternly, 'You're not to bother all of my patients, young man.'

'I'll be good,' Ronnie promised.

Returning to Rosie's bed, Edith told her patient that Sybil was awake, and Ronnie was with her. No sooner were the words out of her mouth than Sally shot off too.

Rosie rolled her eyes in despair. 'Damn!' she muttered crossly.

'I can bring them back if you want,' Edith suggested.

Rosie gave an irritated sigh. 'No, leave it, Sister,' she said wearily. 'Sybil's their hero these days and there's nothing much we can do about it for the moment.'

Feeling sorry for Rosie, Edith went about her duties, only briefly dashing off the ward to see if there was any mail for her in the staff pigeon-holes. When she saw Charles's

elegant copperplate handwriting on an embossed envelope, her heart almost leapt out of her ribcage.

'Hah!' She smothered a cry of joy as she grabbed the
envelope and slipped it into her uniform pocket.

Just the feel of it against her skin made Edith burn with
excitement, she couldn't wait to be alone and in private,
free to read Charles's news. Barely containing her impa-
tience at having to do another bed-bath and change some
more dressings, Edith didn't get a minute alone till nearly
tea-time, when she slipped into her office to slit open the
envelope with trembling fingers. Would this be the one she
had been waiting for, the call to go to Charles, she wondered breathlessly.

My dearest Edith,

I am so sorry for the hiatus in my communications.
The hospital board insisted that we advertised the job of theatre
sister.

Edith's heart leapt into her throat. 'Oh, no! They've gone
and appointed somebody else.'

Be assured, Edith, none of the candidates were of your calibre
and integrity. After going through the tedious procedure of
interviewing several very unsuitable young women, I put my foot
down and absolutely insisted that I could only work with a real
professional – i.e. you, dearest. I stated that it was imperative to
my job, and essential for the good name of the nursing home, that
we appointed somebody of the highest professional standard to the
post and I would brook no further argument or delay.

'Oh, Charles, dearest heart!' Edith murmured adoringly.

I asked expressively for you, using the name Emily Edgecombe, as we agreed, saying I had worked with you previously and had the highest esteem for you. I personally vouched for your character and produced references which I had procured previously from the Leeds nursing home, which I took the precaution of adding your new name to. You officially start working alongside me at your earliest convenience.

Thinking she might faint with sheer joy, Edith gripped the door handle to steady her nerves.

I feel confident that, now you have been officially appointed, albeit under a false identity, we can complete our transference plan as pre-arranged and sail off into the sunset together.

'Oh, please God,' Edith earnestly prayed.

Please write and let me know when you might take up the post. Meanwhile the bungalow awaits your arrival. I enclose terms of employment and your salary scale.

Yours devotedly,
Charles

P.S. Beryl's condition remains stable. I have district nurses visiting her on a daily basis.

Edith folded the letter and locked it in her desk drawer, making a note to herself that she really must clear her office very soon of all her personal possessions. Even though she wanted to run out of the Home, jump in the car and drive away at top speed, Edith knew she had to practise caution and pick her time carefully. If she were to leave not a trace of herself behind, she now had to roll out her very complicated plan.

40. Auntie Sybil

Sybil was increasingly uncomfortable about Ronnie and Sally dashing back and forth between her hospital bed and their mother's and was therefore relieved when the visiting Mary Vale doctor discharged her. Back in her room, unpacking her small bag of belongings, Sybil was pensive. So much had happened since she had last been there. She had been back and forth to London, rescued two lost children, had a baby and was in the process of applying for entirely new war work. In such a short space of time everything had changed, and she had lost the only friend she had ever had in Mary Vale.

'I really don't belong here any more,' Sybil thought to herself.

Gazing out of her window that overlooked Mary Vale's beautiful summer garden, scented with the rich fragrance of rambling roses and stocks, Sybil wished that she had been discharged from the Home as well as the hospital. She knew she wasn't physically up to starting work immediately. Excited as she was about the prospect of working in radar, she knew that first she had to be accepted on to the course and that depended on her passing a mathematics examination that would involve a trip to London. Right now, she needed to concentrate on getting back to her full strength, both physically and mentally, so that she would be in tip-top form just in case she was lucky enough to be interviewed. Plus there was paperwork to be completed on finalizing her baby's adoption.

Opening the window wider so that she could lean out and inhale the fresh tangy sea-salt breeze, Sybil gave a heavy sigh; though she had visited the nursery a few times once she had been notified by Father Ben that he had found suitable parents for her son, she had since ceased her visits. It wasn't fair on the child; the sooner she was gone the sooner the child could start his own life, hopefully in a secure home with parents who loved him.

Then there was Rosie. Sybil let out a little groan. She didn't want to part ways with her only friend on bad terms, but, considering how she had exploited Rosie and her family, what else could she realistically expect? Best to drop the relationship altogether and leave it, like Mary Vale and her baby, in the past.

'If only I hadn't been such a bitch,' Sybil chastised herself. She had certainly learnt a lesson when it came to judging people. 'Never assume you're superior to anyone,' she rebuked herself.

That kind of social arrogance belonged to the Monty Baldwins of this world, and Sybil wanted no more of it. In the process of befriending Rosie and her children, Sybil had learnt humility and understanding, attributes which she hoped would make her a wiser woman in the future.

Sybil's thoughts moved on to Ronnie and Sally, who, she knew, she would really miss; after their turbulent adventure together, she had grown attached to the wild little pair. They made her laugh with their endless babbling: Sally's non-stop chatter about the Hope Farm animals and Ronnie's outrageous imitations of his portly headmaster and the bossy school-dinner ladies. Deep in thought, Sybil jumped in surprise when she heard the children's voices sailing across the lawn.

'Auntie Sybil!'

Leaning further out of the window, Sybil smiled to herself. 'God, they really have got voices like foghorns!'

Standing underneath the window, Sally called up, 'Why've you left the hospital?'

'Because I'm better and somebody else needed my bed,' Sybil explained.

Ronnie waved up at her. 'Come and play,' he cried.

Sybil shook her head. 'You should be visiting your mother, not me,' she told him firmly.

'She's with the doctor,' he replied.

'Please come and look for shells on the marsh with us,' Sally sweetly suggested.

Five minutes later, breathless Sybil, unable to resist, was striding along trying to keep up with Sally and Ronnie, who raced over the sandbanks like lively young puppies. The contrast between finding them filthy dirty and destitute in London and how they looked now, happy, healthy and suntanned in the bright sunshine, was dramatic.

'What if I hadn't found them in Finsbury Park?' Sybil shuddered. 'Would they have ever made their way back to Mary Vale and their mother?'

Sybil was stopped in her tracks by the sound of somebody calling her name, and, turning around, she gasped in surprise when she saw Rosie hurrying towards her.

Girding herself, Sybil thought nervously, 'She's going

to give me a ticking-off for taking her children out of the Home without asking her first.'

As the squealing children chased after each other on the winding sandy path, Rosie, looking stronger and walking a lot more quickly than she previously had, caught up with Sybil.

'I thought I would join the kiddies,' she announced in a voice that was softer and quieter in tone than the one she had used in the days since their falling out.

After a few minutes of awkwardly walking along in silence, Rosie broke the ice. 'I've been discharged from the hospital too.'

'So you'll be heading back to the Home?' Sybil enquired.

Rosie nodded. 'In that big family room without my children.' She pulled down the corners of her mouth. 'Grim.'

Trying to be positive, Sybil said feebly, 'They'll be back with you soon too, surely, now you're better?'

'I don't know,' Rosie answered quickly. 'But I think there are too many bad memories here for them.'

'I'm sorry, I know it's my fault,' Sybil muttered guiltily.

'It's not just what you got up to, though there's no doubting they had a hard time at Mary Vale – plus losing the baby didn't help either,' Rosie said frankly. 'We all know they're much better off at Hope Farm: it's the best home they've ever had, and the Larkins are saints as far as I'm concerned. It seems wrong to drag them away now when they've settled down.'

'Couldn't you move in with them?'

'Me, on a farm?' Rosie actually burst out laughing at the thought. 'Pigs would fly first.' As the smile fell from her face, she murmured, 'And there's no way we can go back to Finsbury Park for a very long time.'

Having seen the carnage done by Hitler's Messer-schmitt bombers, Sybil fervently agreed with Rosie.

'You *definitely* cannot go back there.'

'And I definitely can't stay here forever,' Rosie pointed out. 'So I don't know where I'll go,' she finished gloomily.

The heavy mood vanished as the excited children scooped pebbles and shells from little pools left behind by the outgoing tide.

As excited as the two children, Sybil cried, 'Look, a starfish!'

The breeze, the sunshine and her children's happy laughter brought a glow to Rosie's face, and she, like Sybil, ran about gathering seaside treasures, after which the two women sat on the sandbanks watching Ronnie skim flat pebbles into the sea. Suddenly turning to Sybil, Rosie came straight to the point.

'So when are we going to get our own back on Monty Baldwin?'

Looking thunderstruck, Sybil was momentarily speech-less.

'That's what you want, isn't it?'

Sybil nodded before stuttering, 'B . . . but now that you know the truth about why I was always poking my nose into your business, I rather got the impression that you felt thoroughly exploited.'

'You know, I certainly did,' Rosie answered bluntly.

Seeing Sally throw herself on to Sybil's lap in order to show her the pretty pink shell she had just unearthed brought a grin to Rosie's face. With a knowing twinkle in her eye, she added, 'But, seeing as my kids aren't bearing any grudges, I got to thinking – why should I?'

Back in the Home, Rosie and Sybil colluded. Ironically, because neither of them had a baby to mind, they had plenty of time, though both still had to do the mandatory morning chores; the afternoons, no longer taken up with relaxation and exercise classes, were free. Racking her brains, Sybil explained the problem.

'Are you absolutely sure that Monty gets money from Lady Veronica's family estate?'

'I'd swear on the Bible,' Rosie assured Sybil.

'Servants know *everything*. Who's helping themselves to the port, how much the Stowupland gardener got tipped at Christmas compared with the Dowry House gardener, what her ladyship pays for Marigold's party dresses, his lordship's little flirtation with the new parlour maid. *Nothing* is a secret below stairs. Besides, it's obvious that the Brigadier lives well beyond his means as an Army officer – he's clearly getting money from some other source.'

Rosie dramatically rolled her eyes. 'I ask you! If his lordship only knew what his son-in-law squandered his money on while blackmailing his wife at the same time, he would go mad.'

Excited Sybil sprang to her feet. 'Rosie,' she exclaimed. 'That's it!'

Rosie looked blank. 'That's how we can get to Monty – we have to rub his lordship's nose in it,' Sybil said in a steely voice. 'I wouldn't have a problem telling him how much money Monty lavished on me when I was his mistress.'

Looking nervous but excited, Rosie added, 'And I could tell him how often I've heard the Brigadier threatening to publicly denounce Lady Veronica and Marigold if she ever considered leaving him.' Her voice faltered as she said, 'But will a proud man like Lord Stow believe us?'

'I'm quite sure he must have an inkling of what Monty's up to; after all, he's not stupid and London's a hotbed of gossip.' She paused before she added, 'If we can convince Lord Stow that we're speaking the truth and give him enough accurate information, he would be sufficiently galvanized to approach Monty.'

'Hopefully when his lordship discovers how big a bastard his son-in-law is he'll turn the tables on the Brigadier.'

Sybil popped her friend's little bubble of excitement. 'Fingers crossed he does see it that way, Rosie; knowing Monty, he might just sit tight and ride it out.'

Rosie gave a dismissive snort. 'I bet if Lord Stow offered him enough to go, he would go.'

'Lord Stow has clout; he could subtly drop a word here and there about Monty's abuse of trust and, you never know, Monty might do the right thing and back off gracefully.'

'Leave gracefully!' Rosie hooted scornfully. 'The brute will stick it out until he's pushed out.'

Sybil turned to indignant Rosie, whose cheeks were burning bright red. 'You hate him almost as much as I do, don't you?'

Rosie didn't hesitate in replying. 'I'd do anything that would help her ladyship get rid of him.'

'Then,' said Sybil, 'we had better start planning a trip to

London: what we've got to say can't be done in a letter; it needs to be face to face.'

Rosie gulped nervously. 'I suppose there's no other way.'

'I have to take a mathematics examination in London soon,' Sybil told Rosie. 'Perhaps we can travel down together if you can arrange to come with me.'

'Let me know when and I'll clear it with the kiddies and Mrs Larkin.'

Sybil gave a slow smile of satisfaction. 'Then we'll be on our way and Monty won't know what's hit him!'

41. Short-staffed

Nobody had a clue that Sister Mann had left Mary Vale until Matron, the following morning, went in search of her usually punctual nurse.

'Sorry to bother you, Dora,' Matron said, as she hurried through the nursery, where her colleague, helped by residents on the feeding rota, were busy with the hungry babies. 'Have you seen Sister Mann this morning?'

Looking up from changing Sybil's hefty son's nappy, Dora shook her head. 'No, but I've only been here in the nursery since I clocked on.'

'Can you keep an eye on the wards while I check her room?' Matron asked. 'I shouldn't be more than five minutes.'

Dora smiled. 'I'll pop down there as soon as I've finished changing this bonny lad.'

Hurrying up the stairs to the top-floor rooms, Matron tapped softly on Edith's door. 'Hello,' she called.

Getting no response, she tapped again, this time a little more loudly. 'Hello, anybody there?'

Beginning to feel worried that Edith might suddenly have been taken ill, Matron gently turned the door handle. As the door swung open, she called softly, 'Edith, Sister Mann, are you all right, dear?'

Creeping into the room, Matron, struck by the absolute stillness that greeted her, stopped dead in her tracks. The bright morning sun slanting through the large bay window illuminated an immaculate, tidy, empty space with no evidence anywhere that it had ever been occupied. Matron gazed around, stunned: the bed was stripped, the wardrobe door hung open to reveal an empty clothes rail, and when she opened the drawers they were empty too. Hurrying down the corridor, she checked the bathrooms and lavatories before running back downstairs to peep into the sitting room and dining room. Seeing Sister Mary Paul clearing away the breakfast things, she called out, 'Have you seen Sister Mann this morning?'

The old nun shook her head. 'No,' she replied. 'Come to think of it, I didn't see her last night either.'

Not stopping to explain, Sister Ann ran into the garden, where there was no sign of Edith. Remembering that Sister Mann owned a little car, Matron hurried around to the back of the Home, where cars were usually parked up in the yard. She gasped when she saw that Edith's car was also gone.

'She's taken her car,' she muttered incredulously to Sister Mary Paul, who had just joined her, breathless. 'And her room's stripped bare.'

'Sister Mann wouldn't just leave without an explanation; she's not that kind of person,' Sister Mary Paul insisted. 'Maybe she's left a note explaining where she's gone?'

Dashing back indoors, they checked the pigeon-holes for mail but found no letter waiting for them.

Matron shook her head in bewilderment. 'How on earth could she have left without any of us seeing her go?'

Sister Mary Paul looked worried. 'More to the point, why has she left? Was she unhappy? She went about her duties as usual. In fact, I'd say she's been more cheerful than usual recently – I got no sense that she was brooding or unhappy. Maybe she's taken herself off for a bit of a break?' she suggested.

'That's unlikely, Sister – all her possessions are gone, literally everything. But also Edith is so meticulous that I can't imagine she would take a break, as you say, without notifying us first. To me it looks like Edith didn't want to leave anything to chance; it's clear that every detail has been carefully thought out.'

Outraged, Mary Paul exclaimed, 'You mean all along she's been planning on running away, abandoning her post, right behind our backs?'

Evidently upset by Edith's underhand behaviour, Sister Mary Paul stomped off back to her work in the kitchen muttering under her breath, 'I can't understand why anybody in their right mind would just walk out on their job.'

'Not unless she had a good reason,' Matron thought to herself. 'To disappear so effectively must have taken quite a lot of organizing; it didn't just happen on the spur of the moment.'

Sensing that she was wasting her time, Matron nevertheless checked Edith's office, the sluice room and the delivery suite, but it was clear that the bird had flown the coop – Sister Mann seemed to have disappeared into thin air.

Having a very active baby who rolled and kicked most of the night, Ada found lying in bed (especially once the sun was up heralding yet another hot sunny day) far too uncomfortable. As her delivery date drew ever closer, Ada was usually downstairs in the early morning, drinking tea and eating toast before she slipped into her pretty cottage garden. There, in the cool of the morning, accompanied by her chirpy robin friend and swooping swallows, she deadheaded her flowers, swept the path and did a spot of weeding.

On this particular lovely summer morning Ada decided to take the short walk up to Mary Vale to pick up her daily ration of freshly baked loaf and thereby save Sister Mary Paul the journey later on. Walking into the Home the back way, she found Sister Mary Paul with Sister Theresa in the yard.

'Morning,' Ada called out cheerily as she approached her friends. 'Beautiful day,' she added, then stopped short when she saw the stricken expressions on their faces.

'What's happened?' she gasped. 'Is it bad news from the Front?'

Sister Mary Paul crossed herself. 'No, it's not that, thanks be to God.'

'Then what is it?' Ada asked.

Young Sister Theresa quickly explained, 'It appears that Sister Mann has gone missing.'

'She's gone and run away,' Sister Mary Paul blurted out.

Ada did a startled double-take. 'I don't believe it,' she gasped.

'We've been searching for her all morning, everywhere,' Sister Mary Paul added, as she swept an arm out in a wide circle. 'The Home, gardens, station, marsh, everywhere!'

'There's no sign of her anywhere,' Theresa added.

'Her car's gone too,' Mary Paul muttered crossly.

Theresa gave her colleague's dark robe a gentle tug.

'We'd better get back indoors, Sister, we left the dinner cooking,' she reminded her.

Hurrying after the two nuns, Ada asked a string of questions but got no helpful answers to any of them. Over a cup of tea and while peeling a pile of potatoes, Ada murmured, 'Where on earth could she have gone?'

'We know she comes from Leeds,' Sister Mary Paul remembered. 'She barely mentioned her home life, though she did talk a lot about the nursing home where she used to work, she always said it was smarter than Mary Vale,' the old nun added in a slightly offended voice.

'She might have gone home – maybe there was an emergency?' Ada suggested, as she put the heavy pan of potatoes on top of the Aga stove. 'Something might have come up and she dashed off in the middle of the night.'

'If that were the case, how would she have had the time to clear her room like she did?' Sister Theresa enquired. 'I've just been up there – it's stripped bare.'

Wiping her hands dry on a nearby kitchen towel, Ada said decisively, 'I'm going to see if there's anything I can do to help.'

Looking flustered, Mary Paul cried out, 'Glory be to God, child, don't go overdoing things in your condition; you've got a baby due any time now.'

Ada gave her a sweet smile. 'I know, dearest Mary Paul, but popping on to the wards is not going to harm the baby or me one little bit.'

Ada found Matron washing down the delivery room. Coming straight to the point, Ada said, 'I've heard the news – is there anything I can do to help?'

'Yes, please,' Matron answered eagerly. 'If you're sure

you're up to it? I'd be so grateful if you could collect some instruments from the sterilizing cabinet.'

Ada nodded and went straight off to do as asked, returning to find Matron tending to Josie, an eager young girl who had just gone into labour.

'Ada!' she cried in delight. 'I didn't expect you to be here.'

Ada opened her mouth to say she was just doing an errand, but the very opposite came out. 'Got to keep my hand in,' she smiled, as she caught Matron's eye. 'I'll stay here with Josie,' she said firmly. 'I'm sure you're needed elsewhere, Matron?'

Sister Ann returned a grateful smile. 'Are you sure?' At a firm nod from Ada, Matron breathed a sigh of relief. 'Thank you, that would be grand, I'll be back as quickly as I can,' she promised.

'No rush,' Ada said, then turning her attention to young Josie, adding with easy confidence, 'We're fine here.'

Eighteen-year-old Josie was fit and strong, and better still she had absorbed every instruction issued by Ada in her classes. Ada was impressed and delighted with the young woman's ability to focus on her breathing.

'You're doing so well, dear,' Ada said warmly during a brief break in Josie's increasing contractions.

Sweating but nevertheless cheerful, Josie replied, 'I so well remember what you taught us, Ada.' She gave a cheeky wink. 'I hope you'll remember when your turn comes.'

'If I'm anything like as good as you, Josie, I'll be happy.'

When Matron briefly reappeared to check up on Josie's progress, she found both nurse and patient fairly relaxed.

Beckoning to Ada, she whispered to her in the corridor, 'Are you fine with this?'

Ada beamed. 'Of course, don't worry.'

'It's just that another resident might be starting, and Dora's totally tied up in the nursery. What a day for a member of staff to run away,' she exclaimed in sheer frustration.

'We're fine,' Ada assured her. 'Off you go,' she urged.

'Thank you, Ada, you are a wonder.'

'I'm loving it,' Ada confessed. 'Delivering babies is unquestionably the best job in the world!'

Considering that it was her first birth, Josie's labour wasn't too long; by late afternoon she had delivered a beautiful healthy little girl whom she clasped joyously to her breast.

'She's beautiful,' Josie murmured into her daughter's downy soft hair. 'Perfect,' she sighed as tears slid down her cheeks.

'She's gorgeous,' Ada agreed, as she watched the baby's tiny fingers grip her mother's hand.

'I'd like to call her Ruby, like a little jewel, but I'll wait until I get back to the in-laws. They promised they would help me choose a name that Jack would have liked.'

Ada nodded as she recalled Josie's history. The young girl's RAF fiancé had been shot down over the North Sea when she was only a few months pregnant. Ada remembered how Josie had told her that her fiancé's parents had encouraged her to keep the baby.

'It's all they've got of Jack now,' Josie had tearfully explained.

Looking at mother and daughter, Ada was momentarily overwhelmed by emotion.

'I'm quite sure this little bundle will bring happiness and joy to you and all of Jack's family,' she said softly.

Kissing each of her daughter's tiny pearly fingernails in turn, Josie murmured, 'She's a new beginning; thank God we've got her even if we did lose her dad.'

Later, over a quick cup of tea, Matron told Ada that she had notified the police of Edith's inexplicable disappearance.

Ada, relieved, nodded. 'Good,' she said. 'What did you tell them?'

'I told them that she had disappeared, that her car's gone too, but there's no sign of any foul play, none that I can see anyway,' Matron explained. 'They'll be coming here soon, I should think. When I have a minute, I'll write to the nursing home where Edith previously worked; maybe they can contact her family on our behalf; there's no sign of a home address here anywhere . . .' Matron's tired voice trailed away. 'I really hope she's safe and well,' she finished anxiously.

Utterly exhausted herself, Ada struggled to her feet. 'Hopefully there will be a simple explanation,' she said soothingly.

Seeing her friend worn out by her day's work, Matron said, 'Promise me, dear, that you'll go home straight away and get some rest?'

Ada didn't quibble; her back was hurting after stooping for so long over the delivery bed.

'Don't worry,' Ada assured her. 'I'll be very glad to lie down.'

42. Tobruk

Even though she was exhausted, Ada's eyes as ever drifted to her beloved fells, where the afternoon sun picked out dark hollows and sparkling streams like silver rivulets coursing down the mountainside, frothy with cow parsley and bright-green bracken. Leaning on her garden wall, inhaling the heady perfume of sweet peas and summer lilies, Ada heard a cuckoo calling plaintively for a mate. Remembering the old rhyme, Ada murmured softly,

> In April, come he will.
> In May, he sings all day.
> In June, the cuckoo changes his tune.
> In July, he prepares to fly.
> In August, go he must.

Wishing with all her heart that Jamie could be standing there close beside her listening to the bird in the wood, Ada gave a deep sigh as she recalled her husband's last letter home.

'Africa,' she murmured as a shard of fear shot through her body. What was her husband enduring while she was safe at home, wrapped around on all sides by breathtaking beauty and peace? Was he hungry, thirsty, tired, injured? Ada wanted to wrap around him too, hold him tight in her arms and never let him leave her side. Now he was even further away, on another continent fighting for territory that, so far at least, the Germans had a firm grip on.

Knowing she was overtired and would soon become emotional, Ada hurried indoors intent on making a hot cup of tea, but instead, to her delight, there was a letter from Jamie lying on her doormat. Grasping the letter, she hurried outside to read it in the warm sunshine.

Tobruk

My dearest darling girl,

At last I have a little time to write a proper letter instead of scribbling a note off to you. I hope it gets to you soon – post out here seems to take forever.

Life's been hectic since our arrival: at every turn there's some problem or other. The most pressing is water – the few water wells that exist have been salted by the Germans in order to deny water to the enemy. It's enough to make your blood boil! We gather what little water we can from anywhere we can, and dregs of water bottles can be boiled up in a billy can for sterilizing instruments. The work is hard and gruelling in this climate. One day is much like another in the desert, and I'm told that months can go by with no rain at all. Every surface is covered with a thick layer of dust which rises in clouds when disturbed – it's a real menace to keep at bay when you're performing surgery. We all long for a bath, which is completely out of the question, so we make do with a bar of soap and a flannel – you'd be surprised at how little water is needed if you lather your whole body with soap then wash it off with just a flannel.

Another problem with the continuous heat is our major source of food, bully beef, which we eat with hard tack, dry biscuits, comes out of the tin like lumpy stew, but then it's immediately smothered by a fine film of sand, constantly blown by a dusty hot breeze. I try hard not to think of the lovely fresh produce we eat at home, Farmer Arkwright's tangy Lancashire cheese, fresh milk and creamy butter, not to mention Sister Mary Paul's delicious home-baked bread. As if sand-covered stew isn't bad enough, the flies immediately pounce on our grub, and they're so persistent you simply can't wave them away. They're a danger to health too, causing sand fly fever and terrible desert sores. I try my best to keep my patients' wounds clear of flies, but they regularly descend in a swarm causing bad infection and immense irritation.

That's enough of me! How are you? There's hardly an hour goes by when my thoughts don't drift to you and the baby. How is he or she? The thought that very soon you'll give birth to our son or daughter brings tears to my eyes. I love you so much, my sweetheart, not just because you're clever and beautiful, I love your bravery and strength. Thinking of you steadies my racing fearful thoughts, and when I close my eyes, I see your calm smile and I immediately feel better. I beg you to look after yourself, and our baby when it comes, and please, please, keep me informed, get somebody to write or send a telegram. Kiss the baby when it arrives, tell it Daddy will be home soon. Until then, my treasure, take great care of your sweet self.

Your loving husband,
Jamie
xxxxxxxxxx

Sighing happily, Ada went upstairs, where she lay flat on her bed to ease her throbbing back, and, clasping Jamie's letter to her heart, she fell fast asleep. A few hours later, Ada woke up starving hungry. Blearily making her way down the narrow cottage stairs, she switched on the radio to listen to the evening news before setting about making her supper in the kitchen. Stirring beans in a saucepan and toasting bread, Ada's blood ran cold as she listened to the BBC newsreader's voice announcing to the nation that the city of Tobruk in North Africa had fallen to General Rommel on 21 June after a siege of one day, with 19,000 British soldiers taken prisoner.

As the toast caught fire and started to burn, Ada cried out in despair. 'Oh, my God! Not Jamie, please not Jamie.'

Trembling from head to foot, she flopped down on to the nearest chair, where she gasped as she felt a sudden rush of water trickling down her legs.

'No!' she wailed. 'Not now.'

Desperately trying to steady her nerves, Ada forced herself to breathe deeply; as her heart-beat levelled out, the trembling in her body started to subside. Wobbling uncertainly to her feet, Ada made her way across the kitchen to the back door.

'All I have to do is get to Mary Vale,' she told herself. 'It's only up the road – I can do that.'

As the sun was slowly setting, Ada made her unsteady way along the farm track, with the distance from home to Mary Vale suddenly seeming like miles. Hearing Farmer Arkwright's collie dog barking in the yard, she made her way to the farm gate, which she pushed open.

'Anybody home?' she called out.

When cheery Farmer Arkwright came striding out of the barn, Ada almost sobbed with relief.

'I need to get to Mary Vale,' she told him. A stab of

pain in her lower back took her breath away; when it passed, she said feebly, 'The baby might be coming.'

'Don't move!' Farmer Arkwright commanded. 'I'll get the van and take thee there.'

Minutes later he helped Ada into the van's passenger seat, then, clearly terrified that she was going to give birth right there on the spot, he repeated his initial command, 'Don't thee move, lass.'

Driving the rickety old van that smelt of wet dogs and lanoline up the rutted road, he could hear Ada groaning softly under her breath, as she bounced from side to side. When they reached the Home, Farmer Arkwright slammed on the brakes, then raced out of the van to hammer on the stout back door, which was quickly opened by Sister Mary Paul. Jabbing a thumb in the direction of his van, he spluttered, 'Do summat, woman, yon lass is having a babby!'

The delivery room was already occupied by a resident in labour who couldn't be moved.

'Just put me on one of the wards,' Ada insisted as Sister Mary Paul and Matron guided her along the hospital corridor. Aghast, the old nun exclaimed, 'You need a bit of privacy.'

At this point Ada didn't care if she gave birth in the garden – all she wanted was to lie down and work her way through the contractions that had taken a grip of her body.

'We can use the bed in the doctor's office,' Matron suggested. 'It's been freshly made up.'

Before getting into bed, Ada removed her clothes, exchanging them for a hospital nightdress.

'Oh, that's better,' she murmured thankfully, as she stretched out and relaxed on the cool clean sheets. 'I'm so relieved to be here.'

'You're in safe hands,' Sister Mary Paul assured her beloved Ada. 'Matron and I can handle this together.'

Knowing the kind old nun would not be able to endure the gruesome business of childbirth, Ada offered her an excuse to leave.

'You'll be needed in the kitchen, Sister.'

'Theresa's there, holding the fort; somebody has to, after that Sister Mann abandoned her post,' Mary Paul quietly seethed. 'What a day – three babies in a row and not enough midwives to go around.'

When Ada's stomach tightened hard as a drum, she turned to Sister Mary Paul. 'Please, can you time my next contraction? I just want to concentrate on my breathing.'

Mary Paul nodded as she studied her wristwatch. Remembering how well young Josie had done only that morning, Ada was determined to follow her example. Taking in deep breaths, she rolled with the pain, then exhaled as the contraction receded. Knowing there would be hours to go, Ada tried to conserve her energy for the last stages of labour, which she knew better than anybody were physically the most demanding of all. As the evening wore on, Matron took over from Sister Mary Paul, who was dead on her feet from fatigue.

'I'll pop back later with a cup of cocoa,' the old nun promised, as she bent to kiss Ada on the forehead. 'Take care, dearest girl,' she whispered.

Luckily Matron had arranged that Sister Mary Paul would swap places with Sister Theresa.

Delighted to see her old friend, Ada grinned. 'I seem to have had every nun in the Home sitting with me this evening,' she joked.

'There's a queue of us wanting to help – I wouldn't be surprised if the Reverend Mother turned up next,' Theresa replied with a warm smile.

Theresa was splendidly attentive: offering sips of water, stroking Ada's back, cooling her forehead with a damp flannel, even encouraging her to walk about the room if she felt like it. And in between the ever quickening contractions, they talked of old times, when Theresa, formerly a resident, had been in labour herself.

'It seems like another lifetime ago, before I took Holy Orders,' she said.

'It is a lifetime ago, when you think of all the changes you've undergone,' Ada pointed out.

'I don't think I've ever been happier than I am now,' Theresa smiled, then stopped short as Ada's nails bit into her hand.

'They're getting stronger,' Ada gasped, as she panted through the pain.

'I'm going to get help,' Theresa announced.

Five minutes later she returned with Dora, who was reassuringly calm.

'Come on, sweetheart. Let's see how dilated you are.'

Once Dora established that Ada was well dilated, things happened fast and in no time at all Ada was bearing down hard.

'You know the routine, lovie,' Dora said to Ada. 'When you get the urge, tuck your chin under your chest and give the biggest push you can.'

Ada nodded. 'I know, I've seen it done often enough.'

Dora gave a rueful chuckle. 'That's as may be, but you've never experienced it before. Remember, you must stop pushing on my instruction. If I think you're going too fast and you might tear, I'll get you to pant. Okay?'

'Okay,' Ada gasped, as her body heaved and the urge to push consumed her. Grasping Dora's hand, she pushed so hard she thought her ears would pop.

'Good work, nearly there,' cried Dora. 'Rest now while you can – one more like that and you should see your baby born.'

Suddenly excited, Ada gripped Dora's hand once more. 'I can't wait for that moment,' she cried.

'You won't have to wait long, love. Ready?' Dora, the completely unflappable midwifery nurse, enquired.

Ada nodded, then groaned as another spasm took hold, and, gritting her teeth, she once again tucked in her chin and with one final mighty push she delivered her baby into the world. Dora with practised skill deftly caught the child in her hands.

'A little girl,' she cried. 'A gorgeous little girl!'

Ada wept with joy when Dora placed the tiny, pink squirming body in her arms.

'Hello, darling,' she whispered. 'Welcome to the world.'

Through a curtain of tears Ada watched her daughter blink up at the light, then turn to follow the sound of her voice, gazing up at Ada with new-born filmy-blue baby eyes. Ada thought her heart would burst with love.

'I have a daughter, Dora,' she exclaimed through her sobs. 'A lovely daughter.'

'She's that indeed,' Dora agreed, as she cleaned up the

new arrival, then hurried away to make her tired patient some tea. When she returned with a plate of bread and butter and some strong hot tea, Dora found Matron at Ada's bedside.

'Congratulations, dear,' Matron beamed as she examined the baby now snuggled in a cotton sheet. 'How are you feeling?'

Ada held out her arms for her daughter. 'Never happier,' she exclaimed. 'Sore, exhausted, but so happy.'

When she was finally left alone with her daughter, Ada examined her little hands and feet and stroked the silky wispy hair on her head. Then, holding her to the breast, she called her for the first time by the name that she and Jamie had chosen for her.

'Catherine,' she murmured dreamily. 'Catherine,' she repeated in sheer delight. 'I'm your mummy and you have a daddy too, a wonderful, strong, brave, clever daddy who, please God, is alive and well,' she prayed with a full heart. 'And already loves you very much.'

43. Missing Person

The following morning the police arrived to question the staff about Edith's sudden disappearance. Matron took Dora and Sisters Theresa and Mary Paul to one side.

'I don't want Ada brought into this,' she started. 'We all know how loyal and devoted she is to her friends and colleagues, and how much she would want to help, but right now she must focus all her thoughts and energy on her new baby.'

Sister Mary Paul, who was looking hot and flustered, bobbed her head up and down. 'That's right, Matron, she shouldn't be troubled at all.'

Ever practical Dora added, 'Anyway, Ada wasn't even in the Home at the time of Sister Mann's disappearance.'

'So let's answer the police's questions as best we can, shall we?' Matron continued. 'They might well want to talk with some of the residents too.'

Dora shook her head. 'How do we explain away somebody who has disappeared like a cloud of smoke?'

'And *WHY*?' Mary Paul cried. 'Why do such a wicked, selfish thing?'

Not wanting the old nun to rerun her previous irate grievances, Matron swiftly changed the subject.

'Now that we're one member of staff down, we'll have to rework the rota.'

'I don't mind doing overtime,' Dora volunteered.

'I'll work as many hours as the convent allows me to,' Sister Theresa added.

'Maybe we should advertise for a temporary nurse?' Dora suggested.

Generous-hearted Theresa said, 'You never know, Sister Mann might come back.'

The other three woman looked at her sceptically.

'It's not a bad idea to advertise, Dora,' Matron agreed. 'Let's get the police enquiries over with first and think about advertising the post later.'

In the sitting room the residents were of course aware of Sister Mann's absence.

'She's taken her car,' one of them informed the group.

'Funny, nobody heard her driving away,' another commented.

'Maybe she rolled the car down the drive, then jumped in and started it up once she was clear of the House?' another suggested.

'That would take some doing in the middle of the night,' one of the girls pointed out.

'If that's the case, Nurse Mann must have known what she was doing,' somebody else said.

Upstairs in the family room, Rosie and Sybil were also discussing Edith's actions.

'She was frosty towards me to start with,' Rosie remembered. 'And she certainly didn't like my kids, but she softened up over time, in fact, she was quite chirpy before she took off.'

Sybil looked thoughtful. 'Don't you think that's significant?'

'What?' Rosie puzzled.

'That something made her smile more than she previously had,' Sybil suggested.

'Well, I wouldn't say she was running for the hills and jumping for joy – she just wasn't quite as grumpy,' Rosie recalled. 'But she didn't look like she did when she first arrived here; in those days her face was permanently set like concrete.'

'I know – she tried to befriend me,' Sybil said.

'And you, Mrs Snooty Pants, was having none of it,' Rosie teased.

'I couldn't stand her,' Sybil confessed. 'All her affected airs and graces.'

'There were a lot of folks you couldn't stand in them early days,' Rosie ruthlessly reminded her friend.

'I know, I know,' Sybil said, as she threw her arms up in the air in total defeat. 'I was a snobby cow, that's what your cheeky Ronnie used to call me.'

Both women couldn't help but giggle at the memory. After getting her breath back, Rosie continued, 'Do you think I should mention the change I saw in Sister Mann's manner recently to the police when they come?'

'Why not if it's true?' Sybil reasoned. 'I hope the police won't detain us here for too long – don't forget we're leaving for London in a few days.'

Rosie grinned. 'Fingers crossed we can stick to our plan and travel down together,' she replied with a gleam in her eye.

After questioning all of the staff, and some of the residents, Rosie included, the police assured Matron they would do everything they could to help clarify why Edith had fled Mary Vale so suddenly and in seemingly mysterious circumstances.

'Was she unhappy here?' the sergeant in charge asked.

'I wouldn't say she was terribly happy,' Matron answered honestly. 'But she was a good and conscientious midwife.'

'Did she have any arguments with the staff?' he continued.

'Not that I know of – we're always keen to create a harmonious atmosphere in the Home; it makes life easier for the residents too.'

'Did Miss Mann have friends here?'

'She was a woman who kept herself very much to herself,' Matron told the sergeant.

'Family?' he asked.

Matron shook her head in confusion. 'She never mentioned family.'

Moving rhythmically from his toes to his heels, the portly sergeant pondered the problem. 'We don't know where she's gone and she's made sure we don't know where she's hailed from – bit of a coincidence, wouldn't you say?'

'Aye, sir,' his eager companion agreed. 'Too much of a coincidence.'

'You say you have the address of her former place of employment?'

'Yes, a nursing home in Leeds,' Matron answered. 'That at least is authentic,' she assured the sergeant, as she wrote down the address on a slip of paper.

'We could make a few initial enquiries,' the sergeant said, as he pocketed the information which Matron handed to him.

In a burst of fear, Matron asked, 'Do you think any-thing untoward might have happened to Miss Mann?'

'Difficult to say with the little evidence we have to hand,' he admitted. 'Were there any men involved with Miss Mann?'

'Certainly not that I and my staff know of,' Matron answered.

'Well, we'll see what we unearth in our enquiries, Sister,' the sergeant promised. 'And we'll keep you notified of any significant developments.'

In the post-natal ward, Ada, oblivious to the presence of the police, had been falling in love with her sweet-faced daughter. The breast-feeding, which had been initially tricky, was now well established and Ada was beginning to feel strong and healthy again.

'When can I go home?' she asked Dora, who was help-ing her give little Catherine a bath.

'When Matron says so, missis, so don't go pulling rank.'

After Ada had wrapped her daughter's little wet body in a warm towel, she dried her on her lap, then set about making her nappy.

'When I used to make other babies' nappies,' she said with the safety pin gripped firmly between her teeth, 'I was a dab hand, but with this little wriggle-bottom I feel all fingers and thumbs.'

'Settle her down gently and smooth her skin like this,' Dora said, as she traced a line along Catherine's kicking legs. 'Now lift her bottom on to the terry towelling, do the triangular cross-over and secure the pin in the middle.'

'There, done,' Ada exclaimed in delight.

Taking a small white nightdress with fasteners at the

back, Ada slipped it around her daughter, then held her in her arms for yet another cuddle.

'I could do this all day long,' she purred, as she sniffed her daughter's silky-soft tawny-blonde hair.

'And ruin her,' Dora chided. 'I remember my boys, one on each breast, hungry as lions.'

'You must have been exhausted,' Ada cried.

'Oh, I was,' Dora assured her. 'They were both on the bottle at three months, but you never forget those precious days.'

Ada gazed down at sleeping Catherine, with her delicate eyelashes fanned out over her warm pink cheeks; no, she would never forget these perfect, precious days.

After she had returned Catherine to her crib, Ada set about helping Dora dispose of the bath water and wet towels.

'You should be resting,' Dora yet again chided.

'You're short-staffed, remember?'

Dora nodded. 'Matron's promised to advertise Sister Mann's post,' she informed Ada. 'We can't go on like this, that's for sure.'

'That's a relief,' Ada said. 'Edith's really left us in the lurch.'

Recalling her first meeting with Edith Mann, when she had interviewed her some months previously, Ada remembered how Edith had accepted the post with little joy, slightly as if she had no choice and was going to her doom. She had continued in that joyless mode throughout her time at Mary Vale, doing her duty, proving to be a good nurse but always cold and remote.

As if reading her thoughts, Dora murmured, 'She was a cold fish, though some of the residents noticed a bit of a change in her just before she left here, not that I noticed it myself.'

Replacing the little baby bath on the shelf where it was stored in the sluice room, Ada wondered out loud, 'Edith always was a bit of a mystery – she never seemed to settle here.'

Mopping down the floor with hot water and disinfectant, Dora gave a curt nod. 'God knows where she's flit to.'

Ada gave a heartfelt sigh. 'Wherever she is I hope she's happy.'

44. Whitehall

Before they set off for London, Rosie and Sybil made sure they had discussed and agreed what they'd share of their plans with Matron. Though there was a bit of delicate fudging in what they said, there was also an element of truth.

'I'm going to London to take a maths examination; if I pass it, there's a good chance that I'll be accepted on to a radar-training course,' Sybil started.

Looking cautious, Matron asked, 'Are you strong enough to tackle the journey?'

Sybil smiled. 'Believe me, after the last train journey I endured, with Ronnie and Sally, this one with Rosie should be very straightforward.'

Wanting to be clear about Sybil's plans, Matron asked another question. 'And will you come back here?'

'Yes, I'll return with Rosie,' Sybil replied. 'I plan to leave Mary Vale once my son's adoption is completed.'

Matron nodded, then turned her attention to Rosie. 'And what are your plans, Rosie?'

Rosie explained her situation. 'I left a forwarding address with a couple of neighbours when I moved up here, but, after hearing Sybil's description of Finsbury Park, I'm wondering if there's anybody left there who would even know me and Mick. And,' Rosie pointedly added, 'after the heartache my kiddies put themselves through, I want to make absolutely sure, now that I'm back on my feet, that the authorities in charge of evacuees know exactly where we are, just in case Mick should ever try to get in touch with us.'

'Very well. I wish you both a safe journey,' Matron concluded. 'Take care of each other, and bear in mind that you have both only recently given birth, so don't go overdoing things.'

On the packed train to the South, Sybil and Rosie realized they were both a little nervous. In terms of drawing up a clear plan of action, Rosie was by far the more organized of the two. As the filthy old steam train rumbled through the Midlands, razed to the ground by years of enemy bombing attacks, Rosie laid out her strategy.

'I'll go to Dowry House and make enquiries – don't forget, I still know quite a few people who work there,' she told Sybil. 'Hopefully Lord Stow might be in residence, but if he's at Stowupland I'll just have to sit it out. I'll tell the butler that I have some urgent news for his lordship and arrange with him that, when his lordship returns, he will allow me to speak to him.'

Sybil gave an impatient shrug. 'All that's fine, Rosie, but what if our story doesn't come over as strong enough? What if Lord Stow decides we're hysterical, vindictive women?'

Rosie looked at her friend in amazement. 'Well, I'll be blowed!' she gasped. 'You're the one that got the ball rolling, picking my brains on the Brigadier, telling me how much you wanted to get back at him. Now you sound like you're losing your bottle.'

Sybil flushed indignantly. 'I'm not bottling out, as you

say,' she responded hotly. 'I just want to be sure that we have a good case to present to his lordship.'

Chewing her lower lip, Rosie gazed thoughtfully out of the window, which was splattered with blobs of black greasy rain.

'It's like we discussed before,' she eventually said. 'He'll be angry, so we keep it short and sweet – I tell his lordship how I've got it on good authority that the Brigadier has threatened to blackmail Lady Veronica.'

Sybil quickly chipped in, 'And how he misuses the family money Lord Stow entrusted to him.'

Rosie gave a quick nod. 'Then you come in with your side of things.'

'Right,' Sybil agreed. 'Let's just hope it works.

Later that evening, when they arrived at Euston Station, the two women went their separate ways: Rosie to find a B & B in Finsbury Park and Sybil to a hotel in Whitehall close to the War Office.

'We need to work out where we can next meet up,' Sybil said, as they disembarked from the train that was belching huge puffs of thick black smoke from its sooty engine. 'How about lunch in Lyons' Corner House in Oxford Circus, on Friday? I'll have done my exam by then and hopefully you'll have seen Lord Stow.'

Rosie nodded in agreement; then, after giving each other a quick hug, they parted company, each on her own individual mission.

The next morning, after a meagre breakfast of vile-tasting white margarine and stale bread, the likes of which made

Sybil appreciate the butter and freshly baked bread that was served as often as possible at Mary Vale, she collected up her maths textbooks and set off for the nearest library, where she planned to spend the rest of the day swotting up in readiness for her vital maths exam the following morning. As she hurried down the road beside Downing Street, she sidestepped the sandbagged machine-gun emplacement there, well guarded by armed soldiers wearing tin hats. Loops of barbed wire surrounding government buildings were everywhere, again protected by soldiers on guard, all holding loaded rifles. In her former working days Sybil would have taken all of this in her stride, but after months in the countryside, with the fells and the sea providing her only views, she was surprised at how suddenly jumpy she was.

'Heavens, after all the complaining you've done about Mary Vale,' she mocked herself, 'don't turn into a country bumpkin and start moping for green fields and pretty flowers.'

Cautiously making her way through all the military paraphernalia, Sybil was hardly aware of who she was passing until a voice rang out: 'Sybil Harwood!'

Stopping in her tracks, Sybil turned to see an old chum from the War Office hurrying towards her.

'Alice!' she exclaimed.

'Darling, how are you?' Alice cried, as she wrapped her arms around Sybil and gave her a hug. 'Please tell me you're back?' she asked eagerly.

'No, not really,' Sybil quickly answered. 'In fact, I'm just on my way to the library around the corner – I've got a bit of revising to do.'

Linking her arm through Sybil's, Alice pulled her in the opposite direction.

'Blow the library, let's catch up over a pot of tea — darling, I have so much to tell you!'

After they had placed their order in the steamy café, Alice launched off about the change of staff, their increased hours and her new boyfriend; then, dropping her voice, she poured out the most recent gossip on Brigadier Baldwin.

'Sybil, forgive me, I know you had a thing going with the Brig,' she said confidentially.

'Don't worry, Alice, that part of my life is well in the past; believe me, I haven't seen the man in months,' Sybil replied in all truth.

Alice looked visibly relieved. 'That's excellent,' she blurted out. 'The bounder wasted no time once you had gone.' She suddenly stopped and cocked her head. 'Where exactly did you go, dear?'

Unblinking and lying through her teeth, Sybil smiled. 'I was posted to a military base up in the North.'

Alice gave a quick nod and continued. 'As I was saying, he didn't beat about the bush: promoted his new secretary and in no time at all he was seen all over town with her.'

'Just like me,' Sybil thought to herself. 'Another foolish girl to add to the list.'

Alice lit a cigarette, which she exhaled before adding, 'This one got pregnant and made no secret about who the father was. I can't imagine the Brig's family didn't get wind of it — just about everybody knew. The blighter simply couldn't get the girl out of the building fast enough,' Alice giggled. 'Sent her off to some smart nursing home in

Hove, where, I assume, she's still lingering, awaiting the birth of his illegitimate child.' Alice gave a melodramatic shiver. 'The man's a beast. All of us girls stay well clear of him.'

Sybil smothered a smile. If Monty carried on in this manner, he would very quickly dig his own grave; all that she and Rosie had to do was to add a few finishing touches.

'I'm rather relieved you're not coming back; he'd be on your case in no time,' Alice warned.

'I've no intention of returning to the War Office,' Sybil told her firmly. 'If I pass this maths examination, I'm going to apply to train as a radar operator.'

Alice's eyes all but rolled out of her head. 'RADAR? You'll be posted to the middle of nowhere!' she shrieked.

'That's the general idea,' Sybil smiled.

Rising to go, Alice stubbed out her cigarette. 'Good luck, darling. I'd die if I weren't within spitting distance of Knightsbridge.'

Sybil surprised herself when she spoke the next words. 'I have to admit I've got rather fond of the country.'

45. On a Mission

Though Rosie's memories of leaving Gladstone Gardens were pretty grim, the reality she walked into early the next morning was horrific. Ronnie and Sally had told her in graphic detail of the bomb-site that was their former home, but seeing the decimation first hand took Rosie's breath away. Dodging precarious sagging gable ends that threatened to spew their contents on to the street, she stepped over leaking pipes and smashed concrete slabs as she made her way to the few landmarks that remained upright. The corner shop (which had provided them with 'the tick' for months) was long gone, replaced by a bustling WVS food van. Luckily Mick's favourite pub on a busy street corner was still in business. Not used to entering a pub on her own, Rosie blushed as she stepped inside, but the old men spinning out their pints while playing cards barely noticed her. The landlord certainly didn't recognize her, but he did recall Mick's name when Rosie mentioned it.

Cleaning a pint glass mug with a grimy cloth, he said, 'Yeah, he was a weekend regular.' Suddenly he stopped cleaning to ask sharply, 'Hold on a minute – what did you say your name was?'

'Rosie Pickles, of Gladstone Gardens.'

'I think I might have something for you, wait a minute.'

With her heart pounding in her chest, Rosie stood tensely at the bar waiting for the landlord to return; when he did, he waved a tattered envelope with her name scribbled on the front.

'Somebody left this for you.'

'Mick?' she cried hopefully.

'No, I think I would have recognized him – some fella I've never met, said he was a pal of Mick's.'

With trembling hands Rosie took the envelope. 'When was it delivered?'

'Let's see,' the man considered. 'Maybe two or three months back.'

Quickly thanking him, Rosie hurried out into the street, where she tore the grubby envelope open.

Dear Mrs Pickles,

Your husband and I were good pals. We joined up at the same time and fought together on the Front Line. I'm very sorry to have to tell you that as we retreated under enemy fire I realized that Mick had gone from where I saw him fall, and from where, I'd assumed, he'd lost his life. Unfortunately, shortly after this discovery I had the misfortune to step on a landmine, which killed many of our men and took half my leg off. You will understand that with my injuries I was in no position to search for Mick – all I can say is I sincerely hope he might have managed to crawl away from the crossfire. I'm now a registered invalid and discharged from active service, but I often wonder what happened to my pal Mick and worry that I could have done more for him. I hope he did make it back home and that he is safe and well.

Causing passers-by to stare at her, Rosie exclaimed, 'NO! He didn't come home.' Quickly turning back to the letter, she read on,

Anyway, as I say, the experience has troubled me to such an extent that I felt obliged to make contact with Mick's family, but when I visited his former home (address courtesy of our regimental records) there was nothing left standing. I entrusted this letter to the landlord of the local pub in the hope that one day you, Mick's wife, might read it and make your own enquiries.

Yours,
Arthur Timbs

Rosie slumped against the wall. 'Is he alive or dead?' she wailed.

Trying to pull her thoughts together, Rosie took some deeps breaths; if her husband was confirmed dead, his regiment would have said so; as it was, they had only informed her that Mick was 'Missing in Action'. Now she had to take on board another possibility in this painful story: that Mick had managed to crawl away from a battle scene.

'Missing says it all,' she thought wretchedly. 'He could have been captured, he could be wasting away in a POW camp in Germany, he could be in hiding . . . or he could be dead?' Remembering that she would soon be meeting up with her friend, Rosie rallied.

'Sybil will know what to do,' she muttered, as she slipped the letter into her handbag. 'She's the cleverest person I've ever met,' she thought with a bolt of pride.

'Surely Sybil will have some ideas about how I can set about finding out what really did happen to my poor husband.'

After her extremely challenging maths exam in one of the government offices, Sybil dropped by to say farewell to her former manager, a middle-aged woman (whom she respected) with iron-grey hair and a grim set to her mouth.

'We shall miss you, Miss Harwood.'

'I'm ready for a change, something new and a little more demanding,' Sybil replied brightly.

The manager's bony shoulders bristled. 'Radar-station locations are a far cry from Whitehall,' she informed Sybil, who gave a tight but polite smile.

'I'm aware of that: by definition they're required to be isolated and close to the sea.'

'You might find the work gruelling; it was predominantly a man's world,' the manager told her.

'Women can do mathematics as well as men, and who else is there left to do the work but women?' Sybil asked realistically.

'Fair point,' the manager sniffed.

'Anyway, it's the work I'm keen on, vital war work which I hope I shall be suited to.'

'I'm sure it will suit you very well indeed, if you can bear the isolation.'

'I'm rather good at that these days,' Sybil replied; then, smiling to herself, she thought, 'After months in Mary Vale I've become well acquainted with isolation.'

*

As Sybil talked of her future, Rosie was knocking nervously on the Dowry House's kitchen door, which was opened by a scullery maid whom Rosie had already acquainted herself with.

'This way, he's waiting for you,' the little maid whispered, as she whisked Rosie through the servants' hall to the butler's pantry, where Rosie immediately thanked the butler for arranging her meeting with Lord Stow, who had only just returned from Stowupland.

'I mentioned you would be briefly dropping in,' the butler informed Rosie.

'What did he say?' she enquired.

'He registered his surprise after so many years.'

'But he didn't mind?' Rosie asked anxiously.

The butler shrugged. 'Just make sure you don't overstay your welcome,' he advised, before leading Rosie into the drawing room.

Taking a deep breath, Rosie dipped a curtsey to her former employer, then, after a few curt pleasantries from his lordship, she waded in.

'Sir, there's something that has been on my mind since I left your employment.' Realizing she was trembling with nerves, she took a deep breath before continuing. 'It concerns the well-being of my former mistress, Lady Veronica.'

His lordship's thick grey eyebrows shot up, though his voice remained calm. 'Indeed.'

'Forgive my impertinence, sir . . .' Suddenly overwhelmed by what she was about to say, Rosie just blurted it out. 'Are you aware of how badly Brigadier Baldwin treats your daughter?'

A hard, disapproving look shot across Lord Stow's face. 'Have you come here to blackmail me?'

Flushing, Rosie exclaimed, 'I would never do such a wicked thing, sir!'

'Then what is your purpose?'

Clearing her throat, Rosie tried to explain. 'I've always felt guilty that I didn't do or say more at the time of my employment – I thought it was none of my business.'

'Quite so, it *is* none of your business what goes on in this house – you were paid to do your job – that's all,' he retorted crossly.

'I agree, sir, which is why I held my tongue for so long, but, as I just said, guilt finally got the better of me. I love Lady Veronica – she is the kindest person I have ever met and I feel impelled to speak the truth.'

Stiffening in distaste at what she had said, Lord Stow snapped, 'Why trouble yourself now, years after your employment here ended?'

'Because I have proof, new proof, that the Brigadier's behaviour is getting worse.' Seeing his lordship's expression, Rosie pushed on before he called for the butler to kick her out. 'My family and I were recently evacuated to the North to a Mother and Baby Home, where I met a young woman who worked with the Brigadier in the War Office. She fell pregnant with his child, and he exiled her to the Home, where she recently gave birth to the Brigadier's son. After we got to know each other, we realized we had both had very different experiences of the Brigadier – neither of them good.'

Lord Stow gave a slow cynical smile. 'Ah, I see, it's a case of two outraged women seeking vengeance.'

Rosie shook her head. 'I have only one motive, sir.'

Sweeping his eyes over her shabby clothes and broken shoes, Lord Stow looked deeply unimpressed. Knowing she was fast losing the argument, Rosie starkly stated, 'The Brigadier blackmails her ladyship and misuses family money.'

The look of contempt that had been on Lord Stow's face throughout most of their conversation suddenly changed to shock.

'You should be aware what you are accusing my son-in-law of, young lady – slander could land you inside a court room.'

At the point of no return, Rosie pushed on. 'The Brigadier's not entirely discreet – even you must have heard the gossip.' Ignoring Lord Stow's thunderous expression, Rosie said, 'The truth is, when your daughter threatens to leave the Brigadier, he says he'll publicly announce who Marigold's real father is – he uses blackmail to keep his wife's mouth shut.'

Lord Stow rose from his chair and strode moodily about the room.

'I ask again – why did you never speak to her ladyship yourself?' he demanded.

'As I said, I thought it was not my place, sir.'

'Yet you come here and bother me now?' he repeated himself.

'As I just mentioned, sir, it is only because I recently met one of the Brigadier's ex-mistresses when I was evacuated. It was her story that convinced me that the Brigadier's conduct is worse than it ever was and consequently Lady Veronica must be suffering even more than when I was working as her maid.'

'Who is this friend of yours?'

'A Miss Sybil Harwood, sir.'

'The woman who worked at the War Office with Monty?'

'Yes, sir. She's briefly in London. Would you care to meet her?'

Lord Stow didn't answer yes or no, he simply said, 'Arrange it with the butler.'

At their pre-arranged Friday meeting in the Lyons' Corner House in Oxford Circus, Rosie ran through her terrifying conversation with Lord Stow.

'He thought I was after his money,' she said hotly. 'Asked why it had taken me so long to report the matter.'

Looking up from her plate of baked beans on toast, Sybil smiled. 'Fair point.'

'I said if I hadn't met you, I would have left the whole business in the past, but knowing he was still carrying on with other women made me feel sorrier than ever for Lady Veronica.'

Sybil rolled her big green eyes that had regained their bright sparkle. 'I bumped into an old chum in Whitehall, who told me about yet another silly young woman whom Monty banished after getting her pregnant. God, poor Veronica, tolerating a man like that – I'd have put a bullet between his eyes years ago.'

'You wouldn't if you'd got a little girl to protect,' Rosie said knowingly.

Sybil shrugged. 'Being a woman who seemingly hasn't a maternal bone in her body, I might have considered it,' she replied.

Knowing how detached Sybil had been throughout the

adoption process of her son, Rosie didn't argue about her friend's maternal instincts.

'Anyway, he wants to see you,' Rosie said excitedly. 'This afternoon, before he returns to Stowupland.'

Sybil smiled as she stirred her tea. 'You did well, Rosie.'

Her friend gave her a hard look. 'And so must you, Sybil.'

Before they left the crowded café with its steamy windows, Rosie showed Sybil the letter which she had recently been given by the landlord of the Finsbury Park public house.

'It's about my husband,' she explained as she handed it over. 'I just don't know what to do for the best,' she admitted with tears in her sad dark eyes. Waiting tensely until Sybil had read the letter, Rosie gulped hard as she swallowed her tears. 'Honestly, what chance have I got of finding anything out?'

'You must have made enquiries with Mick's regiment,' Sybil asked.

'Yes, of course I did,' Rosie replied. 'They just kept telling me he's missing in action, but they didn't see him on the ground like his pal who wrote me the letter did: one minute he's there, the next minute' – she snapped her fingers – 'gone, God only knows where.'

'It really is extraordinary,' Sybil agreed, as she gazed at the letter once more. 'It's like he disappeared into thin air.'

Rosie whispered fearfully, 'You hear terrible stories about wounded men who lose their memory – wandering around with no idea where they are, or who they are.'

'Amnesia,' Sybil replied. 'From what I've heard it's not unusual. In which case your Mick might possibly still be alive.'

Seeing Rosie's tired eyes light up with hope, Sybil quickly added, 'But God knows how you trace a missing soldier who has lost his memory. If that's even what happened.'

'To be fair, Mick's regiment may have written to me with more information at my former address in Finsbury Park, but, as you know, that's been razed to the ground. I did notify them that we were being evacuated to the North and left a forwarding address, but there's a chance that any information might have slipped through the cracks,' she finished miserably. 'It makes me feel useless and stupid that I don't even know whether my husband's alive or dead.'

'My dear Rosie,' Sybil said, as she gripped Rosie's trembling hand. 'You must be one of many women who is completely in the dark about their loved one. It's an appalling situation.' Looking thoughtful, Sybil added, 'I have a few friends high up in the War Office, and I don't mean Monty,' she added pointedly. 'I'll make some discreet enquiries on your behalf, but I'll need your husband's full name, date of birth, rank and regiment.'

'I can provide all of those,' Rosie said eagerly.

When it came to meeting Lord Stow, the two women couldn't have presented more contrasting images. Rosie, poorly dressed, nervously fiddling with her cheap handbag, and Sybil, almost back to her pre-baby figure, impeccably dressed in a well-cut military-style black barathea jacket and skirt, with a smart hat set at a jaunty angle on top of her glossy black hair, which was carefully pleated into a popular victory roll. Rosie smiled to herself as she took in Lord Stow's expression when he was introduced to glamorous Sybil, with her posh accent and fine manners. Rosie hadn't been asked to sit down when she had come to pay him a visit on her own, but this time, with Sybil at her side, they were both ushered to a comfortable sofa in a wide bay window which looked over the splendid gardens bathed in bright summer sunlight. Sitting with her trim ankles neatly crossed, Sybil came straight to the point.

'I believe Rosie has talked to you about Brigadier Baldwin?'

Lord Stow said nothing but gave an abrupt nod.

'I worked for Monty for almost a year at the War Office, where he courted me, flattered me and finally seduced me,' she said, without as much as a blush or a hesitation. Sybil simply recited the cold facts. 'He had a reputation for womanizing; I just happened to be one in a long line of many.'

'Did you know he was married?' Lord Stow asked.

Sybil nodded. 'He made no secret of his marriage to Lady Veronica – quite the opposite. He seemed immensely proud to be her husband; the relationship clearly enhanced his own swollen ego.'

'So even though he was a married man you allowed the situation to continue?' Lord Stow cut in.

Sybil raised a perfectly arched dark eyebrow as if to say, you are a man of the world, before she continued in her clipped, elegant voice. 'Yes. We became lovers and I got pregnant.'

Blushing Rosie, who could never have spoken to his lordship in such a cold, matter-of-fact manner, stared shame-faced at her own trembling hands.

'Monty said he would take care of things, which was the only gentlemanly thing he could do in the circumstances. I imagined he would send me to some genteel nursing home near to my family and friends; instead he sent me to the opposite end of the country, to a Mother and Baby Home run by nuns. In effect Monty got me out of the way, exiled me there so that nobody would know of my condition, especially *your daughter*,' she added pointedly.

Seeing Lord Stow moving uneasily in his chair, Sybil concluded, 'Your son-in-law is an unscrupulous cad, sir. I know nothing personally of his relationship with your daughter, but I have heard from Rosie of the further wrongs he committed. We're coming from two very different perspectives: Rosie was your servant, I was Monty's lover, but both of us have exactly the same opinion of him.'

'I'm surprised that a woman like you, a woman clearly of the world, should suddenly have scruples,' Lord Stow scoffed. 'Why involve yourself now?'

'I'm involving myself, as you put it, because I want to punish Monty for what he did to me. I paid the price for being a little fool. Rosie may have other, kinder motives: her devotion to Lady Veronica and Miss Marigold. Believe me, my motives are not quite so charitable.'

Seeing Lord Stow visibly slumping in his chair, Sybil said quietly, 'Sir, your daughter's reputation goes before her; she is obviously a proud and loyal woman who would never let her family down.'

'Never!' he exclaimed.

'I have not witnessed what Rosie has described to you, but you cannot doubt her testimony; she comes here only to help the mistress she is still devoted to – surely that is significant in itself?'

Stow turned his brooding sad eyes on Rosie. 'You say the Brigadier uses Marigold to blackmail my daughter?'

'Yes, sir.'

'What do you know of Marigold's parentage?'

Rosie hardly dared to breathe as she answered. 'I know the truth, but I have told no one apart from Sybil here.'

'Would you swear on the Bible that all you have revealed to me is God's honest truth?'

'Yes, sir, I would swear on my children's lives that I am speaking the truth.'

'And you, young lady,' he continued as he turned to Sybil, 'you who did my daughter a great disservice, would you swear in a court of law that what you've told me is the truth?'

'Certainly, sir.'

'I shall have to speak with Lady Veronica,' Lord Stow said, as he rose and stood to attention. 'I would prefer it if neither of you visited the house again unless otherwise invited.'

Before they left the room, Sybil turned to Lord Stow. 'Sir, may I suggest that you urge the Brigadier, as an act of goodwill to the Mary Vale community where Rosie and I lived, to continue to do all he can to keep the Army from requisitioning the Home which he himself said was "vital" to the women who seek succour there?'

Stunned by Sybil's off-script comments, Rosie studiously avoided eye contact with her bold friend, who confidently cruised on. 'It would be a great loss to close down an institution the Brigadier has fought so valiantly to keep open,' she added with a cynical raise of an eyebrow.

*

Once outside and at a safe distance from Dowry House, both women felt weak at the knees.

'I couldn't believe my ears at what you just said,' Rosie squeaked.

'Shhh! There's a park just opposite,' Sybil gasped. 'Let's go and sit down before I collapse.'

Finding a café in the park, they both immediately ordered tea. 'I could do with a brandy and soda right now,' Sybil admitted.

Pouring out the hot strong tea, Rosie spluttered, 'Oh, my God, there was one point in there when I thought I'd faint clean away. You talking to his lordship like that, telling him all the mucky truth,' she exclaimed.

'It wouldn't have worked otherwise: he needed to know the hard facts, even if I did come across as a whore.'

'You were so brave, Sybs,' Rosie cried. 'I was so proud to be sitting there as your friend, and when you told his lordship that I was there only because of how fond I am of Lady Veronica, I all but burst into tears!'

'I wanted to stress that you weren't there for anything other than your loyalty and concern. Stow's kind of people always think ex-servants are out to make a quick buck.'

Rosie nearly choked on her tea. 'I would *NEVER* do that!'

'I know that, darling, but he needed to be told,' Sybil answered firmly.

'And then,' Rosie spluttered on, 'right out of the blue, you telling Lord Stow how good it would be if the Brigadier continues to fight the good fight to keep Mary Vale open – oh, my God, I thought I'd have hysterics!'

Sybil giggled in sheer delight.

'I just couldn't stop myself,' she exclaimed. 'The idea of dumping Monty on Mary Vale was irresistible. He might not give a damn about the place, but he could be saddled with the task of at least looking like he's trying to keep the place open,' she crowed.

Looking pulverized, Rosie slumped back against the wooden chair she was sitting on. On a quieter note she mused, 'I wonder how his talk with Lady Veronica will go. She'll be difficult. She's a proud woman.'

'Maybe,' Sybil agreed. 'But she might be getting sick and tired of Monty – as I've often said, I would have shot him by now.'

'She was sick of him when I was there before the war started,' Rosie recalled.

'Then let's hope that she's so worn down by Monty's infidelity she's prepared to finally tell the truth about their marriage.'

Round-eyed Rosie stared at Sybil. 'Do you think we really influenced Lord Stow?'

Sybil laughed. 'Well, he didn't kick us out! It's all down to Lady Veronica now,' she added thoughtfully. 'It's up to her to make the next move.'

46. Motherhood

Ada stayed on the post-natal ward with her baby daughter for a week before she was declared fit enough to go home. Sister Mary Paul would have kept her in for a month if she had had her way. Having fallen in love with sweet little Catherine, the old devoted nun wanted her favourite girl and her favourite baby to stay close by, so she could fuss over the pair of them from dawn till dusk. The new arrival, with her sweet rose-bud lips and curious blinking baby eyes, had completely captivated Sister Mary Paul, who loved both mother and daughter to distraction.

Forever popping into the ward to check on Ada, she would make some excuse about needing to see Dora, which was her way of getting into the nursery to kiss and cuddle Ada's baby, until Dora firmly removed her.

'Isn't she the most beautiful child you have ever seen in your life?' the nun raved. 'You can already see how intelligent she's going to be – those bright little eyes following you around the room.'

Dora sweetly indulged Sister Mary Paul, and, if the truth were told, she was pretty besotted by Ada's lovely daughter too. As was Matron. It wasn't uncommon to find the three of them cooing over Catherine, who thrived on their praise and attention. When Ada walked into the nursery one day, she surprised all three women, who were peering adoringly into her daughter's cot. When they saw Ada's teasing smile, they quickly made a feeble excuse.

'She's due for a change,' Dora announced.

'She seems to be thriving,' Matron said in professional mode.

'She's a beauty, a little angel!' Sister Mary Paul gushed.

Sitting on one of the feeding chairs, Ada opened up her nightdress so that Dora could place Catherine on her breast.

'You spoil her,' she said fondly.

'Rubbish! We're her guardian angels,' Sister Mary Paul protested.

Before Ada left the Home, she had a quiet word with her friend, Matron.

'You're going to be under-staffed if you don't get some temporary help,' she fretted.

'We've been that way since Edith disappeared into the night,' Matron answered crossly. 'Not a word from her, nobody knows where she's gone, not even the police, though they have managed to track down the family home in Morley.'

'Really? That could be useful,' Ada said eagerly.

'It wasn't – that's what the police officer told me. Mrs Mann – Edith's mother – is a drunk; they couldn't get a word of sense out of her. Apparently, she just shouted and swore at them for not finding her daughter, who, she said, had left her penniless and destitute.'

'Heavens, that's quite shocking,' Ada exclaimed.

'Even the police officer said he would have run away and left no forwarding address if he lived with a tyrant like Edith's mother.'

'I suppose it explains something,' Ada considered. 'Why she never talked of home or family.'

'The police also discovered that Edith was sending money home every week, but it's stopped since her disappearance. From the amount they quoted, it sounded like she sent her mother most of her pay packet.'

'She must have left herself short,' Ada reasoned. 'Why would she do that?'

Matron shrugged. 'Who knows what power the mother had over her?'

Ada looked thoughtful. 'Ann, have you considered that Edith might have been paying her mother to stay out of her life?'

'Maybe, it's definitely a possibility,' Matron answered, then appeared deep in thought. 'The police sergeant told me that it wasn't uncommon these days for women from strict families to suddenly run away from home in order to join up.'

'Run away in order to serve their country,' Ada murmured.

Matron nodded. 'The sergeant said that in his experience they nearly always re-establish contact once they've been conscripted, when it's too late for the family to do anything about it.'

'Is that what they think Edith might have done?' Ada asked.

Matron shrugged. 'Who knows? He said that these days it's a common occurrence.'

Bringing the conversation back to where it had originally started, Matron informed Ada that they would make finding temporary nursing help a priority.

'Actually,' she started awkwardly, 'in time, we were hoping that . . .' Blushing, she left the sentence hanging.

'That I'd carry on where I left off,' Ada teased.

Matron nodded before quickly saying, 'When the time is right, of course.'

'You know I'd love to come back,' Ada smiled. 'I've always said that was what I wanted to do.'

'No pressure, dear,' Matron insisted. 'You and the baby come first.'

'I know that,' Ada earnestly agreed.

Matron beamed. 'So, for the time being, we'll settle for a supply nurse, then,' she said happily.

'But you must promise to get somebody as soon as possible,' Ada urged. 'I don't want my nearest and dearest wearing themselves out.'

'Promise,' Matron replied, before she flung her arms around Ada. 'Dearest girl, it will be lovely to have you back among us once more – we've missed you so much.'

Sister Theresa walked Ada back to her cottage.

'I'm fine,' Ada insisted, as she pushed sleeping Catherine in the pram that she had borrowed from the Home.

'We can see that,' Theresa giggled. 'But, as you know, we always see our patients off the premises.'

Remembering the many times she had accompanied patients to a waiting car or to Kents Bank Station, Ada nodded in agreement with Theresa.

'Thank you, for a minute there I had forgotten the protocol.'

Peering into the pram at the peaceful baby, Theresa

said, 'She's got your mouth and nose; she'll be a beauty like her mother.'

Using Theresa's old name, the one that was hers before she became a nun, Ada exclaimed, 'Oh, Shirley, I'm just so very happy – if my darling were here with me, my life would be perfect.' She stopped short as guilt swept over her. 'Life can't be perfect when there's a world war raging, can it?' she muttered miserably.

'Darling, you must seize every moment of joy that there is to be found in these dark days,' Theresa cried. 'A new baby, a new life, is something to rejoice about, war or not. And look at her, so sweet and innocent, she's a wonder to behold.'

After Theresa had safely deposited her patient back home, Ada felt a rush of deep emotion. Imagining that her beloved Jamie was beside her, she murmured, 'This is your home, sweetheart, this is where you'll live with your mummy and your daddy.'

Ada's heart gave a skip as she said the word 'Daddy' out loud. Would Catherine, born on the same day the city where her father was fighting fell to the enemy, ever meet Jamie? Suddenly afraid, tearful Ada held her baby tighter. Jamie would come back – her entire life, and her daughter's too, would be halved, devastated and destroyed, without his vibrant, loving presence. A little wail from her daughter clutched in her arms brought Ada's attention swiftly back to the here and now.

'Are you hungry, darling?' she murmured.

Sitting under the old gnarled apple tree, Ada fed the baby until she dozed off, warm, full and contented. Rising slowly so as not to disturb the sleeping infant, Ada laid Catherine in the pram, then, gently bouncing the pram, she sat with the sun on her face until she fell asleep too. When she woke up, ravenously hungry, she was grateful for the basket of food Sister Mary Paul had packed for her: a warm pasty, a slice of fresh bread, even a handful of strawberries fresh from the garden allotment. These, combined with Farmer Arkwright's delivery of milk, an egg and a tiny pat of butter, were all she needed for a good few days.

When Catherine woke up, Ada popped her in her pram and set off down the lane for a walk. After introducing Catherine to the frisking lambs and bleating sheep in the nearby fields, she walked along the path that edged Cartmel Forest. Stopping to listen to a red-and-white greater spotted woodpecker's tapping on tree bark competing with a green woodpecker's incessant cackling call from deep within the forest, Ada's thoughts, as always on her walks, flew to Jamie.

'I have to stay strong,' she said out loud. 'I mustn't give in to fear,' she announced to a robin redbreast who was singing his heart out in a nearby blackberry bush.

Being a mother, albeit a new one, further strengthened Ada's resolve to stay firm and focused. Catherine needed her now, and Jamie more than ever before. She was glad she had her job to look forward to. She would have less time to mope and worry when she was back in the hustle and bustle of hospital life – not that that ever stopped her worrying about her beloved, but when she was on duty the needs of others completely engulfed her own and she felt like she was doing her bit for the war effort.

As she turned the pram around and set off for home, Ada's eyes came to rest on the distant fells, now hazy gold in the summer heat. Standing still for a moment, she imagined the numerous sheep paths zigzagging up the hillsides dotted with ancient cairns, guiding fell-walkers safely on their way. Tracks would give way to crags and hollows, deep and cool even in the summer sun; she could see in her mind's eye banks of gorse, heather and bracken, falling steeply to roaring waterfalls and black slate gorges brimming with pure spring water. She remembered one such spot, Black Moor Pot, where she and Jamie after a strenuous walk over the Borrowdale Fells had stripped off and jumped into the deep rocky pool, whose icy-cold waters had stung their white bodies. Shivering and giggling, they had clambered out and flopped naked on to the grass, where the scorching sun had baked them dry. Memories of their happiness flooded back to Ada in a sweet rush which she hugged to herself. These precious moments she had shared with Jamie formed their past, precious memories of their love that she would cherish forever and that she would take to the grave.

47. Triumph

Back at the Home, the event Sybil had been longing for over so many months – walking out of Mary Vale without a backward glance – was now looming large. It was also proving to be an increasingly painful one because of Sally and Ronnie, whom Sybil loved more with every passing day.

One fine summer morning she was horrified to find Rosie sitting on a bench in the garden sobbing her heart out. Hurrying to sit down beside her distraught friend, Sybil exclaimed, 'Darling! What on earth has happened? Have you had more news?'

Rosie gulped. 'No, it's not that . . .' Racked with sobs, she couldn't continue; when she finally regained her composure, she gazed up at Sybil with her dark eyes full of tears. 'I just can't bear the thought of you leaving us; we'll be bereft without you; me and the kids have grown to love and need you so much.'

The thought of leaving Sally and Ronnie, two kiddies who only months ago she would have happily handed into police custody, brought tears rushing into Sybil's witch-green eyes too. How could this emotional metamorphosis have come about? Now Sybil enjoyed every minute she spent with the children: walking, fishing, hunting in rock pools, skimming pebbles over the ocean at sunset; this afternoon they were all looking forward to going swimming together, then having ice-creams (albeit made from evaporated milk and flour) on the beach.

On summer evenings, when the children visited the Home, Sybil read to them in the shady garden steeped in the perfume of phlox and delphiniums. As swifts darted back and forth feeding their chirruping young nesting in Mary Vale's many ancient eaves, Sybil enthralled the two suntanned kiddies with tales from Beatrix Potter, Just William, *Wind in the Willows* and *Alice in Wonderland*. Sybil knew that their relationship had turned into something more profound after she had rescued the pair of them from the bombed-out streets of Finsbury Park; what she never expected to feel was the huge love that now engulfed her every time she saw them running towards her, calling her name, '*AUNTIE SYBIL!*' and rushing into her arms, eager for a hug, a kiss and a cuddle.

'Oh, Rosie,' she sighed in despair. 'What are we going to do?'

In her typical tough London way, Rosie straightened her scrawny shoulders and wiped away her tears. 'Get on with it, as usual,' she answered, blinking away tears. 'What else can we do in these bleedin' awful times?'

Sybil seriously wondered how her friend could, in fact, 'get on with it', with no home, potentially no husband, and no money.

'One thing I do know,' Rosie announced, 'I'm not taking the kids away from here.'

'What?' Sybil cried in alarm. 'You're going to leave them with the Larkins? They'd be much happier living with you, Rosie. And you – without them – surely you'd be distraught?'

'It's best for them, though, not me, and it wouldn't be forever, just while I find my feet and get a job, perhaps in service, close by.'

Looking less alarmed, Sybil listened intently to what Rosie was saying.

'They could be with no better family than where they are now. Nobody could deny how happy and healthy they are these days – they're bonnier, fitter, brighter, stronger – need I go on? All that good grub and running about on the fells, climbing trees, herding sheep, then coming here to play by the seaside. Life's never been better for them. No,' she said firmly. 'They're staying put – at least for now. They came here as evacuees in the first place and that's what they still are, wartime evacuees.'

Sybil couldn't argue with any of the facts that Rosie had listed – in fact, she completely agreed with her – but she still thought her friend's decision was a huge act of selfless love.

Reaching for her hand she squeezed it. 'You're a good mum,' she murmured.

Rosie returned the squeeze. 'And you're the best friend I've ever had.'

'Where will you go?' Sybil nervously enquired.

'Well, I can't stay here any more,' Rosie told her. 'I don't want to either – too many bad memories – but I hope to stay local.'

Remembering the baby Rosie had lost and what she herself had put her through, Sybil could only nod her head in agreement.

'I've worked in service before,' Rosie continued. 'If I could pick up work in one of the big houses in Kendal or Lancaster, I wouldn't be far away from the children.'

'That's a possibility,' Sybil agreed, though she secretly wondered how much hard physical graft her frail friend could actually undertake: mopping flag floors, clearing and setting fires, working in a busy kitchen, lifting heavy pots and pans would very soon exhaust Rosie. She decided to consciously change the subject, at least for now.

'I'm looking forward to our swim later on.'

Rosie gave a shudder. 'You won't catch me in that dangerous seawater,' she declared.

'It's only dangerous when you don't check the tide,' Sybil told her. 'I've checked today's tides – we'll be fine.'

'I'll sit it out and keep an eye on the picnic,' Rosie joked. Rising, she shook out her creased dress. 'Can't hang around here, I've got chores to do.'

'Me too,' Sybil groaned. 'That's one thing I won't miss when I leave here: all the wretched laundry!'

After finishing her laundry work a little earlier than usual, Sybil headed into the sitting room, where some of the morning papers were often left lying around. Perched in the window seat of the large bay window that overlooked the sweep of garden that ran down to the sea, now at high tide and swilling over the marsh, Sybil read the front-page war news, then turned to the society page, which she regularly skimmed for the occasional gossip about former debutante friends. Her eyes grew large as she read the headlines in a column at the bottom of the page: BRIGADIER MONTY BALDWIN AND LADY VERONICA BALDWIN TO SEPARATE.

'Oh, my God!' Sybil gasped, as she held the paper close to her flushed face so she could read the report. *It has come as a shock to hear that the glittering couple, well known for their love of the arts and fine entertainment, are to separate. I'm told by close friends that it is an amicable arrangement between Brigadier Baldwin and his wife, Lady Veronica, who will have custody of their only child, Marigold.*

Speechless Sybil could only clutch the paper with trembling hands.

'I don't believe it,' she managed to splutter, before running out of the room in search of Rosie, whom she found covered in soot from her morning's work cleaning out the Home's grates. 'Look!' she cried and thrust the paper in Rosie's face. 'Read it!'

Rosie, who was a very slow reader and pretty shortsighted too, squinted at the paper. 'What?' she mumbled.

Impatient Sybil read the headlines for her. 'Lady Veronica and Monty are divorcing.'

With a loud clang Rosie dropped the poker she was holding.

'Can you believe it?'

Looking stunned, Rosie tried to take in the information. 'Lord Stow took us seriously,' she gasped incredulously.

'He must have done,' incredulous too, Sybil agreed. 'He must have had a word with Veronica fairly quickly after seeing us; after all, it's not that long ago.'

'I bet she would have been tight-lipped to start with,' Rosie said knowingly.

'His lordship must have winkled the truth out of her; otherwise we wouldn't be reading this article,' Sybil realistically pointed out. 'I wonder if he paid the bastard off or just sent him packing with his tail between his legs?'

Still unable to absorb the news and the enormous victory they had achieved, Rosie gave a loud jubilant laugh. 'We did it, against all the odds,' she exclaimed.

Sybil joined in the happy laughter. 'YEAH! We did it, Rosie!'

Their picnic that afternoon on Grange Beach was one of the happiest days of Rosie's life. She certainly didn't swim, but she did paddle in the shallows, where she stood watching her laughing children play tag in the deeper water further out. Chasing Sybil, who was wearing a clinging red swimsuit, Ronnie and Sally dived under the waves in order to catch her out, but she was a strong swimmer and dodged most of their advances. Afterwards, lying on the warm sand eating meat-paste-and-cucumber sandwiches and oatmeal gingerbread washed down with a flask of strong tea, they listened to the tide shushing against the pebbles as it softly slipped away from the shore.

'Can we swim again, Auntie Sybil?' Sally asked, as she tickled Sybil's tummy, which was pleasingly returning to its former shape.

'Yes, but first I must digest my food,' Sybil answered sleepily. 'Go and build a sandcastle with a deep moat and I promise I'll come and decorate it with shells as soon as it's finished.'

'Yeah!' exuberant Ronnie cried. 'Let's build two castles, Sal, and a connecting drawbridge.'

Listening to the children's happy chatter, Sybil turned to Rosie. 'I told them I'm leaving this week,' she said with a lump in her throat.

Rosie struggled to sit up before she answered, 'I know.'

Sitting up too, Sybil watched the redshanks and other waders pecking for worms at the water's edge.

'They're upset,' Rosie continued, 'but they knew this was coming, just like they know that I'll have to leave here soon too. Anyway,' she added cheerfully, 'look on the bright side: a fancy new job – don't tell me you're not looking forward to that?'

'I'm really looking forward to it,' Sybil assured her. 'God knows what I would have done if I'd been turned down for the training.'

Impressed, Rosie murmured, 'I'd never even heard the word "radar" until you mentioned it.'

'Please, God, it will help to speed up an end to this wretched war,' Sybil said earnestly.

'Please, God,' Rosie echoed; then, looking a bit sheepish, she asked, 'I know it's been a busy time for you, lovie, but did you manage to uncover anything about my Mick?'

Remembering the promises of help she had given Rosie during their stay in London, Sybil quickly explained. 'I did make some initial enquiries on your behalf when I was in London,' she started apologetically. 'But leaving so quickly with the children and everything that followed took my eye off the ball.'

'Of course it did,' Rosie answered fondly. 'You'd got more important things to cope with.'

'But I promise,' Sybil continued, 'once I'm back in London I will probe further, get a few friends to make enquiries, do a bit of snooping.' Laying a comforting arm around her friend's shoulder, Sybil said softly, 'We've got to keep hoping, sweetheart, and never give up.'

Rosie nodded. 'Keep smiling through, as the song goes,' she said bravely.

'For I know we'll meet again, some sunny day,' they sang in unison.

48. One Good Turn
Deserves Another

Shortly before Sybil was due to leave Mary Vale, she beckoned Rosie into her room and handed her a bag of clothes.

'I really don't need them any more,' she said. 'Would you like them?'

Looking at the pile of expensive cashmere jumpers, tweed skirts, silk blouses and summer frocks, Rosie refused point-blank to take them.

'They're too good for me!'

'Don't be silly,' Sybil urged. 'You'll need some smart clothes if you go for any job interviews. Anyway, to be honest, you'd be doing me a favour. I really don't want to ever see any of them again; they remind me of Monty or being pregnant – both of which make me feel miserable for very different reasons.'

Knowing that Sybil's son's adoption had been finalized and the little boy was due to leave Mary Vale shortly after his mother, Rosie (who had asked the question more than once) nevertheless asked it again.

'You're quite sure about having your baby adopted?'

'Without a doubt,' Sybil declared.

'But you're so wonderful with my children,' Rosie reminded her.

'I wasn't,' Sybil firmly reminded her. 'And, bear in mind, I didn't actually give birth to them,' she pointed out. 'Rosie, I know that right now I simply wouldn't be a good mother; it's not the poor little blighter's fault but entirely my own. The least I can do is to give him a fresh beginning with a family who loves him.'

Rosie smiled. 'I'm quite sure Father Ben will have found a good family for him.'

'I'm sure he has,' Sybil agreed. 'I trust him completely.'

Turning back to the pile of clothes she had just been presented with, Rosie asked, 'What are you going to wear if I take all of your old clothes?'

Opening the wardrobe door Sybil took out a couple of outfits. 'I recently bought these in Lancaster; they'll do for the time being and I can always pick up more when I'm passing through London.'

Wide-eyed Rosie gazed at the fashionably short black-and-white crêpe pleated skirt and matching top which Sybil held in one hand and the navy cotton shirtwaister she held in the other.

'Gorgeous!' she laughed. 'You'll look very smart and professional.'

'That's exactly the look I want,' Sybil replied. 'No frills and flounces in this wartime bunker – my flirting days are over.'

'You always look gorgeous whatever you wear,' Rosie said, as she headed towards the door. 'The children told me they're meeting you later for a swim.'

'Do you mind my seeing them without you?' Sybil asked anxiously.

'Of course I don't mind – you must make the most of every moment while you're here, close to them.'

Sybil found Sally and Ronnie in their favourite spot, by a rock pool where little crabs scuttled and insects skimmed the surface of the water. Both of them were sitting side by side looking very glum. Hurrying towards them, she plonked the basket she had brought along with her down on the ground before gathering the children into her arms.

'I've brought your goodbye presents,' she said brightly.

Close to tears, Sally gulped, 'We're sad because you're leaving, Auntie Sybil.'

'We don't want you to go,' growled Ronnie, who was struggling to keep his emotions in check.

Determined to keep the mood cheerful, Sybil rummaged in the basket.

'I've already told you, it's not forever, just a temporary break,' Sybil started. 'Come on, kids, after all that we've been through, do you really think I'd turn my back on my two best friends?'

Considerably brightened, Ronnie and Sally beamed.

'It was exciting when you were having your baby on the train,' Sally giggled.

'For you, maybe,' Sybil grinned. 'Now look,' she added in a louder voice as she peered into her basket. 'What have we here?'

With a swagger Ronnie read the names on the little tags Sybil had attached to the parcels.

'That's for Sally, this is for me,' he said as he distributed them. Both children smiled with pleasure when they unwrapped their gifts.

'Mrs Tiggy-Winkle!' Sally cried, as she stared in delight at her brand-new book, which in the past she had only read with Sybil in Kendal Library.

'*William and the Evacuees*,' Ronnie chuckled. 'I can read this on my own now,' he added proudly.

Hunkering down between the children, Sybil said, 'What you two little terrors need to understand is that I *have* to go away in order to do my war work; it's a duty we must all do if we're to win this terrible war.'

Resorting to his favourite expression, Ronnie muttered darkly, 'Bleedin' Hitler!'

'Quite so.' Sybil smiled in agreement as she handed the children another present. 'Writing sets. I've got one too. Look inside the wallets,' she instructed. 'They contain a writing pad, envelopes, postage stamps and a pen. Now you have no excuse not to write to me, and I've got no excuse not to write to you.'

'How do we know where to send our letters?' Ronnie asked.

'I'll leave a forwarding address with your mother,' Sybil explained.

'I'm not a very good writer,' Sally confessed. 'Could I draw pictures instead?'

'Yes, one of your lovely pictures,' Sybil agreed. 'Just so long as we keep in touch, that's really all that matters.' Looking from one child to the other, she added, 'Promise you'll both write.'

'Cross my heart and hope to die,' Ronnie declared, as he made the sign of the Cross over his heart.

'Me too,' Sally said as she followed suit.

'Good,' Sybil said, as she got to her feet. 'Now let's go for a swim.'

*

Later that afternoon, after the children, proudly clutching their new books and writing sets, had returned to Hope Farm, Rosie joined Sybil in the garden, where they took a stroll before the gong went for supper.

'How did it go?' Rosie asked.

'I gave them both writing sets and they promised to keep in touch,' Sybil told her. 'I hope you will write too,' she added with a hopeful smile.

'Me, I can't spell for toffee!' Rosie exclaimed.

'Get Ronnie to teach you – his reading has come on in leaps and bounds since we got back from London.'

Rosie grinned. 'He used to be a big mouth, but these days he's more of a bookworm . . .'

Her voiced trailed away as a large open-topped silver Daimler came cruising down the drive.

'Who's come visiting in a swanky car like that?'

The car pulled up at the door of Mary Vale House and the smartly dressed chauffeur leapt from his seat to open the passenger door for a tall, elegant lady who was wearing a cream chiffon tea dress and an exquisite canvas-and-straw boater decorated with pink silk roses. Stepping out of the car, the woman turned her head in order to survey the sweep of garden that ran down to the sea, at which point Rosie visibly swayed on her feet.

'Oh, my God!'

Clutching her friend before she stumbled, Sybil cried, 'Rosie, what is it? What's the matter?'

Flushed and trembling, Rosie burst into a run. 'Your ladyship!' she cried. 'Lady Veronica!'

Sybil stopped dead in her tracks as she watched the two

women greet each other: poor Rosie in her faded pinafore and the glamorous new arrival.

'Rose!' the woman exclaimed. 'We were beginning to think that we might have got the address wrong.' Hurrying forwards, Lady Veronica shook an astounded Rosie by the hand. 'How wonderful to see you.'

Flabbergasted, Rosie was seriously struggling to find words. 'Your ladyship,' she said, as she bobbed the customary curtsy. 'What on earth are you doing here at Mary Vale House?' Realizing that up until recently the singular purpose of the Home was a hide-away for unmarried mothers, Rosie clamped a hand over her mouth. Could it be that Lady Veronica was here to have a baby too? The very thought brought a blazing blush to her cheeks. As if reading her embarrassed thoughts, Lady Veronica smiled.

'Don't worry, darling, I'm here solely for one purpose – to see you, of course.'

Completely overcome, Rosie turned to Sybil, who was hanging back some way behind her.

'Please let me introduce you to my closest friend.'

Extending her hand, ever confident Sybil stepped forward, saying, 'Delighted to meet you, Lady Veronica.'

The two women locked eyes.

'You must be Sybil Harwood,' the visitor said. 'My father mentioned you.'

Knowing what Lord Stow might have said about her, certainly nothing good, Sybil managed to remain calm and composed.

'I had the honour of meeting Lord Stow recently,' she replied diplomatically.

Looking Sybil straight in the eye, Lady Veronica said, 'I'll come straight to the point – it's so much simpler.'

Rosie trembled in fear at what would come next, while Sybil stuck out her small determined chin – she could take what was coming. But, surprisingly, what she wasn't expecting was gratitude.

'I came here to thank you both from the bottom of my heart,' Lady Veronica explained.

Rosie gaped at her in disbelief. 'You drove all the way from London to thank us?'

'No, of course not,' Lady Veronica laughed. 'I'm staying with friends in the Windermere area. I knew of your address from Dowry House's trusty butler,' she said with a sly smile. 'Seeing as I was in your neck of the woods, I thought I'd swing by to say hello.'

Seeing Rosie completely out of her depth, Sybil took charge. 'Would you like a cup of tea or something to eat?' she asked politely.

'No, thanks, that's most kind, but I'd love it if we could find somewhere nice and private to talk,' Lady Veronica replied.

After settling their visitor on a bench facing the sea and as far away from the House as possible, Rosie and Sybil waited, sitting on the lawn in front of her, for their visitor to speak.

'As I said,' Lady Veronica started, 'I'm here to thank you both. I always knew you were a devoted maid, Rose, but what you have done, and years after you left my service, was an act of deep kindness.'

'The truth always preyed on my mind, your ladyship,'

Rosie mumbled. 'It was only when I met Sybil' – she nodded in her friend's direction – 'that I felt strong enough, and bold enough, to approach Lord Stow.'

Turning to Sybil, Lady Veronica said kindly, 'You stuck your neck out too, I hear?'

Sybil didn't flinch. 'I feel I must apologize for my relationship with your husband.'

Lady Veronica waved a dismissive hand. 'Don't worry, dear, there were so many.'

'Which makes me all the more ashamed,' Sybil confessed; then, before she could stop herself, she said, 'I'm delighted that your father took the initiative and spoke to you of our concerns.'

'He was awkward and angry in turns,' Lady Veronica recalled. 'Having never spoken a word to my father about my husband's infidelities and his threats to blackmail me, I asked him how he knew; that's when he told me about your visit to Dowry House.'

Rosie spoke in a voice quivering with happiness and disbelief. 'We weren't at all sure if his lordship had taken us seriously.'

'Don't you worry, he took you very seriously, Rose,' the visitor replied. 'Once my father had established the facts, he was relentless. He hired the best lawyers in the land to handle the case.'

Poor Rosie blushed as she blurted out, 'He said I was pre . . .' She turned to Sybil.

'Presumptuous,' Sybil clarified.

'Presumptuous to suggest you even wanted a divorce,' Rosie concluded.

Lady Veronica didn't hesitate for a moment. 'You

weren't presumptuous, Rose dear,' she cried. 'You were spot on. I had begged Monty over and over again for a divorce – frowned upon as they are, I preferred the scandal that would follow to a lifetime with Monty – but he would never agree.' Holding up a hand, she gave a self-deprecating smile. 'Please believe me, it wasn't devotion on his part; he simply wanted the titled connection and the income.'

'I knew it all along,' Rosie said with a delighted smile. 'We all knew it below stairs.'

'Anyway, enough of me – tell me how you come to be here, Rose.'

Looking like she didn't quite know where to start, Rosie answered bluntly, 'My husband was conscripted into the Army. Sadly me and the kiddies saw him only a few times before he was reported missing in action, then we got evacuated. I came here, expecting, but recently lost the baby,' she concluded with a heavy sigh.

'My dear, how absolutely awful for you all,' Lady Veronica commiserated. 'You've been through hell!'

With tears pricking her eyes, Rosie nodded. 'We have been through hell, ma'am,' she agreed. 'And I've not even told you a third of the story,' she thought. 'But we struggle on – what else can folks like us do?'

'Brave girl, that's the wartime spirit; but even so, dear girl, you've certainly had a basin full.'

After Rosie had told her tragic story, Lady Veronica asked Sybil what her plans for the future were.

'I'm leaving the Home this week to begin my training in radar.'

'No more War Office?' Lady Veronica asked with a knowing smile.

'No more War Office,' Sybil answered firmly. 'Time to move on.'

'And you, Rose, what are your plans?'

'I'm looking for work in service.'

'Here, locally?' Lady Veronica asked.

'Yes, I need to be close to my children, who are staying at a local farm.'

Lady Veronica clapped her hands in delight. 'Marvellous — you're available for work?'

'Yes, indeed, ma'am.'

'Would you consider working for me again?'

Rosie looked embarrassed.

'Much as I'd love to, ma'am, I really don't want to be in London — it's too far away from my children.'

'I'm not talking about London, dear girl,' Lady Veronica explained. 'I've just taken over the lease of the lakeside home where I'm presently staying in Windermere, and I'm in need of a reliable housekeeper. There is nobody in the world whom I would prefer to you.'

At this point Rosie, overcome with gratitude and excitement, burst into tears.

'Yes, yes, please,' she sobbed, as she took the clean handkerchief Sybil extended to her. 'But I've only been a lady's maid before, and a scullery maid before that.'

'Then it's time you were promoted to higher things,' Lady Veronica insisted. 'Now, if you'll excuse me,' she said, as she rose from the bench, 'it's time for us to drive back to Windermere, where my friends are waiting for me to join them for supper. I'll be in touch very soon, Rose dear,' she promised.

'Thank you, your ladyship, I would love to work for you again,' Rosie blurted out. 'It's like a dream come true.'

Lady Veronica gave a radiant smile. 'Well, then, we've both had our prayers answered, for which I'll always be eternally grateful.'

After Lady Veronica had cruised away in her sparkling silver Daimler, Sybil and Rosie stared at each other with tears in their eyes.

'Dreams really do come true,' Rosie gulped.

Sybil gave her a warm hug. 'If anybody deserves happiness it's you, my darling.'

The following wet and breezy morning seemed to herald the end of the long, hot summer they had enjoyed. Carrying her suitcase, Sybil said goodbye to the staff; then, with only Rosie and the children for company, she made her way through the little wood that led to Kents Bank Station. Though Rosie had instructed her children to bear up, Sally was crying before they even got on the platform, and when the train pulled in Ronnie started too.

'We're such a bunch of softies,' Rosie said apologetically.

'I'm no better,' Sybil murmured as tears slid down her pink cheeks. Swiping them away, she turned to the children. 'You remember what I said about writing to me and keeping in touch?'

They both nodded mutely.

'You won't forget, will you?'

In answer Ronnie and Sally flung themselves into Sybil's arms, where they sobbed their hearts out, and it was only the loud shunting of the train that brought them all to their senses.

'All aboard,' called the impatient guard.

'Goodbye, darlings,' Sybil cried, as she leapt on to the train. 'Be good for Mummy,' she said, waving out of the window.

'Bye, Auntie Sybil,' Ronnie and Sally called out, as they waved farewell.

'I love you!' Sybil sobbed, while the train gathered speed and a cloud of black smoke snatched the children she had grown to love so much from sight.

49. Zophony House

Shortly after Sybil's departure, Rosie, taking a stroll in the garden, saw a smart little Ford drive up to Mary Vale's front door; then an equally smart couple climbed out of the car; and less than an hour later Rosie watched them drive away with Sybil's baby boy, clutched in his new mother's arms. Feeling like a spy, Rosie observed their coming and going closely just in case one day – if Sybil ever enquired – she could tell her what happened the day her son left the place where his mother had given birth to him.

In the Home itself Sybil was barely missed. Never popular among her fellow residents, some even gleefully mocked Sybil.

'A relief all round now that Her Majesty has gone.'

'You can say that again.'

'I certainly won't miss her snooty looks.'

'Nor her swanning around swinging her posh handbag.'

Rosie quickly put a stop to the girls' catty remarks. 'She was good to me and my kids,' she reminded them.

'Yeah, and it took some time,' said one of the older residents, who had witnessed Sybil's previous vindictive behaviour towards the Pickles family.

'She made up for it a thousand-fold,' loyal Rosie protested.

Because the residents unanimously liked Rosie they did

as she requested and kept their unkind thoughts to themselves, but if the truth were told not one of them regretted seeing the back of Sybil Harwood.

A few days after Sybil's departure a telegram arrived for Rosie, which sent the blood draining from her pale face.

'I hope it's not bad news, dear,' said Sister Mary Paul, who had picked up the telegram from the telegram boy, who was standing on the front step waiting for an answer.

Knowing she was a slow reader, Rosie thrust it back at the nun. 'You read it – it'll be quicker.'

Adjusting her little wire-framed spectacles, the nun carefully read the contents of the telegram.

'It's from somebody called Lady Veronica Baldwin.'

Rosie crumpled with relief. 'Thank God! I thought it was going to be bad news about Mick, my husband,' she explained.

Mary Paul squinted at the tiny print. 'She says, *Dear Rose, can you please come to Windermere tomorrow? Would be grateful. Address below. Best regards, V.*'

Sister Mary Paul looked up. 'Shall we send a telegram back?'

Flushing with excitement, Rosie nodded. 'Yes, please,' she exclaimed.

'What's the message?'

Rosie looked flustered. 'Is there a daily bus to Windermere?'

'Yes,' the nun replied.

'How long does it take?'

'About two hours,' Sister Mary Paul guessed.

Rosie smiled. 'Then please say that I'll be at . . . where am I going?' she laughed excitedly.

Referring to the telegram, the nun said, 'Zophony House, Lakeside, Windermere, it says here.'

Rosie smiled. 'Tell her ladyship I'll be there before noon.'

Grateful that Sybil had given her so many lovely clothes, Rosie sat on the Windermere bus feeling very fine indeed. Because it was a hot day, she was wearing one of Sybil's pretty little crêpe dresses which she didn't fill out, but the soft sage-green colour and the shape flattered her skinny body. One of the residents had lent her a pair of smart court shoes and a decent handbag, so all in all Rosie felt like chic personified when she started out on her journey.

The chauffeur, whom she immediately recognized, met her at the bus station in Windermere, and Rosie blushed as she stepped into the gleaming Daimler, drawing envious glances from several passers-by. Sitting back against the creamy leather upholstery, Rosie stared in wonder at the endless stretch of Lake Windermere, which seemed to her as vast as Brighton Beach, which she had visited once as a child.

'Beautiful,' she said out loud.

'It's that all right,' the chatty chauffeur agreed. 'Wait till you see Zophony House – you're in for a right treat.'

He couldn't have spoken a truer word. The house that was to be her responsibility was about a mile outside of the little grey-slate town of Bowness. Built on a gentle rise overlooking the lake, turreted windows reflected the sun rising high in the bright summer sky. The curving drive from the country lane wound around banks of dense rhododendron bushes, before it opened out in a wide sweep in front of the house. Unlike the grand London houses Rosie had known in her time in service, Zophony House was a simpler structure built entirely of timber and red brick. Wide and rambling, its many windows opened on to the woods, the lake, the towering fells and the splendid gardens that rolled down to a deck at the water's edge, against which a couple of motorboats at anchor rocked.

'Oh, my God!' Rosie sighed as she tried to take it all in.

The chauffeur gave a smug smile. 'Told you, didn't I?'

Lady Veronica, cool and elegant in a floating navy linen dress decorated with a crisp white sailor's collar, came hurrying out of the wide carved front door overhung with jewel-red roses.

'Rose, so good of you to come at such short notice.' Ushering her visitor into the house, she added, 'I have to go back to London tomorrow, to tie up a few urgent details concerning my separation.'

Rosie tried to hide a smile; hearing Lady Veronica talking about 'her separation' gave her a sense of deep satisfaction.

'I wanted to give you a guided tour of my new country residence before I left, as I was rather hoping you might be in residence when I return.'

Delighted that she would soon be living in such a glorious place, Rosie blushed with pleasure.

'That's kind of you, your ladyship.'

Lady Veronica, clearly excited, called over her shoulder, 'Let's start with the drawing room.'

Rosie's jaw dropped as she walked into the lovely room, decorated with old oil paintings and furnished with deep-plush, pale-blue sofas and comfortable chairs. Charming as the room was, with its elaborate white marble fireplace and wooden parquet floor polished to a shine, it was the view that drew Rosie. The French doors were flung wide open, giving on to a patio smelling of pungent wild herbs, then the lawn overlooking the lake sparkling azure-blue in the sunlight.

'I fell in love with the place the moment I first laid eyes on it,' Lady Veronica confessed.

'I can believe it, ma'am, it's the loveliest place I've ever seen.'

'I was so lucky to be able to take over the lease,' Lady Veronica continued.

'Am I to understand that you won't be here all of the time, ma'am?' Rosie asked, as they moved on to the kitchen, which, though old-fashioned, was large and well equipped.

'To be honest, while the war rages on, I would prefer to spend most of my time here,' Lady Veronica replied. 'Plus, for the moment I think it might be wise if Marigold and I were out of the public eye, at least until the divorce is finalized and everything is official.'

Rosie gave a quick nod. 'I quite understand,' she said, while at the same time wondering how she could introduce the subject of her own kiddies. As if reading her thoughts, kindly Lady Veronica said, 'I've been thinking about where your two children might stay when they come to visit you at Zophony House.'

Rosie quickly glanced up at her employer. 'That's nice of you,' she murmured.

'There's the sweetest little turret bedroom in the east

tower with a couple of single beds. It's a rather thrilling set-up, tucked away up a spiral staircase. I suspect any child would love it.'

Thrilled, Rosie cried, 'Really, you wouldn't mind them staying here?'

'Why should I?' Veronica smiled. 'They're your children after all.'

After arrangements for Ronnie and Sally had been settled, Lady Veronica asked a rather direct question. 'Will you be happy managing an entire household, Rose?'

Rosie took a deep breath before she said firmly, 'I think so, ma'am.'

Understanding some of her anxieties, Lady Veronica quickly clarified the situation. 'It won't be like Dowry House. I plan to keep the staff down to a minimum; I don't want a servant at every turn. A cook, scullery maid, gardener-cum-chauffeur and you as housekeeper-cum-lady's maid should do it, wouldn't you think?'

Realizing that she was being given serious responsibility, Rosie felt a blush of pride colour her cheeks. 'I'll certainly do my best, your ladyship.'

'We can live simply, frugally here; after all, we have no choice these days. There won't be endless splendid parties like we had at Dowry House, nor society dinners, just a simple quiet life.' Lady Veronica's eyes strayed to the view through the kitchen windows. 'We're lucky enough to find peace in these awful times.'

After viewing her own room – neat and pretty with blue chintz curtains and a matching bedspread, plus stunning views out over the lake – Rosie was escorted to the east tower. After ascending the echoing stone staircase, Rosie gazed in rapt delight at the narrow slitted windows which lined the circular space looking out over the forest and the sloping emerald lawn.

'It's like a fairy-tale,' Rosie cried in delight. 'It's just perfect!'

Shortly before Rosie left to catch the bus back to Mary Vale, she and Lady Veronica enjoyed a pot of tea, which Rosie, longing to explore the kitchen on her own, more than willingly brewed.

'Would you mind if I left all the hiring to you, Rose? It's really not my territory,' Lady Veronica said, as she popped a cigarette into a long silver holder and lit it with a silver lighter which was on the coffee table before them.

Though Rosie slightly quailed at the awesome thought of hiring and firing staff, she straightened her back. 'If you think I'm up to the job, and you trust me with your instructions, who am I to disagree?'

'Excellent,' Lady Veronica replied. 'I'll never forget the trust I had in you during your time at Dowry House. You were always such a devoted maid.'

'I loved my time with you, ma'am.'

Veronica smiled. 'Not withstanding certain marital flies in the ointment,' she teased.

Seeing Rosie blush at her mention of the Brigadier, Lady Veronica politely asked, 'Have there been any developments on your husband's whereabouts since we last met, Rose?'

'No, but Sybil's promised to make further enquiries while she's in London,' Rosie said hopefully. 'She has a few influential connections and she's going to approach them.'

'I have a few whom I could approach too,' Lady Veronica promised; then, reaching into her handbag, she pulled out a set of keys for Zophony House, which she handed to Rosie.

'All yours,' she smiled. 'I've arranged with the chauffeur to keep an eye on the place until your arrival, which I hope will be very soon.'

Rosie took the keys and gripped them in her hands. 'I've a few things to sort out with the children and Mrs Larkin, who looks after them; once that's done, I can move in immediately to take up my post,' Rosie promised.

'I look forward to seeing you in residence on my return. Here are the terms of your employment and your rate of pay,' Veronica added, as she slipped a buff envelope into Rosie's hands. 'Any problems, phone me on my direct line – I've written it down on the envelope.'

Shaking her mistress by the hand, Rosie said earnestly, 'Thank you, ma'am, I can never thank you enough for this wonderful opportunity.'

'Rose, dear,' Lady Veronica smiled. 'I think the shoe is on the other foot; it is *I* who can never thank *you* enough.'

50. A Deal is Struck

Timid Rosie, the little mouse of a woman who had been so ill and had shrunk in fear and shame on her arrival at Mary Vale, was hugely missed by all when she left for Windermere, this time on the train, which she could now afford. Sister Theresa and Ada (along with baby Catherine, cosily sleeping in her big old-fashioned pram) were there to wave her off, along with Mrs Larkin, Ronnie and Sally.

Before she talked to her children about her new plans, Rosie had made sure she and Mrs Larkin had a quiet word in private.

'I can only do this if I have your backing and support,' Rosie started. 'Is it wrong of me to leave my children?'

Mrs Larkin was as ever pragmatic. 'Well, sweetheart,' she said, as she lit up a cigarette and poured tea from the big brown pot that was always brewing on the ancient Aga in her cluttered but comfortable kitchen, 'you're caught between a rock and a hard place, I'd say.'

Rosie's brow crinkled. 'What do you mean?'

'Well, you can't stay here on the farm – there's no room for a start, and what would you do? Feed the sheep, milk the cows?'

Rosie shuddered at the thought. 'I'd be hopeless,' she confessed.

'But that's not the point, really, is it?' Mrs Larkin said realistically. 'In effect it would be two families living together, not Sally and Ronnie living with *me*.' She left the sentence hanging before she added, 'There would inevitably be arguments, your children playing you off against me, or the other way around. It's predictable, of course, but it would get very tedious.'

Rosa nodded in agreement with her sentiments. 'You have created a safe place for my kiddies – they're happier here than they were at Mary Vale, and, though they go on about Finsbury Park, to tell the truth it was a slum and now it's just a bomb-site. Ronnie and Sally have flourished with you and your lovely family, and amazingly they now love going to school. I would hate to take them away from all of this,' she finished.

Mrs Larkin gave a warm reassuring smile. 'You know I'm happy to have them here. Windermere is a new start for you – and the children can visit and come and stay. What's there to worry about?'

Rosie suddenly grinned. 'Nothing!' she exclaimed. 'I'm so used to life going wrong I can't get used to life going right.'

Mrs Larkin grinned back. 'Then it's about time you started, lovie.'

Rosie told Ronnie and Sally about her new appointment when they next came to visit her at Mary Vale. Without Sybil's lively energetic presence, the atmosphere was flat and the light summer drizzle misting the garden and the view of the bay didn't help to lift the mood either. In the sitting room, which smelt of cabbage and custard, Sally blurted out, 'I don't like it here any more.'

'I never much liked it anyway,' Ronnie growled.

Seizing the moment, Rosie nodded in agreement with

both of them. 'I feel the same – it's time to move on,' she announced.

'Like Auntie Sybil, she's moved on and gone,' Sally said wisely.

'I'm thinking of doing exactly the same thing,' Rosie said.

'What?' Ronnie asked in complete astonishment. 'You're going to take a maths examination and train to work in radar, like Auntie Sybil?'

The very thought made Rosie burst out laughing. 'Don't be daft, son, I'm not as brainy as your Auntie Sybil, but I can do other things.'

'Like what?' Sally asked.

'Well, before you two were born, I worked for a lovely lady in London,' Rosie explained. 'Do you remember the stories I used to tell you about her lovely frocks and her diamonds in a safe-box which I had the key to?'

Sally's eyes grew round as she recalled the stories. 'She was like the Queen; she had a tiara and lots of jewels.'

'That's right, lovie,' Rosie nodded. 'Her name is Lady Veronica and she came to see me here at Mary Vale the other day.'

'Was she wearing her jewels?' Sally asked breathlessly.

Rosie smiled. 'No, but she drove here in a big posh silver car, with a chauffeur.'

Now it was Ronnie's eyes that grew as round as saucers. 'WOWWWW!'

'She came to see me because she wants me to work for her again, not in London but up the road, in a place called Windermere,' Rosie explained.

'That's where Mr Larkin sells his cattle,' Ronnie said knowledgeably.

'She's asked me to go and be her housekeeper in a big house by the lake.' Holding her breath, Rosie waited for a reaction.

'Can we come too?' Sally asked.

'Yes, you can, but Mrs Larkin wants you to stay with her some of the time, which is good, as I'll be busy some of the time too, working in Windermere.'

With a solemn expression on her face Sally said, 'I don't want to leave May and the cows and the sheep and the rabbits and the kittens – they need me.'

'Of course they do,' Rosie assured her earnest daughter. Turning to Ronnie, she continued, 'Me and Mrs Larkin don't want you to leave your school either, son, not when you're doing so well and you're due to go back there at the start of the new term.'

'I don't want to move school again,' Ronnie answered without hesitation.

'That's what I thought,' Rosie answered. 'So what do you say to a plan where you spend some of the time with Mrs Larkin and some of your time with me?'

Ronnie looked around the chilly room. 'Will it be in a house like Mary Vale, full of women having babies?'

'No!' Rosie cried. 'Zophony House is one of the most beautiful houses I've ever seen. Look,' she said and presented them with a postcard of the house which she had bought in a local bookshop. 'It's got a wood, a huge garden and private boats anchored by the lakeside.'

The children gaped in wonder at the black-and-white postcard of Zophony House, which gave some idea of its size and beautiful location.

'And best of all,' Rosie said, as excited as a child herself, 'you'll have your very own bedroom in *that* tower, the east tower,' she said, pointing to the postcard.

'Just like Rapunzel in the fairy-tale,' Sally sighed dreamily.

'Can I go fishing in one of the boats?' Ronnie asked.

'We'll have to ask Lady Veronica's permission,' Rosie answered honestly. 'But she's a nice lady, I'm sure she'll say yes.'

So it was agreed with surprising ease that Ronnie and Sally would spend their life going back and forth between Hope Farm and Zophony House.

Ever the realist, Ronnie asked, 'What will happen when the war ends, and Dad comes home?'

Rosie pulled her son close to give him a kiss. 'Let's talk about that when it happens, son, but meanwhile we'll stick together and keep on doing our best, eh?'

Ronnie grinned at his mum. 'What is it that you and Auntie Sybil always say?'

Thinking of darling Sybil, whom she missed so much, Rosie repeated the familiar words with a catch in her voice, 'Keep smiling through.'

'Yeah,' he agreed. 'Let's keep smiling through.'

Less than a week later, standing on the platform dressed in another of Sybil's little crêpe dresses, plus a jaunty felt hat that Sybil had also bequeathed to her, Rosie was unrecognizable as the impoverished woman who had arrived at the Home only months ago. Rosie wondered if her children might have a last-minute tearful panic when the moment of farewell finally arrived, but Mrs Larkin, with her thoughtful foresight, had arranged a picnic on the beach with the rest of her family, followed by a swim. After hugging her children and giving them some money to buy lollipops for all the Larkin children, Rosie said her goodbyes.

'I'll see you both next week at Zophony House.'

Turning to Ada and Sister Theresa, she said, 'I can never thank you enough for everything you have done for me and my kids.'

Sister Theresa smiled. 'I'll miss you all,' she said truthfully.

'Take care of your little girl,' Rosie said to Ada. 'Bring her to Zophony House when you can.'

'I will,' Ada promised. 'I can't wait to see the place.'

Finally, Rosie said to Mrs Larkin, 'Thank you from the bottom of my heart for all that you've done for us.'

As the train hooted and lurched forward on the tracks, Rosie jumped aboard and blew kisses, while her children blew kisses back. Waving, she called out, 'Love you, see you soon, byeee!'

Waving they all called back, 'GOODBYE, MUM – GOOD LUCK!'

51. Shocks and Surprises

As summer came to an end, Rosie settled into her new role as housekeeper. Though Zophony House was nothing like as big as Dowry House, it was nevertheless large and rambling. On her housekeeper's phone Rosie contacted Dora at Mary Vale, asking where best to advertise the domestic roles which Lady Veronica required.

'The *Westmoreland Gazette*,' Dora immediately answered. Knowing that Rosie wasn't confident about her reading and writing skills, Dora thoughtfully offered to help her with the wording.

'That would be marvellous,' Rosie gratefully accepted.

'Now that we've got a short-term supply nurse until Ada's back, I could take a bit of time off and pop over to sift through the replies with you,' Dora suggested. 'It would make a day out for me.'

'Yes, please,' Rosie enthused. 'You'll love Zophony House. If the weather's fine, we can have tea on the lawn,' she added excitedly.

'OOOH!' Dora teased. 'Aren't we all lah-di-dah now that we're a housekeeper?'

Rosie blushed. 'Stop it, Dora,' she begged. 'I'd really appreciate your help. I do want to pick the right people for her ladyship,' she finished nervously.

'You're not daft, lovie, you can spot a bad 'un, I'm sure,' Dora said encouragingly. 'You've got to believe in yourself more,' she urged. 'You don't think Lady Veronica would have given you the job if she thought you were a dunce, do you?'

Rosie laughed at Dora's choice of words. 'She said she trusted me to sort it out.'

'There you are, then,' Dora replied. 'Follow your instincts!'

With Dora's guidance and her own common sense, Rosie gave the cook's job to a local middle-aged woman who lived in Bowness and had cooked in some of the grander houses in the area. She came with good references, a warm smile and had excellent contacts with the local farmers and suppliers. The scullery maid Rosie chose actually reminded Rosie of herself as a teenager, eager, shy, young and gawky, except that this girl had a thick Cumbrian accent and cycled from her family's sheep farm to start work at seven o'clock every morning.

The very best and most unexpected thing to happen, and one which Rosie had never even thought possible so soon after saying goodbye to Sybil, was her friend phoning up announcing she was going to pay her a visit.

'We recruits are being sent to Manchester on a short training course,' Sybil told Rosie. 'I thought if I came ahead of the others, I could get the train to Windermere and spend a few days with you.'

'Oh, yes, yes!' Rosie exclaimed.

'I know it seems like I've only just left, but I've so much to tell you and also,' she blurted out emotionally, 'I miss you so much.'

Tears sprang to Rosie's eyes. 'I miss you too,' she sighed.

'Let me know what time your train gets in and I'll come and meet you at the station.'

'See you soon,' Sybil cried excitedly, as she put down the phone.

Rosie was as excited as a child at the prospect of Sybil's visit. She wanted to share her lovely new home with her and show her all the wonderful places she had discovered. But something happened the day before Sybil's arrival which took the wind out of Rosie's sails. As she was arranging vases of the last of the summer blooms in the hallway and morning room, the housekeeper's phone rang out.

'Windermere 836.'

'It's Dora, Rosie. Listen, lovie, I'm so sorry but I'm afraid I have some bad news.'

Rosie's heart dropped like a stone. 'Ronnie and Sally?' she gasped.

'No, sorry, they're fine,' Dora quickly apologized. 'It's Sister Mann, Edith, remember her?'

'The nurse that ran away,' Rosie recalled.

'That's right, her, well, the truth is the police think she's taken her own life,' Dora answered in a low whisper.

'*WHAT?*' Rosie exclaimed.

'You probably didn't get a chance to read about it in the papers,' Dora suggested. 'Apparently the police have found Edith's car on an isolated track just off the Manchester Ship Canal; it's been left there abandoned for some time, it would seem.'

Flabbergasted, Rosie couldn't believe that she was hearing correctly.

'But how can they be sure that Edith isn't alive somewhere just because she happened to abandon the car?'

'They found incriminating documents inside the car, a suicide note from the sound of things,' Dora, still whispering, replied. 'The police are due here sometime soon; you can imagine the state the nuns are in. I'd better go, I'm needed,' she said urgently. 'I'll call you later.'

From the minute that the chauffeur picked up Sybil in the shiny silver Daimler, the two women barely stopped talking, and of course the very first topic of conversation was Edith Mann.

'What a shock,' Sybil said, as the driver threaded his way through the winding, narrow streets of Windermere. 'The whole of Mary Vale must be very upset.'

'I've only talked to Dora – she did say the nuns were in a terrible state. The police are due to visit today. They'll all blame themselves, that's for sure,' Rosie said knowingly.

'Poor Matron, she has such a big heart, she's bound to be racked with guilt.' Rosie gave a heavy sigh. 'I suppose the mystery of Edith's Mann midnight flit is finally solved.'

'It feels like none of us ever really knew her,' Sybil mused.

Rosie nodded. 'And now we never will.'

Cook had set out a delicious lunch in the big warm kitchen; she'd managed to drum up fresh bread, home-made tomato soup with fresh herbs and even a crumble made with apples from the Zophony House orchard. Rosie was impressed by how fit and well Sybil looked, while Sybil was astonished at the change in Rosie.

'You've filled out,' she cried, as she eagerly accepted more hot soup from the cook. 'Your hair's longer too, and you're certainly a lot more energetic.'

'I feel marvellous. Running this place gives me energy and pleasure too,' beaming Rosie replied. 'Moving here is the best thing that ever happened to me. My only worry was how the children would react long term to me leaving Mary Vale.'

'Did they threaten to run away to London again?' Sybil teased.

Rosie gave a proud smile. 'Nothing of the sort – they've been here a couple of times now and they love Zophony House as much as I do.'

'Who wouldn't?' Sybil asked, as she gazed out of the window which looked out over the fells.

'They like the lake and the mountains, of course, but they're sort of used to that now, having been at Hope Farm for so long,' Rosie explained. 'What they especially love is having their own room in one of the turrets. Sally thinks she's a princess, while Ronnie thinks he's a wizard. They make up all sorts of games and play up there for hours and hours,' she finished happily.

'Bless them,' Sybil sighed. 'I miss them so much.'

'Will you have time to visit them at the farm?'

'Not this time, but next, I hope,' Sybil promised.

'I know they write to you,' Rosie said.

Sybil chuckled. 'Ronnie's letters are more like Just William book reviews, and Sally's letters are full of drawings of rabbits and fairies – sometimes the occasional cow makes an appearance. Their letters make my day when they arrive.'

After lunch, as they walked in the garden, Rosie asked about Sybil's training.

'All the recruits are frightfully brainy.'

'Just like you,' Rosie teased.

'After our short stint in Manchester it looks like we're going to be posted to somewhere on the east coast – it's all terribly hush-hush. Even now we don't know exactly where and won't until we fetch up there. I do know that it's mixed, men and women working together side by side around the clock.'

'You might get to meet Mr Wonderful yet,' Rosie teased again.

Sybil wagged a warning finger in the air. 'Don't run away with yourself: there'll be no young men, just middle-aged boffins in underground bunkers.'

'Not so romantic, then?' Rosie decided.

Sybil turned down the corners of her pretty mouth. 'I don't give a fig about men and romance right now,' she declared. 'I'm so pleased I was accepted for radar work; it feels like at last I'm doing something really important instead of frittering away my life with fools like Monty.'

'I'm quite sure Lady Veronica must be feeling the same: she's in London right now sorting out her separation,' Rosie said with some satisfaction. 'Have you heard any news on the Brigadier?'

'I occasionally hear gossip about Monty from my chums in London,' Sybil replied. 'Apparently he's not changed a jot, still chasing after the next pretty thing in a skirt, though apparently without his aristocratic connections he's not quite so irresistible any more,' she said with a gleeful smile. 'In fact, somebody mentioned he's living in a flat in Earls Court.' Sybil smirked. 'Not quite Dowry House, eh?'

The two women exchanged a wicked conspiratorial smile.

'My, how the mighty have fallen,' Rosie purred.

Rosie made sure that she had completed all her chores so that on their last day together, when there was just a whisper of autumn in the air, the two women could set off for a walk along the lakeside. Taking a picnic in a rucksack, they followed the path that meandered around the edges of the vast lake, on which fishing boats bobbed. After a few miles they climbed up to a high crag that commanded spectacular views of Windermere. Spreading a picnic blanket for them both to sit on, Rosie handed out meat-paste-and-cucumber sandwiches, while Sybil poured tea from a Thermos.

Carefully choosing the right moment to open a topic that was painful to her friend, Sybil started tentatively.

'So, Rosie, remember I said I would make enquiries on your behalf about Mick?'

Holding a sandwich, Rosie's hand froze in mid-air as she waited to hear what Sybil would say next.

'Don't get your hopes up,' she warned. 'I wasn't able to do as much digging as I hoped, but I did discover that it's not all that uncommon for wounded concussed men to disappear from the battleground.'

Voicing her worst fears, Rosie gasped, 'So my poor boy could be wandering around not knowing who he is or where he is?'

Sybil continued in a firm voice, 'Let me explain. According to some of the records I read, wounded soldiers, especially those suffering from amnesia, have been found and protected by allies or partisan workers.'

'They risk their lives to save our boys,' Rosie cried.

Sybil gave a grim nod. 'The punishment doesn't bear thinking about,' she murmured. 'For all we know your Mick, if he did crawl away as his pal suggested when he wrote to you, could be holed up somewhere in France or Belgium and posing under a new identity.'

Hardly daring to breathe, Rosie murmured, 'Mick might be alive, then?'

Sybil answered cautiously, 'If he were very lucky and was helped by partisan workers on the ground, he could be alive.'

'But . . .' Rosie continued fearfully, 'if he was wounded and found wandering around the countryside half crazed, he could have been picked up by the enemy and sent to a prisoner-of-war camp.' Rosie fought back angry tears. 'I know I keep saying this, but if Mick was in a camp, wouldn't I know about it? After all, there are means of identification, discs and papers that can be traced – why not Mick's?'

'I agree,' Sybil answered. 'That's why I personally think Mick – if he's still alive – got away and might, even as we speak, be being shielded by some kind soul. You mustn't lose hope, darling.'

'It's hard to always be brave,' Rosie wailed as tears overcame her.

Stroking her hand, Sybil said earnestly, 'In the reports I read, some soldiers suffering from amnesia suddenly regained their memory and made it home under cover, just as Ronnie always imagined! Wouldn't that be something?'

Rosie gave a grateful smile. 'It would be nothing short of a blessed miracle,' she said. 'Thank you, lovie, for making those enquiries.'

Sybil gripped her hand firmly in her own. 'Don't give

up hope,' she said again. 'Not now, after all you've suffered – and keep in touch with his regiment. It's important that they should be able to track you down,' she reminded Rosie, who gave a quick nod.

'I've informed them of my new address here, but I might contact them again to make sure they received that information.'

'Good girl,' Sybil smiled. 'You never know, miracles happen in love and war.'

'I just miss him,' Rosie blurted out. 'There's not a day goes by when I don't think of him – where he is, is he safe, is he suffering? I've been hoping and praying for so long, and so have my children. Look at the mad risk Ronnie took to find his dad.'

'You don't need to remind me,' Sybil laughed.

'My poor little lad,' Rosie said with tears in her eyes. 'That's how much he loves his dad.'

Rosie and Sybil's last evening together (when cook had gone home) was spent cooking corned-beef fritters and drinking sherry.

'This is the life,' Rosie sighed, as they sat in comfortable chairs by the crackling log fire with the curtains open so they could watch the light fading fast over the lake.

'It's been so lovely to have these unexpected few days together,' Sybil sighed. 'I've no idea when it will happen again, but I've enjoyed every minute here with you.'

Rosie reached over to grip her friend's hand. 'Thanks again for throwing a bit of light on what might have happened to my husband. At least it gives me some hope, which is better than none at all.'

'I only hope it helps,' Sybil said, then, raising her cut-crystal stemmed sherry glass, she toasted, 'Here's to our days at Mary Vale, and to friends, wherever they are.'

Raising her glass while blinking through tears, Rosie echoed Sybil's strong sentiments. 'To friends, God love them, wherever they are.'

52. Golden Autumn Days

On a fine early-autumn morning, Ada, dressed in her freshly starched and ironed sister's uniform, wheeled Catherine (wearing a pretty new dress knitted by Sister Mary Paul) up the farm track towards Mary Vale House.

'We're starting work today, my precious,' she beamed at her gurgling baby. Little Catherine, now nearly three months old, flashed a toothless smile at her mother. 'You'll be fine in the nursery with Dora,' Ada assured herself more than her daughter. 'She'll be looking after you while I'm working on the wards, though I will pop in to feed you from time to time.'

She didn't add, 'And because I cannot bear the thought of being away from you for more than two hours at a time.' Ada marvelled at the enormity of her love for Catherine; it filled her life with joy and laughter, and every stage in her development was a marvel. The only sadness, as ever, was that she had had no recent news from Jamie, and that her darling husband couldn't see his baby grow and thrive as she could. Ada had borrowed Matron's camera and taken a few black-and-white photographs, which she had immediately posted off in the hope that her husband would eventually receive them. Post to and from North Africa was wildly erratic, though Ada had heard from Jamie after he had been notified of his daughter's birth. With tears streaming down her face and her heart aching with love, she had read the letter that had taken so long to get through to her.

My wonderful girl,

I am so happy and relieved that all went well and that you didn't suffer too much giving birth to Catherine. A daughter — how wonderful! Does she have your sparkling eyes and a little dimple in her chin? My heart is so full of love and pride, I can't stop talking to the chaps about you and our baby. Everybody is very kind and patient with me forever rambling on about how beautiful my little girl is, especially so now, when we have low energy due to the scorching heat, reduced rations and water is always a problem. But at least I'm not in a POW camp, where I'm told the conditions are appalling. We're still ministering to the sick and the wounded, and there are plenty of those. General Montgomery's influence promises to be huge; he's quite the tour de force, boosting morale and planning to retrain the troops for the next attack, which will have to come soon if we're to stop Rommel and his men from reaching Alexandria and the Suez Canal. Enough of all that. I just want to think of you and the baby for the moment, I'm closing my eyes and imagining you first, the smell of your hair, your lovely long legs and that radiant smile that melts my heart, then my sweet Catherine, lying sleeping — or crying — in the crook of my arm. One day, please God, let that be so; I count the hours and pray the good Lord will keep you both safe until I'm home. Please send me more photos of our baby, and you too, my most beloved.

Your devoted husband,
Jamie.

That was the last letter Ada had received. Though the increasing joy of motherhood was now a constant in her life, she still woke up every morning with a sick feeling in the pit of her stomach. Where was her beloved, was he sick, hungry, still able to work? Or had something gone wrong since that last letter? None of the possibilities brought any comfort to her nervous state; she had to do what millions of women were forced to do every day that war continued: buckle down and get on with it, and wear a smile even though her heart was breaking.

Fortunately, as summer gave way to autumn, the landscape of the war in North Africa radically changed. In early September, at the Battle of Alam el Halfa, General Montgomery had his first victory after taking command of the Eighth Army, while the German Commander, General Rommel, suffered a humiliating loss. For a change the Allies were winning rather than losing in North Africa, which brought a broad smile to everyone's face when the news broke. Montgomery was seen as a hero who would reshape and empower his Eighth Army, leading them on to further victories.

The news had brought both pride and joy to Ada, but she would only rest easy when Jamie was granted leave, if only to see his daughter for a few days. Recently, her thoughts ricocheted between returning to work and news from the Front, and when she wasn't preoccupied with those, Ada was busy feeding, washing, cleaning, gardening and cooking. It had unquestionably been a long and very happy summer for her and Catherine, but now it was time to re-enter the real world, where Ada knew her presence and support were urgently needed, especially so since the news of Edith Mann's suicide had been in the news.

After settling Catherine in the nursery, gurgling and bouncing on Dora's knee as her nappy was changed, Ada blew her dear trusted friend a kiss before hurrying down the hospital corridor to Matron's office.

'Good-morning,' she said as she opened the door. Seeing Matron with her head in her hands, Ada rushed to her side.

'Dearest, what is it?'

'I should have done more for Edith,' Matron said in a choked voice. 'I just can't get the poor woman out of my mind. It's my job to look after my staff – why didn't I see it coming?' she wailed.

Stroking her hand, Ada said soothingly, 'Nobody could have second guessed Edith's thoughts; none of us had a clue of what she was planning; she was a very private woman.'

'I just can't believe she would take her own life,' Matron insisted. 'She might not have been compassionate, but she was tough, she was used to life's knocks; even the police officer who broke the news of Edith's suspected suicide said she had suffered terrible hardship at her mother's hands.' Looking sad, Matron sighed. 'It gives me a bit of satisfaction knowing that Edith was seemingly a little happier in the lead-up to her leaving. Can you believe that her mother actually told the policeman that Edith had killed herself just to spite her? Imagine anybody saying such a wicked thing when they had just been informed of their daughter's death?'

Thinking of her sweet blue-eyed daughter, Ada shivered at the thought.

'No, I certainly cannot,' she exclaimed.

Wanting to rouse her friend from her painful reverie, Ada helped her to her feet, after which she faced Matron square on.

'Listen, dearest Ann,' she urged, 'the best thing we can do now is to pray for Edith's immortal soul.'

Knowing this was the language that Sister Ann understood, she waited for the nun's troubled eyes to clear.

'You're right, Ada, absolutely right,' Matron replied with a weak smile. 'Life goes on.'

'It certainly does,' Ada agreed. 'But before you get down on your knees, I'd like you to inspect my uniform – is it up to scratch for my first day at work?' Ada asked, as she turned a full circle for Matron's benefit.

'You look wonderful,' Sister Ann said, as she embraced Ada. 'We've missed you more than words can say – it's such a relief to have you back. And where is that darling baby of yours?' she asked, suddenly brightening up. 'Is she with Dora?'

Knowing that a quick visit to the nursery would do Matron the world of good, Ada nodded. 'Indeed, she is. Why don't you run along there and welcome the latest little recruit back to Mary Vale?'

'I most certainly will,' Matron answered, as she bustled off down the corridor.

Ada fondly watched Matron go, then turned her attention to the urgency of the here and now. All but a couple of the residents that she had previously nursed would have left by now, their places taken by the constant flow of new arrivals whom she needed to get to know immediately. Ada knew better than anybody how important it was to spend time with each patient, familiarizing herself with their backgrounds and medical history, helping them build up relationships with the other women in the Home, and encouraging them to join her exercise and breathing classes, which she planned to reinstate now that she was back on the job.

Entering the post-natal ward, Ada's heart gave a happy little flip of excitement; smiling, confident and happy, she made her way along the line of beds, calling as she went, 'Good-morning, and how are we today?'

Nobody could resist Ada's charm and natural warmth; it was impossible not to want to be her friend. Ada's patients grew to love and trust her from the moment they met her, and in the months that led up to their giving birth that bond grew stronger and stronger. She would always be there for them, putting their needs first, listening and soothing, comforting and encouraging like the natural-born nurse she was. Ada could now add motherhood to her professional expertise; bringing her own baby into the world had made her even more compassionate and understanding. She knew what it was like to hold a new-born infant in her arms, to feel the pulse of her milk coming through her breasts and, even after the agony of childbirth, to know the euphoric bliss of smiling into your baby's misty pale eyes for the very first time.

Nobody could have been happier than Ada as she walked along the wards; supervising the care of young pregnant women was a task she loved. Added to which she had the joy and support of friends who enhanced her daily life at Mary Vale; solid as a rock Dora, adorable young Sister Theresa, darling Sister Mary Paul and last of all Matron, dearest Sister Ann, whom she had worked alongside for years. They had unquestionably had their bad times during 1942 – Rosie's poor husband lost in mysterious circumstances in the midst of warfare, her darling Jamie fighting the war in North Africa, losing Sister Mann, not to mention Ronnie and Sally running off to London – but better times had followed, like Ronnie assisting Sybil throughout her labour and Sybil now serving her country working in radar.

'That's Mary Vale's grace working within us,' Ada thought. 'A surprise around every corner.'

Once a sacred priory, Mary Vale had withstood many wars over the centuries, including this present one that gripped the entire world. Standing at the window, Ada gazed at the autumn leaves floating down in golden showers on to the lawn that sloped down to the sea. With an unexpected surge of emotion, Ada felt a rush of love for Mary Vale, which had never failed those who entered its walls. It was a place she loved with all her heart, in a country that millions were fighting to save from tyranny. A land where she hoped her daughter, sleeping peacefully in the nursery, would grow up free and where families destroyed by war would be reunited.

'Life will go on and love will return,' Ada prayed.

As the low-lying autumn light slanted through the falling leaves, she quietly hummed to herself, *We'll meet again . . . one sunny day.*

Then, smiling, Ada went about her daily duties.

Acknowledgements

The Daisy Styles series, now ten books in total, would never have happened without a great team who work tirelessly and meticulously with me, especially so during Covid times when it's proved to be even more important to have open channels of communication. So, it's huge thanks to my editors at Penguin, Rebecca Hilsdon and Clare Bowron, for their energy, enthusiasm and focus, and to Donna Poppy, my copy-editor – an amazing perfectionist. My grateful thanks also go to Dr Clive Glazebook and Senior Midwife Patsy Glazebrook for their obstetrics knowledge and their patience with my questions about childbirth in the Second World War, which was vastly different to how maternity units operate now. And finally, as ever, this book is for all of those wonderful nameless women conscripted to work where they were sent and do their duty without question or complaint. I salute you all.

He just wanted a decent book to read ...

Not too much to ask, is it? It was in 1935 when Allen Lane, Managing Director of Bodley Head Publishers, stood on a platform at Exeter railway station looking for something good to read on his journey back to London. His choice was limited to popular magazines and poor-quality paperbacks – the same choice faced every day by the vast majority of readers, few of whom could afford hardbacks. Lane's disappointment and subsequent anger at the range of books generally available led him to found a company – and change the world.

'We believed in the existence in this country of a vast reading public for intelligent books at a low price, and staked everything on it'
Sir Allen Lane, 1902–1970, founder of Penguin Books

The quality paperback had arrived – and not just in bookshops. Lane was adamant that his Penguins should appear in chain stores and tobacconists, and should cost no more than a packet of cigarettes.

Reading habits (and cigarette prices) have changed since 1935, but Penguin still believes in publishing the best books for everybody to enjoy. We still believe that good design costs no more than bad design, and we still believe that quality books published passionately and responsibly make the world a better place.

So wherever you see the little bird – whether it's on a piece of prize-winning literary fiction or a celebrity autobiography, political tour de force or historical masterpiece, a serial-killer thriller, reference book, world classic or a piece of pure escapism – you can bet that it represents the very best that the genre has to offer.

Whatever you like to read – trust Penguin.